To.

Hope you enjoy "Incense."

INCENSE
& PEPPERMINTS

CAROLE BELLACERA

Best,

Carole Bellacera

FOR DANNY

Also by Carole Bellacera

Border Crossings
Spotlight
East of the Sun, West of the Moon
Understudy
Chocolate on a Stick
Tango's Edge
Lily of the Springs

Praise for INCENSE & PEPPERMINTS

Like a classic rock ballad, Carole Bellacera's *INCENSE & PEPPERMINTS skillfully transports the readers back to the turbulent seventies, and the heartbreak and passions of warm, as seen through the eyes of a nurse serving in Vietnam. I couldn't put down INCENSE & PEPPERMINTS.—Cindy Myers, author of* THE VIEW FROM HERE

Settle into a comfortable chair and grab the box of tissue because this book will touch your heart like no other. Incense & Peppermints combines romance and history like I haven't seen in a very long time. The reader has the front row seat on this fantastic roller coaster ride of love, danger, and drama. 5 stars of 5 stars. **Annette M G Nishimoto, Book Reviewer, Independent Writer, Editor and Proofreader.**

"With intelligent and absorbing writing, Carole Bellacera places a courageous and inspiring young woman at the intense and dangerous center of the Vietnam War. Bellacera's account of the seventies is heartfelt and real, yet her moving story of love, loss and healing is timeless."

--**Diane Chamberlain**, best-selling author of **Necessary Lies**

"A stirring and heartbreaking story of love--of all kinds--in the middle of a devastating war. You won't be able to put it down.**"--Stephanie Elliott, Head of Editorial, US, Working Partners Ltd.**

"Carole Bellacera gives readers what they love; a story as rich in plot as it is in character. You will not regret reading Incense & Peppermints."— **Jennifer McMurrain, Author of *The Divine Heart* and *Winter Song*.**

PROLOGUE

Memphis, Tennessee, February 2011

With a beep, the instant message popped up on her Facebook page.

For a moment, 62-year-old Cindy Sweet stared at the name, and her heart did a slow somersault. *Ryan Paul Quinlan.*

No, it can't be.

Maybe her bleary eyes were deceiving her. She'd arrived home after getting off the 11-7 shift at St. Jude's, and driving home in a cold, near-freezing rain. Her only thought had been of falling into her king-sized bed fitted with soft Egyptian cotton sheets, and snuggling under the fluffy down comforter. On her way upstairs, on impulse, she'd stopped off in the office to double-check the time of a dental appointment that afternoon, and Facebook had popped up when she'd moved the mouse.

And before she could switch to her calendar, the instant message appeared–from Ryan Paul Quinlan.

Her heart began to pound, her hand hovering over the mouse. She couldn't bring herself to click on the link. To see if it was really him.

But it couldn't be. *How* could it be?

Quin had died in Vietnam forty years ago.

SEPTEMBER 1970

Dear Cindy,

This is really hard for me to admit, but I miss you. I thought it'd be really cool to have the room to myself, and it is—no lie! I have to confess, I couldn't wait until you left for nursing school, but I do miss having you in the house. I know we fought a lot but <u>everybody</u> fights with their big sister, don't they? You remember my friend, Sherry? She's the one whose birthday is the day after mine. Can you believe I'll...<u>we'll</u>...be turning 14 next month? I'm so bummed you won't be here for my party. Anyway, Sherry *and her big sister, Chris, have knock-down-drag-outs all the time. And she'd give <u>anything</u> if Chris would move out.*

Last night I was watching the Miss America pageant, and it just wasn't the same without you. Remember how we'd always hope that one of those ditzy chicks would fall on their butts? Ha! Didn't happen last night either. Miss Texas won...as usual. I don't get why Miss Indiana never wins. It's not like she was a skag or anything! Oh, well...

Hey, I gotta go. Homework to do...as usual! You know Mom...gotta get homework done before I can go out and play Kick-the-Can before it gets dark. (Can't do homework after supper because I want to watch 'The Brady Bunch.' Geez, I bet you miss TV, don't you?) By the way, Mom says hi—and to be careful! (She just popped her head in my room to remind me about homework. Geez!!!) I <u>hate</u> school! Did I mention that?

Love, Joanie.

P.S. I love you, Cindy. I really do. And I'm sorry about all our fights.

CHAPTER ONE

From high in the air, it looked beautiful below, a lush green oasis. Like a photo out of the travel magazines Aunt Terri kept on the coffee table so she'd look like the sophisticated traveler she'd always wanted to be. But a few minutes later, when Cindy saw the defoliated gouges of earth and pitted, dusty roads—by rocket blasts?—she realized what she'd been gazing at before must've been the last of Thailand, not Vietnam at all.

It was closing on two in the afternoon, and after twenty-five hours of flight, dressed in her rumpled, sweat-stained Class-A uniform, complete with clammy nylons and high-heeled pumps, Cindy felt about as rank as a dirty sock in the bottom of a gym bag. Her cinnamon-brown hair had long since escaped from what used to be a tidy French roll, and now hung in damp tendrils on her neck. She'd have to do something about that before they landed. After all, she *was* in the military, and God knew what kind of officers would be there to greet her at Bien Hoa Air Force Base. There'd probably be some gung-ho types, just watching for serious "infractions" like—*God forbid!*—a nurse having her hair touching the collar of her Class-A. *Something like that would surely make us lose the war!*

Cindy didn't know where such bitter thoughts were coming from. When she'd left home for Travis Air Force Base, she'd felt proud and excited to be going to Vietnam—to make a difference there. To save some lives, or at the very least, to give comfort to those who couldn't be saved.

Her heart panged, and a wave of sadness settled over her as she thought of Gary. So many years ago. She tried to shake off the melancholy, tried to remember she'd *wanted* to come to Vietnam. She'd volunteered for it. And now, the moment of truth was about to arrive.

The engine of the 727 decelerated and Cindy felt a sinking sensation in her stomach. The captain's voice crackled over the muted roar of the engines, "Stewardesses, please prepare for landing."

Around her, the atmosphere changed as soldiers began to wake up and rustle about, studiously avoiding each other's eyes. The four other nurses aboard exchanged nervous glances, and Cindy recognized various emotions emanating from them—excitement, wariness, outright fear—and she wondered how she looked to them. Like the self-assured 21-year-old nursing grad who'd finished at the top of her class at Niagara University? Like the confident young woman who'd gone through basic training at Fort Sam Houston, learning to shoot an M-16–and doing it pretty accurately–before serving ten months at Walter Reed Army Hospital in Washington DC? Or did she look the way she felt—a terrified girl not quite sure of her medical skills, thrust into a world she was absolutely positive she wasn't at all prepared for?

The whining of the landing gear as it locked into place alerted her to reality–she was here in 'Nam, and down there, a war was going on. Within moments, it would be her new world—a world that hadn't existed for her until that hot summer night in 1965 when a young soldier bound for Vietnam had so briefly entered her life.

Ω

The stench hit her as she stepped off the plane. It was like a fetid oven—a furnace blast filled with the stomach-churning odors of animal feces, rotting vegetation and molding garbage overlaid with exhaust fumes from trucks, jeeps and airplanes. As Cindy descended the roll-away steps placed against the 727, the heat curled around her, wilting her already-damp hair, pooling inside her panty-hose and turning her bra into a wet, constricting bandage. During the flight, her feet had swollen, and as she hobbled across the tarmac toward the terminal at Bien Hoa, weighed down by the over-stuffed duffle bag she'd slung over her shoulder, the two-inch heels of her pumps felt like stilettos.

She heard a roar, like an enthusiastic crowd at a football game, and startled, looked to her left. The noise had erupted from waving and cheering soldiers outside the terminal. That's when it hit her. They were going home. Probably on the very plane from which she'd just disembarked—their "freedom bird" home. It would be one long year before there'd be one for her.

As she drew closer to the homebound soldiers, she saw they were mostly all young, like her, in their early twenties. Their eyes weren't young at all, though; they were ancient. Eyes that had seen way too many horrors. The "thousand yard stare." She'd heard about it from one of the GI's on the plane, returning for his second tour of duty. How long did it take to develop a thousand yard stare? Would *she* have one, too, at the end of her tour?

Chaos reigned inside the terminal. Male bodies pressed together like magnets, most of them incoming soldiers, inching their way toward the counter manned by three uniformed soldiers. Cindy got in what she hoped was a line, the only woman in sight. The tangible scent of maleness surrounded her, arousing a primal feeling of excitement mixed with fear. Perspiration trickled down the back of her neck under hair escaping its French roll. She felt vulnerable, almost hunted. Where were the other four nurses from the plane? Craning her sore neck, she caught a glimpse of one of them, a redhead with freckles, big blue eyes and a wide friendly mouth. Probably right off a Minnesota farm. They exchanged a glance that spoke more than words ever could. *What the hell are we doing here?* No doubt, like her, she was wishing she was back home, milking a cow, and wondering why she'd ever joined the Army.

Overhead, a gigantic fan moved lazily, doing nothing to cool the air, but creating an odd, flickering shadow in the dust-molted room that reminded Cindy of the dark atmosphere in an old Hollywood B-movie. The earthy smell of stale male sweat wafted over her, and something—a *hand?*--brushed against her buttock; she flinched.

"Sorry," a gruff voice muttered.

She barely suppressed a shudder and looked to her left—right into the hungry eyes of a young marine.

But he wasn't the only one looking at her, she realized. She felt the stares—from everywhere, men *ogling* her. That wasn't something she was used to. Men usually shied away from her because of her height, five-foot-eight…well, closer to five-foot-nine. She'd always been the tallest girl in school, even nursing school. She'd loomed over every boy she'd ever dated, which wasn't many.

Only Gary had been taller.

Her cheeks burned. *Jesus, why are they staring?* Surely it hadn't been that long since they'd seen a female. It wasn't as if these guys had been out in the jungle for months; they were fresh off the plane from The World. She ran a cautious hand down the back of her skirt to make sure she hadn't managed to get it tucked into her panty-hose during her last visit to the toilet on the plane. No, everything seemed to be in order.

And speaking of toilet, she would soon have to go. She glanced around the terminal, hoping to see a restroom. But, apparently, that was another American luxury unavailable at the moment. She sighed.

After a twenty-minute wait, she finally made it to the counter. A bored private stamped her paperwork and gestured to another line forming at the end of the room. Toes pinching from the torture devices the US Army referred to as "dress pumps," Cindy made her way over to it, relieved to see the red-haired nurse already there.

Her blue eyes lit up when she saw Cindy. She waved, and suddenly Cindy felt better about everything. The girl was just so apple-pie American, so *comforting*, like she was a little bit of home. Cindy had a gut feeling they'd be the best of friends as they helped each other get through this year in Vietnam.

Ω

After a briefing—and a bathroom break in the less-than-luxurious one-holer in the building-- Cindy followed the others to a row of green Army buses for the short ride to the 90th Replacement Battalion, a holding facility for soldiers and nurses until their individual unit assignments came through. The bus, its windows covered with wire mesh, rumbled through narrow streets, protected by jeeps mounted with M60 machine guns in front and behind the convoy. Heat pulsated inside the bus like something alive—an entity bent on sapping every ounce of energy out of the bedraggled human cargo.

A hard-bitten soldier caught Cindy's eye and nodded toward the screens. "That's to protect us from grenades thrown by our friendly South Vietnamese gooks."

Cindy wiped the sweat from her brow and tried to summon a grin, even though she didn't think that was something he should be joking about. He stared back, iron-jawed, and with a sudden queasiness, she realized he wasn't joking. Trying to dispel her dread, she turned away from him and looked out the window.

Vietnam looked pretty much like it did on TV. Bare-footed peasants trudged along the road, carrying baskets filled with unidentifiable items. Others dressed in black pajama-like clothes and conical hats toiled in rice paddies. A scrawny water buffalo lumbered through one of those paddies, an old man following with a switch that for the glimpse Cindy caught, he seemed to be using quite liberally. An ancient-looking woman squatted at the roadside, appearing to be selling something. Clearly, this country, beyond the war, was mired in poverty.

"So, where are you from?" the redhead next to her asked.

Cindy turned and smiled. "Plainfield, Indiana. You?"

By the time the buses pulled through the gates of the 90th, she felt as if she'd known Shelley forever. She wasn't, in fact, from Minnesota, but from New Hampshire, but she *had* had experience milking a cow. Her father owned a dairy farm.

"Who can we talk to about seeing if we can be sent to the same hospital?" Cindy asked the sergeant who appeared to be in charge inside the Quonset hut to which they were led.

He gave her a blank look, and then said flatly, "You haven't been in the Army long, have you, Lieutenant?"

Two days later, Cindy found herself assigned to the 24th Evacuation Hospital in Long Binh. Shelley went to the 71st Evacuation Hospital in Pleiku, hundreds of miles up-country.

And that's when Cindy learned her first harsh lesson in Vietnam.

You could count on nothing.

CHAPTER TWO

The pain grabbed her with talon-like claws. Cindy bolted from her cot, clutching her mid-section. She waited for the spasm to subside before scrambling up and heading for the back door that led to the foul-smelling latrine containing two pit toilets, three rusty sinks and a battered shower head. On her first visit there two nights ago, she'd noticed with apathetic horror—who knew there could *be* such a thing as apathetic horror?—that the women shared it with frogs, lizards and all varieties of bugs.

But right now, the creepy Vietnamese fauna was the least of her concerns. This getting up in the night to run to the toilet was a real bummer! Those damn M11's–malaria pills they'd been issued upon arrival. No one had bothered to warn her about the lovely side effect of diarrhea.

With the nasty business finished, Cindy lugged herself back into the women's quarters, meeting another nurse in anguish on the other side of the door—a newbie who'd arrived the day after Cindy.

"Oh, my God," she gasped, cradling her midsection as she stumbled toward the door. "Third time tonight!"

"Good luck," Cindy said, and with a sigh, trudged back to her cot.

Her stomach was finally at ease—for the moment—but the dreamless sleep from which she'd been so rudely awakened refused to return. Maybe it was the artillery rumbling in the distance. For the past three nights, it had started about midnight and continued through the early hours. She hadn't slept at all the first night because of it—well, that and the urgent runs to the toilet. But by the second night, she'd been so exhausted, she probably would've slept through a bombardment of the base itself.

Now, though, sleep eluded her. She lay on the cot, staring up at the mosquito netting. What was Shelley doing right now? Had she reached Pleiku yet? The disappointment of knowing they would be going to different hospitals still lingered. Shelley had shipped out within hours of getting her assignment. Cindy didn't have to report to the 24th until tomorrow morning…which was, she estimated, a few hours away.

Oh, God! What if they put me in that hospital and I don't know what I'm doing? She'd never worked trauma cases before. Even at Walter Reed, she'd worked on the internal medicine ward doing basic nursing care. What if she didn't have the skill to do it? After all, she'd only been out of nursing school less than a year.

The door creaked open and shuffling footsteps alerted her that the nurse she'd passed a few minutes ago was back in the building. Cindy propped her head on her hand and glanced over to see her moving to a cot across from hers.

"You okay?" Cindy whispered, trying not to wake the other sleeping nurses.

A soft groan came from the semi-darkness. "I once competed in a hotdog-eating contest...and won it. Felt a thousand times better than now. And I'd *kill* for a cigarette."

Ω

"So, that's how I ended up here." 2nd Lieutenant Jennifer Yu's cigarette tip flared in the darkness as she took a long drag. "Happy Birthday to me!"

They were on their third cigarettes. It had been 45 minutes since they'd left the women's quarters and come outside for a smoke. Nearby, a soldier kept guard at the entrance of their quarters, and no doubt he'd heard every word they'd said. Cindy wondered why the women's quarters needed a guard, anyway, and then remembered the hungry look in the troops' eyes at the terminal.

"Bummer that you're celebrating your birthday on your third day in 'Nam." Cindy released a stream of smoke and tapped her cigarette on the side of the wall to get rid of the growing ash.

Jenny grinned. "Yeah, but at least now I can drink…legally."

"For sure! So…five brothers and four sisters? No wonder you joined the Army. This must seem like the calm in the eye of the storm for you."

She nodded. "Oh, yeah. My parents were the only Chinese-American Roman Catholics in my neighborhood. We lived in a little apartment in San Diego; our room was so tiny we girls had to turn in unison at night just so we didn't get popped with somebody's elbow. In the summer, the boys slept up on the roof just to get a little breathing room."

Jenny, a petite girl with long, straight black hair and velvety-brown almond-shaped eyes, was as smart as she was pretty. So tiny she barely reached Cindy's shoulder, Jenny struck her as a little firecracker, somebody who wouldn't take any crap from anyone. Maybe that was because she'd grown up with five brothers.

Even though it was almost four in the morning, the night had brought no relief from the sweltering air. The monsoon rains that had fallen every afternoon since Cindy's arrival did nothing to relieve the encompassing heat. In the gray, pearl light of approaching dawn, a gecko skittered up the wall of the barracks, and Cindy didn't flinch. Ten hours ago, the sight of the lizard would've sent her running inside, screeching. She dropped her cigarette butt and ground it out with the heel of her combat boot, then remembered one of the silly military rules. She snatched up the smashed cigarette, crumbled it between her fingers to release the tobacco, and then tucked the wrapper into her pocket. "I guess we should try to get some sleep. I have to report to the 24th Evac at 0800."

"Maybe I'll get stationed there, too," Jenny said hopefully.

Cindy opened her mouth to tell her not to count on it, but something in the other girl's expression stopped her. Suddenly she didn't look so strong and sure of herself.

"It would be nice to have someone...you know...a good friend to go through the year with," Jenny added.

Cindy nodded and gave her a smile. "Yes, it would."

More artillery boomed in the distance, sounding closer than before, and strobes of light flickered on the horizon. It looked like lightning, but both of them knew it wasn't. Lightning didn't create skinny white streaks spinning haphazardly across the sky. Out there, someone was probably getting killed right now. The morbid thought was at contrast with the gentle swaying of coconut palms under a crescent moon.

Jenny, glancing in the same direction, seemed to read her thoughts. "It would be beautiful, wouldn't it? If it weren't for the war. Reminds me of Hawaii. I got to spend a night there because of mechanical problems."

Cindy nodded. "Maybe someday when the war is over, it'll be a tourist destination. You never know." But she didn't really believe that. Who'd want to come to a country where so many people had died?

She placed her arm around Jenny's shoulder, knowing if anyone could see them, they'd probably think they were looking at Mutt and Jeff. She grinned at the thought. "Come on, let's go get some sleep."

As she stepped back inside the women's quarters, her stomach gave a tell-tale rumble. "Crap," she muttered. "Guess I'll be heading right out the back door."

Jenny gave a short, bitter laugh. "'Crap' is right. I'll be right behind you."

Ω

The chief nurse, Lieutenant Colonel Eugenia Kairos, looked like Cindy's mother, but smelled like her late grandmother. An over-indulgence in an old lady's perfume, judging by the flowery stench in the room. Evening in Paris? Well, probably not *that* cheap. Probably Chanel No. 5…after all, she *was* a full bird, which meant she could afford it.

But the resemblance to her mother was uncanny—the dark brown bouffant hairdo, the sparkling dark eyes, the high cheekbones, even the little corkscrew curls that snaked down beyond her earlobes. She could've been Mom's older sister, despite the fact that her mother didn't have a drop of Greek blood in her—that she *knew* of, anyway.

On first sight, Cindy had been delighted, feeling an immediate kinship with the woman. But that all changed the minute Colonel Kairos opened her mouth. "I'm going to put you on Ward 2, surgical intensive care, Lieutenant. But when you're needed during mass-casualty pushes in the ER, you'll be expected to report to the ER on the double." Malice, pure and simple, glimmered in the depths of her beautiful brown eyes. "I don't care what you're doing. Sleeping, masturbating, taking a dump…whatever. You get the word, you get your ass to the ER. If you should prove to be especially adept in the ER, I may transfer you there permanently." Her eyes narrowed. "I can usually tell which nurses have what it takes to work the ER. Not many do." Her tone insinuated that Cindy fell into the latter.

Cindy stood at attention, resisting the urge to wipe away sweat from her forehead. The hospital was air-conditioned, but at the moment she wouldn't have believed it. Her fatigue shirt clung to her skin, feeling as thick and uncomfortable as an Army-issue blanket. Why couldn't the uniforms be more appropriate to the tropical climate?

"I have rules," Colonel Kairos went on, "and as long as you follow them, we'll get along just fine. Rule # 1—my nurses are ladies, and will comport themselves as such. That means you don't make a spectacle of yourself at the Officer's Club."

Her jaw tightened. "If I had my way, my nurses wouldn't be indulging in *any* alcoholic beverages, but since I can't stop you from doing so, I will say that I will *not* tolerate public drunkenness. So just watch yourself when you're at the O Club. Same thing goes for entertaining male company in the nurses' quarters. I simply *won't* have it!"

Her eyes flashed indignantly like the mere thought of a nurse "entertaining" a male was a personal offense. "Now, I'm not so blind as to think it *doesn't* happen, but you'd just better not get caught. Because I guarantee you, I won't go easy on you if you do. As for fraternization with the enlisted men, do I even need to go there?" She stared Cindy down, apparently waiting for an answer.

Cindy swallowed hard. "No, Ma'am!" She tried to bark it out like she'd done in boot camp, but it came out as a squeak.

Colonel Kairos nodded and said, "Not too long after I got here, I had a nurse who was sleeping around with a corpsman. I had her ass booted right out of the 24th."

Oooh, and she got to go home? The thought ballooned in Cindy's mind, and she couldn't help but smile. Immediately realizing that wasn't the response the Lt. Colonel hoped to elicit, she sobered. But it was too late.

"You find something funny about that, Lieutenant?"

"No, *Ma'am!*"

The woman's dark eyes skewered her for an endless moment. Beneath her fatigue shirt, sweat trickled down Cindy's back, and she prayed she wouldn't have a sudden attack of the runs; it had been several hours, and she was due. *Oh, God, please let me out of this maniac's presence.*

Finally, the Colonel spoke again, "Good. Because she ended up at a field hospital somewhere near the DMZ. And another thing…I won't tolerate a potty mouth. You're a young lady in the Army, not a foul-mouthed sailor. I have spies everywhere, so keep it clean."

Like you? Talk about the pot calling the kettle black.

As if reading her mind, the lieutenant colonel's gaze daggered into Cindy, making her feel like a butterfly pinned to a cork board. "You may have noticed you have an extra piece of material under your fatigue shirt, Lieutenant. That's called a 'modesty panel,' and it's issued to every nurse under my command. I've heard some nurses are cutting them out, and I won't have it. They're there for a reason; I won't have my nurses strutting around with their nipples showing through the sheer bras you girls wear today. You clear on that, Lieutenant?"

"Yes, Ma'am."

She gave a stiff nod. "Okay, good. Report to Capt. Martin in Ward 2. *Dismissed!*"

After saluting, Cindy stepped out of Colonel Kairos' office and took a deep breath of Vietnam's foul air; it felt refreshing after being in Chanel hell for the past fifteen minutes.

Ω

Captain Rosalie Martin looked up from the nurse's station and gave Cindy a big smile. "Ah, you must be the FNG! Welcome to Ward 2, Lieutenant Sweet. What's your first name?"

"Cindy," she said, surprised by the nurse's friendliness—especially after dealing with The Wicked Witch of the 24th.

The pretty redheaded nurse, not much older than Cindy, laughed. "Cindy Sweet! I love it! Well, Cindy Sweet, we don't stand on ceremony around here, despite what Cruella told you. I'm Rosalie." She extended her hand. "Yeah, I can tell by the pale look on your face that you just came from her office. Between you and me..." Her grin grew sly. "I don't think she's been laid since JFK took office."

Cindy almost choked on the laughter that wanted to bubble up out of her throat. She held it back, afraid that her supervisor's affability was all a big trick. That as she soon as she responded with laughter, the smile would disappear from the captain's face and Cindy would be flailing in hot water.

Rosalie's hazel eyes focused on someone beyond Cindy's right shoulder, and her smile grew bigger. "Oh, there you are, David. This is Lieutenant Cindy Sweet, the replacement for Carolyn. Could you give her a tour of the hospital? It's pretty quiet here right now; I'll hold down the fort."

Cindy turned to see a young man in fatigues and sergeant's stripes behind her-- a corpsman. The name on his shirt read *Ansgar*. His blue eyes and sandy blond hair fit with the Scandinavian name.

He gave her an easy smile and extended his hand. "Nice to meet you, L.T." He grasped her hand in a firm shake. "We're glad to have you here. You're joining one of the best teams in the hospital with the Captain and Doc Moss."

"David is right, Cindy," Rosalie said. "We're a great team…well, with one or two exceptions…" She exchanged a knowing glance with David. Cindy figured it was better not to ask.

He gave her a shy smile. "Shall we start in the ER?"

She nodded and they turned to go, but just as they reached the door of the ward, Rosalie called out, "Oh, Cindy? That rigmarole Cruella told you about the modesty panel? You can cut it out with bandage shears. The record for any nurse keeping it is about a week, I think."

David grinned. "That's what I hear."

They walked outside under the covered walkway toward the ER. Immediately the sopping heat enveloped Cindy. *Guess the hospital* had *been air-conditioned.* She could practically feel her hair escaping her once neat bun, and clinging to her neck as if she'd just climbed out of a swimming pool.

As they headed down the walkway side by side, Cindy stared at David from the corner of her eye. *Nice looking guy.* Ever since Gary, she'd been a sucker for blond-haired men. And David was tall like Gary. Too bad he was enlisted. But then if cavorting with an enlisted guy would get her sent home...oh, yeah, they hadn't sent that nurse home, but to the DMZ.

She shook the thought away. No way would she ever do something like that, anyway— sleeping with a guy just to get out of the military. In fact, she was probably the last remaining virgin in the U.S. Army. Archaic as it sounded, she was waiting for the right guy before she had sex. Mom's constant warnings about men "taking advantage" had sunk into her brain. But it wasn't just that. A card-carrying romantic, reader of

Victoria Holt and Anya Seton, Cindy wanted to wait until she was in love. Of course, if she'd had the opportunity, she would've lost her virginity to Gary in a heartbeat, despite Mom's dire warnings.

But here she was--probably the only female virgin in Vietnam. *Thanks a lot, Mom.*

Shaking her head, she glanced at David and saw him gazing at her, a curious look in his eyes. Her face grew warm, and she searched for something to say to fill the silence. "Can I ask you a question, David?"

He smiled. "Sure."

"Captain Martin called me a FNG. What's that?"

David's face reddened. "The 'F' stands for a word I don't normally use in mixed company; the 'NG' is 'new guy.' Or in your case, 'new *girl.*'" He grinned at her discomfiture. "Don't worry, though. You won't be one for long."

F…new girl? What…? And then she realized what word he was talking about, and her own cheeks grew hot.

Nice. Really charming.

CHAPTER THREE

"**C**aptain Hendricksen, this is our new nurse, Lt. Sweet," said David at the nurse's station back on Ward 2 after their tour of the hospital.

A willowy Nordic-looking blonde looked up from her paperwork, her blue eyes as arctic as her heritage. Brenda Hendricksen gave Cindy an indifferent appraisal. "Just what we need," she snapped. "Another FNG to train."

Cindy bristled. The acronym had been light and unthreatening coming out of Rosalie's mouth, but from this haughty bitch, it could be taken in no other way but insulting. In civilian life, Cindy would've had no problem retorting, but not here. Captain Hendrickson outranked— and face it—intimidated her.

"Captain Hendricksen is on her second tour of duty here at the 24th," David added, his blue eyes holding Cindy's.

She got the message. "Pleased to meet you, Captain." She held out her hand, and then dropped it when Hendrickson refused to look up.

Instead, the nurse grunted and scribbled something in a patient's chart. "David, you might as well put her to work. O'Sullivan needs an I.V. Tell her to use an intracath."

Panic bubbled up inside Cindy. *I've never done that before! I haven't got the foggiest idea how to do it!*

David must've sensed her alarm. He gave her a wink of reassurance and spoke to the nurse. "Right away, Captain."

As they moved away from the nurse's station, he said under his breath, "Don't worry, L.T. I'll show you how to do it. It's a snap."

God, the guy must be a mind-reader, she thought. As he'd promised, he walked her through the procedure. It wasn't as difficult as she'd expected. Under his guidance, she inserted the sheath of the intracath into the soldier's vein on the underside of his elbow, withdrew the needle, attached the IV line and secured the site. After that, he took her from patient to patient with a cart to change dressings and take care of Foley catheters—a routine that would be reenacted several times throughout the shift. Wounds had to be cleaned, dabbed and dressed four times a day. Patients with tracheotomies had to be suctioned frequently to clear out mucous.

Vital signs had to be monitored. And finally, bodies had to be bagged for the morgue—a chore Cindy knew she'd never get used to.

The hours flew by, and although she was exhausted, she felt a gratifying sense of accomplishment. She *could* do this. All she had to do was take one day at a time, one patient at a time. The most difficult thing would be her tendency to get too close to the patients, rather than stay detached. Most of the boys here were barely out of high school. One minute they'd been healthy and whole, and in the next, their bodies were torn apart and mutilated. Here, in the ICU, once conscious, they'd be glad to be alive. It would only be later, when they realized the extent of their injuries that they'd wish they'd died. But that wouldn't happen until after they'd moved on to one of the other wards. It would be another nurse's problem.

The door to the ward opened and a lanky man in surgical scrubs stepped in. Cap Bren, the name everyone called Hendricksen behind her back, according to David, looked up and gave him a 500-watt smile, looking like a model in a Swedish toothpaste commercial. They exchanged a few words and Brenda rolled her eyes, giving a terse nod to Cindy and David.

The surgeon loped toward them, his craggy movie-star face creased in a smile. "You must be the new girl," he said, stopping in front of them. His piercing blue eyes swept over her, and something about his gaze made Cindy conscious that she was a woman—and not only that, but an attractive woman. He stuck out a hand, totally ignoring David at her side. "I'm Dr. Jackson Stalik, but you can call me Jack," he said with a thick mid-western accent. Not Indiana, though. Michigan, maybe.

"Hi," Cindy said with a smile. His grasp was warm and strong—typical surgeon hands. "I'm Cindy Sweet."

His grin widened, wolf-like. "And I'll bet you are," he said in a seductive purr.

She felt David stiffen next to her. Suddenly the surgeon seemed to remember where they were. The come-on look disappeared from his eyes, replaced with formal politeness. "I'm looking forward to working with you, Lieutenant. You're going to learn a lot here."

He turned and ambled off toward one of the patient's beds. Cindy stared after him, unsettled by his flirting, yet, intrigued.

David cleared his throat. "Watch out for him, L.T. He eats girls like you for breakfast. Even sleeping with Cap Bren doesn't stop him from sampling all the new nurses that come through the 24th."

Cindy looked at him. "He's sleeping with *her*?"

He nodded, his eyes filled with disgust. "Among others, and he's got a wife and three kids back in Detroit. But that's not the worst of it." He watched the surgeon through steely eyes. "He's a drunk. Couldn't you smell the whiskey on him?"

Stunned, Cindy shook her head. "I didn't notice anything. Are you telling me he's drunk on duty?"

David shrugged. "Wouldn't put it past him. But maybe my sense of smell is more sensitive than yours. Or maybe he drinks so much that the smell comes through his pores. Just be careful around him."

She gave him a sidelong glance, and smiled. "Are you always so protective of FNGs?"

He grinned back. "Only FNGs who look like you." As soon as the words were out of his mouth, he blanched, and then slowly, his face flushed. "Sorry, Ma'am. I didn't mean…"

Poor guy. He looked miserable. "Don't worry about it," she said. "I'm not easily offended."

Relief washed over his face. He glanced up at the clock on the wall. "Looks like our shift is about over. The Colonel told you we work 12-hour shifts, six days a week, right?" At her nod, he went on, "First three weeks, you'll have orientation, one week on days, one week on nights and one week on IV duty." He gave a wry grin. "The most hated job on the floor. Nights you'll usually be working with four to five corpsmen and at least one other RN. Maybe…" He stopped at the sound of chopper blades thrumming outside.

At the nurse's station, Cap Bren looked up, her body tensing. The phone on her desk shrilled out. She grabbed it, listened, and then her chilly blue gaze fastened on Cindy. "We've got incoming, Lieutenant. You might as well get your first mass-cal push out of the way right now, so get your ass to the ER *stat!*"

Ω

Mass carnage. On some level, Cindy had known to expect that inside the ER. She'd been told what would happen during a push. But experiencing it first-hand—that was something she could never have imagined. The *whop-whop* of the Hueys, one after another, as they landed and discharged the wounded pulsed through the cloying, jungle-rich air—a sound that would echo in her ears for the rest of her life. The ghastly sight of discarded limbs piled up outside the doors of pre-op sent her stomach plunging. With those macabre clues of what awaited her inside, Cindy entered, and bile rose in her throat.

Blood everywhere, saturating the bodies of the wounded soldiers, and seeping onto the concrete floor. Doctors and nurses ran from one casualty to another, cutting away uniforms, washing grimy bodies to flush away blood and tissue in order to determine the gravity of wounds. Soldiers sobbed for their mothers or shrieked in pain as medical staff efficiently barked orders, amazingly calm in the mayhem. The stench of unwashed bodies, blood, feces, and worst of all—burned flesh—permeated the room.

Cindy stood paralyzed, knowing she needed to react, but unsure of what to do. Nursing school hadn't prepared her for *this*. She fought an irresistible urge to run screaming out of the building…head straight for the flight line and back home to Indiana. Who cared if they declared her AWOL? Nothing could be worse than this!

"*Nurse*!" A hand grabbed her arm. "Need some help here!"

A doctor—she assumed he was a doctor—steered her to a gurney holding a bloodied GI.

"Bouncing Betty wound," the dark-haired doctor said. "Draw some blood and type-cross it, then get it to the lab *stat*."

Cindy stared at the wounded soldier, and her stomach dropped. He was covered to his chest with a bloody sheet—a sheet that went disconcertingly flat around the hips. Incredibly, he was still conscious. His brown eyes gazed at her in confusion. He couldn't be older than 19, Cindy thought. Probably hadn't even been shaving that long.

"Poor bastard doesn't stand a chance," the doctor muttered. He looked at her suddenly. "Why are you just standing there? Draw his blood and get it to the lab for a type-cross—and hang a bag of O-Neg stat!"

Cindy moved. With trembling fingers, she started his IV using an intercath—thank God David had showed her how a few hours earlier—then drew the soldier's blood, thankful that his arms were intact, thankful that somehow, her fingers knew how to perform that single task. She studied his face. Unmarked, just filthy from the field. As she drew the tube of blood, his eyes focused on her.

"I'm not going to make it, am I, nurse?" he whispered with a southern accent. She knew that accent—had heard it every day for the first 16 years of her life.

Her heart drummed. What could she say? What *should* she say? She tried to summon an encouraging smile. "We're going to take good care of you, soldier."

Her words sounded hollow, even to herself. She gave his shoulder a reassuring pat and turned to go. But he reached out and grabbed her arm, his grip surprisingly strong.

"Don't go!" His voice rasped with emotion. "Please, ma'am…" he added as she turned back to him. His brown eyes swam with tears. "Stay with me…I don't want to die alone…"

Cindy swallowed a lump as big as Georgia. For a moment, she felt as if she'd time-traveled back to 1966, hearing Gary pleading with her to stay with him for a while. Her hand covered the GI's and gently loosened it from her arm.

"You're not going to die, soldier." *Please, God, don't let that be a lie!*

Incredibly, the boy gave a half-hearted smile, but it didn't diminish the fear in his eyes. "Just in case…" he whispered. "Stay with me?"

Beneath the grime of battle in his hair, Cindy could almost make out glints of gold. Again, she thought of Gary. She squeezed his hand and placed it by his side. "Where you from, soldier?"

"Conway, South Carolina," he said, closing his eyes and grimacing.

Probably the morphine the medic had given him on the battlefield was beginning to wear off. She tried to summon a smile. "I grew up in Little River."

His eyes fluttered, and incredibly, a grin flickered over his bluish lips. "Lucky you. Always…envied the kids…near the water."

"Well, I wasn't lucky enough to live that close to the water. Our house was on the other side of 17." She glanced toward the lab, and then met his gaze. "Look, I'm going to run this blood down to the lab, and when I get back, we're going to talk about the good old times on The Strand. And don't tell me you didn't spend a lot of time there, because I know you did. I'll be right back…won't be a minute, I promise."

Slowly he opened his eyes. "Yeah, the Strand…did some hell-raising there," he muttered, then grimaced. "Sorry, ma'am. I reckon I've…forgotten how to speak when there's a…lady present."

Cindy smiled down at him, trying to hold back tears. "I want to hear all about it. I'll be right back." She gave him a final pat and rushed to the lab.

Later, she would wonder how much time had actually passed. Not more than a few minutes, she was sure. She stepped back into the chaos of the ER and headed toward the soldier from Conway. She didn't feel so much at sea now; she had a purpose, and that was to stick by her promise to be with him, whatever happened. She knew, deep in her heart, that he probably wasn't going to make it. Otherwise, they would've taken him directly to the OR. But damn it, he wouldn't die alone!

She stopped, her heart giving a lurch. His gurney had disappeared. Her gaze whipped around the room; she saw other soldiers—way too many to count. But none of them looked like the boy from Conway. Then she saw the doctor who'd ordered his blood drawn, working feverishly over another GI.

"What happened to that boy?" she blurted out, reaching his side. "The one you had me draw his blood?"

The blood-splattered doctor gave a weary nod toward a yellow curtain at the rear of the tunnel-like room. "Back there. With the other expectants."

Cindy's heart dropped. This wasn't news.

He'd said from the first moment that the boy probably wouldn't live. That he was "expected" to die. Why, then, had he ordered the blood work? That had given her hope.

She whirled around and raced toward the curtained area. *Please be alive, please...please.* But out of the six gurneys behind the yellow curtain, only one was uncovered, and the occupant was a black GI, eyes closed, breathing shallow. The other five figures were draped by sheets. Cindy's gaze fell upon one of them—the one with blood covering most of the bottom half...where the sheet went flat.

No. Her heart froze in her chest. She took a step forward, her knees trembling. It would be so easy just to turn and leave. Never knowing. Maybe she could convince herself that the doctor out there was wrong, that perhaps a surgeon had come in while she was in the lab and had taken the boy to surgery. Maybe even now, he was being worked on...being saved.

She took a deep breath, and with a trembling hand, she gently drew away the sheet.

His wide brown eyes stared up at her. He didn't look at peace at all. Only terrified.

Ω

The heat pressed around her; not a whisper of a breeze pierced the night. Cindy sat on a bench outside the ER, leaning back against the corrugated tin wall, her eyes closed, and tried to dispel the nightmare images running through her brain. All of them began and ended with one face—the boy from Conway. The boy she'd let down by ignoring his simple plea to stay with him in his last moments of life. Had he known? Was that why he'd been so insistent? Why hadn't she realized that? The blood could've waited. The doctor had surely known he was an expectant— that no matter what they'd done, he was going to die anyway. And all he'd wanted was someone to stay with him for his last moments.

Cindy groaned. *Stupid, stupid, stupid!*

"I thought I might find you here."

She opened her eyes and saw David Ansgar standing in front of her. But he looked completely different than he had when she'd last seen him during the push. He'd changed into civilian clothes—jeans and a Steppenwolf T-shirt, and his hair, which had been slicked back on the ward, looked freshly washed and somehow longer and blonder.

"What are you doing hanging around here?" she asked. "You should be out at the NCO Club, chugging back a few beers."

"I could ask you the same thing." He placed a small Styrofoam cooler on the bench beside her and took a seat. "I thought I'd bring a PBR to you. Figured you could use one." He opened the cooler and drew out a chilled Pabst Blue Ribbon.

"God bless you." Cindy took the beer, popped

the top and took a long quenching swallow. She wasn't normally a beer drinker; in fact, she wasn't much of a drinker at all, but since she'd turned 21 in May, she'd sampled a few tasty sweet drinks like pina coladas and Singapore slings. Right now, though, this beer tasted just as good as the sweetest drink she'd ever had.

David watched her. "So, was it as bad as you expected?"

She closed her eyes and nodded. "Worse."

He sat silently for a long moment, and then said, "I wish I could tell you that's as bad as it's going to get. But I'd never lie to you like that."

A wave of panic swept through her. "Oh, God! I don't know if I can do this."

"You can." His voice was quiet, firm. "One thing I can guarantee, L.T., the more you deal with stuff like that, the more competent you'll become. Some of the things you'll see…" He stopped and shook his head, his eyes taking on an odd expression. Haunted, Cindy thought. Then he continued, "You'll do what needs to be done. And you'll know you're making a difference."

Cindy looked at him. "Really? Well, I didn't make a difference today. I screwed up. *Royally* screwed up."

His gaze met hers. "You want to talk about it?"

She told him about the soldier from Conway. By the time she finished, tears streamed down her face. "So, I couldn't do that one thing he asked of me. Just a few minutes, David! That's all it would've taken. Instead of taking that blood to the lab..." She bit back a sob.

He reached out and gave her hand a quick squeeze, then released it as if he'd suddenly realized he was overstepping his boundaries. Disappointment flickered through her. His touch had been reassuring, made her feel as if she weren't quite so alone.

For a long moment, he didn't speak. What had she expected, she wondered? Reassurance that what she'd done—or hadn't done—wasn't so horrible? He was probably trying to find a tactful way to tell her she didn't deserve to be wearing the uniform of a combat nurse.

"You *feel* like you screwed up," he said finally. "But what you did was follow orders. Here's the thing, L.T., you learned that next time, you'll try to never leave a dying soldier alone when he begs you to stay with him. But sometimes, no matter how much you want to do something, you can't. There's too many of them dying, and not enough of us. And you'll deal with that, too."

She stared at him. "I don't know if I can handle that."

"You'll be surprised what you can handle." He tipped back his can of beer and drank the last of it, and then he stood. "Well, got another early shift tomorrow, so I guess I'll try to get a few winks." He gave her his quick smile. "You should try to do that, too."

Again, Cindy felt that odd flicker of disappointment. She'd hoped they could talk longer. She had so many questions. Where was he from? How long had he been in-country? How come he seemed more like a doctor than a corpsman?

"Yeah, I guess you're right," she said, standing. She swayed wearily, and he reached out to steady her. She gave a little laugh. "Now, I *know* you're right. So, we're working together tomorrow?" she asked hopefully.

He nodded. "Yeah, I've got three more day shifts then I switch to nights after my day off." He turned to head back to his barracks. "Take care, L.T. See you tomorrow."

"Hey, David," she called after him. He turned and looked back. "Thanks,"

Cindy said. "You know…for the pep talk—and the beer."

He smiled. "Anytime."

Cindy watched him go. If she'd be working with David, surely she wouldn't screw up too badly.

October 1970

Dear Cindy,

I hope you're doing okay over there. I've got to tell you—I'm worried sick about you. Over there so far away, and that fighting going on. Every night I watch Walter Kronkite, and it just looks like the war is never going to end. Of course, I know we <u>have</u> to be there. We've got to stop Communism from coming here and brainwashing all of us. But still, I don't understand why you had to go join the Army and get sent over there. That's not a place for a nice young woman like you. I can understand why you wanted to be a nurse, but why couldn't you just stay here in Indiana and work at Methodist Hospital like Sylvia Dixon's daughter does? Well, I know I might as well be talking to the wall. You always were the most hard-headed girl I ever saw!

Anyway, at least they caught that Communist, Angela Davis, in New York the other day. I hope to God they throw her in prison and toss the key away. They should do that to every one of them peace freaks who're always marching on Washington. If they had their way, we'd all be singing the Russian national anthem and eating Beef

Stroganoff. (That is Russian, isn't it?)

Well, anyway, we're all doing okay here. Joanie's looking forward to Halloween. The school's having this big party, and then she's going out trick-or-treating with that Sherry friend of hers. Wild girl, that one. Definitely a bad influence on Joanie. Anyway, I think she's decided to dress up as a hobo. Joanie, not Sherry. That one will probably dress as a tramp down on The Circle. You should see some of the stuff she wears to school—skirts that barely cover her hiney and big old platform shoes!!! But back to Halloween…those kids are so lazy these days! When I was a kid, I used to go all out…planned my costume for months. Well, at least Joanie didn't ask to take one of my white sheets so she could cut two holes in it. She really misses you, Cindy. We all do. I sure hope you're doing okay over there. You'd better be careful, you hear me? How come you don't write much? Only one letter so far, and you've been there for over a month now.

Guess I'd better close, hon. I've got to get over to the Kroger—working evenings all week. You take care, sweetie. We love you. And we're praying to God to keep you safe.

Love, Mommy

CHAPTER FOUR

The stench seemed to be coming from the unvented air conditioner duct. Or maybe it was from the hallway. Wrinkling her nose, Cindy tucked the last of her clothing into a drawer and slammed it shut. "Okay, I can't take it anymore. What *is* that horrible smell?"

She stepped into the hallway of her new quarters, Hooch # 4, and scanned up and down. Nothing she could see to account for the noxious odor. But it was definitely getting worse.

Relieved at finally moving into the nurse's quarters so she didn't have to find a ride for the two-mile trip to the hospital every morning, she was even more thrilled to learn that the quarters had been recently renovated, and were blessedly air-conditioned. Her room wasn't just cool; it was downright cold! She'd dug out her thick

Niagara U sweatshirt from her duffle bag and put it on. Amazing she'd actually had the foresight to pack it.

But this smell? What, on God's green earth could smell that bad? It was worse than Myrtle Beach at low tide after a hurricane had deposited a bunch of rotting dead fish in the sand.

From down the hall, she heard music starting to play on a stereo—Joni Mitchell. Wasn't that coming from Jenny's room? But she was working the 2nd shift this week, so she should still be sleeping. Cindy glanced at her wristwatch. Well, it *was* just after noon. The morning had flown by with all the unpacking and organizing.

She tapped at Jenny's door. "Hey, you up, Jen?"

"Come on in!" she called.

Cindy opened it. "*Yikes!*" She pretended to shade her eyes. "That's what I call *bright*. No wonder you're awake. How could anybody sleep in here?"

Jenny's room had been painted a bright sunshine-yellow with orange trim. Either the former occupant had exceptionally bad taste or had been in a chemically-induced fog when she'd decided on these colors.

Surrounded by packing boxes, Jenny sat on the floor, dressed only in an Army tee and red heart-print panties. "It's not the paint that's keeping me awake." She wore a welcoming smile, but dark smudges shadowed her almond-shaped eyes.

Cindy knew she looked the same. On her first three nights after duty in Surgical ICU, she'd cried herself to sleep. After that, she'd stopped crying, but every time she slept, the nightmares would come.

"I know," she said. "It's hard to sleep when you see their faces every time you close your eyes."

Jenny nodded and took a rolled-up poster out of a box. "Hand me that box of thumbtacks, will you?" She got to her feet and stepped onto her cot, positioning the poster against the wall.

Cindy couldn't hold back a snicker. "Bobby Sherman?"

Jenny threw her a dark look. "Hey, he's cute! Make yourself useful and give me a pin, will you?"

"Sorry." Cindy bit her lip and handed her a push-pin. "Sometimes I forget how young you are."

"I'm 21!" she said, with a look of outrage. "That means I have to stop liking Bobby Sherman?" She pushed the pin into the poster and held out her hand for more.

"*Just* 21," Cindy corrected. "You're still a baby. *God*! What *is* that smell? It's like something died in this place."

Jenny smirked and pushed in the final pin. "Finally! I know something you don't." She flopped down onto her cot, sending it creaking under her 98 pounds. "It woke me up yesterday. So thick I thought it was coming out of my pores…thought I'd caught some strange Vietnamese disease. But a girl down the hall told me it's *nuoc ma*—something the mama sans eat for lunch every day. 'Armpit sauce," she calls it. They cook it on hot plates down in the community room."

"God!" Cindy wrinkled her nose. "But what *is* it? And how could anyone eat something that smells that bad?"

"It's a seasoning they use that comes from…are you ready? Decayed fish."

So, that explains the rotting fish on the beach smell.

Jenny rolled onto her back and stared up at the ceiling, her straight, glossy-black hair splayed around her head in a shiny ribbon. "And I thought *my* relatives ate some weird stuff."

On the stereo, Joni Mitchell sang about a big yellow taxi.

"Gross." Cindy perched on Jenny's footlocker. "So, they do this every day? That's what we have to put up with to get clean laundry?"

Jenny shrugged. "Hey, if it'll get me out of doing laundry, I can handle it."

"I suppose you're right," Cindy gave a sigh. "I can't believe I'm saying this, but I'm hungry. You want to head down to the mess hall?" Her gaze centered on her friend as she just realized something. "You're practically *naked*! Aren't you *freezing* in here?"

"Not anymore." She glanced up at the air duct, and Cindy followed her gaze. A small neck pillow had been inserted into the opening. "*That's* how I adjust my thermostat, and I have an extra pillow if you're interested." She sat up and reached for her fatigue trousers draped on her footlocker. "Yeah, let's go eat. No matter what crap they're serving, it's got to be better than what the mama sans are having."

Ω

"You're right," Jenny said, taking a bite of mashed potatoes and gravy. "I see the faces, too. Every night. But at least with you, most of your patients can communicate. Mine? Some of them might as well be mannequins in a store window."

Cindy nodded, reaching for her Coke. "I don't know how you do it."

A sizzle of frying grease erupted from the kitchen, and the smell of French fries permeated through the dining hall. As Cindy ate, she felt the stares of men all around her. At first, it had been disconcerting to be one of just a few women in the mess hall, but now the stares had become commonplace. She was a round-eyed woman in a world of men, and therefore, an object of curiosity—and desire. And if she were totally honest with herself, she had to admit it was a heady feeling; she'd never felt attractive to the opposite sex. After all, who wanted to date Lurch?

Many of the other nurses—Rosalie, for one—were clearly put out by it. Probably because as pretty as she was, she'd never had a lack of male attention. Jenny, too, was annoyed by the stares, but insisted it wasn't because she was pretty, but because she was Chinese-American—the enemy, and the looks they gave her were ones of disgust, not lust. Cindy thought she was crazy.

Jenny shook her head and reached for her glass of milk. "But then…maybe it would be worse to be where *you* are. All those expectants…" She shuddered. "I don't know how you deal with that."

"What choice do you have?" Cindy stared at the Indiana state flag hanging next to others circumventing the cavernous room and thought of the expectant from last night's shift. Only 19, from Vincentown, New Jersey. Multiple gunshot wounds. Nothing anyone could do for him. He'd died calling for his mother. And Cindy had refused to leave him until he'd taken his last breath, much to the disgust of Cap Bren. It had been awful, but still, Cindy wouldn't change places with Jenny.

Her friend had been assigned to Ward 5, the Neurosurgical ICU. Everyone knew it was one of the worst places to work in the hospital because of the "gorks"—men with horrific brain injuries, left comatose or worse. Still alive but with brains so damaged they no longer functioned. It took a strong nurse to cope with that. Cindy didn't know if she could do it. After Jenny's first day of duty, they'd run into each other in the temporary quarters and had gone outside for a cigarette. It had been clear by looking at Jenny's shell-shocked face that she hadn't been prepared for what she'd encountered, and Cindy knew her own face looked exactly the same.

Between jerky puffs of her cigarette, Jenny explained the eight levels of consciousness in which her patients were classified. Cindy was familiar with the first five—"alert: normal," "awake: spontaneous eye opening," "lethargic: greater than normal sleeping but easy to arouse," "stuporous: greater than normal sleeping, but hard to arouse" and "semi-comatose: won't awaken but have purposeful movements." The others were new to her—"decorticates" were patients in a coma but who curled up to pain; "decerebrates," also comatose, stretched out to pain. Those classified as "flaccid" didn't respond at all, even to extreme pain.

Just listening to those definitions made Cindy want to cry. Who'd want to live like that? The boys, the ones who survived, would be sent home to live out the remainder of their lives in nursing homes. For the first time since she'd arrived here, Cindy felt lucky to be working in Surgical

ICU; at least *some* of their patients recovered. The lucky ones would be sent home; the not-so-lucky would go back to their units to fight again.

"What's weird is that many of them *look* so normal," Jenny was saying through a bite of fried chicken. "I mean, except for the bandaged heads. Last night, they brought a new guy in, a decerebrate…and God, Cindy! I found myself thinking he was *cute*! I mean, he was a nice-looking guy. Twenty years old. Just the kind of guy I'd be attracted to if I saw him in the O Club. Isn't that just *sick*?" She put down her fork as if suddenly realizing that she did, indeed, feel sick.

"You know what?" Cindy tucked a lock of damp hair behind her ear; she knew it had been a mistake to wear it down, but she was so sick of always having to twist it up for work. But God, it was so hot on her neck. The mess hall wasn't air-conditioned like the barracks. Only a few ceiling fans turned lazily, doing little—if anything—to cool the humid heat that clung to her skin like mold. "I'm going over to the beauty salon and get my hair cut," she said, making the decision there and then. "Short hair has got to make you feel cooler. Why don't you come with me? Then maybe we can take a bus into Saigon. Check it out."

Jenny was already shaking her head. "Not enough time to go into Saigon; I'm back on duty at 7:00. But I'll come to the salon with you. If we ever get a day off together, maybe we can do

Saigon then."

Cindy sighed. "Yeah, like *that* will ever happen. "

Ω

"*Hot toc!*" The smiling Vietnamese hairdresser pointed at Cindy's new do and handed her a mirror.

Cindy checked out the back of her short layered haircut and grinned. "It's cute!"

"And it really accentuates those gorgeous green eyes of yours," Jenny said, swinging her new chin-length bob and admiring herself in the mirror. "I wish I had the nerve to go that short, but Michael would go ape if he knew I'd cut it at all!"

"Well, Michael's not here, is he?" Cindy said, turning her head back and forth and gazing into the mirror. Jenny was right. This short cut did make her eyes look large and elfin. "Besides, you're planning to break up with him, right?"

"Thinking about it. My mother will die, though. She loves him. She's already planning the wedding."

"Thanks, Mai," Cindy said as the hairdresser removed the plastic cape from around her neck.

She followed the pretty Vietnamese girl to the cash register and paid for her haircut with MPC's—Military Payment Certificates which she'd received in exchange for the real money she'd arrived with. MPCs were the only legal currency accepted on military bases in Vietnam. It looked like Monopoly money, but it spent just as well as real—and prices at the PX were good.

Cindy had discovered there were six PXs on base, and they offered everything from toiletries to snacks and alcohol. And what you couldn't get at the PX you could order through the PACEX catalog.

Mai smiled and with a slight bow, tried to hand Cindy her change. Cindy shook her head. "You keep. For you."

Mai's smile widened, her brown eyes sparkling. *"Cảm ơn bạn."* Thank you. She tucked the money in the pocket of her apron.

Beautiful girl, Cindy thought. Even with that smallpox scar on her forehead. She knew she'd tipped her more than she should have, but these people were dirt-poor. A few extra bucks would go a long way to feed a Vietnamese family, and it wasn't like Cindy was hurting for money. With her paycheck every two weeks from the Army, and not much to spend it on, by the time she was back in The World, she'd have a nice little nest egg built up...maybe enough to buy that GTO she'd been salivating over since she'd first got a driver's license.

"So, what are you going to do now?" Jenny asked as they stepped out of the fragrant salon into the decayed stench of the post. It was raining...as usual. The afternoon monsoon would ruin their new hairdos, but the rain felt good on Cindy's heated skin.

"Well, I thought I'd stop by the PX and see if they have anything new," she said. "Want to come?"

"No. I think I'll go back to the barracks and get a nap before work."

Just as she spoke, the strobe of helicopter blades broke through the sound of the rain—not just one chopper, but several. Cindy and Jenny locked gazes.

"Or maybe not," Jenny said.

CHAPTER FIVE

Almost twelve hours later, Cindy closed her eyes, leaned against the wall of the hospital facing the covered walkway, and took a long drag of her Virginia Slim. Beside her on the bench sat a new nurse, Lt. Shyanne Rooney. Cindy wondered if Shyanne had finally stopped trembling, but she was too tired to open her eyes and see.

God, it was hot as Hades. She tugged at the modesty panel beneath her fatigue shirt, drawing it away from her skin in a futile attempt to get some semblance of relief.

The wounded coming from surgery had been nonstop until about fifteen minutes ago. It was going on two in the morning, and Cindy felt like she could sleep forever. Now, anyway. As soon as she got into her bed back at the barracks, she knew what would happen. Her brain would click on, and all of the horrors she'd seen in the past hours would re-play, over and over like an 8-track tape on a constant loop.

"Oh, Lord a-mighty," Shyanne said softly in her thick Kentucky accent. "Russell Springs feels like it's on another planet. How can this be the same Earth? What we just went through...they'd never believe it. I mean, what they see on their TV screens..."

Cindy stirred herself to respond, but kept her eyes closed. "Probably would rather not know the truth; I know my mother wouldn't."

"Oh, here comes Cap Bren," said Shyanne as if she were welcoming her new best friend.

Cindy opened her eyes, and stifling an inward groan, straightened up as the willowy blond nurse took a seat a few benches over and lit a cigarette. Blood spattered her fatigues, just as it did Cindy's and Shyanne's. Only difference was, Cap Bren probably didn't even care. In fact, she probably got off on it. *The cold bitch.* If vampires were real, she'd be one. The woman was still as haughty and distant as she'd been on the day they'd met, and Cindy's dislike for her had only grown. Not to mention, her disgust. Sleeping with a married man! Inexcusable! Cindy knew what it was like to have her family torn apart by a home wrecker. As soon as the divorce was final, Daddy had married his little dish, and now Cindy had a half-brother not even out of elementary school and a toddler half-sister.

Cindy and Shyanne sat silently, inhibited by

Cap Bren's presence, even though they might as well have been invisible since she hadn't even acknowledged them. But if they did something wrong–to her way of thinking–she'd notice all right. She was probably just waiting to call them out on something, the gung-ho witch!

The doors to Ward 3 opened, and two corpsmen came out to smoke under the covered walkway. Their cigarettes flared in the darkness, and their conversations carried on the night's sultry breeze.

"Man, did you see that Amber Summers is coming next week? Doing a show, too. Right here."

He was referring to the quadrangle at the end of the walkway where all the shows were held.

The other corpsman gave a deep groan. "The Playmate? Shit, I want a piece of that! Did you see that centerfold?"

In the greenish-yellow halo of a security light anchored on the covered walkway, Cindy watched Cap Bren straighten up and glare toward the two men. "Just what the troops need," she said, her voice dripping with condemnation. "A little tart in a mini-skirt and go-go boots prancing around the ward and driving the sex-starved guys crazier than they already are. Yeah, that's good for morale."

The two corpsmen looked startled, then muttered apologies. For what, Cindy didn't know, and was sure they didn't either. They beat feet down the walkway, no doubt to escape the nutty RN before she entirely went off on them.

An awkward silence fell; Shyanne broke it, much to Cindy's horror.

"I hear Bob Hope puts on a really great Christmas show," she said brightly, aiming her remark at Cap Bren. Apparently, she hadn't been around long enough to know better.

Cap Bren raised her head, took a long drag on her cigarette and stared balefully at Shyanne. Incredibly, the Kentucky FNG wasn't at all fazed by her superior's cold demeanor because she gave the nurse a 100-watt smile. "Why, I'm just tickled to death to be here in time for Christmas. They say nobody puts on a show like Bob Hope."

Cap Bren's icy gaze didn't veer from Shyanne's animated face. It was just a good thing looks couldn't kill because poor Shyanne, as oblivious as could be, would be lying in the morgue with all the other stiffs. Trying to stop her, Cindy gave her a nudge with her elbow.

"*What?*" she said, turning her smile on Cindy. "Maybe it's not cool, but I *love* Bob Hope! Why, we used to watch his show; the whole family would get together, and we'd make us a big bowl of popcorn and have a good old time." She looked back at Cap Bren. "Captain, is it true that Long Binh gets the best acts here? You know, because it's such a big important post? Oh, Lord! I heard even *Mrs. Nixon* came to the hospital last year. Is that true? Did you get to meet her?"

Cap Bren stood, dropped her cigarette and ground it beneath the toe of her combat boot. Apparently, rules weren't all that important to her. But if Cindy or Shyanne had done it, God help them. "Hell, no, I didn't get to meet her! The Red Cross wouldn't let her anywhere near our wards. God forbid that the First Lady should have to see the ugly reality of war. No, she had a 'meet and greet' with GI's on the malaria ward." She wore the expression of someone who had a vile taste in her mouth. Her arctic gaze skewered them. "You two on vacation? If not, I suggest you get back to work." She turned and headed to the ward.

In the northwest, flashes of artillery lights illuminated the night, and flares floated to earth, looking like festive lanterns. Cindy wearily got to her feet. She waited until the nurse disappeared, and then muttered, "Bitch."

Shyanne drew in a sharp, shocked breath. "Why, Cindy! Shame on you! The Lord tells us not to judge others unless we've walked a mile in their shoes."

"*You* walk a mile in her shoes." Cindy headed toward the hospital doors. "Personally, I'd rather put a two-step in one of them."

"What's that?"

Cindy turned and gave her new friend a smile. "A poisonous snake they have here. A bite from one, you take two steps, then drop dead."

Ω

Cindy didn't get off duty for another three hours. When she finally entered her room at 5:15 am, her fatigues were so soaked with sweat and blood, she felt as if she'd stepped out of a horror movie set in a rain forest. She stripped them off and stood in her underwear, staring down at the sodden, gore-saturated mess. Suddenly she bent down and grabbed her fatigue shirt, and turned to her bureau where she kept an extra pair of bandage shears.

Seconds later, the modesty panel inside her shirt fell to the floor. Cindy felt a measure of satisfaction, but it still wasn't good enough. She grabbed it and gleefully cut it into little pieces. Then she dropped facedown onto her cot and fell into a blissful, dreamless sleep.

Ω

Cindy sat, cross-legged, on her cot, eyes closed. Tears streamed down her face as the singer's voice washed over her from the 8-track stereo she'd bought at the PX and set up on a make-shift shelf of boards and cement blocks against the wall.

It wasn't just his voice that moved her, which was incredibly beautiful and full of passion for his girl, Jennifer. It was the memories his voice awakened in her. Memories of a weekend last summer on a mud-soaked farm in upstate New York. A million years ago.

A knock on her door startled her. Wiping away tears, she called out, "Come on in!"

The door opened and a bedraggled-looking Jenny stepped in, still in her blood-stained fatigues. "Hey," she said, eyes weary. Then her gaze sharpened. "What's wrong?"

"Oh, nothing!" Cindy gave her a sheepish smile. "This song always makes me cry."

Jenny looked at the stereo. "Nice voice. Who is it?"

"Bert Sommer. I saw him at Woodstock." She scrambled off the bed and opened the door of the mini-fridge she'd bought at the PX the other day. "PBR? You look like you could use one."

Jenny's jaw had dropped. "First of all, yes, to the beer. Second, *you* were at Woodstock? Are you shitting me? *You?*"

Cindy grinned, popping the top of the Pabst Blue Ribbon and handing it to her. "You really think I'm Debbie Reynolds, don't you?"

Jenny laughed. "I was thinking Pollyanna." Sprawling onto Cindy's cot, she took a long draw from her beer.

Grinning, Cindy threw a pillow at her. "Well, I *was* at Woodstock. I was in New York State visiting my old college roommate and we decided, kind of on the spur of the moment, to go to this huge outdoor concert we'd heard about. There were so many acts I was excited to see—Joan Baez, The Who, Jimi Hendrix, but it turned out the one that impressed me most was a guy I'd never heard of—Bert Sommer. Something about him just captured me. It made me wish my name was Jennifer. As soon as I got back to town, I bought his album."

"Well, for God's sake, play it again," Jenny said. "I've got to hear this song about me."

Jenny listened to it, a look of awe on her pretty face, and Cindy knew she "got it." After the song ended, Cindy rose from the cot to turn down the volume.

"Wow," Jenny murmured. "What does he look like? His voice makes me want him to strip off my clothes and fuck me senseless."

Cindy felt her face go scarlet at Jenny's profanity. Pollyanna, she wasn't—especially since arriving here in 'Nam and learning all kinds of new curse words, but that particular one was just so coarse! And it seemed especially so coming from the mouth of a sweetheart like Jenny.

"You *do* get it. I knew you would. And he *is* cute. Oh, my God! You should see his hair. Here." She grabbed the 8-track cover and passed it over. "In fact, he was a cast member in the West Coast version of 'Hair.'" She stopped, seeing the amazement on Jenny's face when she looked up from the album cover. "*What?*"

Jenny shook her head. "*You.* At Woodstock. I just can't get over it. And how is it possible you're still a virgin?"

Cindy felt blood rush to her cheeks. Jenny was the only one who knew her secret. But that was cool; she was glad to have a good friend to share secrets with. She gave her a sly grin. "Believe me, Jen, if I could've got up on that stage with Bert, I wouldn't be a virgin today."

Ω

"Lieutenant," snapped Cap Bren the minute Cindy walked onto the ward. "That Playboy bunny will be arriving for a tour of the ward at 0900—and I want you to escort her. Show her the ropes. I can't stomach it."

"No problem, Captain."

And it *wasn't* a problem. Cindy welcomed a change to the daily routine—one that didn't involve a mass-cal. Anyway, she was curious to learn what a pin-up girl would be like—not that she was familiar with **Playboy**, but everyone knew it was filled with photos of naked girls. Or nearly naked. It seemed an odd choice, though, for a celebrity visit. That was one of the few things she agreed with Cap Bren about. How could having a little sex-pot strutting around the ward in a mini-skirt be a good thing for these poor guys?

As if reading her thoughts, Cap Bren glared at her as if *she* were responsible for the Playboy playmate's visit. "Well, what are you standing there for? Get the dressing tray and get busy. Work doesn't stop just because a blonde with big boobs is visiting."

The two hours flew by. Cindy was in the middle of suctioning a soldier's trach when she heard a commotion at the ward entrance. She turned to see a major in dress uniform and a couple of civilians standing just inside the doors with a curvy brunette. She wore a ridiculous black crinkle-patent sleeveless mini-dress and black knee-high boots, and looked like she'd just stepped out of the pages of **Photoplay**.

"I'll be right with you," Cindy called out. She finished with the soldier, and hurried over to the group. "Hi. I'm Lieutenant Sweet, and I'll be taking you around to meet our patients." She tried not to recoil from the cloying perfume that emanated from the girl. Chanel # 5? Could Cap Bren smell it over at her desk? Probably not. If so, she'd be flying over here, demanding that she take a shower before meeting the guys and making them nauseated.

The red-faced major, obviously a REMF–rear echelon motherfucker, as they were called because of their cushy jobs far from the front— gave the playmate a gushy smile and introduced her, his gob-smacked eyes never veering from her pretty face, except for the occasional sly glance at her generous boobs. Cindy supposed he was congratulating himself for being lucky enough to get bimbo-duty for the day.

"Pleased to meet you, Lt. Sweet." Amber Summers gave Cindy a bright smile, her false-lashed brown eyes sweeping over her fatigues and combat boots.

Cindy smiled back and shook her hand. Was that pity she saw in her gaze? Why? That she wasn't dressed like a tart?

"I just want to say, I'm *so* grateful for all you do for our fighting troops," the playmate went on in a chirpy mid-western twang, her gaze sweeping the ward, and finally resting on Cap Bren who sat diligently working at her desk, her back rigid with what Cindy knew to be disdain. "All of you! You're so brave…" She gave a delicate shudder. "I could never do it…"

Damn right. Cindy tried to imagine the buxom brunette changing a bedpan—or bagging a body for the morgue—and couldn't. Amber wore her hair "I Dream of Jeannie-style," all piled up and braided on top with a fat, shimmering pony-tail falling to her shoulders, but she didn't have an iota of Barbara Eden's girl-next-door sweetness. Pancake make-up shellacked her face, and her eyes were lined dramatically in electric blue—not a flattering shade, even for a playmate.

Suddenly Cap Bren's blonde head shot up, and her gaze skewered Cindy. "Lieutenant Sweet, Miss Summers doesn't have all day. Go ahead and start the tour."

The quicker to get her out of here. It was left unsaid, but Cindy got the message loud and clear.

"Right. We'll start over here." Cindy led the playmate and her entourage—the two civilians, one obviously a bodyguard and the other, a press secretary or something, and the major—over to one of the few conscious patients, a triple amputee. Some of the stronger guys on the ward called out to Amber, begging her to come over to their beds. "Wait your turn, guys," Cindy admonished. "She's only one person."

The two corpsman on duty, taking vital signs, looked longingly at Amber from across the ward. Sooner or later, they'd each find an excuse to come over and ask Cindy a question or to give an unnecessary report on a patient. It was inevitable. And why not? They were human, and with the exception of the nurses who were technically "off-limits," it had been a long time since they'd seen a round-eyed female.

The playmate looked around at the various machines and tubes that kept the soldiers functioning and Cindy became aware of the cacophony of beeps, hisses, clicks and alarms of the hospital—a sound that had become white noise to her. She thought she saw the playmate shudder. Cindy placed her hand on the amputee's remaining arm. "This is Private First Class Reggie Carpenter," she said. "He won a Purple Heart for dragging a wounded soldier to safety just before an incoming round hit their bunker. Private Carpenter was the only other survivor."

She watched Amber's eyes widen as she stood

on the other side of his bed and took in the sight of the nearly limbless soldier. He looked up at her like an excited school boy, his blue eyes gleaming. "Wow! You're so pretty!"

Amber looked disconcerted, then took a deep breath and leaned to give him a kiss on the cheek. "Thank you, soldier. You're pretty handsome, yourself."

Cindy noticed that Amber's voluptuous breasts brushed against him for a brief moment before she pulled away. The soldier had obviously noticed it, too, because his face turned scarlet. To save him from further embarrassment, Cindy moved away from his bed. "Let's move on to the third bed down on the left. These next two guys are heavily sedated."

Before she was out of ear-shot, she heard a laugh come from the bed of the amputee. "Damn! I guess I'm not as bad-off as I thought. First boner I've had since the firefight."

Cindy stifled a laugh. Maybe a playmate wasn't such bad medicine after all. Just as this thought went through her head, Amber came to a frozen stop in front of another patient's bed. One of the corpsmen, Derek Stevens, was in the middle of changing the dressing on a soldier's face. A grenade had taken off his nose, mouth and half his jaw, but somehow, he'd survived.

Amber stood there, staring in revulsion at the wounded G.I., the blood draining from her face. He stared back at her, and Cindy watched the appreciative gleam in his eyes disappear, replaced by a wintry flatness. Her heart gave a pang. She could almost read his thoughts. *I forgot! I'm a monster now. Is this how my girlfriend will look when she sees me?*

Cap Bren was right. This was no place for a Hollywood sexpot. These guys didn't need to be reminded that their lives had been forever changed by a grenade or a claymore mine or artillery rounds. Especially if the gal couldn't hide the horror she felt by looking at them!

"Why don't we let Private Stevens finish with Lt. Boniventure, and we'll come back later," Cindy said, walking toward the playmate. "Right down here, we have---"

Amber's eyes rolled back in her head, and she swayed. Cindy lurched to grab her before she fell, but her bodyguard got to her first. He swooped her off her feet and headed toward the door.

"For Christ's sake!" Cap Bren snarled from her chair, glaring at the shocked major. "Don't just stand there, gaping like an idiot, Major! Better go check on your little bimbo. I'm sure you're really good at hand-holding."

Instead of reprimanding her for speaking to a superior officer in such a manner, the major wiped at his suddenly perspiring face and scurried after the starlet and her bodyguard. The promotions guy followed meekly behind him.

Cindy's gaze met Cap Bren's, and for once, she

didn't see disdain in the captain's face. In fact, she wasn't positively sure, but she thought she saw a glimmer of a smile on her lips. But it was gone almost immediately, if it had ever been there at all.

"And what are *you* just standing there for?" she said. "Get back to work!"

"Yes, ma'am." Cindy hurried over to the corpsman finishing up on Lt. Boniventure.

I'll never like you, Cap Bren. But I just might be starting to respect you.

November 1970

Dear Cindy,

I hope all is well with you over there. Your mother just worries about you all the time. I keep telling her you have a good head on your shoulders, that you'll be fine. But I don't think she hears me. You know how she is—she'd worry a wart off a toad. I love my sister, but she just drives me nuts sometimes. Well, you remember. You saw us fighting like cats and dogs, didn't you? And over the silliest things. Remember that time we didn't speak for days because I was watching **Rowen & Martin's Laugh In***, and she said it was obscene? Said it was a bad influence on you girls. And I told her if she didn't like what I watched on TV, she could move out and find her own place. I guess that <u>was</u> a mean thing to say— considering she and your daddy had just got divorced, and she was all messed up over that. Well...you know what it's like having a sister that bugs the heck out of you, right? Sometimes, you just lose it. So, sue me.*

And speaking of Joanie, I think she misses you even more than Ellen and I do. Poor thing just mopes around all the time. And every time a letter from you arrives, she just brightens up like a Christmas tree. Not that we get many letters from you. (Hint, hint.) But I guess they're keeping you pretty busy over there. Apparently, that peace plan that sounded so good back in September has come to *nothing, huh? I figured that's what would happen. I'm beginning to think we're never going to get out of Vietnam. Seeing all those boys dying on the news every night just makes me sick. Of course, if I say anything against the war, Ellen starts accusing me of being a communist. She reminds me of your Grandpa Van more every day. Lord, he suspected <u>everybody</u> of being a commie. Just between you and me, I'd love to go on a protest march…maybe go to DC and give Nixon a piece of my mind. Yeah, <u>that'll</u> happen! Ha!*

Not much going on around here. Same old, same old. Ellen is still working at the Kroger…still talking about moving out and finding her own place. Ha! Like <u>that will</u> happen! Heck, I don't want her to, anyway. I'd miss her too much. Joanie is still hanging out with that little Sherry girl down the street—thick as thieves, those two. Ellen can't stand her…thinks she's boy-crazy, and is going to turn Joanie into a little streetwalker. I keep telling her to lighten up, but you know she never listens to me.

I'm still working at the telephone company, still saving money for that trip to Hawaii I'm going to take some day. Hey, wouldn't it be great if we could meet there for your R&R? Isn't that what it's called? But shoot! I don't think there's any way I'll have enough money in time. Oh, I bought a new record the other day—B.J. Thomas—the one with "Raindrops Keep Fallin' on My Head." It's from **Butch Cassidy & the Sundance Kid.** *Do you remember when we went and saw that movie at the Brownie Theater last fall? I just love Robert Redford!*

But Paul Newman is pretty darn good-looking, too, in this movie. Do you have any theaters there? I hope so! I don't know what I'd do without the Brownie Theater. Be bored to death, I guess. Of course, I'm still dating Tommy. You remember him, right? He works down the hall in Accounting. He's okay, I guess. No Robert Redford if you know what I mean...but what can I expect, living here in the cornfields of Indiana?

Well, I guess I'd better run. Got to get up early tomorrow for work. You take care, you hear? And just know we're all thinking about you—and praying you're okay—every day. Love you, hon.

Aunt Terri

CHAPTER SIX

Dr. Charley Moss, the surgeon she'd encountered at that first devastating mass-cal where she'd left the boy from South Carolina, hit the ping pong ball, sending it in a slow-moving arc over the net. Cindy grinned and hammered it, blasting it across the net where it hit the edge of the table at a perfect, un-gettable angle. The officers hanging around the table in the Officers' Club cheered and hooted over the blare of Steppenwolf's "Magic Carpet Ride."

"*Yes!* I win *again!*" Cindy slammed the paddle down on the table, and then tried to wipe the smug grin off her face. "Want to go again?" she asked sweetly.

"*Hell*, no!" Charley gave her a mock glare and handed his paddle over to a red-headed 2nd lieutenant. "I'm sick of being humiliated by a *girl*.

You could've warned me you were a ping pong champion."

"In high school," Cindy corrected.

His warm brown eyes twinkled. "And when was that? Last year?"

"Smartass." Cindy playfully threw a ping pong ball at him which he caught in one giant hand. "I happen to be 21!"

"Don't remind me," Charley quipped. "Jailbait. That's why I'm outta here. Too much temptation." He winked, tossed her the ball and headed off toward the bar.

Cindy laughed. She liked flirting with Charley. In his early-thirties with his wavy, dark brown hair and rugged, square-jawed face, he was the kind of guy that turned girls' heads. But it wasn't just his looks that made him so attractive. He was intelligent, funny, respectful and a talented surgeon who didn't act like he thought he was a god. Unfortunately, he was also happily married. Not only that, but he was the father of four-year-old twin girls and a newborn baby boy back in Tampa. And maybe that was another reason Cindy liked to flirt with him. She knew it wouldn't go any further than that.

As "Magic Carpet Ride" trailed off, another song began to play, and Cindy's heart gave a pang of homesickness…nostalgia…something indefinable. The image of a blond, blue-eyed boy in army fatigues drifted through her mind. Gary. The song, "Incense & Peppermints," always made her think of him. It had come out long after he'd died, but there was just something about it—maybe the peppermints. She still remembered that kiss, the feel of his soft, tentative lips, the hint of peppermint on his breath. She wondered if that flavor—and that song—would always make her feel sad? As if something beautiful and real had been ripped away from her before she really got the chance to savor it.

"You ready to play, Cindy?" asked the redheaded lieutenant, tapping his paddle against his hand.

"I believe it's my turn," said a voice with a slow, southern drawl.

Cindy's gaze shot to an officer in a pilot's drab green uniform. The name scrawled on his chest read *Quinlan*. But it wasn't his name or the gold rising eagle insignia on his collar that drew her attention. It was his intense gaze. She'd never seen eyes that color, more green than blue, a shade that reminded her of one of Aunt Terri's postcard photos, an aerial shot of the sea surrounding a coral reef off a Caribbean island.

Paul Newman, this guy puts your baby blues to shame!

He grinned and gave her a wink—and she realized she'd been staring. Her face grew hot.

"You're not afraid I'll beat you, are you?" he said.

Cindy's eyes narrowed. "Hasn't happened yet." She served—a good one that even a professional would've had a hard time returning. But Quinlan was ready. He hit it back and the game was on.

Ten minutes later, the score stood at 19-18, Quinlan's favor. The game had been fast-paced. No conversation had accompanied it, only cheers and laughter from the growing mass of officers who'd crowded around to watch and place bets— most of them on Cindy—because almost every one of them had been beaten by her.

But she wasn't sure she'd be able to pull it off. Yeah, she'd stayed close, trading the lead with the pilot several times. But every time she had the lead, he'd take it over again. And Cindy knew why. His curly sun-streaked brown hair and structured cheekbones that spoke of an American Indian bloodline kept distracting her. And his smile when he won a point—revealing straight white teeth and a firm, strong mouth above a delectable movie star-like cleft in his chin...well, it was just a crime to be that good-looking!

And she didn't even know his first name.

It was Quinlan's serve. He grinned at her from across the ping pong table, his mesmerizing eyes sparkling. He gave her a slow wink, and her knees went weak. Then he served. The ball skipped just over the net and hit the upper right corner. Cindy lunged for it, but knew it was pointless. The ball bounced away, out of reach.

Quinlan's grin widened. "Nice try, Cinnamon."

"Good serve," Cindy said grudgingly. She wanted to ask why he kept calling her Cinnamon but figured now wasn't the time for chit-chat. The tantalizing smell of grilled hamburgers wafted toward her, and her stomach growled. She hadn't eaten since 1100 hours, but it would have to wait. Until after she beat him.

He grabbed the ball and gave it a bounce. "20-18. Game point."

"*Quin*!" A voice shouted from the door of the officer's club. "Just got the call. Platoon under fire, at least three casualties, maybe four. Hot LZ!"

Quinlan threw down the ball and paddle, and ran toward the door. Cindy stared after him. And just like that, he was gone. The red-headed 2nd lieutenant grabbed the ball. "My turn."

"Who *is* that guy?" Cindy asked.

"Who? Quinlan?" The lieutenant served the ball, and Cindy mechanically hit it back. "Dust off pilot. He's in here all the time when he's not out flying missions."

If that were true, why had she never noticed him before?

The lieutenant won the point. And ten minutes later, the game.

Ω

"*Bastards*!" Jenny downed a rum and Coke in one swig. Her almond-shaped brown eyes swam with tears. "I hate them!"

Cindy reached across the table and gave her hand a squeeze, trying not to sneak a glance at her wristwatch. She knew it was almost time to go on duty, but Jenny had come into the Officer's Club ten minutes ago in a state of fury, and she still hadn't calmed down.

"I just don't get it!" she ranted. "I'm there to help them, and this...*jerk* has the nerve to tell Captain Burke he doesn't want me to touch him! Cindy, he called me a *gook*!"

"Hon, he's a *gork*! His brain isn't working right!"

"No!" She shook her head, sending her sleek black hair flying. "Not this guy. His injury isn't that serious. He's fully conscious and very vocal. And he thinks I'm the enemy! And it's not just him, you know." She glanced around at the male officers in the club. "It's *them*, too. I can see it in their eyes when they look at me. They don't say it out loud but I know what they're thinking. Gook."

Cindy held back a sigh. "Now you're being silly, Jen. Believe me, the only thing they're thinking is how to get you in the sack. And speaking of that, look who just walked in."

Jenny looked toward the door and despite the tears, her face brightened. "Hey, Simon! Over here."

A lanky black captain ambled over to their table, an easy grin on his bespectacled face, his warm brown eyes fixed upon Jenny as if she were the only person who existed in the place. They'd met at the PX a few weeks ago after a supply of small refrigerators had come in. By the time Jenny got there and joined the long line of eager customers, only one fridge remained. Simon Forrester, who'd been in line in front of her, had graciously allowed Jenny to have it, and they'd been dating ever since. He worked in Personnel, and even though everyone teased her about going out with a REMF, she didn't give a rat's ass. She'd fallen head over heels, and apparently, so had he.

He sat down and ordered a beer. Jenny immediately turned to him and began telling him about "the jerk" on the ward who'd had the audacity to call her a gook. *My cue to leave.* Cindy stood. Simon looked up and caught her questioning gaze. *You got this?*

He nodded and gave her a reassuring smile, revealing deep dimples grooved in smooth mahogany skin. Jenny had caught herself a handsome one, that was for sure.

"Time to clock in," Cindy said. "Jenny, have another beer. Or…" she gave her a wink. "Go smoke something."

Recently, they'd discovered the joys of weed, thanks to an enterprising corpsman who worked with Jenny. Just an occasional toke helped to take the edge off. Jenny giggled, nestling her head against Simon's neck. Cindy grinned and headed for the door. They were so cute. So much for poor Michael back in California. She wondered if Jenny had written the "Dear John" letter yet.

And when is it going to happen for me? The thought came out of nowhere. And just as quickly, an image replaced it—one of a handsome pilot with sea-green eyes and sun-streaked hair.

Stupid, Cindy admonished herself. *You'll probably never even see him again.*

CHAPTER SEVEN

Another mass-cal.   Cindy, disheveled, bloody and exhausted, began her ninth hour of duty trying to calm a little Vietnamese girl who writhed on a gurney, secured by restraints. Blood-stained dressings covered her abdomen and thighs. Gunshot wounds.   No evacuation tag to reveal whether or not she'd had morphine.   Cindy had no idea how much to give her, and all the doctors were occupied with incoming.

Eyes glazed with pain, the girl, six years old, Cindy guessed, surely no older than eight, flinched from her touch, fearful of being hurt worse, no doubt. Poor thing.   God knows what events had occurred to bring her here in this shape.   Where was the rest of her family?   Or was she one of the many orphans who roamed the villes near the base?

"It'll be all right, sweetie," Cindy said. "One of the doctors will fix you up good as new." She reached out to brush a piece of matted blue-black hair from her grimy, blood-streaked face.

The little girl hissed, her lips drawing back in a snarl. "*Du ma nhieu!*"

Heart thumping, Cindy withdrew her hand. She didn't speak Vietnamese, but she was pretty damn sure the little girl hadn't given her a compliment. Her beautiful brown eyes blazed hatred. And she wasn't done.

"*Americano putain!*" she screamed, thrashing on the gurney.

Now, Cindy understood why she was restrained. The silver doors from surgery popped open, and David Ansgar burst through, looking as exhausted as Cindy felt. His gaze shot from her to the child.

"What're you doing wasting time with her?" he snarled. "Our guys need your attention!"

Cindy's jaw dropped. She wasn't used to David speaking to her like that. Out of all the corpsmen, he was the one most conscientious about upholding protocol between himself and the nurses.

"She's critical," Cindy said, summoning her most authoritative officer's voice—and it still came out sounding like a girl playing at being a nurse. "Her temp is through the roof, and she's obviously in incredible pain. I don't know if she's had morphine, or how much to give her if she hasn't."

David strode over to another soldier who'd just been wheeled in. "Forget her! Let the little bitch die! Need some help over here!" He began cutting a blood-soaked pant leg off the unconscious G.I.

Cindy stared from David to the little girl. Her breathing was growing shallow—five rapid, deep, gasping breaths followed by a few seconds of silence. Cheyne-Stokes respirations. Until her arrival in Vietnam, Cindy had only read about terminal respirations. Now, she witnessed them every day. Blood oozed out the corner of the child's mouth. Her eyes, so full of hatred and fury a moment before, had become fixed and dilated.

"David, she's dying!"

"Get the fuck over here, Lieutenant!"

Cindy knew an order when she heard one, even if issued by someone she outranked. She ran to his side. There wasn't time to discuss anything. The casualties just kept exploding through the ER doors. Sucking chest wounds, blown off limbs, gory head wounds with pieces of skull missing, revealing the mottled grey of exposed brains, bodies Swiss-cheesed by shrapnel. A smell permeated the ER—beyond the usual ones of blood, antiseptic, and in one horrible case, burned flesh from a white phosphorous wound—the burn that just kept on giving, scorching through each layer of tissue until deprived of oxygen. All these stenches were of the field, clinging to the bodies of every wounded soldier—a loamy, green smell, the essence of the earth mixed with the blood of the wounded, the sweat and grime of days spent out in the bush. It was downright nauseating.

She worked feverishly, cutting off uniforms to identify wounds that weren't immediately evident and triaging for surgery. Somewhere in the back of her mind, she only vaguely remembered a young girl who'd been sickened and squeamish by the atrocious wounds she'd seen that first mass-cal. Today, she was nothing more than a robot.

Finally, the incoming dwindled, and two hours later, Cindy stood in the anteroom to the ER, washing the blood and grime from her fingernails. The doors swung open, and David stepped inside, his scrubs darkened with sweat, eyes blood-shot, lips grim. He ran his fingers through his damp blond hair and said, "Sorry about yelling at you, LT. I'll understand if you want to write me up."

Cindy dried her hands. "Forget it, David. I just want to know why you were so…mean. It's not like you. She was just a little girl." The memory of the child's last moment lingered in her mind. The dilated eyes, the blood seeping from her lips, that last horrible rattle of breath like the clatter of palm fronds in a stiff wind.

David gave her a measured look. "Those two expectants lying on gurneys behind the yellow curtain? That 'little girl' is the one who put them there. Three more casualties are in surgery, and last I heard, it's doubtful if two of them will make it."

Cindy drew in a shocked breath.

He nodded. "Yeah, that little gook tossed a grenade into a group of soldiers as they were doing a search-and-clear in her ville. That's how she got shot—by one of the wounded guys…he's the one who just might survive." At the sink, he turned on the hot water full blast and began to soap up. "Why the hell they brought her here, I don't know. They should've just left her there."

Cindy's stomach had gone hollow at his words. Now, she understood his anger. And it burned deep within her, too, as she thought of all the wounded soldiers they'd worked to save this afternoon. Yet, she couldn't help but wonder what had driven a little girl to such measures? How could one so young be so poisoned by hatred?

She opened her mouth to say something— what, she didn't know. But David turned around, his blue eyes bright with tears. "You know what? We live in a really fucked up world."

Cindy swallowed hard, her throat tightening. "Yeah, it sure is…when a little girl becomes a killer and dies so young."

David shook his head, a muscle in his jaw tensing—and that's when Cindy realized his tears were not of sadness, but of fury. "No, not because of that. Because I don't *give* a shit that she died."

Ω

"Here." Captain Rosalie Martin handed a tightly-wrapped joint to Cindy. "Montagnard Gold. Charley snagged it for me on his last med-cap."

Inside Rosalie's quarters, the scent of sandalwood incense swirled around Cindy and the other three nurses sprawled on cushions and beanbag chairs. Outside, the monsoon rains beat down on the corrugated tin roof, almost drowning out Joni Mitchell singing "Chelsea Morning." Black-light posters of Jimi Hendrix and The Doors hung on the walls, a surprising revelation of Rosalie's musical tastes. Cindy had figured the Alaskan nurse a Gordon Lightfoot kind of girl.

Cindy took a long drag of the joint, and passed it to Jenny. The fragrant weed filled her lungs, and the reality of Vietnam receded just a bit. One hit, not bad. She grinned at Rosalie, thinking how *unlikely* a pothead she was. Well, not that she *was* a pothead. None of them were. But Rosalie, with her penny-red hair, dimples and hazel eyes, looked like the antithesis of someone who enjoyed an occasional toke.

For that matter—Cindy looked over at Jenny and Shyanne—neither did they. But since that first evening a few weeks ago that Rosalie had invited them into her quarters and passed around what she said was the best marijuana Vietnam had to offer, it had become an escape they all looked forward to. Drinking was good, but smoking was better. No toilet hugging in the night and no hangover the next morning. Win-win.

Cindy released the drag she'd held in as long as possible and said, "Charley snagged some Mary Jane from *Charlie?*" She giggled at her joke.

One beautiful eyebrow arched, and Rosalie grinned. "No more for you, Sweet. How can you get stoned on one drag? And no, he didn't get it from Charlie, you idiot. He's got some friends up in the foothills. Very grateful friends who appreciate his medical skills. They call him # 1 *Bac Si* Charley."

"I know what that means!" Shyanne's pretty face lit up. "Vietnamese for 'doctor.'" She took a small puff and let it out immediately.

Cindy couldn't help but grin. Shyanne still hadn't got the hang of toking. But then, she was high all the time, anyway. It came naturally to the Kentucky girl.

"I can't believe Dr. Moss does this stuff," Shyanne went on. "He seems so straight and narrow."

Cindy, Jenny and Rosalie all burst out laughing. Shyanne stared at them in astonishment. "*What?* What did I say?"

Jenny recovered first. "Charley, straight and narrow. He's the least gung-ho doctor at the 24th. How long have you been here, Rooney?"

"A month tomorrow," she said, big green eyes wide and innocent. Wearing baby-doll pajamas, and with her freshly-scrubbed face and blond hair pulled back in a ponytail, she looked about 14.

That sent off another riot of laughter. With the drumming of the rain, and the swell of Joni's clear soprano, it was a moment before Cindy realized someone was banging at Rosalie's door. With authority.

Rosalie's face paled, and all four of them went into action. Rosalie ground the joint into the ashtray and slid it under the bed. The other girls grabbed their cans of beer, and tried to look innocent as Rosalie scrambled to the door.

A collective silent groan filled the room as Cap Bren walked in, still wearing her surgical scrubs. Her suspicious gaze swept over them. "What's going on in here, Captain?"

Cindy wondered if Cap Bren had been promoted overnight. She sure sounded like she thought she outranked Rosalie.

Rosalie stared her down, her chin lifting with just a hint of arrogance. "Just having a little girl-time, Brenda. We would've invited you if you hadn't been on-duty."

Yeah, right, Cindy thought. *The same day we'd be downhill skiing in hell.*

Cap Bren held each of their gazes for one icy moment that felt like an eon. Shyanne's face turned bright red, and Cindy wanted to shake her. *Can you look any guiltier?* Jenny stared back, an "I-don't-give-a-shit" look on her face. Cindy tried to keep her expression neutral, but wasn't sure if she'd accomplished it. No doubt, she looked as guilty as poor Shyanne. She *felt* like she'd been caught stealing from the offering plate.

Cap Bren looked at the wisp of incense smoke curling out of a small brass elephant on Rosalie's desk. "Nice scent," she said. "Sandalwood or patchouli?" Her ice-dagger gaze fixed upon Rosalie.

Rosalie smiled, holding onto her composure. "You must have a good nose, Brenda. It *is* sandalwood."

"Oh, I *do* have a good nose, Rosalie. An extremely *sensitive* sense of smell."

They eyeballed each other. Tension crackled in the room, as thick as the smoke from the incense. Poor Shyanne looked like she was about to faint. And Jenny's "I-don't-give-a-shit" expression had become more of an "oh-fuck-we're-up-shit-creek now" kind of look.

Incredibly, Cap Bren broke eye contact first. "Anyway, I just stopped in to give you some news. In fact, this concerns you all." Her gaze swept over them. "There's a Dining In with some important generals and a few South Vietnam politicians in Saigon tomorrow night, and we need at least five or six nurses to attend— Top Brass orders. I'm volunteering all of you."

"But I'm on-duty tomorrow," Cindy blurted out.

"So am I," Jenny said.

Shyanne beamed. "I'm not, Captain! And I'd love to go! What do we wear?"

"A nice dress and high heels," Cap Bren said. "And if you don't have a nice dress, I suggest you get to the PX tomorrow morning as soon as it opens, and get one. The car will pick you up outside the Officer's Club at 1800 hours." She stared at Cindy, and then Jenny. "And don't worry, you two. I'll find someone to cover for you. This isn't an invitation. Consider it an order."

She whirled around and left the room, slamming the door behind her. All four of them slumped in relief. Jenny reached under the bed and drew out the ashtray. "Where's the lighter?"

Cindy took a sip of her tepid Pabst. "Ah, well...how bad can it be? Hobnobbing with the brass and some politicians? At least, we get a decent dinner and a few hours away from the war."

Rosalie slumped into her beanbag chair, disgust written all over her face. "Just wait," she said. "We'll see how you feel about that on Friday morning."

CHAPTER EIGHT

If he doesn't remove his hand from my butt, I'm going to go ape-shit.

The one-star general was old enough to be her father. No, her *grandfather.* Cindy moved stiffly in his arms. Make that his *one* arm—the other one, with its attached hand, had firmly adhered itself to her left buttock. Would Shirley Bassey *ever* make it to the end of "Something?"

"You sure are a sweet thing," General Fardon whispered into her neck. Since he was several inches shorter, that was as far as he could reach. The brush of his bushy grey mustache sent a barely restrained shudder through her. "Where did you say you're from, honey?"

Cindy drew away from him, trying not to wince from the strong cologne he'd apparently bathed in. "Plainfield, Indiana, sir."

He leered up at her, his blue eyes—fatherly,

she'd thought, when he'd first asked her to dance—sparkling with booze-enhanced lust. "Then where on earth did you get that darling southern accent?"

His hand traveled in a lazy circle around her butt cheek. Cindy gritted her teeth and tried to smile. "I moved to Indiana from South Carolina when I was 16. Guess I haven't lost my southern charm."

He giggled. Yes, the general *giggled*. "Oh, you *do* have southern charm, my dear. You most certainly do." His fingers gave her butt a little pinch.

She flinched, wanting to haul off and knock his stupid—and obvious—toupee' from his head. But if she did that, she'd be standing in front of Colonel Kairos tomorrow morning, breathing in her toxic smell and getting the dressing down of her life.

It sounded like Shirley was finally winding down. *Thank God!* This evening had been a nightmare—just as Rosalie had warned. But when the official car had pulled up in front of the lavish French villa in Saigon, and she'd walked into the air-conditioned ballroom, she'd been impressed. Tuxedo-clad waiters circulated among the guests with silver trays of champagne and savory appetizers under glittering cut-glass chandeliers. An orchestra played on a stage, mostly Frank Sinatra and Perry Como songs that made Cindy feel like she was on the set of

Lawrence Welk. A sit-down dinner of lobster and filet mignon on a linen-covered table set with crystal and silver made it almost impossible to believe a war was going on. After dinner, the orchestra took their leave, and more popular music issued from the PA system—and the dancing began.

It hadn't taken Cindy long to realize that the top brass officers and politicians at this shindig all had their mind on one thing—sex. Although it was unspoken, she got the clear impression they were expecting the nurses to make their evening worthwhile. Rosalie had said as much, of course. But Cindy hadn't quite believed it…until now. Since when did the US Army pimp out its nurses?

She glanced over at Shyanne, dancing in a close embrace with a full bird, a corpulent, bald-headed man who looked like he'd really enjoyed his lobster and steak dinner. Typical Shyanne. She was smiling up at him like she thought he was the most darling man she'd ever met, and chatting a mile a minute. Jenny and Rosalie were dancing, too, but as far as Cindy could see, their partners, both lieutenant colonels, seemed to be behaving appropriately. Cap Bren was nowhere to be seen, and Cindy tried not to think dirty thoughts about what, exactly, she might be doing. After all, if what David said was true, she was sleeping with Dr. Stalik, whom everyone knew was a skuzzbucket and a drunk.

The General's hand made a final tour of her butt as Shirley Bassey's song finally ended. Cindy pulled away from him. "Thank you for the dance, General."

He grinned, keeping a firm grasp on her hand. "Thank *you*, honey. The first of many, I hope."

Cindy forced a smile, wondering how he could possibly think it was sincere. With what seemed like considerable effort, she pulled her hand away, and turned to go back to the table where she'd left her glass of champagne.

"Colonel MacKenzie, you should be ashamed of yourself, sir!"

Shyanne's indignant cry erupted from the dance floor, and everyone turned to see what was going on. Oblivious to the stares, the petite blonde glared up at the colonel, her hands planted on her curvy hips, two bright spots of red on her freckled cheeks. "First of all, sir, you're the same age as my grandpappy down in Kentucky, and second of all, what kind of girl do you think I am? Not that it's any of your beeswax, but I'm saving myself for the man I'm going to marry, and that most certainly wouldn't be an old man like you. I don't care if you *are* a colonel. You could be the president of the United States, and I still wouldn't go all the way with you. That's just *disgusting!*" Her cry ended in a wail, and she burst into tears.

From all directions, Cindy and the other nurses descended on her. Rosalie reached her first and took the weeping girl into her arms. Sending the stunned colonel a reproachful look, she led Shyanne off the dance floor.

The colonel finally found his voice. "That's *insubordination*, young woman!" he yelled over the voice of Glen Campbell singing, "Honey, Come Back." "I could write you up for talking to me like that!"

Shyanne cried harder. Cindy wanted to belt the creep. And then Rosalie did something that stunned them all. She stopped, her arm still around Shyanne's shuddering shoulders, and turned to face the colonel. "Then you'll have to write me up, too, Colonel MacKenzie. But if you do, remember this. I can write, too, and the person I'll write will be your wife back in wherever the hell you come from! And I'll tell her exactly why my nurse was insubordinate to you."

The colonel stared at her, his Adam's apple bobbling like a cork in a pond.

Maybe it was the couple of glasses of champagne she'd had, but before Cindy knew it was happening, she heard herself speak out in a strong, clear voice, "You can write me up, too."

"And me," Jenny said, glaring at the colonel.

His lizard-like eyes roved from one nurse to the other. "What is this, a mutiny?"

"You can add my name to the list as well, Colonel MacKenzie," said a new voice, one Cindy usually heard belting out orders on Ward 2.

She turned in astonishment and saw Cap Bren skewering the colonel with a gaze as icy as the fjords of Norway. "My nurses are here to help entertain you tonight, but that doesn't mean they're going to whore themselves out to you. And if you have a problem with that, Colonel, you can take it up with me later." She turned to the nurses. "Come on, ladies. We're leaving."

Cindy followed Cap Bren and the other three nurses toward the doors. As she passed the general, she saw him glaring at the colonel, his ruddy cheeks like balls of fire. *Oh, boy. The shit's going to hit the fan.* Not because he thought the colonel had done anything wrong by propositioning the cute young nurse, she was sure. But because he'd ruined *his* chance with the nurses. The candy had been snatched from the baby.

As the five nurses climbed into the car to take them back to post, Shyanne tried to thank Cap Bren for speaking up for them, but the head nurse brushed her off with a terse, "That old goat had it coming."

Her eyes red, Shyanne murmured, "I just hope I didn't get you in trouble." And she burst into fresh tears. "Oh, Cap Bren, if they want to discharge me, that's fine, but if you get in trouble, too, I'll just die!"

Cindy winced. No one *ever* called her Cap Bren to her face. But amazingly, the head nurse looked over at Shyanne with a glimmer of warmth in her eyes. "Don't worry about it, Lieutenant. I've been around the block a few times, and I can handle myself with the likes of MacKenzie."

The next morning, almost as soon as Cindy walked into the ward, the phone rang. It was Colonel Kairos's secretary, ordering Cap Bren to report to her office. Fifteen minutes later, she returned to the ward, her face as expressionless as the Sphinx.

CHAPTER NINE

The boy was going to die. That's why they'd put him behind the yellow curtain. Horribly wounded by a mortar shell to the chest, neck and extremities, his trachea had been smashed beyond repair. Yet, he was conscious, struggling to breathe—and terrified.

His wild brown eyes pleaded with her. *Help me!*

He knew he was dying. Bad enough. But no one deserved to suffer like this. It was beyond cruel. She had to do something.

Cindy whirled around and left the curtained area, her gaze searching the ward. Thank God! Jackson Stalik stood at the nurses' station, flirting with Cap Bren. And she was eating it up, as usual, flashing her seldom-seen toothpaste commercial smile and batting her baby-blues. Something she said apparently cracked him up because he threw back his head, bared his yellow horse teeth and brayed like a donkey. Cindy wanted to gag. Hard to believe she'd ever found him attractive.

Well, good. He obviously had some free time on his hands. She approached the desk, knowing she risked drawing the wrath of the moody head nurse, but she didn't care. Cap Bren noticed her first. Her eyes, fixed with rapturous attention on Stalik's craggy Charlton Heston face, lost their warmth as soon as they focused on Cindy.

"What is it, Lieutenant?" If her voice could sound any colder, it would be an iceberg.

"Excuse me, Captain." Cindy turned her gaze to the doctor. "Dr. Stalik, the expectant behind the curtain is really struggling. I know he doesn't have much time left, but couldn't you intubate him to ease his suffering?"

Even before she finished speaking, a pained look crossed his face. "No, I cannot. I just finished ten hours of surgery, and I'm damn well not going to spend my precious free time working on a lost cause." His gaze sharpened. "And might I ask, Lieutenant, don't you have enough work without spending your energy on a dead man? Because if you don't, I'm sure I can find something for you to do."

If Cindy had been a cartoon, her jaw would've dropped to the floor. She couldn't believe her ears. And this guy had taken the

Hippocratic Oath? She felt Cap Bren's irritated gaze burning into her, but ignored it. "Doctor, the kid isn't dead *yet*. Can't you help make his passing a little easier? That's all I'm asking."

He gave a world-weary sigh and exchanged a look with Cap Bren—one that clearly said, *God save us from young Pollyanna nurses who don't know an endotracheal tube from a catheter.*

But Cindy did, and she'd already decided she'd intubate the dying soldier herself if Stalik wouldn't change his mind.

He looked at her name-tag, pointedly telling her he didn't have a clue who she was, even though she'd been working on Ward 2 for two months. "Lieutenant Sweet, I know you haven't been here long, so take what I'm going to say as a valuable lesson. You can't save them all. And most of the ones you don't save are going to die messy, horrible deaths. That's what war is all about. Senseless, ugly, painful deaths. Accept it. Concentrate on the ones who're going to live. Now, get back to work!"

Cindy stood frozen, trembling with rage. She stared at the callous doctor, allowing all her hatred to drill into him. She wanted to call him every name in the book, but some semblance of sanity kept her silent. She knew her expression said it all.

He glared at her. "That's an order, Lieutenant."

Cindy whirled around and marched to the

supply closet. She grabbed an endotracheal tube, and ignoring the stares of Stalik and Cap Bren from across the room, headed back to the yellow curtain.

"*Lieutenant*!" Dr. Stalik barked. "I wouldn't do that if I were you!"

Cindy whipped back the curtain and stepped inside. One glance told her nothing had changed. The GI was still struggling to breathe. The tortured, gurgling sound reverberated throughout the enclosure.

Cindy stripped open the sterile package, then adjusted his head so she could insert the scope. She took a deep breath, her heart pounding. She'd done this only once before, but with Rosalie supervising. And the patient had been unconscious. This kid flailed on the gurney, his eyes rolling in panic. And what made it even worse, the blood and torn tissue would make it almost impossible to see the vocal cords. But she had to try.

"I'm going to help make it easier for you to breathe, sergeant, but you have to be very still, okay?" She crossed her right forefinger and thumb and inserted them into his mouth, applying pressure to the upper teeth with her forefinger, and to the lower teeth with her thumb.

The curtain ripped open. Cindy looked up, readying for a fight. Cap Bren stood there. Dr. Stalik stood behind her, his face grim. He spoke first, "Lt. Sweet, are you blatantly disobeying my order?"

Her heartbeat sped up. Resolutely, she looked back down at her patient. "You can have me courts-martial if you want, Doctor," she said through gritted teeth. "But I'm going to make sure this boy dies in peace." As carefully as possible, she inserted the blade into the GI's mangled mouth, her hand trembling.

She concentrated hard, easing the curved Mcintosh blade into the vallecula at the base of the tongue.

"Jack, leave us," Cap Bren said in a brittle voice. "I'll take care of this."

Cindy heard the curtain swish. Dr. Stalik had left. As she worked over the boy, she felt movement behind her and knew it was Cap Bren. The head nurse stood silently, watching as Cindy inserted the straight Miller blade past the epiglottis, exposing the larynx.

"You're doing fine, Lieutenant," Cap Bren said quietly, and handed her the ET tube.

Shocked, Cindy met her gaze. Cap Bren gave a brief nod, her expression unreadable. Cindy looked back down and guided the ET tube into what was left of the boy's trachea, then carefully, removed the laryngoscope. She attached the ambu bag and began squeezing.

Immediately, the horrible gurgling sounds ceased, and the boy began breathing easier. His expression revealed relief. He stared up at her, and Cindy felt his gratitude. She blinked hard to hold back tears. With her free hand, she brushed a lock of grimy dark hair away from his forehead.

Suddenly she realized Cap Bren had left the enclosure. Cindy knew that later, she'd have to deal with her, accept whatever punishment she and Dr. Stalik would cook up. But what could they do? Send her stateside for a courts martial? That actually sounded as good as a trip to the Bahamas. Besides, Cap Bren…she'd given her unspoken consent simply by her encouragement. Maybe she'd stick up for her?

The GI moved, one hand fumbling at his bloodied fatigue pants. Desperation flared in his eyes, and she wondered if, after all, she'd done something wrong when she'd intubated him. But then she realized he was searching for something in his pant pocket. She stilled his hand, and leaning over him, slid her fingers into the pocket, drawing out a small black & white photograph of a smiling brunette, her arm wrapped around the neck of a big black dog with a white ruff.

"Is this what you're looking for?" She held the photo in front of him. On the back, she read the words scrawled in ink–"Sherry & Bailey—my two best friends."

He nodded, once again quelled of panic.

"Your girlfriend?" Cindy asked quietly.

An infinitesimal shake of his head.

"Wife?"

A nod. His eyes filled with tears. Cindy swallowed hard, and this time she couldn't stop her own tears. She brushed her hand over his head. "She's very proud of you," she murmured. "You're an American hero...she knows that. And you'll always live in her heart."

Peace, finally. By now, the tears were streaming down her face. For fifteen minutes, she stood at his side, squeezing the ambu bag. His eyes had closed some time ago.

She heard movement at the curtain, and Cap Bren stepped inside. Without speaking, she went to the GI's side, pressing her fingers against his blood-streaked throat. Her gaze met Cindy's, and finally, Cindy saw the humanity she'd so often thought was missing in the head nurse.

Cap Bren reached out and took the ambu bag from Cindy's grasp. Then with one arm wrapped around her shoulders, she led her out of the curtained area.

December 1970

November 26, 1970

Dear Cindy:

I am so bored. It's Thanksgiving afternoon, and everybody in this house is napping except me. By which, I mean...Mom and Terri. Her stupid boyfriend came over for Thanksgiving dinner and ate like a pig. And then he left Mom and Terri and me to clean up. What a jerk! I don't know what she sees in him.

Anyway, it's pouring outside. Has been all day. Mom said it's supposed to turn to sleet tonight—and we might even get snow tomorrow. I hope so. I hope it snows so deep they'll have to cancel school on Monday. Wouldn't that be cool?

How was your Thanksgiving? We really missed you. It just wasn't the same here without you. Not to get mushy or anything. But holidays are just no fun without you. I can't believe you won't be here for Christmas! I'm going to be bored out of my mind. Sherry is going on a ski vacation to Colorado. Can you believe it? She doesn't even know how to ski!

Oh, well...hey, I got a new poster of David Cassidy

and hung it right over my bed. He's SOOOOOO gorgeous! Every night while I'm trying to fall asleep, I make up a story where The Partridge Family's tour bus breaks down right in front of our house. And it takes several weeks to get it fixed, so they move in with us. Of course, David falls madly in love with me…and we…well, you get the idea. By the way, this is just between you and me. Anyway, we don't do anything but kiss. David is way too much of a gentleman to take advantage of me.

Listen, I gotta go. The pumpkin pie in the kitchen is calling out to me. Wish you could be here to have some with me. I decorated it with candy corn just the way you like it. I love you, Cindy. And I miss you.

Your Sister,
Joanie

CHAPTER TEN

"**D**id you hear the news?" Jenny raised her voice over the sound of CCR's "Travelin' Band" when Cindy walked up to her table in the Officer's Club. "Cap Bren broke it off with Stalik. They had a huge fight out in the quad this afternoon, and Sue Stevens, that black chick who works on Ward 9, heard it all."

"Wow." Cindy placed her beer on the table and sank into a chair, exhausted from her 12-hour shift. She took a healthy swig of her Pabst Blue Ribbon. "You got details?"

Jenny lit a cigarette and took a long draw. "Just that Cap Bren was yelling at him, calling him a callous bastard, and he was standing there with a hangdog look on his face and pleading with her to calm down. Sue said he looked like he was two sheets to the wind—not that *that's* unusual. Anyway, it ended with Cap Bren telling him he wasn't good enough to wipe dog-shit off her combat boot and then stalked off."

Cindy shrugged. "It could've just been a little tiff." But she wondered. Could it possibly have anything to do with her insistence to intubate the dying soldier? If so, well…Cindy would definitely have to revise her opinion of Cap Bren— something she'd been well on the way of doing, anyway. And if she'd dumped that son-of-a-bitch Stalik…well, Cindy just might have to become her new best buddy.

The thought made her grin. As if Cap Bren would allow that.

"So, how was your day?" Jenny asked. "Better than mine, I hope."

Cindy turned her beer can on the table, her gaze fixed on the wet circles of condensation welling around its base. The yeasty aroma of the Pabst wafted through the smoky air of the club. "I helped somebody today," she said softly. And just like that, tears filled her eyes. She blinked to hold them back. The face of that poor boy—the way he'd looked when he could breathe again refused to dislodge from her mind. She gazed at Jenny. "He died, anyway, but I made it easier for him."

Jenny's face softened. She reached out and gave Cindy's hand a gentle squeeze. "You feel like talking about it?"

Cindy nodded. "It was an expectant—horribly messed up–"

"I've been looking for you, Cinnamon," said a soft southern accent behind her.

She turned, and her heart jolted. There he stood—the dust off pilot she hadn't been able to get out of her mind for the past two weeks. Every time she'd come into the Officer's Club, she'd searched for him. Casually, of course. And had always been disappointed when she hadn't seen him.

His unusual green eyes twinkled. "I think you owe me a re-match at ping pong. If you'll remember, I was getting ready to cream you when I got called out on a mission."

Cindy's heart somersaulted at his slow, easy grin. "Ah, Captain Quinlan," she said, finally finding her voice. "I hardly think 'creamed' is the right verb. You were ahead by only a couple of points, if I remember correctly."

"It's Quin," he said, and extended a hand. "There's an empty table over in the corner. I'll buy you a drink if you beat me."

Cindy and Jenny exchanged glances. Jenny grinned and mouthed, "Go!"

Oh, why not? She'd be a fool to waste this opportunity. Cindy grabbed her beer and stood. Instead of dropping his hand, he crooked a finger, and gave her a slow wink. Cindy's heart plummeted to her knees, and she felt heat rise upon her cheeks. *He knows exactly how he affects me.*

She placed her hand in his, and electricity jittered up her arm. He turned, leading her through the crowd toward the ping pong tables. Cindy's gaze fastened on his broad shoulders and decidedly sexy butt in his olive-green jumpsuit.

It was the best sight she'd seen all day.

Ω

"So, how are you at pinball?" Quin asked.

He slanted a grin at her as they walked toward one of the post's swimming pools–off-limits at night. Some idiotic rule by a high-ranked REMF. But nobody cared. On these hot, humid tropical nights, especially now that the monsoon season had passed, more often than not, someone was making use of the tepid water.

"Terrible," Cindy said, then added with a teasing grin, "Why? Do you think you've found something you can beat me at?"

He shrugged, eyes twinkling. "Maybe. You know, it's hard on a guy's ego when the prettiest girl in the club creams him in front of his buddies. I've got to find something to beat you at."

Cindy smirked. "Maybe swimming?"

He studied her face. "Yeah, right. I see that mischievous look in your eyes, Cinnamon. What? Did you train for the Olympics?"

She giggled, and then cringed. God, she sounded like a schoolgirl. And not for the first time tonight. "Of course not," she said, grateful the darkness would hide the blush she felt on her cheeks. "But I'm not bad."

He chuckled. "Famous last words."

For the past two hours, they'd played ping pong and pool at the O Club, and she'd won two out of three games. Amazing how being with Quin had revived her. Walking her back to the nurse's quarters, he'd suggested a swim, and she hadn't thought twice about it. After a quick stop in their respective rooms to get swimsuits, they'd headed for the pool.

The splash of water alerted them. Apparently, they weren't the only ones with the idea of cooling off on this sultry night. One solitary guy swam its length with bold breaststrokes. Apparently sensing their presence, he stopped swimming, and treading water, looked up at them with an expression as guilty as the one Joanie had the time Mom caught her eating chocolate icing off a freshly frosted cake.

Did they look so much like officers even in their swimwear?

"Sorry, ma'am...sir. I'm just leaving." The boy swam to the edge of the pool and pulled himself out of the water.

"No problem, soldier," said Quin with an easy grin. "We aren't going to report you...as long as you don't report us."

"You don't have to go," Cindy said. As much as she was attracted to Quin, she wasn't sure she was ready to be alone with him. Especially in a state of half-nakedness.

But the soldier was out of the pool, toweling off. "I was finished anyway," he mumbled. He loped off into the darkness.

Quin's eyes glimmered in the moonlight. "Ah…alone at last." He held out a hand.

Her cheeks burning, she reached for it. He moved quickly, scooping her up in his arms, and barreling both of them into the pool. As the tepid water closed over her head, Cindy wondered if this was what it was like to have an annoying big brother. But as soon as he grabbed her around the waist and pulled her against his cool, wet body, that thought melted away like ice cream in the heat of the jungle.

"Brotherly" would never be in her vocabulary when it came to Quin.

Ω

"So, what's it like to be a dust off pilot?" she asked him. "Scary, I bet."

They sat on the edge of the pool, their feet in the lukewarm water, sucking on peppermints Quin had produced from his backpack. Funny that he loved peppermints, just as Gary had. An odd coincidence. Cindy could take them or leave them. Chocolate was her favorite—especially M&Ms.

Muted moonlight filtered down from a cloud-obscured sky, playing hide & seek on the pool's placid surface. A warm, humid breeze caressed Cindy's wet skin, blessedly cool from the swim.

Quin grinned and ran a hand through his slicked-back hair. "Scary? Not for a NAFOD. We don't scare easily."

"Okay, I'll bite. What's a NAFOD?"

His grin widened, became charmingly wolfish. He popped another peppermint in his mouth. "That's what they call us. It means 'No apparent fear of death.'"

Cindi felt a kick in her stomach. She didn't know if it was caused by his nonchalance or the significance of his words. Suddenly the candy she'd been enjoying didn't taste quite so good. "And is that true? You don't have a fear of death?"

He shrugged and gazed off at a stately palm tree, its fronds swaying in the breeze. "I don't think about it. What's the point? If it happens, it happens."

Silence. Suppressing a shiver, Cindy stared down at her feet in the water. She gave a gentle kick, watching the resulting eddying circles. *You're a complete idiot to get involved with this man. If something happened to him...*

"It's hard to describe what it's like landing in a hot LZ," he went on. "You're so pumped up with adrenaline. You're coming in, and it looks like the 4th of July down there. Radio's squawking, in constant communication with the pilots of the gunships providing cover fire; we're talking to the guys on the ground, asking for a smoke grenade or a flare to guide us in. Talking to the artillery guys, making sure they hold their fire so we don't end up getting blown up by 'friendlys.'" His voice grew in excitement. "Man, it's boss. The thunder of artillery, the pounding of the rotors, the 'whump' of grenades from the gunships clearing our paths. The heat in the chopper is unreal. I'm literally soaking in sweat, but my mouth is dry as sand. And the sight below, especially at night—man, it's bitchin."

Cindy tried to imagine it. And she almost could. But what she couldn't imagine was being exhilarated like he sounded. *Terrified* seemed more like it.

"You got the flash of cannon," he went on. "The tracer spray from automatic weapons, the red fire from the gunships. Illuminating everything, you've got parachute flares launched from artillery. And you're in the middle of it all, Cinnamon." He looked at her, his eyes alight with excitement. "I've never felt so alive."

Cindy stared at him. He was a full-grown man, but at the moment, he looked like a nine-year-old boy opening the Christmas gift he'd been longing for all year. Despite the unsettled feeling in the pit of her stomach, she managed to give him a half-hearted smile. "Surely there must be *something* you like about your job."

He grinned, and shook his head. "Nah. The job is a bummer." His gaze scanned her face, grew softer, and Cindy's pulse quickened. "Enough about me, Cinnamon. I want to know more about you."

She shrugged and looked away. His appraising gaze made her feel like an awkward 12-year-old. Her cheeks burned, and she knew the moonlight was probably bright enough to reveal her agitation. "Not much to tell," she murmured. "I grew up in South Carolina, moved to Indiana when I was 16, went to college and nursing school then ended up here."

"Why?" he asked, holding out the bag of peppermints. "What made you join the Army? You could've got a nursing job anywhere, right?"

An image of Gary appeared in her mind. Sitting on that park bench on a hot Indiana night. Asking her to write him because he didn't expect to get much mail from home.

She popped a mint into her mouth, moving her feet back and forth in the warm, silken water. "I fell in love with a boy on the night he left for 'Nam," she said quietly. For a moment, she couldn't believe she'd actually spoken. But the words hung in the sultry air; Quin remained silent. Cindy fixed her gaze on the stars glittering in an unusually cloudless sky. "It was just that one night. That's all we had. He came into the diner where I worked…on his way to Camp Pendleton. He had a few hours to kill before his bus, and I kept him company." She shook her head, dipping her hand into the pool.

"I know it's crazy, but I fell for him that night. I loved him with all my heart. Everyone thinks you can't really fall in love at 16, not for real, but for the next few months, Gary was all I could think about. I dreamed of the day he'd come home, and then our real life together could start." She stopped, choking back a thickening lump in her throat. How could it still affect her like this? After so many years.

Quin's hand covered hers and squeezed. "How did he die?"

Cindy blinked back tears and took a tremulous breath. "They said a grenade flew into his foxhole. He grabbed it, jumped out of the foxhole and ran with it, saving the lives of the two other soldiers. He was awarded the Medal of Honor."

Quin didn't speak. After a long moment, Cindy shook her head and said, "I still don't get it. Why would he do that? Why would he try to run with it? It just doesn't make sense. Why wouldn't he have thrown it out of the foxhole?"

"You don't know what you're going to do when the adrenaline kicks in," Quin said quietly. "I guess all he was thinking about was protecting his buddies. Sometimes, that feels like all that matters." He fell silent. Then he squeezed her hand again. "And that's what made you join the Army?"

She nodded, staring into the pool water. "I wanted to try to help boys like Gary. Try to save them if I could." She shook her head. "But I know…" her voice trailed away.

"Cinnamon, look at me."

She did. His face was solemn, his green eyes intense as they gazed into hers. His thumb brushed away a tear. He opened his mouth to speak, but nothing came out. His gaze moved from her eyes to her mouth, and her pulse quickened. Like a magnet, his lips drew her; she leaned into him, and they kissed. His breath tasted of peppermints.

When they broke apart, Quin smiled, his sober expression replaced by a mischievous one. Cindy knew what was coming but before she could react, he slid an arm around her waist, and nudged her into the water. With one big hand on the top of her head, he dunked her. Luckily, she'd had just enough warning to take a breath first.

With the flat of her hands, she pushed him under the water, and then surfaced. "You *jerk*!" Laughing, she splashed him right in the face.

He laughed and grabbed her, pulling her up against his slick, cool body. His hands clamped around her face, anchoring her mouth for another kiss.

If Cindy hadn't known she was standing in waist-high water, she would've sworn she was drowning.

Ω

"So…are you going to invite me in?" Quin asked as they made their way to the nurse's quarters.

Cindy's heart practically stopped; her cheeks burned.

Quin laughed and squeezed her hand. "I'm just yanking your chain, Cinnamon. It wouldn't be gentlemanly of me to make a move on you when we're just getting to know each other."

For a second, Cindy felt almost disappointed. After making out with Quin on the edge of the pool for a good twenty minutes, she'd pretty much decided virginity was for the birds and it was high time she got rid of that particular obstacle to her love life.

"Of course, I think we got a good start on 'getting to know each other' back at the pool," he added, a grin evident in his voice. "Where did you learn to kiss like that?"

Cindy's cheeks burned hotter. *Could the man read her mind?* Before she could think of a response, he went on, "Just a good thing it's dark out here. I'm still having trouble walking."

"What…?" Cindy started to ask, and then it dawned on her what he meant. "Oh." To cover her embarrassment, she said the first thing that popped into her head. "Well, even if I wanted to, I couldn't invite you in. Colonel Kairos would have a cow if she found out. You're heard about her, haven't you?"

"No, what?"

"She patrols the nurse's quarters several times a night with a huge black dog who, incidentally, hates men. Rumor has it he's tracked down quite a few of those nasty creatures being entertained by nurses."

Quin guffawed. "Filthy, disgusting men! They oughta be locked up."

"If Kairos had their way, they probably *would* be."

Quin squeezed her hand again, sending a shiver up her arm despite the heat of the sultry night. "One of those humorless, gungho REMFs, is she? Sounds like somebody ought to remove the cattle prod from her ass."

Cindy grinned. "And I guess you're just the man to do it?"

He snickered. "Sounds like you already know me better than I thought. It's just too bad Halloween is over. Me and the guys were looking for a REMF to prank. Somebody nobody likes."

"Hey, you're only about six weeks late," Cindy said. "And April Fools is still three months away. I say you go for it."

They'd reached the quad between the hospital and the nurse's quarters.

"I like the way you think, Cinnamon," Quin said.

Cindy smiled. "Just don't give her my name when you get caught."

"I don't *get* caught."

At the end of the quad, she turned to him. "You'd better not go any further. I'm serious about Kairos and her black dog. And he seriously does not like men."

As if on cue, in the distance, a dog began to bark. Probably one of the German Shepherds the MPs patrolled with, but it might well be Cruella's mutt. Quin cupped her face in his hands and gave her a hard kiss that took her breath away. "That's so you don't forget me," he said.

As if.

"Hey, will you go to the Bob Hope show with me next week? That is, if I'm not off on a mission?"

At the gleam of excitement in his eyes, Cindy suspected he'd be equally happy about either possibility—the show with her or the mission. She nodded. "I'd love to…if I'm not on-duty."

"Okay, then it's a plan." He gave her a hug and released her.

But when she turned to go, he grabbed her hand, his face alight with a grin. "Hey, wait! I just had an idea how to prank Kairos. And I know how you can help me."

"Oka…ay. What is it you want me to do?"

His grin widened. "Get your nurse friends to donate some bras and panties for the cause. As many as you can get."

CHAPTER ELEVEN

The mess hall reeked of typical military breakfast fare—bacon, eggs, hash browns and toast. Not a bad smell, but one that promised more than it gave; Cindy had learned that by experience. The bacon was fatty and chewy, not crisp like she liked, and the unseasoned scrambled eggs tasted like…well, not the eggs Mom used to make. The cooks put big, slimy onions in the hash browns-- because of the meatloaf incident in which she'd been forced to sit at the table to finish said dinner as a child, Cindy detested onions. And the toast never seemed to be brown enough to be called "toast."

As usual, Cindy found herself in the chow hall line, watching a white-clad Vietnamese cafeteria worker ladle a glutinous mass of gray oatmeal into a ceramic bowl and hand it to her. Cindy peered down at the unappetizing substance. *Good thing it tastes better than it looks.* Especially after being doctored with a heaping tablespoon of brown sugar and dolloped with butter. She made her way through the mess hall toward a table in the corner where Jenny and Rosalie sat. As she reached the table, Jenny and Rosalie burst into gales of laughter.

"What's so funny?" Cindy asked, placing her tray on the table and sliding into a vacant chair.

Still giggling, Rosalie gave her a bright smile. "Oh, just a rumor Jenny says is going around the post this morning. Tell her, Jen."

Jenny's almond eyes danced. "Apparently Kairos is up in arms about finding a bunch of bras and panties decorating the outside of her quarters this morning. She's on the warpath, vowing to hunt down the culprits and punish them to the extent of the law…whatever *that* is."

Cindy chuckled, stirring brown sugar into her oatmeal. "Imagine getting so upset over a reverse panty-raid. You'd think she'd find something better to do with her time."

"I just wish I'd been there to see her face when she stepped outside this morning," Rosalie said with a grin. She looked at Cindy. "That 'Cross My Heart' bra was one of my favorites, but it was definitely worth the sacrifice."

Cindy nodded. "I'm going to the PX before my shift this afternoon. Something tells me there's going to be a big run on the lingerie department."

The three of them burst out laughing.

Ω

On the stage at the end of the quadrangle, Bob Hope made a joke about the hidden delights beneath Joey Heatherton's mini-skirt, and the audience cracked up. So did Cindy, even though she secretly thought Hope was an old lech, and couldn't understand why all those starlets like Heatherton and Nancy Sinatra fawned all over him. One thing was for sure. This wasn't the fatherly, hilarious man she'd watched on TV all her life. Her mother would be horrified.

Still, despite the fake snow and Christmas lights on the stage, the Vegas-pretty elves in their short green dresses and white go-go boots, the hokey-looking reindeer and sleighs, the voices raised in choruses of "Walking in a Winter Wonderland" and "It's Beginning to Look a Lot Like Christmas," Cindy had to admit she was enjoying the holiday show. Or…was it simply that she was enjoying the man sitting beside her? That it didn't matter what they were doing or watching or experiencing–if he was beside her, it might as well be Heaven. She glanced at Quin. He turned and gave her a wink. Her heart skipped a beat, as it always did when he looked at her like that.

On stage, Joey Heatherton began to sing "Santa, Baby," and Quin returned his attention to the star. For a moment, Cindy felt an irrational jealousy, but when his hand closed over hers, his thumb moving lazily over the tender spot between her thumb and forefinger, she immediately forgave him for his momentary preoccupation with the sultry blonde singer. After all, he was here with *her*, wasn't he? And she wouldn't trade her life for Joey's...not even if it meant going back to The World.

The annual USO Christmas show had drawn GIs from all over the post–medical staff and patients from the hospital, high-ranking brass from Saigon, and civilians from who knew where? Even non-ambulatory patients were enjoying the show, having been wheeled out in their beds by corpsmen. Everywhere she looked, Cindy saw the blue pajamas of patients, and was thrilled for them because any chance to get out of the wards, even for a little while, had to be a morale-lifter. She just wished there weren't so many left inside that were in no shape, physically or mentally, to have a few moments of "real life" again.

Quin leaned over and whispered in her ear, "You know Bob Hope has never spent a night in 'Nam? The old coot flies to Thailand to spend the night after every show."

Cindy rolled her eyes. "Not luxurious enough for him, I guess."

"Hey!" His eyes glittered. "I have an idea. You want to book?"

Cindy didn't question him. She nodded and

stood. Holding hands, they worked their way through the crowd, down past the chapel until they reached the front of the hospital. Finally, with just the muted sound of Joey singing, it was quiet enough for her to ask where they were going.

He grinned. "Be patient, Cinnamon. You'll see."

Cindy smiled back. It didn't matter. She was perfectly happy being with him. Holding his hand. Unbelievable that she'd known the man for only a few weeks, and yet, she was undeniably, head-over-heels in love with him. He was *the one*.

He led her to a jeep parked outside the NCO Club, told her he'd be a minute, and disappeared inside. True to his word, he appeared a moment later with a tow-headed sergeant. Cindy recognized him as Sergeant Clancy, the guy who'd taken Quin away for a mission on that first day she'd met him. He quirked a bashful grin at her and crawled into the back of the Jeep.

Quin ushered Cindy into the passenger seat and got behind the wheel. "This is costing me half my paycheck," he said, turning the ignition.

"Damn right," said the sergeant from the back. "Making me work on my day off."

Cindy looked from one to the other, mystified. "What are we doing?" Quin laughed and gunned the Jeep. A minute later, they were passing through the gates of Long Binh. The Jeep bumped down the dusty road, past Quonset huts and shacks, past peasants working in the rice paddies. In the west, the sun sank toward the horizon, casting a golden glow on a bank of clouds hovering low in the red-dusted sky over Cambodia. *Where on earth is he taking me?*

The wind from the Jeep's speed felt blessedly cool against her sweat-dampened face. But before she could get used to it, Quin braked and turned into Bien Hoa Air Force Base. Cindy glanced at him. He grinned, eyes sparkling with anticipation.

A moment later, he parked and led her across the blistering tarmac toward a dust off with its big red cross emblazoned on its nose. The sergeant loped along behind them.

Cindy squeezed Quin's hand. "So, I'm finally going to get a tour of your office, Warrant Officer Quinlan?"

He laughed, revealing straight white teeth, and boosted her into the chopper. Cindy looked around in wonder. No frills here. No seats, just space for litters. What had she expected? A Learjet? Quin settled her into the co-pilot's seat and buckled her seatbelt.

She stared at him. "What are you doing?"

He brushed his lips across her cheek, sending a delicious shiver down her back. "We're going for a ride, honey-chile," he said, thickening his Southeastern Texas accent. He scrambled into the pilot's seat and buckled in.

Her jaw dropped. "Are you crazy? This can't be legal." Behind her, Sergeant Clancy climbed into the dust off, holding an M-60 machine gun. "You guys could get into serious trouble!"

Quin and Clancy exchanged an amused glance. Then Quin guffawed, and drawled, "What're they gonna do? Send us to Vietnam?"

Ω

Cindy sucked in a deep breath at the sight below. Miles and miles of rice paddies broken by jungle canopies so thick it looked like she could fall onto them and bounce back up to the chopper. Mud-brown rivers snaked through the lush carpet of green interspersed by small Quonset-hutted villes and occasional American outposts designated by concertina wire and sandbags. In the west, the setting sun shot vivid beams of coral pink and violet-purple through the dark-honey sky, so beautiful it almost hurt to look at it.

The acrid smell of fuel competed with the woodsy musk of Quin's cologne—Revlon's Pub. No contest, Cindy thought. She found his delicious scent so powerful, it could drive away the stench of *nuoc ma*. Her headset crackled over the throb of the pulsating engine and the whop of the blades, and Quin's voice came through, somewhat tinny. "Milady, if you'll glance to your right, in just a minute, you'll see the crystal blue waters of the South China Sea."

True to his word, a vivid sapphire blue bay came into view bordered on the left by a strip of white sand beachfront. "That's China Beach down there," Quin said. "Maybe on your next two days off, I'll take you there. We'll forget we're in a war zone."

Cindy's heart skipped a beat at the thought of being alone with Quin on a white, sandy beach. War zone? When she was with him, no matter where they were, the war faded away.

Ever since the night they'd made out at the deserted pool, she hadn't been able to get him off her mind. It had been three weeks of wild highs and desperate lows. When she wasn't on duty or sleeping, she was at the O Club, waiting for him, praying for his arrival. When he didn't appear, she imagined the worst. Hated herself for it. Wanted to claw out her brain for having such gruesome thoughts. Three, four days would go by at a time with no word of him. And then, one afternoon or evening, she'd walk in the club, and there he'd be—playing pool, laughing and drinking beer with his buddies—and all her anxieties would melt away. She'd go immediately to his side, and watch his amazing green eyes brighten at the sight of her.

They established a routine on those incredible nights at the club. An hour or so of drinking beer, playing ping pong or pool, slow dancing to "Never My Love" by The Association, the first song they'd ever slow-danced to, and that had now become "their song." Afterwards, inevitably, they'd go for a walk and end up making out on a bench near the water tower. His peppermint kisses drove her crazy, turned her inside out. He was *the one*. This, she knew. She wanted him to make love to her, but when he'd ask her to take him back to her room, she always balked, reminding him about Colonel Kairos patrolling with her big black dog. Deep inside, Cindy knew it wasn't the lieutenant colonel or her dog that stopped her. Quin seemed so worldly, so sophisticated, despite his down-home Texas accent. What if, in her inexperience, she disappointed him?

The chopper banked left and headed northwest toward the central highlands. Down below, Cindy saw flashes of light among the green carpet of jungle. Were they being shot at? She glanced back at Sergeant Clancy who sat on his helmet with legs dangling from the open side of the chopper, watching the ground intently with his weapon readied for action. He didn't seem concerned, just watchful, so she decided not to be either. She felt safe with Quin—like nothing bad could ever happen as long as they were together. Soon the jungle disappeared and they were flying over acres of defoliated, scarred earth. An overwhelming sickly-sweet stench filled the cockpit.

"Agent Orange," Quin said to her unspoken

question. "It gets rid of the cover where Charlie hides."

Cindy nodded. She'd heard of it. It sure stunk to high heaven. The sun had finally sunk below the horizon. Darkness arrived quickly in Vietnam. Within moments, it had become full dark.

Quin reached over, grabbed her hand and gave it a squeeze. "Check this out."

The chopper ascended into a bank of low-lying clouds. When it broke above them, Cindy gasped in delight at the sight of a full moon illuminating the billowy carpet of clouds below them. For a moment, they hovered there, taking in the magnificent beauty of the tropical night. The scent of Quin's Pub cologne teased her nostrils, driving out any lingering odor of the Agent Orange. She felt his gaze upon her and turned.

"You know what this is, Cinnamon?" he said. Slowly, his right hand lifted in the peace sign. "It's peace."

Her heart swelled. She took in his handsome, sharp-boned face, his warm green eyes, his soft smile—and felt overcome with love. She forgot Sergeant Clancy's presence, didn't even care if he could hear her through the headset.

"I want you to be my first, Quin," she said softly. "Tonight."

CHAPTER TWELVE

Even before she opened her eyes, she inhaled the scent of Quin's cologne—and smiled. Never would she smell Pub again without thinking of this wonderful night. She stretched out her legs on the double bed, loving the soft caress of the sheets against her bare skin. Amazing that such a hotel existed here in Saigon. It must've cost hundreds of dollars.

Her eyes flashed open. For the first time, it occurred to her that Quin might have come from money. Maybe he was the son of a Texas oilman. He hadn't talked much about his home in Texas, except to say he lived near Galveston. In fact, he…*they*…hadn't talked much at all last night. She smiled and drew in a deep, cleansing breath.

Last night, a girl; today, a woman.

She turned on her side toward the middle of the bed, and with the flat of her palm, traced the sheet where he'd slept. She could almost imagine his imprint still there, the indentation of his sun-streaked brown head on the pillow. The scent of Pub permeated the sheets. She drank it in, wishing she could bathe in the stuff, just to hold onto his presence.

His pager had gone off sometime before dawn, and he'd kissed her gently, told her he had to make a run. *Go back to sleep,* he'd whispered. *I'll be back before you even miss me.*

But a quick scan of the room and the bathroom beyond told her he wasn't back yet—and she *did* miss him. She'd missed him the moment he'd left the room.

She sat up and pulled the sheet around her. What time was it? Sunlight streamed through the half-opened bamboo shutters, creating a dancing pattern on the carpeted floor from the fronds of a palm tree in the courtyard. A ceiling fan with wide rattan blades rotated overhead, sending a cool balm of air over her flushed skin. Cindy saw a note on the bedside table, and beneath it, a pile of *piasters*. She frowned. He'd left *money* for her?

But his sweeping handwritten note—almost feminine for a big hunk of man like him--drove away any thoughts of being paid for last night.

Hey, Cinnamon Girl! Last night...oh, hell! I don't have time to tell you how much it meant to me. But you know, don't you? I'm leaving you some taxi money...just in case I can't get back before you go on duty. But I will be. I know it! I can't wait to be with you again…I think I could be happy for the rest of my life with my Cinnamon girl.

Cindy smiled, her eyes blurring with tears. One night in the O Club, Neil Young's "Cinnamon Girl" had played, and with a broad grin, Quin had sung it all the way through, his gaze glued to hers. It had been excruciatingly embarrassing, but oh, so sweet. She couldn't imagine any other guy having the balls to do something like that. Just her Quin. Her finger traced the ink, the swirl of his handwriting. *Do you mean that, Warrant Officer Quinlan?*

A key clicked in the lock, and her heart leapt. Wrapping the sheet around her, she jumped up from the bed. The door opened, and Quin stepped inside, still wearing his pilot jumpsuit, hair tousled. His sea-green eyes sparkled, his grin becoming rakish as he looked her up and down.

"Now, *that's* what I'm talking about…a beautiful, naked girl wrapped in a sheet."

Cindy laughed and ran to him. He snuggled her against him, his lips brushing against her forehead. "Just the reward I need after a successful mission…even beats a nice, cold beer."

He swept her up and carried her back to bed.

Ω

"Nurse! Please…I'm so thirsty," rasped the

19-year-old private behind the yellow curtain.

He was bleeding out from numerous wounds zippered from his neck to his thighs. Not a thing they could do to save him. Yet, incredibly enough, he hadn't lost consciousness. He stretched out a grimy hand to her, his blue eyes dazed with shock. "Please…I'd give anything for a Coke right now."

Cindy hesitated. She'd been on-duty for 12 hours, and the last of the casualties from the afternoon's push had been taken to surgery. Many had died on the table. This poor boy had been brought in just a few minutes ago, and determined by Triage to be an expectant. No hope for survival. But the note from the triage doctor clearly read NPO. Nothing by mouth.

The G.I. grimaced, and Cindy realized he was trying to smile.

"Just one little Coke," he whispered. "What's it going to hurt?"

Her heart panged. He knew he was dying. She choked back the thickening lump in her throat and nodded. "I'll be right back."

She got the bottle of Coca-Cola from the supply room fridge and opened it. Shielding it from Cap Bren at the nurse's station, she strode back to the curtained area, half-expecting to find the private dead. But he was still hanging on.

Holding the back of his head, she guided the Coke bottle to his lips, and he took a healthy swig. His eyes burned from the carbonation, but when she drew back the bottle, he shook his head, and gasped, "Please…another sip."

He drank and then drew away from the bottle. She released him, and he dropped back to the gurney. "Thanks," he whispered, his eyes closed.

She stroked his wavy red hair from his gray forehead. "You're a brave soldier," she murmured.

His eyes fluttered open. "God bless you, nurse," he whispered. He took another ragged breath, released it and was still, his pupils fixed and dilated.

Cindy covered him with the sheet and left the curtained area. Cap Bren looked up from her paperwork, and her gaze fixed upon the nearly full Coke bottle in Cindy's hand. She stared at it a moment, and then turned back to her work without comment.

Ω

"It's beginning to look a lot like Christmas…"

Off-duty nurses were caroling on the wards where some of the patients were strong enough to appreciate the holiday spirit. A nice sentiment, Cindy thought, but she suspected the forced frivolity made the boys even more homesick than they already were. She knew *she* was…except, of course, when she was in Quin's arms. Nothing else mattered then. But she couldn't blame the nursing staff who tried to make the best of a bleak Christmas in a war-torn place like this. She'd even done her part, helping to put up decorations on the ward—construction paper snowflakes, bells and reindeer. Someone had even brought in a flimsy-looking artificial tree of silver metallic. God knows where they'd found it, and they'd decorated it with medical items from supply—tubing, plastic gloves, bulb syringes, and of course, the construction paper decorations—and they'd added the finishing touch of tinsel from the PX so it looked almost like a real Christmas tree.

"O come, all ye faithful…"

Cindy had just finished changing the dressing of a semi-conscious G.I. when the ward doors opened, and David Ansgar strode in, his face an odd shade of gray. He looked from Cindy to Rosalie, his blue eyes anxious. Cindy's heart plunged.

Quin! Something had happened to him.

She took a step toward him and tried to speak. Nothing came out.

The corpsman cast a glance at Rosalie and then back at Cindy. "Charley needs another volunteer in surgery."

Rosalie shrugged, scribbling something in a patient's chart. "It's finally slowed down here. I can spare Cindy." But then her head lifted and she stared at David. "Surgery? Where's the surgical team?"

He swallowed hard, glanced at Cindy, and then

turned back to Rosalie. "He's ordered them out. But Rose, he can't do this alone. He needs a scrub and circulator."

Slowly, she rolled back from her desk, eyeing him. Cindy moved closer. Relief that Quin wasn't involved had been replaced by a different fear—unidentifiable, but strong.

"You'd better tell me what's going on, David," Rosalie said quietly.

"They just brought in a G.I.," David said. "…with a live RPG lodged in his abdomen."

CHAPTER THIRTEEN

When Cindy entered the surgery behind David, Charley Moss looked up, his tanned face beaded with sweat. An uncharacteristic anger flared in his brown eyes. "What the *fuck* are you two doing here?" He kept his voice low, as if a noise of any kind could set off the grenade. "I ordered an evacuation."

David stared him down. "You need a scrub and circulating nurse, *sir*."

Cindy's eyes locked on the blood-stained G.I. on the operating table. He was unconscious, from a large dose of morphine, no doubt. Or perhaps he'd already been put under. But Dr. Moss and Dr. Pete Finnegan, the anesthesiologist, weren't the only ones in the room. Hovering over the hapless victim, a young man in a bomb disposal suit waited to take custody of the RPG once Charley had dislodged it. *Please God, let him get it out quickly—and safely.*

Charley's face whitened—with anger or fear, she couldn't guess. "Let me make this perfectly *fucking* clear. This thing goes off, we're all pink mist. You got it?"

David gave a terse nod. "Got it, sir."

Charley looked at Cindy, his eyes like black bullets. "Lt. Sweet? You can turn around and walk out of here right now. Maybe live another day to make love to your fly-boy. That's the smart thing to do, and I know you're a smart girl."

He knows about Quin? The illogical thought raced through her mind. Odd, the things one thinks about during moments of crisis.

But Charley was waiting for an answer. Her chin lifted. "I'm staying, sir." *Sir.* She'd never called Charley "sir" since the first day she'd met him, and he'd firmly informed her he answered to "Charley," not "sir."

His gaze seared into her. For a long, tense moment, he stared at the two of them, and finally, Cindy saw resignation wash over his face. He nodded. "Then God be with us." He closed his eyes briefly, made the sign of the cross, and said, "Scrub in."

Cindy exchanged a glance with David, and they moved toward the sinks. As they lathered up, he stared down at his fingernails and murmured, "I'll be scrub. That okay, L.T.?"

Cindy nodded. Even though he was a corpsman, he had more experience in surgery than she. And it wasn't a time to let ego get in the way. Not that it mattered to her. What mattered was saving the life of that poor boy on the table–and not killing themselves in the process.

Rinsing off, David looked up at her. "Just in case something…happens, L.T. I want you to know I'm…really proud to serve with you." His blue eyes glimmered with sincerity mixed with something else…fatalism? "I think you're…pretty fantastic."

Cindy had to blink to hold back tears. "Thanks. I think you are, too. And thanks for not speaking in the past tense." Suddenly her pulse jolted. "We must be crazy, huh?"

Incredibly, his face lit up in a grin. *"Beaucoup dinky dau."*

A G.I. bastardization of French-Vietnamese slang meaning "very crazy."

Despite her racing heart, Cindy grinned back. "Ah, hell! It don't mean nothin'."

Ω

"Careful now, sir. Nice and easy…" murmured the bomb disposal technician.

Cindy held her breath as Charley, with amazingly steady hands, lifted the rocket propelled grenade out of the ravaged cavity in the

G.I.'s stomach. A trickle of sweat rolled down his forehead, and she couldn't move to wipe it away—one of her responsibilities as the circulating nurse. Terrified that any movement would jar him, make him lose his grip on the grenade and...

She felt David's eyes upon her and risked a glance at him. He nodded, gave her a wink. She could almost hear his thoughts. *It'll be okay, L.T. Almost over now.* But she knew better. Even if the bomb disposal technician got the RPG out before it exploded, they still had to work on the boy. Her gaze shot to his gaping wound. Would it be too late?

An alarm sounded.

"Blood pressure dropping," murmured Finnegan.

Her heart jolted. *No!* She didn't think she could stand it if he died now. Not after all this. His blood pressure had dropped to a dangerous level.

"Turn off that alarm," Charley growled. It went silent.

He continued to move with a steadfast surety, lifting the RPG away from the boy's body. Seconds ticked by on the wall clock, monotonous and loud in the sudden eerie silence of the OR.

"Easy, sir," murmured the bomb disposal technician. "Easy..."

Time passed like a thick river of molasses as Charley turned to the bomb disposal technician who held out a towel, ready to take custody of the grenade. A *towel?* Cindy held back a hysterical giggle. Like *a towel* would protect them if the device went off.

Charley obviously hadn't picked up on the incongruity. Moving like a diver underwater, he placed the RPG into the technician's outstretched towel-covered hands. No one breathed. Even as they watched him turn to the OR doors and walk gingerly away. The OR doors closed behind him.

Charley recovered first. "I need some suction here."

David went into action. Cindy sponged away the sweat from Charley's forehead.

"Cindy, hang another liter of Ringers, please," Charley said, clamping off blood vessels. "If it's the last thing we do, we're going to save this boy."

Ω

It was 0200 when Cindy finally got off duty. After changing out of her scrubs, she stepped out of the hospital and saw David on the covered walkway. Somehow, she knew he was waiting for her. Something about the way his eyes lit up when he saw her. Sweet guy, Cindy thought. But all she wanted to do was get to the O Club to see Quin. *Please let him be there tonight. I need to feel his arms around me.*

"Hey, L.T." David gave her a weary smile.

"Just wanted to say you were amazing in there."

Cindy laughed. "Oh, yeah. *Nobody* can hang an I.V. bag like me. And did you see how I was on top of sponging off Charley's forehead? Clearly, that's a result of four years of training in one of the best nursing schools in America!" She gave him a playful punch on the shoulder. "No, David, *you* were the amazing one. You knew exactly what Charley needed before he could even ask for it."

David shrugged, the color in his cheeks heightening. "Okay, *we* were amazing. All of us. He's going to live, you know. Charley is sure of it. Hope to God they send him back home with a medal."

Cindy studied him a moment. "You know, David, when you get home, you need to use the G.I. Bill and go to medical school. I think you'd make a great doctor."

His blush deepened. "Oh, come on."

"No, I mean it. You've got that special something—like Charley. Compassion combined with technical skill. We need more doctors like that. You should really think about it. I'm serious!"

He gazed at her for a long moment, and then nodded. "Maybe I will. I've already volunteered to go on some med-caps with Charley. You've heard of them, right? He goes into remote villes to give basic health care to the villagers. Strictly a volunteer thing. Maybe you should come, too."

"Yeah, I might do that." Cindy looked longingly in the direction of the O Club. She didn't want to be rude, but she needed to go.

"Hey, want a beer?" David asked. "I've got some Pabst in my room. Only take me a minute to run get it."

"Well, I----"

"Hey, Cindy!" Quin stepped out of the balmy darkness. "Some nurse in the O Club just told me what you did tonight."

He looked as gorgeous as always, except his usual easy smile was missing. But Cindy's heart melted all the same.

"*Quin!*" She ran to him, throwing her arms around his neck. "Oh, it's so good to see you!" She lifted her lips for his kiss. But his hands tightened on her upper arms like steel clamps. He stared at her, his body rigid. She drew away and peered at him. "What's wrong?"

He glared, his jaw tense, and that's when it hit her. He was *furious*! She'd never seen Quin mad. Never seen him irritated or even impatient. She started to speak, but before she could get a word out, he gave her a hard shake.

"What the *fuck* were you thinking? You could've been *killed*."

"Quin, I--"

He shook her again. "Putting yourself at risk like that?"

"Sir," David spoke from behind her. "Take it easy. Cindy felt like it was her duty—"

"Her *duty?*" He shot David a baleful glance. "To *what?* Commit suicide? And who the hell are *you*, anyway?"

"Quin, please." Cindy disengaged herself and frowned up at the man she loved. "This is Corpsman David Ansgar, and if it weren't for his nursing skill, that boy would've died on the table tonight. So, don't you *dare* be disrespectful to him."

"It's okay, L.T.," David said.

"No, it's *not* okay!" she said over her shoulder, and then turned back to Quin. The green fire in his eyes hadn't dissipated. "Quin, I love you, but I won't have you talking to my friend like that. He's one of the best corpsman in this hospital, and what he did today was as heroic as it gets! Charley ordered everybody out of surgery; he was going to risk his life to save that boy, but David insisted on scrubbing in—and so did I. I'm sorry if that frightened you, but this is what I'm here for. I volunteered for the Army just like you did. Don't you think I live in fear every single time you go out on a mission? But I don't berate you for doing your duty!"

She watched as the anger drained from his face, his eyes softening. "Oh, Christ! I'm sorry, babe. It just scared the hell out of me, hearing you were in there, and what could've happened…" He folded her into his arms and kissed her temple. She nestled into his warmth. "I don't know what I'd do if I lost you," he whispered. Suddenly he drew away from her. "I apologize for my tone, Sgt. Ansgar. Just thinking about what could've…" He shook his head. "I guess I went a little crazy."

Cindy, to her shame, had forgotten all about David standing behind them. But when she turned around, the corpsman was already walking away into the darkness.

"No problem, sir," he said. "Just be good to her. She's a special girl."

After he'd disappeared, Quin grinned down at her, all trace of anger gone. "Smart guy. You better watch out for him, sweetheart; I think he's half in love you."

"Oh, shut up…" Cindy smiled. "…and kiss me."

January 1971

December 25, 1970

Dear Cindy,

Merry Christmas, Freckleface. How come you haven't written to your old dad lately? I know you're busy over there, and I'm so proud of you, serving your country like you are. But I sure would like to hear from you more often.

Hey, I can't wait until you come home, and come on down here for a visit. You aren't going to believe how big Scotty is. He turns five on January 2nd, you know? And Nancy is toddling all over the place. Getting into everything. Seems like it was just the other day she was born. Where does the time go? I sure wish you'd had the chance to get to know the kids better. You're such a great big sister. Joanie worships the ground you walk on. Did you know that? (I know she doesn't show it.)

Lesley says hello, and hopes you're keeping yourself safe. We can hardly wait to move into the new house down in Murrells Inlet. Four bedrooms, two and a half baths. Lesley is thrilled to death with her big kitchen. You know how much she loves to cook. (Hope you got that care package she sent early this month. That woman has been baking cookies since Thanksgiving.) And the kids have their own rooms, and that leaves a nice guest bedroom for when you come to visit. How about that? We close on January 15th. Counting the days! Working *for the airlines is a pretty good deal...well, except for all the traveling. Lesley's not thrilled about that, but I keep telling her 'it's the paycheck that's getting you that new $45,000 house on the water, so quit complaining!'*

Well, I'd better wrap this up, Freckleface. The kids will be up from their naps soon, and then all hell will break loose. You should've seen them this morning, opening their gifts from Santa. Of course, Nancy didn't really know what to make of it, but Scotty tore through those presents like a locomotive! Just goes to show how different boys are from girls. You always took your time unwrapping Santa's gifts. I think you liked the anticipation more than the present. But come to think of it, Joanie was a lot like Scotty. She couldn't get the presents opened fast enough. Ah, we had some nice Christmases, didn't we, hon?

You take care of yourself, you hear me? And <u>write</u> your old dad. I'm hungry for news.

Happy New Year, sweetheart.

Love,
Dad

CHAPTER FOURTEEN

"**H**ey, Lieutenant. How about some company? I can't sleep."

The voice came out of the semi-darkness from a bed in the corner of the ward. Cindy glanced at the wall clock. 0210. Working the night shift, she and Rosalie were the only RNs on duty, along with one corpsman, a shy black guy named Rudy who, when not busy, sat in a corner of the nurse's station, writing a science fiction novel in long hand on a legal pad. Tonight's shift had been quiet, a relaxing change of pace from the usual. Cindy had just finished her rounds, taking vital signs and checking IVs, and was headed back to the nurse's station when the patient in Bed # 12 called out to her. She turned and walked over to 1st Sergeant Roger Stevens.

"Are you in pain, Sergeant? I can give you something to help you sleep."

The marine was recovering from an emergency appendectomy. A member of Marine Reconnaissance, he'd been flown in from the bush five days ago, suffering from a burst appendix, and had barely survived the surgery. His condition had improved enough that tomorrow he'd be transferred to Ward 4.

"Nah, not in pain," he said in a distinct Minnesota accent. "Just need some company. You too busy to sit and talk?"

Cindy glanced at the nurse's station to see Rosalie engrossed in a paperback copy of Hunter S. Thompson's "Fear and Loathing in Las Vegas." And Rudy, of course, was busy scribbling on his legal pad, his mind obviously off on an alternate universe somewhere.

"Yeah, I can spare a few minutes, I guess." She pulled up a chair near his bed.

Stevens was a good-looking man in his early-thirties with dark hair and a Clint Eastwood squinty-eyed, steel-jawed face. Looked like a marine straight out of Hollywood casting.

"Want to see some pictures?" he asked, reaching for a box on the stand next to his bed.

He obviously had forgotten he'd already shown her photos of his family. But if it helped him get through the night…

She *oooed* and *ahhed* over his three freckle-faced boys, ranging in age from a toddler to a six-year-old. They all looked like Daddy.

"And this is Rita." He handed her a well-thumbed picture of a gorgeous redhead in an emerald green swimsuit standing under a coconut palm tree. "I took this photo of her during my last R&R in Hawaii."

Stevens was on his third tour of 'Nam. How he could do that, leaving a family back home, Cindy couldn't understand. It wasn't like they'd forced him. But she knew some of these guys got addicted to the danger, especially the battle-toughened Marines in Recon. But they weren't just adrenalin addicts; many of them were heroin junkies.

She hoped that wasn't the case with this guy, Stevens. He didn't look like the typical GI Joe-type. Was way too affable and easy-going. Cindy nodded and smiled over his family pictures, and ten minutes stretched to twenty. He showed no sign of wearing down. In fact, something in his brown eyes seemed almost manic. Just as she was about to make an excuse to get back to the nurse's station and get him a sleeping pill, he pulled out another picture.

"Check this out, Lieutenant."

At first, she wasn't sure what, exactly, was the big deal—just three Marines in camo gear and "boonies," each wearing big grins on their grimy faces out in the jungle.

"You and your buddies, right?" she asked.

He grinned. "Yeah, but take a look at our necklaces."

She peered closer at the grainy black & white

image, and saw that the three men were wearing some odd-shaped, grayish-looking necklaces. "Yeah? I really can't tell…"

His grin grew wider, wolfish. "Charlie ears," he said. "Every time we get a kill, we cut off their ears and string 'em on nylon. You can only wear them about three days before they start stinking and turning green, but we still hold onto them. I have a shoebox half-full of dried-out Charlie ears."

Cindy's stomach turned over. Stevens gazed at her serenely. She wondered if *she* was, in fact, turning green? From the next bed, the hushed, rhythmical sound of a breathing tube filled the silence—a quadriplegic who might never regain consciousness—and probably wouldn't want to if he knew what kind of life lay before him.

"You want to see?" Sergeant Stevens leaned towards the bed tray, reaching for another box.

Cindy jumped up from her chair, almost knocking it over in her haste. "Some other time. I've got work to do."

He laughed out loud, but his eyes glinted with something close to malice. Or was that her imagination? "What's wrong, Lieutenant? Have I upset you?"

She backed away from his bed, her stomach roiling. "No, I just…"

His grin disappeared. "Oh, cut the crap, why don't you? I know what you're thinking. Well, don't go getting judgmental on me, nursie.

You have no fucking idea what it's like out there in the bush. The things you see…the things Charlie does to *us*. I went to relieve my buddy on sentry duty at our perimeter and found him bleeding to death. They'd cut off his penis and stuffed it in his mouth. He was still alive when I found him."

Cindy's legs grew weak. She cast a desperate glance back at the nurse's station. Nothing had changed there. Rosalie was still engrossed in her paperback and Rudy was scribbling away like mad. How could two realities be so different? They, carrying on their work like it was just a normal night, and she…thrust into a nightmare of the atrocities humans committed against each other. It wasn't that she was a total innocent. She'd known war was horrific and senseless and cruel, but…oh, dear God, she'd never imagined such vile things as was coming out of Stevens' mouth. And it was as if he were delighting in the shock she knew she couldn't hide.

"Shit like that happens all the time out there," Stevens went on, his cheekbones burnished red, eyes wild and glittering.

My God…the man is insane!

"You getting all spazzed out about a few ears on a string? *Shit!* That's mild stuff. Working recon, we'd come across a gook ville, capture the sonuvabitches, and make them talk. Tell us where the NVA are holed up. Most of the time, all it took was a gun to the little gook's head. But with the stubborn ones, we'd take his wife or his daughter and make him watch as we took turns with her. You know what I'm talking about, Lieutenant?" He leered at her.

Cindy shook her head, her horror growing. "Please! I can't...I don't..."

He grinned. "Don't want to hear my story? Why not, sweetheart? Don't have the stomach for it? Tough shit. Yeah, we'd fuck her right in front of the gook. And then when he finally told us what he knew—and they always did—we'd put a bullet through her brain. And then his."

Cindy whirled around, choking to hold back the bile rising in her throat.

"Hey, where you going, nurse? We're just getting started. I have all kinds of stories to share with you!"

She headed unsteadily to the nurse's station.

"Don't judge me, Lieutenant!" he shouted, his voice rising in fury. "Not until you've walked a moment in my combat boots, don't you fucking judge *me*!"

Ω

She hadn't seen Quin in over a week. He'd left on some secretive mission eight days ago, and with each passing moment, the dread in the pit of her stomach grew. Something was wrong. She knew it!

The first unsettling premonition came on the night First Sergeant Stevens had verbally assaulted her. She'd imagined Quin captured in the bush by VC, tortured and mutilated as the American troops had done to them. She shuddered at the thought of Quin's beautiful ears hanging on a string around some Charlie's neck—and then had wanted to rip her brain out to obliterate the hideous thought.

He'd never been gone this long before. And there was no one she could go to for information. The other nurses—Jenny, Shyanne and Rosalie, saw her growing anguish and tried to reassure her. Sitting in one of their rooms, late at night, they'd smoke grass and urge her not to think the worst—that there were probably all kinds of innocuous reasons why he hadn't returned. Why he was unable to contact her. Cindy nodded, but didn't miss the barely disguised anxiety in their eyes. They, too, knew there was cause to worry.

On the tenth day of his absence, the blaring of a voice on the base PA system accompanied by the teeth-chattering thunder of chopper blades announced incoming casualties. Cindy bolted up from her bed, threw on her fatigues and combat boots, and raced to the hospital.

Charley Moss was working triage, and he

immediately put her to work, cutting away uniforms from the mangled troops. She worked feverishly, ignoring the blood on her hands, unable to take time to wash between patients. Another casualty—and her heart froze when she saw the flight uniform he wore. *Oh, God, oh, God, oh, God!* But no, the name read Morgan. She moved from one patient to another, hanging I.V.s for blood and plasma, inserting Foleys for patients not making urine, putting in airways, suctioning trachs. The casualties surged into the ER, one chopper after another bringing in more. All the ORs were in use. Every surgeon on the base had been called in for duty. Patients awaiting surgery were lined up in the halls, some barely holding onto a sliver of life. Others, expectants, had already been relegated to the yellow curtain. And still, the wounded kept coming.

Two more pilots were rolled through the double doors of the ER, and each time, Cindy felt her stomach drop to her ankles. Every fiber of her being screamed at her not to approach them, to let one of the other nurses or corpsmen deal with them. She knew she couldn't bear it if she saw that one of those bloodied uniforms wore the name of Quinlan. But her sense of duty—or her sense of decency—forced her to go to them, to do what she was trained to do to save their lives. And each time, thank the Lord above, the names on the flight suits wasn't the one she'd prayed not to see. And yet, when she did see an unfamiliar name, she felt almost guilty at her relief. Someone back in The World loved this guy—a sweetheart, a wife, a mother, a father, maybe a son or daughter. But thank God, *thank God*, it wasn't Quin.

By five p.m., the last of the casualties had been relegated to surgery or the yellow curtain, and there was nothing left to do but clean the ER. The nurses and corpsmen worked together silently, too weary to speak. Cindy felt numb with fatigue as she picked up bloodied dressings, discarded tubes and basins filled with shrapnel. She couldn't wait to drop into her bed and blot out the day's horrific memories with the oblivion of sleep…if she *could* sleep.

Just as David Ansgar began to spray down the blood-soaked floor, the chopping blades of a Huey split the silence. Everyone stopped what they were doing and stared at each other. Cindy met the resigned gaze of David, her heart dropping. *Oh, no. More?* To her shame, she felt her eyes fill with tears, and she turned away, not wanting him to see her weakness. *I can't take anymore. Not today. I just can't.*

The chopper grew louder, and everyone went into action, gathering supplies, readying for more wounded. Cindy did the same. There was no choice. Just because she couldn't take it didn't mean she *wouldn't* take it. Charley Moss, having just finished the last surgery, raced out to the landing pad to triage the incoming.

He returned moments later, relief on his craggy face. "Relax, people. No wounded." His brown eyes settled on Cindy. "Just a dust off returning to home base."

Cindy's heart leapt. Did he mean...?

A figure appeared behind Charley, wearing a green flight suit, his sandy hair rumpled, his face smudged with grime. But his green eyes were sparkling, and his smile brightened Cindy's world, driving all the shadows away.

Her throat choked with tears, she ran to Quin, and he took her into his arms, his warmth folding around her like a thermal blanket. Trembling, she pressed her cheek against his chest, hearing the soft, regular thud of his heartbeat. He smelled like the jungle, a green, earthy, almost primitive smell. Usually, she found the smell offensive, but because it was Quin, because he was *here*, whole and unharmed, and in her arms, it didn't matter.

Nothing in the world mattered except that he was here.

February 1971

February 9, 1971

Dear Cindy,

It's a quiet evening here, so I thought I'd write you a line or two. Terri is out with her boyfriend...well, I guess I can't really call him that anymore. He proposed to her on Saturday night, and she said yes. They're planning a Christmas wedding, and I'm sure she's going to want you to be a bridesmaid. Ooops. I probably shouldn't have written that. She'll kill me. Oh, well, too late now. Besides, she's probably already written you to tell you the news, so I'm sure she's already asked you. I'll bet she wrote you on Sunday morning and got it into the mail yesterday. Anyway, I'm excited for her. Not because I particularly like Tom. If you ask me, he's a little dull...but he has a good job, and the two of them seem to get along well. Only thing is...now that they're getting married, I guess I'm going to have to knuckle down and find a new place for me and Joanie. Can't afford a house, so it looks like I'll have to find an apartment to rent.

It just galls me...really, it does...that Joe and his floozy are living in a $50,000 house on the water in Myrtle Beach. You'd think he'd be a little more generous with alimony and child support, wouldn't you? So the *mother of his children and minor daughter wouldn't have to live in a tiny little apartment, just getting by. But that's your father. I guess his new wife and kids come first. Of course, I know it's not all his fault. That Lesley! I'm sure she screams bloody murder if he wants to give a little extra to Joanie. Oh, dear. I can just see your face. I know how you hate it when I say the slightest negative thing about your father. I'm sorry. Forget I said anything.*

So, I watched Apollo 14 return to earth on TV today. Pretty exciting! Those astronauts are just so brave. I can't imagine how they have the nerve to go up in space like that. I don't suppose you got to see it over there? I don't know if they televise that stuff or not for you.

Speaking of television, I just don't know what it's coming to. Terri got me to watching "All in the Family," and usually, it's pretty funny, but tonight's episode was just disgusting! One of Archie's friends turned out to…well, like boys more than girls. Yes, I know there are weird people in the world like that, but do I want to see it on TV? Absolutely <u>not</u>! When I realized what the show was about, I made Joanie leave the room, and she was mad as a wet hen. But I don't want her exposed to stuff like that. (And by the way, you watch out for women like that over there; I've heard the military is full of those thespians.)

Well, it's going on 10:30, so I'd better wrap this up and get to bed. Working at Kroger tomorrow. Sometimes, I feel like I live there. I love you, Cindy. You take care of yourself.

> *Love,*
> *Mommy*

P.S. You tell your young man, Quin, that he'd better respect you. You hear? Be a good girl now. Take it from me, boys want only one thing, and once they get it, they'll drop you like a hot potato.

CHAPTER FIFTEEN

"*No, damn it!!!*"

Quin threw down his ping pong paddle and ran his fingers through his tousled hair as Cindy bent over double, laughing. She'd just slammed the ball straight down the line at 20-18, and it had blistered past him like a bullet. Nothing he could do but let it go. That ended their tiebreaker match, she having won the first, and now, the third game.

Cindy knew she shouldn't laugh at his frustration. They'd been down this road many, many times before. He'd never beaten her in two out of three, much to his chagrin. But what was she supposed to do? Let him win just to save his pride? She hadn't been raised like that; her father had been an All-American from Duke. He'd disown her if he knew she'd lost on purpose to assuage a man's ego. Besides, Quin's aggravation was put on. Cindy had never known a guy so easy-going and self-confident. Just another reason why she was crazy-head-over-heels in love with him.

He grinned from across the ping pong table. "*Someday* I'm going to find something I'm better at than you."

Cindy rolled her eyes. "Oh, quit whining! I can't fly a dust off while dodging fire. Come on, I'll buy you a beer."

Arm in arm, they headed toward the bar. The delectable aroma of freshly prepared French fries from the kitchen wafted through the club, and Cindy's stomach growled. She was just about to suggest ordering some when The Guess Who began singing *American Woman.* "Oooh!" In mid-step, Cindy turned and tugged Quin to the dance floor. "I love this song! Let's dance."

But Quin's attention, for once, wasn't upon her. He was staring over at a commotion at the bar. She followed his gaze and saw a large man flailing about, obviously in some kind of distress. Another man, clearly panicked, was beating him on the back. "Help! He's choking!" he screamed out.

Cindy and Quin leapt toward them, as did several other officers. Quin got there first. He grabbed the man from behind—a four-star general, Cindy saw with surprise—and tightened his arms around him, thrusting upwards to dislodge whatever had blocked his airway. But it wasn't working. The general's granite face was already tinged with blue.

Cindy looked around frantically. "Isn't there a doctor in here?" But no. Not one doctor in the entire place. How was that *possible?* "Somebody call the hospital and get a doctor over here *stat!* I mean, *right now!*" She maneuvered in front of Quin. *No time for a doctor. This man is going to die if I don't do something.*

"*Somebody get me a knife!*" she shouted, then tugged on Quin's sleeve. "Help me get him on a table."

The officer with him, a colonel, she saw now, looked at her as if she'd lost her mind. "*Who the hell are you and what do you think you're going to do?*"

Quin ignored him, helping Cindy get the choking general on a table that some quick-thinking lieutenant had cleared off with a sweep of his hands. Someone handed her a sharp-tipped steak knife. "Help me rip his collar away," she ordered.

Quin held down the thrashing general while another officer ripped his collar open. The colonel's face had drained of color. He tried to get to the general, but several other officers restrained him. "What're you doing?" he screamed.

"She's a nurse!" someone yelled back. "Let her help him!"

"Somebody get me a straw...or a ball-point pen…something with an opening at each end," Cindy called out.

The general's body had gone limp. He'd lost consciousness. With steady fingers, she found the indentation between the Adam's apple and Cricoid cartilage, and then pointed the tip of the steak knife downward.

The colonel let out a strangled cry. "She's going to kill him!"

Cindy sensed him struggling to rid himself of the arms holding him back, but concentrated on what she was about to do. This man's life depended upon it. She started to lower the knife. Something jostled against her, and it was only by the grace of God that she stopped the knife from stabbing the general through the gullet. A scuffle broke out behind her, but still, she took a deep, steadying breath and prepared to make the incision for the emergency tracheotomy. A thud followed by a louder one brought a sudden silence, and then she felt Quin's presence beside her.

"Go ahead, Cinnamon. Do what you gotta do."

"Here's a straw, Lieutenant," said a breathless voice.

Cindy nodded. "Good. Somebody call for a gurney. As soon as I get this done, we've got to get him to the hospital."

She took a deep breath, closed her eyes and said a quick prayer. Then, with a steady hand, she used the knife to make a half-inch incision. Blood trickled down the general's neck. She slipped a finger inside the slit to open it, then, carefully, eased in the straw, about an inch deep.

American woman...mama let me be...

Cindy took the other end of the straw into her mouth and gave it two quick breaths. Paused for five seconds, then another breath. The general's eyes opened. Confused but not panicked. Cindy drew her mouth away from the straw and watched him. *Gonna leave you woman...*

His chest rose ever so slightly. He was breathing on his own.

Cheers rose from the officers crowded around the table. Quin grinned at her, pride shining in his eyes. He drew her close and kissed her forehead. She wilted against him in relief. She'd done it. She'd saved the man's life. And surely he hadn't been without oxygen so long that it had affected his brain. How much time had passed?

Bye-bye...bye-bye. American Woman was still playing, so it couldn't have been that long. She stepped back from the table. "Did someone notify the hospital?"

Just as she spoke, the doors flew open and two corpsmen ran in with a stretcher. It wasn't until they'd left with the general that reaction took over. Cindy began to tremble, and Quin eased her down into a chair. That's when her eyes fell on the colonel lying flat on the floor, out cold.

Quin followed her gaze and then looked back at her. He nodded, then gave an abashed grin. "Yeah, it appears I'm in a shitload of trouble."

CHAPTER SIXTEEN

The doors from the OR burst open and yet another gurney rolled in with a semi-conscious patient. Cindy suppressed a weary sigh and hurried over to meet the attendants. It had been one of those mornings—worse than usual. She'd come on duty at 0700 to find eight new patients, all critical, had been med-evaced in during the night. The following hours had blurred by in a frenzy of hanging IVs, suctioning traches, inserting Foleys, taking vital signs, and changing dressings. And now, just when it seemed like she might actually get a moment to breathe, maybe even down a cup of coffee or smoke a cigarette, here came another one.

"APC ran over a mine," said the OR tech. "This kid was the only survivor. We did what we could but…" His voice trailed off. His grim face said it all. The kid probably wouldn't survive.

Taking the chart from atop the soldier's sheeted form, Cindy glanced at it. Nineteen-year-old Pfc. Patrick Cummings from Stowe, Vermont. She looked at the boy and felt a sinking sensation at the sight of a bandage covering half his face and skull. His left side had gotten the worst of it. His arm and leg had been amputated and God only knew what his face looked like under that bandage. The boy whimpered as the effects of the anesthesia wore off. His head moved back and forth. A tear trickled down the undamaged side of his face.

"Mama!" he cried out so mournfully that Cindy's heart gave a twinge.

She imagined a woman in Vermont, perhaps pulling a tray of maple sugar cookies from the oven in her farmhouse kitchen. Outside, snow would be drifting from gray skies, but the kitchen was warm and toasty. Maybe she had a view of the ski slopes out her window. Would she wonder if her boy was homesick for his mountains? Would she have any inkling that her Patrick had been wounded, that he was barely clinging to life in an evac hospital halfway across the world? Would that severed umbilical cord which connected mother and child hold some kind of psychic power that would warn her of impending loss, the same way twins could sense their other half was in trouble?

David Ansgar appeared at her side. She took one end of the gurney and said, "Let's put him over here near the nurse's station."

His blue eyes met hers. She knew what he was thinking. *Not behind the yellow curtain?* She shook her head, biting hard on her lip. "This one's going to live," she said firmly. *No black car pulling up in front of that mother's house in Stowe, Vermont.*

By 1500 hours, Cindy had started to believe it. Patrick's vital signs had stabilized, and Charley Moss had offered cautious hope that he just might make it. Ample doses of morphine finally had the G.I. resting easily. No more crying out for his mother, thank God. As toughened as she'd become in these past four months, Cindy's heart broke every time a grown man called out for mom. It always brought to mind an image of a young mother cuddling her little boy. How wrong that a society would send those boys, barely out of their teens, to war in a country across the ocean, only to die, crying out for their mothers.

The anti-war thought came out of nowhere, shocking her. Not that she'd ever been *pro*-war; but the Vietnam "police action" had been going on since her early teens—a fact of life. Even when Gary had been killed, she hadn't denounced the war or questioned why America was fighting in Vietnam. In fact, it had spurred her decision to go to nursing school and ultimately, to join the Army. Why, *now*, were these thoughts popping in her mind? She *had* to believe they were here for a reason—that these guys weren't dying for nothing. Otherwise, how could she get up and come into this hospital every day?

Close to the end of her shift, Cindy sat at the nurse's station desk with Rosalie, making notes in Patrick's chart. The GI was still holding his own. If he could survive the night, that faceless mother in Vermont might see her son again. The phone on the desk shrilled out, and Cindy stiffened. Not more incoming wounded, she prayed. She'd surely lose her mind if she had to stay another second past 1900 hours.

Rosalie picked it up. Her hazel eyes fixed upon Cindy as she listened to the caller. "Yes, sir. She's on-duty until 1900." Her eyes widened. "Oh, of course. I'll send her over right away. Thank you, sir." She hung up the phone and looked at Cindy, speechless.

"What?" Cindy demanded. "Who was that?"

Her eyes wide as cereal bowls, Rosalie said, "Colonel Simpson, the attaché for General Hopper. Cindy, I heard all about you saving a general in the O Club, but I had no idea it was *the* General Hopper, for God's sake!"

Cindy stared at her. Rosalie had just returned from an R&R in Bangkok, so she'd come late to the news about the general's near brush with death and Cindy's emergency tracheotomy. "What do you mean, *the* General Hopper? Is he someone special? Besides being a four-star, of course."

"Oh, not really!" Rosalie's eyes sparkled.

"He's just the highest-ranking brass at headquarters in Saigon. Oh, and by the way, he wants to see you."

Cindy put down her pen, her heart dropping to the soles of her combat boots. "The attaché wants to see me?" she asked hopefully.

Rosalie snorted. "No, you silly girl. The *general* wants to see you." She grinned. "So, if I were you, I'd get my ass over to Ward 7 pronto. You don't keep a four-star waiting."

Ω

Colonel Simpson met her outside the single private room on Ward 7. Cindy recognized him immediately as the priggish, narrow-faced colonel who'd tried to stop her from doing the trach on the general. A fading purplish-green bruise still marked his left cheekbone where Quin had decked him. For days, they'd both waited for the ax to fall, but had heard nothing. Was that ax about to descend now?

The colonel's dark gaze flicked over her, his jaw tightening. Clearly, he hadn't forgiven the incident, even now when he surely knew their actions had saved his commander's life. Typical REMF. Kissing ass to officers who out-ranked him and despising the ones who didn't.

"This way," he said stiffly, ushering her into the General's room.

Cindy stepped inside, heart pounding. It

wasn't every day that she came face-to-face with a four-star general. And clearly, this wasn't the room of an ordinary patient. The four stars of his insignia were displayed on his chart and above his bed along with his unit badge. Bouquets of flowers covered every available surface; the room smelled like a funeral parlor. A shiver skittered up her back. The man could well have been *in* a funeral parlor rather than a hospital room, no thanks to that idiot colonel standing at his bedside, managing to look both smug and disdainful at the same time.

The man in the bed spoke with a thick southern drawl, "So, this is the young lady who saved my ornery behind the other day?"

As soon as Cindy saw his generous smile, her anxiety eased, and she smiled back.

Colonel Simpson nodded stiffly. "Yes, sir. Lieutenant Cynthia Sweet."

Cindy wondered if she was imagining the condescension in his voice. But the sour look on his angular pock-marked face made that doubtful.

General Hopper stuck out a bedpan-sized hand. "Well, howdy, young lady. Come on over here and let me shake your hand. I'm mighty grateful you were in that O Club the other night. That piece of sirloin damn near killed me. But you know that, don't you?"

"I figured it out, sir. And I was happy to be of service." Smiling, Cindy approached him and took his extended hand. He looked grandfatherly, but not like a feeble, close-to-death kind of grandfather, despite the thick Kerlix bandage covering his throat. More like a virile movie-star grandfather with his craggy good looks, crinkling blue eyes and buzz-cut iron-gray hair. He was a big a man, that much she remembered from the night at the O Club—a real John Wayne type.

He looked deeply into her eyes. "Just so you know, I'm not all talk and no cider, young miss. I am *sincerely* grateful for what you did, and so is my wife back in Wichita Falls. You are a credit to the Army Nursing Corp, and I'm going to see you're properly rewarded. All you have to do is ask, and if it's in my power, I'll move heaven and earth to get it for you."

Cindy didn't know what to say. *Send me home?* She almost had to bite back the words. Somehow, she didn't think he'd appreciate that particular request. "Just doing my job, General Hopper. That's what they train us for...to be of service wherever we can."

He nodded with satisfaction and finally released her hand. "Our boys are lucky to have a fine nurse like you. I'll bet they really appreciate you in triage. I have a daughter about your age, and just between you and me, she's a fritter-minded little thing, though I love her to pieces. In her sixth year at Baylor and still don't know beans when the poke is open, bless her heart."

Cindy didn't know whether to laugh or

commiserate so she just continued to smile.

"And I understand there was a young man with you that night who had a hand in my rescue? An egg-beater pilot, they tell me."

Cindy's heart dropped and her gaze flew to Colonel Simpson. *Oh, shit.* His jaw tightened, and the bruise on his jaw almost seemed to glow under the fluorescent lights. He stared at her with icy eyes. Clearly, if it were up to him, she and Quin would both be in the stockade.

"Yes, sir," Cindy stammered. "It was my…er…Warrant Officer Ryan Quinlan, a friend of mine."

The general glanced at Colonel Simpson, then turned back to her with a barely concealed grin. "And I understand he had to take…extraordinary measures to…assist you in keeping me from the Grim Reaper?"

Cindy felt her cheeks grow hot. She studiously avoided looking at the colonel. "Yes, sir. He did what he felt he had to do. Every second counted, you understand?"

"'Course I do, young lady! And I'm mighty glad that young man took matters into his own hands to help move things along. Colonel Simpson here agrees, don't you, Bob?"

"Yes, *sir!*" the colonel barked, staring straight ahead.

"So, if you happen to run into that dust off pilot again, hon, I want you to thank him personally for me, you hear?" He shook his gray head and gave an abashed grin. "I still can't believe I almost died. Lord, I survived the battles at Chosin Reservoir in Korea and D-Day in Normandy. I've climbed Mt. McKinley and the Matterhorn, and got home snug as a bug in a rug–and to think, I almost met my maker because a piece of Texas Black Angus steak got stuck in my craw. If not for you…" To Cindy's astonishment, his eyes grew misty. He swallowed hard, blinked a few times, and then gave her a wink. "Well, I just had to say thank you. And I meant what I said…anything you need, you just call me, you hear, young miss? Bob, give her my personal phone number."

Colonel Simpson drew a card out of his uniform pocket and extended it to her, his gaze focused somewhere behind her left shoulder. Then he escorted her to the door.

With her mind still spinning, Cindy stepped out of Ward 7 to head back across the quad toward Ward 2. She still had fifteen minutes of her shift to complete. Besides, she couldn't wait to tell Rosalie about her conversation with the general. *Damn it!* Why hadn't she thought of something to ask for? The general had said *anything*. Now, of course, all kinds of things came to mind—chocolates, good French soap, champagne.

She stepped under the covered walkway, and the world shuddered under her feet. A blast of heat surrounded her. She hit the ground with the sound of an explosion still reverberating through the humid tropical evening.

CHAPTER SEVENTEEN

Coughing from the thick, black smoke roiling over her, Cindy sat up. The explosion seemed to have come from beyond the hospital. Somewhere past the morgue. A mortar attack? Her stomach dropped to her toes. *The chemical dump.* Where the Army buried toxic materials. *Jesus! What am I breathing?*

Covering her mouth and nose with her shirt, she scrambled to her feet. Panicked, people were emerging from the buildings. The post siren moaned out a warning—too late. Unless there was more coming. That thought sent her heart hammering.

"*Attention, all personnel! Red alert, red alert!*" crackled the loudspeaker. "*The post is under attack! Take cover immediately! Condition Red Alert!*"

Keeping her mouth and nose covered, she ran toward Ward 2. They'd be going crazy in there, trying to get the patients to a place of safety—if there *was* one. No way would they be able to get everyone out and into the emergency bunkers. Impossible to evacuate the entire hospital!

Just as she reached the door of the ward, a gunshot split the air. Someone in the quadrangle shrieked. And then more cries of horror and panic. Cindy whirled around and saw a form clad in fatigues sprawled on the grass. Even from a distance, Cindy could see the red bloom on the soldier's shirt. More shots rang out. Everyone in the quad ran for cover. Cindy bolted toward the injured soldier.

Behind her, she heard the horrified shouts of the staff on Ward 2. Rosalie, she thought, and one of the corpsmen. "Cindy! *No!*"

She ignored them and ran toward the fallen GI. More shots rang out. She flinched but kept going. Reached him just as another shot rang out followed by whoops of victory. She glanced up at the water tower in time to see a figure topple off with a scream. Wincing, she turned back to the soldier on the ground. The blood on his back had spread to the size of a football. Her heart dropped as she turned him over. It wasn't a *he,* but a *she,* a FNG nurse who worked with Jenny on Ward 5. Cindy had just met her at the O Club only a few days ago. She'd been shot just inside the covered walkway, probably had been on her way either to or from the nurse's quarters.

"I'm sorry," Cindy murmured, her eyes blurring with tears. Gently, she closed the young woman's staring brown eyes. The bullet had gone straight through her heart; death had been instantaneous.

She stood and looked around for other wounded, but didn't see any. Marines ran with cocked weapons toward the water tower. A bitter taste rose in Cindy's mouth, and she hoped with all her heart the sniper had died—in agony.

Remembering they were still under a red alert, and she would be needed in the ward, she loped back across the quad. When she burst into the ward, she saw Rosalie and the two on-duty corpsmen wearing flak jackets and helmets, grabbing mattresses from extra beds and covering patients. The instructions about red alerts clicked into her mind, and she donned her helmet and flak jacket and joined them in dragging mattresses from the few empty beds. Not enough for all the patients, but like in triage, they'd save the ones who were in the best condition, the most likely to survive. She hated playing God like this, but what choice did she have?

Still, without thinking too much about it, she headed straight for Pfc. Patrick Cummings, clumsily dragging the mattress. She'd be damned if she'd let him die like this, not after all he'd been through. But just as she started to place the mattress on top of him, the sirens outside stopped abruptly.

"Attention, all personnel," rang out the voice on the loudspeaker. "*All clear*! Red alert is canceled!"

Cindy froze, watching as Rosalie and the corpsmen matter-of-factly slipped out of their flak jackets and helmets, and then began to remove the mattresses from the patients. "Just like that?" she said. "I saw they got the sniper, but what about the explosion? And how do they know it's over?"

One of the corpsmen, Sgt. Randall Stevenson, a short-timer due to ship out the end of the month, shrugged. "Probably caught the sapper."

Rosalie moved past Cindy, tugging a mattress back onto an empty bed. She seemed calm, composed. Cindy couldn't believe it. "Excuse my ignorance, but what's a sapper?" she asked.

"A VC demolition expert," Randall explained, helping Rosalie with the mattress. "But in this case, he probably wasn't an expert. Sounds like the explosion was a decoy to draw people out onto the quad for the sniper. It was probably someone who's worked on post for months. You've heard of Russian 'sleepers,' right? Same thing." He shook his head in disgust. "Some mama-san working in the laundry, vetted by security, finally shows her true colors after months of being a kiss-ass to every American she comes in contact with. That's how the VC work. Fucking bastards."

Stunned, Cindy stared at him. In all the

months she'd been working with him, she'd never heard him say more than two sentences at a time. Out of all the corpsmen on Ward 2, Randall was the one who kept the most distance, never involving himself in small talk or joking around. He worked competently without obvious emotion. Until now.

"The sniper killed one of the new nurses," Cindy said, slipping out of her flak jacket. "I think her name was Janice." She swallowed hard. "She works...*worked*...on Ward 5."

Randall's eyes met hers. His jaw tightened. "Like I said, fucking bastards."

Turned out Randall was right. The official report came in from the ER a few minutes later. The sapper had been apprehended—a 14-year-old shoeshine boy who worked at one of the PXs. After detonating the charge near the chemical dump, he hadn't been able to get away fast enough, suffering shrapnel wounds on both legs. Thankfully, no one else had been injured in the explosion. The sniper, an older boy who'd worked in the motor pool, had died from his wound. And it had been a stomach wound, so Cindy's wish for an agonizing death had, no doubt, come true.

Cindy wondered about all the other Vietnamese who worked on-post. How many were actually VC who'd infiltrated the post under the guise of being allies? She thought of her friendly hairdresser, Mai. Always so sweet and embarrassingly submissive. And Papa-san Song who worked as a cashier at the PX, always wearing a big, toothless grin and greeting her with "Hello, Tall Pretty Lady." But behind those smiles, how did they really feel? Hatred for Americans? Anger that they had come to their country, ostensibly to help the South Vietnamese, but waging war, all the same?

Finally off-duty, Cindy prepared to leave the ward after one final check on Patrick Cummings, who appeared to be sleeping comfortably, his vital signs stable. She prayed he'd make it through the night. He *had* to. She didn't know why she felt so strongly about this particular GI, but somehow he'd touched a chord in her, and she just didn't know how she'd stand it if he died. Crazy and unprofessional, she knew. Rule # 1—never get emotionally attached to a patient. But too late—she already was.

"Hope you have a quiet night," Cindy called out to Cap Bren and the FNG, Lieutenant Mona Young, and headed for the door. A tiny mama-san mopping the floor looked up as she approached, and gave her a black-toothed smile. "Goodnight, Nurse Cindy." She reeked of "tiger balm," a foul-smelling oil the Vietnamese used to ward off evil spirits.

Cindy forced a smile and murmured, "Thank you." *Are you with us, Mama-san? Or are you just waiting for the right moment to kill us?*

Ω

Clad in her dark green dress uniform, Cindy stood at attention in front of Colonel Kairos, trying not to inhale her flowery odor as the woman's cold gaze swept over her from the top of her jaunty green cap to her neat black pumps. To an onlooker, it would seem by the grim look on the commander's face that Cindy was mired in deep shit, about to get the dressing down of her life. Colonel Kairos' dark brown eyes revealed not a glimmer of warmth.

Yet, Cindy stood before her commanding officer to receive a Certificate of Achievement for the valor she'd portrayed in going to the aide of a fellow soldier under fire. Her actions in trying to rescue the fallen nurse had resulted in a request by Dr. Charley Moss to have Cindy awarded with The Soldier's Medal, an award that rewarded heroism in the face of great danger. But the request had been denied by Headquarters because "she is a woman, and women don't get rewarded for heroism." Instead, they presented her with a "Certificate of Achievement." Whatever that was.

Obviously, Colonel Kairos felt as if she didn't deserve either. After presenting the certificate to her and returning Cindy's crisp salute, she turned on her heel with a brusque, "Dis-*missed*!"

But just as Cindy turned to go, the colonel spoke again. "Oh, Sweet! I almost forgot." She grabbed an envelope from her desk and extended it to her. "A message from General Hopper." She looked put out and mildly curious, as if wondering why a four-star general would be sending a personal message to a peon like Cindy.

Cindy took it with a curt "thank you."

Colonel Kairos glared at her. "It's rather unusual for someone of your rank to get correspondence from a four-star general." She waited for Cindy's response, not even trying to disguise her curiosity.

Cindy wasn't about to alleviate it. "Yes, Ma'am," she snapped, then gave her a smart salute. "Is that all, Ma'am?"

Colonel Kairos looked startled, and two bright spots of red appeared on her sharp cheekbones. But she must've realized she couldn't force Cindy to tell her. Her jaw tightened and she returned Cindy's salute in a way that seemed more like a "fuck you" than a sign of respect. "Go! Get the hell out of here!"

Cindy turned and strode out of her office, feeling the woman's disdainful gaze burning into her back. Once outside, she rolled her eyes, praying she wouldn't be put up for any more awards. After an encounter with Kairos, she felt lower than pond scum—and in need of a few hours of oxygen therapy to clear her brain of Chanel No. 5.

In the quad, she sat down on a bench and opened the envelope. The note was short and to the point, scrawled in black ink: *It should've been the*

Soldier's Medal. Two of them actually—one for the nurse, and one for me. Anything you need, young lady, you call me—anytime. My direct line: 078546. Joseph.

Ω

"Patrick, you're looking quite handsome today!" Cindy grinned down at her favorite patient as she wrapped the blood pressure cuff around his remaining arm. It had been a week since he'd come in from surgery, barely clinging to life. Now, although half his face was still heavily bandaged, as were the stumps of his left arm and leg, he looked like a different boy. Like a survivor. In fact, if his vital signs remained stable, he'd be evacuated stateside within the next few days. Cindy prayed for that, but she was going to miss him like hell. Intelligent and blessed with a droll sense of humor, Patrick had become the favorite of all the staff, but Cindy knew she was *his* favorite nurse. In the late hours when the ward was quiet, he'd taught her how to play Blackjack—and he beat her consistently at it. Quin was delighted to learn someone had found something they could beat her at, and took great pleasure in teasing her about it.

Patrick's right blue eye gleamed up at her, and the vestiges of a grin twitched on the side of his mouth she could see. "Yeah, they were finally able to wash my hair. I'm ready for my Breck commercial."

Cindy laughed, then listened to the thud of his heart through her stethoscope. "120/75," she said with satisfaction, releasing the inflatable pump. Her gaze scanned the silky tumble of reddish-gold curls on the right side of his head. Hair a girl would kill for. "I see that. Where did you get such gorgeous color hair? And it's so long! You don't even look like you're in the military."

He shrugged. "Not many barbers out in the bush. Got the red from my mom. Comes from the Irish side of the family. Hey, L.T., I got a letter from my girlfriend yesterday. You want to see her picture? I know I've been talking your ear off about her all week."

Cindy removed the blood pressure cuff. "Of course I want to see Nancy. I feel like I know her already."

He nodded and reached for a letter on his bedside table. A rosy blush covered his cheekbone. Cindy felt a pang. Patrick had been an extremely handsome boy. That much was obvious from the side of his face unmarked by the explosion. He had sparkling blue eyes, carved cheekbones, a strong, straight nose and a square cleft chin—movie-star perfect looks. In fact, he kind of reminded her of James Dean in *Rebel without a Cause*. *Still* handsome, she reminded herself. She just hoped his Nancy would feel the same way.

He removed a color photograph from the letter and handed it to her. A pretty blonde with sultry blue eyes smiled into the camera with an intimate, "come hither" look, reminding Cindy of a young Brigitte Bardot. *A little sex kitten.* Would a girl like that want a man who wasn't her equal in the looks department? Immediately Cindy felt guilty for her thoughts. Who was she to judge the girl? If she really loved him…

"She's beautiful," Cindy said, handing the photo back to him.

He smiled down at it, a soft look in his eye. "She hopes to make the U.S ski team for the Winter Olympics in Japan. Alpine skiing. I know she's going to do it. She's been skiing since she was four."

"Oh, I hope so! I love watching the Winter Olympics. Do *you* ski?" The question slipped out before she realized it, and she almost bit her lip. *Stupid question. Of course he doesn't* now.

He didn't seem to notice. "Everybody who lives near Stowe skis. But for me, it's purely recreational. If I want speed, I'll race cars, not ski down a mountain at 60 miles per hour on fiberglass sticks." He gave a short laugh that held only a touch of irony. "Course, I don't have to worry about that anymore, do I? Wonder how much I can get for my Rossignols?"

Cindy gave his arm a gentle pat, searching for something to say that would comfort him. Problem was…there wasn't anything. Across the ward, a patient moaned and called out for a nurse. With relief, Cindy turned to go to him, but before she could move, Rosalie appeared at his bedside.

Cindy turned back to Patrick and saw his face had brightened.

"I know. I'll give my skis to you. If you come and visit me and Nancy in Vermont after you get back to The World. Do *you* ski, L.T.?"

"I've only tried it once," Cindy said with a grin. "When I was in college, some of us went to a ski resort in the Catskills. I caught on pretty quick but I stuck to the bunny slopes. I'd like to try it again someday."

But it seemed as if Patrick had stopped listening. He was staring at Nancy's photo again, his face pensive. And then he asked the question that echoed her earlier thoughts. "What's she going to do when she sees me, L.T.?" He looked up at her, all traces of a smile gone. "Is she going to run away, screaming?"

Cindy's heart lurched. Her throat felt tight, and she knew she was on the verge of tears. *And that couldn't happen.* She owed it to Patrick to maintain a positive, life-affirming attitude. She reached out and brushed a stray gold-red curl from his forehead. "If she's the girl you believe her to be, Patrick, she won't run away. She'll love you, no matter what."

Cindy only hoped with all her heart she was speaking the truth.

March 1971

February 25, 1971

Dear Cindy:

Well, I just couldn't believe it when Ellen let it slip that she wrote you my happy news before I got a chance to. That's why I sent that postcard, hoping it would make it to you before her letter did. Did it? I'm guessing not. Oh, well…yes, I'm engaged! Tom and I have set a date for December 18th—a week before Christmas. He wanted to get married this summer, but I said no way! Cindy has to be home, and she has to be my bridesmaid.

So…only ten months to wait! Of course, what I'm <u>really</u> waiting for is September when you'll be back home. Oh, Cindy, I miss you so much.

The news every night is so grim. All that footage of the GIs wading through swamps and jungles. And the horrific images of dead Viet Cong. All they talk about is the body count. Theirs, of course. Oh, they say how many Americans died, but they always counter it with how many more Viet Cong died. I guess that's supposed to make us feel better! Tell that to Hazel Sharepeace down the road. Her 19-year-old son, Bobby, was killed in An Khe last week. Her only son. God, I hate this war. Hate it! Of course, if I say anything like that around here, I get the stink-eye from Ellen. Was it your father who turned her into such a rigid conservative?

We got into a huge fight yesterday after we read the account in the paper about William Calley's testimony during his court martial. He's trying to put the whole blame for that atrocious massacre on his commanding officer. Not that Medina is innocent, but come on! Anyway, I said something like "they should take both of them and string them up from the highest tree," and your mom just lost it. Started screaming about how unpatriotic I am, and how <u>dare</u> I talk like that while you're over there risking your life, and how I should support the troops, no matter what they do, and remember it's a war and bad things happen in wars…etc. She went on and on. And when I finally was able to get a word in edgewise, I asked her if "supporting the troops" included condoning the murder of babies? Well, I thought she was going to blow a gasket. Needless to say, we're not speaking to each other right now. (But we'll get over it; we always do.)

Cindy, I enjoy reading your letters so much. I'm just tickled pink that you're in love. Quin sounds like a fantastic young man. I can't wait to meet him. You said he's been there several months longer than you, right? So, he'll be coming back home before you do. I'll bet you're not looking forward to that. Well, of course, you want him back in the States so he'll be safe, but I know you're going to miss him like crazy! If this is as serious as you say it is, you might get married and move to Texas. I'll probably <u>never</u> get to see you. Oh, well, as long as you're happy…

I'd better close and get this in the mail. Ellen and I are supposed to go look at wedding gowns today, but since we're not exactly on speaking terms, who knows? Oh, Joni just walked in and saw I was writing you. She said she'll write you real soon. She has BIG NEWS! (And I know what it is. Ha!)

Take care, Cindy. Love you bunches.

Aunt Terri

CHAPTER EIGHTEEN

Cindy pushed Quin into a frothy wave washing onto the sand, and took off running as fast as she could. The seaweed-flecked surf hit him mid-calf, slowing him down as he raced after her. She knew if he caught her, she'd be swimming in the China Sea much earlier than she wanted to. It was early morning, and the water temperature would be way too cool for a dip–to her way of thinking, anyway. Quin would have other ideas.

"*You little*…when I catch you, you're going to be so sorry!" Laughing, he chased after her, splashing through the wavelets.

She made an abrupt turn and headed away from the ocean, onto the hard-packed wet sand— and immediately realized her mistake. Fast, she was, but not as fast as the high school track star he'd been back in Karnes City, Texas. She could feel him gaining on her. And then, his warm arms wrapped around her from behind, and her backside was plastered up against his muscular body.

"Okay, now you're going to pay, Cinnamon Sweet," he growled. He twirled her around, threaded his long, strong fingers into her shaggy hair and angled her face up so he could capture her mouth with his.

Cindy's hands tightened on his back as she gave herself up to his kiss. Suddenly everything—the beach, the ocean, the cloudless sapphire sky—even the war—disappeared. It was just Quin, and the magic of his kiss. It took her away just as the ocean had yesterday afternoon when she'd floated on her back in its tropical embrace, gazing up at white, billowy clouds, secure in the presence of her man nearby. They could've been anywhere else in the world— Hawaii, the Bahamas, Tahiti. Impossible to believe they were still in 'Nam.

But they were–even though, admittedly, it was a far cry from the 24th Evac at Long Binh. By some miracle, they'd been able to take a mini R&R at China Beach, a recreational facility for GIs to give them a respite from the war. Quin had managed to secure a tiny cottage for two nights. They'd arrived yesterday afternoon, and the beach had been so crowded with GIs that Quin had refused to let her wear her bikini. Fine with her. Females were few and far between, and Cindy had no desire to flaunt her near-naked body in front of those hungry male eyes. Even in a pair of shorts and an Army tee-shirt, she felt exposed and uncomfortable. If it hadn't been for Quin's presence, she would've spent the rest of the day in the cottage.

Now, at 0600 hours, the beach was practically deserted—probably because all the GIs were sleeping off hangovers in their quarters. Which was what Cindy had been doing…well, not sleeping off a hangover, but *sleeping*—the first decent, uninterrupted sleep she'd had in weeks–when Quin roused her from bed, tossed her shorts and T-shirt at her and declared they had to go for a walk to see the sunrise. He'd barely given her the chance to go to the bathroom first.

And there it was—the salmon pink rays of the sun glimmering just above the luminous South China Sea, promising a new day of bliss with Quin. *Bliss.* Who knew she'd use a word like that—that she could find bliss here, in a country ravaged by war? But yesterday as she'd submerged her non-bikinied body in the warm, green waters—yes, the same exact shade as Quin's magnetic eyes—something had invaded her soul which had been missing for months. Peace.

She knew it was an illusion, that as soon as they returned to the 24th, it would be gone, disappearing like the melted remnants of cotton candy on the tongue, leaving little more than the tantalizing taste of sugar behind. But this sugar—

this peace—she would savor for the next sixteen hours…when it would be time to check out of the cottage and head back to Long Binh.

Quin drew away and gazed down at her, his eyes sparkling with amusement. "You know what I want to do right now?" he asked.

Feeling the bulge in his shorts, Cindy pressed against him, giving a short laugh. "I have an idea."

His eyes widened in feigned shock. "Cynthia Marie Sweet, you are a *bad girl!*"

"I was an innocent little girl before I met you," Cindy shot back, grinding against him suggestively. She laughed at the flush deepening on his cheekbones. "You corrupted me."

"Enough of that, woman! You have to focus." He set her apart from him, a determined look on his face.

Cindy grinned, allowing her gaze to drift to his obvious erection. "Seems to me *you're* the one who needs to focus."

"Shame on you! Calling attention to my…*ahem*…debilitating physical affliction like that. What are you? Some kind of…*nurse* or something?" He placed his arm around her shoulder and turned her to face the way they'd come.

Cindy giggled. "As a matter of fact…I *do* know a bit about nursing. And I have just the thing to take care of your problem. Where are we going?"

"Back to the cottage. I have a surprise for you."

"Oh? Besides the one in your pants?" She reached up and ruffled his damp, sun-streaked hair. The humid air of the coast had turned it to springy curls.

He gave her bottom a slap. "I really *have* corrupted you, haven't I? I've turned you into a sex maniac." He sighed. "Why does that always happen to me?"

Cindy stopped in her tracks. "*What?*" She pulled away and turned to face him with a mock glare. "You turn all your women into sex maniacs? How many women are we talking about?"

He gave her a wink, his grin widening. "Only the ones I really like…and that would be you." He grabbed her hand and tugged her forward. "Come on, Cinnamon. We're wasting time." He pulled her along the sand.

Cindy stumbled after him, trying to keep up. "What's the big hurry? Don't we have all day?"

"Not for what I have in mind. Come on!"

A breeze, heavy with the tang of salt water, caressed her skin turned away from the beach. Approaching the cottage, Cindy heard the sound of music coming from inside–The Association singing "Never My Love," the song they'd first slow-danced to at the Officers Club. "Quin!" She pulled on his hand to stop him. "There's someone in the cottage!"

Oddly enough, he didn't seem at all concerned. Until he looked at the picnic table outside the front of the cottage. *"Oh, son of a bitch!"*

Cindy followed his gaze to where a little white bird—a sandpiper, she thought it was called—stood pecking at colorful bits of *something.* Quin dropped her hand and ran at the bird, waving his arms like a wildman. *"Get out of here, you dadburned varmit!"*

"Quin! What's wrong with you? It's just a bird! Did you *hear* me? There is someone in our cottage playing music!" She glanced fearfully toward the door of the cottage. "He might be dangerous!"

Quin rolled his eyes. "Yeah, a dangerous maniac who likes The Association. *Wooo!* I'm terrified." He turned back to the table, glaring down at whatever the bird had been feasting on. "Damn it! All that planning, and it's *ruined!*"

"What's ruined?" She approached the table. "Oh, look! It's M&Ms! Who knew a bird would like M&Ms? But why…" She looked up at him. "Did you leave M&Ms on our picnic table?"

Quin shook his head, a resigned look on his face. "Not me. I paid some guy to do it. I was going to use peppermints, but you said M&Ms were your favorite."

"Huh?" Cindy stared at him. "You had M&Ms last night and didn't *tell* me?"

"Because I'm an idiot, that's why." He stared forlornly at the scattered bits of candy. "I thought it would be romantic."

"Romantic? *Sharing* your M&Ms would be the romantic thing to do, not leave them out here for the birds to eat." She looked back at the multi-colored candies. "Hey, look! That looks like an 'M.' And isn't that an 'E?'"

He gave her a glum look. "You don't have a clue, do you, Cinnamon? Oh, hell. It was a stupid idea, anyway. I was just trying to think of something original. That's what I get for paying some joker twenty bucks to do what I should've done myself. And who knew a stupid bird would like M&Ms? Oh, hell with it." He gave a deep sigh, fished something out of his shorts pocket and dropped to one knee. "Will you marry me, Cynthia Sweet?"

At first, it didn't quite compute. Then she thought she'd imagined the words. But when she saw the box he was holding, her heart raced. She stared at a glittering diamond ring the size of one of the M&Ms on the table. Her gaze shot from the ring to Quin. He gazed up at her with hopeful eyes and a look on his face she'd never seen before--vulnerability.

"This isn't a joke, is it?" she whispered.

He shook his head, and in his luminous green eyes, she saw the truth. It most definitely was not a joke. He swallowed hard, and said huskily, "I love you, Cinnamon. And I want to spend the rest of my life with you…" Deliberately thickening his Texas accent, he added, "…if you'll have this good old country boy from Texas."

Tears misted Cindy's eyes as she reached down, grabbed his hands and pulled him to his feet. "Yes, you good old country boy, I'll marry you. *Yes!*"

Laughing and crying at the same time, she watched as he slipped the engagement ring on her finger, his hand trembling. Then his warm mouth closed over hers. Her fingers entwining in his curls, she kissed him back. Mouths locked, he picked her up and twirled her around. Finally, after a long, sweet moment, he set her down and they broke apart. She gazed at him breathlessly, her fingertips caressing the crinkly lines at the edges of his eyes.

"I still don't get it, though," she said. "What were you trying to do with the M&Ms?"

"Oh, man." He sighed. "I really screwed that up, didn't I? See, we were supposed to come back and you'd find 'Marry Me' spelled out in M&Ms on the table. *Daggonit!* I shoulda used peppermints. Remember that first night at the pool when we sat and ate a whole bag of 'em?"

"Yes, but…"

"But no! I remembered how much you liked those dang M&Ms. And apparently these doggone Vietnamese birds like 'em, too. See, I paid this G.I. to arrange them on the table while we were out to watch the sunrise, but either he couldn't spell or that blasted bird ate a hell of a lot of letters." Quin sighed, his arms tightening around her. "But at least one thing went right—I told that G.I. to start playing "Never My Love" on the cassette player. The first song we slow-danced to, remember?" Cupping her face, he lowered his forehead to hers. "God, I'm such an inept idiot, aren't I? I wanted this to be the most romantic proposal ever, and I totally screwed it up."

"Hey!" Cindy fastened her hands on his and drew away so she could meet his gaze. "Watch it, buster. You're talking about my fiance' and I won't have you bad-mouthing him. I think he's the most romantic man in the world…and this is a story I'm going to love to tell our grandchildren someday."

He gave a reluctant grin. "Great. Our grandchildren will find out what a doofus Old Grandpa is."

A gentle breeze sent the reeds of a bamboo wind chime clacking from the eaves of their cottage. Cindy cupped his square jaw in her hands, her lips quirking. "You *are* a doofus," she muttered. "*My* doofus. Now shut up and kiss me."

CHAPTER NINETEEN

Cindy couldn't wait to get to the ward to show off her diamond. It flashed on her finger with every movement of her hand, and she couldn't stop staring at it. With a smile, she envisioned a huge wedding in Texas…maybe on the beach at Corpus Christi. Although Quin's immediate family lived in Karnes City, his grandparents—the wealthy ones on his mother's side–had an estate in the famous coastal city. And according to him, his grandmother doted on him, the only grandson. Yes, she was sure they'd give them a huge white wedding.

Of course, it didn't matter to Cindy. She'd marry Quin in front of a Justice of the Peace with no one in attendance, if that was what he wanted. But knowing him and his Texas state of mind, the bigger, the better.

She burst onto the ward, hoping Rosalie would

be on duty, but instead, she saw Cap Bren at the nurse's station. Trying to mask her disappointment, she approached the desk with dissipating enthusiasm. "Hi, Captain. Looks like things are quiet this afternoon."

Cap Bren looked up from a patient's chart, her blue eyes smudged with lavender circles. "It is now. Big push last night. Sixteen casualties. Nine made it." She nodded toward the ward where eight corpsmen and five nurses checked vitals and hung I.V.s. "So far."

Cindy decided not to mention her engagement. Cap Bren wouldn't give a crap either way, so why bother? "I don't come on duty until seven," she said, knowing what she was about to say, and regretting it already. "But I could help you out right now if…"

Cap Bren shook her head. "We're good. Enjoy your time off." She started to turn to her paperwork, but when Cindy brushed back her too-long bangs, the captain's gaze sharpened, centering on the dazzling ring on Cindy's left hand. "So! Your dust off pilot proposed, huh?"

A squeal came from behind Cindy, and then Shyanne Rooney swooped down on her. "Oh, my *God!*" she belted out in her thick Kentucky drawl, her cherubic face gleaming. "Let me see that rock!" As the other nurses gathered around in excitement, Shyanne grabbed Cindy's hand and examined the ring. "Holy *moly!* It's big enough to choke my granddaddy's donkey!" The blonde nurse wrapped her arms around Cindy. "Oh, *Cinnndddy*, I'm so dadgummed *happy* for you!"

Laughing, Cindy hugged her back. "When can we get together so I can tell you all about the proposal, Shy? It's so hard getting together with you and Jenny and Rosalie. One of us is always working!"

"Did someone say my name?"

Cindy turned to see Rosalie step into the ward, looking more like a beauty queen than ever in her light green summer cords, cap and pumps. What was up? Had she been promoted? But no, she still wore the double silver bars of captain on her collar. "Rosie, where are *you* off to?"

Rosalie grinned. "Guess you haven't heard. They moved my DEROS up. I'm catching my freedom bird home in..." She peered at her wristwatch. "...exactly two hours. I just stopped in to say my final goodbyes–and I'm so glad you got back in time, Cindy."

Unexpected emotion washed over Cindy. She'd known Rosalie was due to go home soon, but when Cindy had left for China Beach with Quin, she'd thought there would still be plenty of time for them to get together before she shipped out.

"Oh, Rosalie!" Her eyes blurred with tears as she hurried over to her friend. "I'm so happy for you, but I'm going to miss you so much!" She hugged her, and then drew back. "You think there's any chance at all you can come down from

Alaska for my wedding?"

Rosalie's hazel eyes widened. "*What?*"

Grinning, Cindy waved her hand, sending the diamond flashing.

"*Oh, my God!*" Rosalie grabbed her hand and peered at the ring like it was the Holy Grail. "It's *gorgeous*, Cindy! Congratulations!" She hugged her. "I know you and Quin are going to be so happy! And yes, I'll try my best to be at your wedding! Just let me know when and where."

All the nurses drew in close, laughing and taking turns examining Cindy's ring. Except for Cap Bren. Her face stone-like, she sat at her desk, briskly writing in a chart. With a loud snap, she closed the chart and stood.

"Let's hope there *is* a wedding," she said, her eyes blazing with undisguised emotion. "Can someone please cover the desk?" And she strode down the corridor and stepped into the restroom, slamming the door behind her.

Stunned silence fell among the nurses. Cindy stared at Rosalie. "What the hell is that all about?"

Rosalie shook her head, a somber look on her face. "I guess you never heard the story. It was during her first tour of duty here in '67. I don't know how true it is, but this is what I heard...Brenda was just like us then. Young, idealistic, insecure. Scared." She gazed off down the corridor where Cap Bren had disappeared. "Hard to believe, huh? Anyway, the story is that she fell hard for a dust off pilot. They met early in their tours, and had the same DEROS, give or take a week. They got engaged and were planning to marry back in the World."

Cindy's stomach started to churn. She didn't want to hear the end of the story. She wanted to run, screaming, back to the nurse's quarters, bury her head in her pillow and pretend she hadn't heard any of this.

"Brenda shipped out first," Rosalie went on.

Cindy shook her head. "No. I don't want to hear…please."

Rosalie grabbed her arm and squeezed, her gaze locked with Cindy's. "You can't run from this, Cindy. It explains a lot about Brenda, and why she's the way she is. Her pilot was shot down during the siege of Khe Sanh, trying to evacuate the wounded. Just a few days before he was due to ship out."

Cindy's heart felt as if it had dropped to her feet. She'd known this was coming from the moment Rosalie started the story, but hearing the words spoken out loud felt like a nauseating punch to her gut.

"Oh, Jesus," whispered Lt. Ariane Mitchell, a new nurse on the ward.

Cindy couldn't find her voice. Rosalie was right. This did explain a lot about Cap Bren.

Finally, Lt. Natalie Wilkins, a nurse who'd been on the ward the longest, and due to ship home in another month, cleared her throat. "My heart goes out to her, but that doesn't excuse her trying to put a damper on Cindy's news." She gave Cindy's arm a squeeze. "Don't let her mess with your mind, Cindy. You and Quin are going to have a beautiful wedding!"

Cindy took a deep breath and summoned a smile. "I know that."

"Hey, L.T.! Congratulations!" David Ansgar joined the group of nurses and extended his hand to her. "I hope Quin knows what a lucky man he is."

Cindy smiled and took his hand. "Thanks, David. But I'm the lucky one."

His blue eyes locked with hers. "Don't sell yourself short, L.T. Any man would be lucky to have you." He dropped her hand, his cheekbones reddening as if he'd just realized he may have stepped over a line he shouldn't have crossed. Cindy felt sorry for him. It had been obvious for some time that David had a huge crush on her. Poor guy. Nothing worse than a hopeless crush.

Except a dead fiancé. Her stomach plunged at the thought. *No! Don't think that!*

Footsteps sounded from down the corridor, and Cindy turned to see Cap Bren approaching, her eyes puffy and red. Cindy felt a twinge in her heart. Clearly, the captain had been crying in the restroom, but now her face wore its usual remote mask. Her chilly gaze fastened on Cindy.

"I'm sorry for that comment, lieutenant. It

was unprofessional and uncalled for." Her eyes softened. "I do wish the very best for you and Quin. Congratulations on your engagement." With that, she turned and walked back to her desk. She sat down and reached for another chart. "Get some rest, Sweet. You're going to need all your energy tonight."

CHAPTER TWENTY

"Hey, did you hear the news, L.T.? Cap Bren is no longer a captain. I guess we're going to have to come up with a new nickname for her."

Cindy looked up from irrigating a trach to grin at David Ansgar a few beds down. "Yeah, I've been raking my brain, trying to come up with something. So far, I've got nothing."

He shook his head and hung a new bag of Ringers for a comatose patient. "Her getting promoted really screws with us. I mean, what can you do with Major?"

Cindy laughed. A few months ago, she could've thought of all kinds of nicknames for Cap Bren. *Hard Ass. Bitchy Bren. Gung Ho Gertie.* But after learning about the tragic death of her fiancé, she understood how Brenda had evolved into the stoic, hard-nosed nurse she was. But what she couldn't understand was why she had returned to Vietnam for another tour of duty. Having lost the man she loved here, it seemed like that would be the last thing she'd want to do.

"I guess we'll just have to bite the bullet and call her Major Hendricksen," Cindy said, moving on to the next patient. "Boring, I know, but what can you do?"

The ward doors burst open and two OR techs rolled in a gurney. Charley Moss in blood-splattered surgical scrubs followed. He walked over to Cap Bren...*Major* Bren, Cindy reminded herself, and gave her a chart. Cindy hurried over to get the details of the new admission as David took the gurney from the OR techs.

"...survived the surgery, but it's touch and go," Dr. Moss was saying. He glanced at Cindy and gave her a nod. His face looked drawn and haggard, his brown eyes weary. How long had he been in surgery? "The bullet severed her spinal cord just below the neck, so even if she does survive, she'll be a quadriplegic." He shook his head.

"*She?* It's a girl?" Cindy asked. It wasn't often they got a female patient in ICU. She thought of that poor nurse who'd been killed by the sniper last month, and her stomach dipped. *Please, God, don't let it be a nurse that I know.*

Charley nodded. "Somebody says she's a hairdresser on post. Unfortunately for her, though, that wasn't her only occupation. The guys who brought her in said she works in a whorehouse just off post. According to the GI who shot her, she'd lured three of them into the hooch, and then left them with some excuse. When he stepped out to urinate, he found her getting ready to toss in a grenade. He shot her point-blank and then had the guts to grab the grenade and throw it off out of harm's way. Brave guy."

Hairdresser on post? Cindy thought of Mai. Just this morning, she'd thought about making an appointment with her for a haircut. It had been a couple months since she'd had a trim. Pretty, vivacious Mai, a genius with a pair of scissors. Impossible that she was a prostitute. Or worse, a VC terrorist. Cindy whirled around and headed for the patient bay, trying to ignore the disquiet in the pit of her stomach. David was checking the vitals of the new patient. Cindy saw the glossy black hair first. *But they all have glossy black hair.* And she was tiny, just like Mai. Again, not unusual. All the hairdressers in the post's only beauty shop were tiny.

Cindy stood at the patient's bedside. Surgical bandages covered her neck where the bullet had entered. Amazing, really, she'd survived this long. Was it hatred for Americans that was fueling her struggle to live? Cindy stared down at her. The girl's skin was the color of a grey pearl, almost translucent. The color of imminent death. In contrast, her long black bangs gleamed with a healthy blue sheen. Cindy reached out and brushed her bangs away from her clammy forehead. When she saw the smallpox scar, she didn't feel anything at all. Not even surprise.

Feeling David's gaze upon her, she looked up and gave a shrug. "Who am I going to get to cut my hair now?" The joke was crass, and she immediately felt ashamed. But that was followed by a rage so profound that her hands tightened into fists. She wanted to rip out the tubes and the respirator regulating Mai's breathing. It hissed its life-giving oxygen in and out, clicking and clacking its methodical rhythm, a sound comforting to Cindy when it concerned other patients. But now, with this one, it sounded obscene.

"You treacherous *bitch*!" she spat. Her gaze flashed to David. "I gave her *money* because I thought her family needed it. She was probably handing it over to the VC. I taught her to say 'Mark Lindsay is fab' and 'You have Hershey bars?' in English. I gave her all my old movie magazines my Aunt Terri sent me because she's so crazy about American movie stars. And all the time, she was working for the VC? We can't trust anyone, can we, David? Because they may be smiling to our faces, but they'd just as soon be sticking a knife into our backs."

David didn't respond, but his sympathetic expression showed he understood where she was coming from. Cindy was glad he didn't offer any meant-to-be comforting platitudes. He turned back to the I.V. bag and adjusted the flow. Without another glance at Mai, Cindy left her bedside and went to check on another patient.

Two hours later, Mai died, and Cindy volunteered to roll her body to the morgue. As the morgue attendant accepted it, jotting the information on his clipboard, Cindy felt the last of her pre-Nam innocence and idealism disappear.

Ω

The scent of sandalwood incense permeated Cindy's dorm room, masking, she hoped, the pungent aroma of the rich Montagnard Gold weed Quin had commandeered on his last trip to the central highlands. Naked and entwined, they lay smoking the joint in Cindy's twin bed after making love. He'd been sneaking into her room since January, and despite the rumors of Colonel Kairos patrolling outside the women's quarters with her man-hating dog, he hadn't been caught. The nurses had devised a system to warn each other that a man was in their room to prevent unnecessary embarrassment—a sign that read *Just worked Mass-cal. Do Not Disturb*. That way, if Kairos decided to do a sudden inspection of their quarters, with any luck, she'd respect the sign and leave said nurse alone. Of course, the nurses all joked that her smell would precede her, so any nurse who happened to be entertaining a gentleman would have time to hide him.

But if anyone was keeping track, since Cindy had met Quin, she'd worked a *lot* of mass-cals. Nestled against his warm, damp body, she took another drag of the joint, giving herself up to the lovely floating sensation it gave her. At this moment, thanks to the grass—and Quin, all was right with her world.

Summer-like weather had arrived with a vengeance in Vietnam with day-time temperatures topping out at 101 degrees. Even with the room air conditioner pumping out a constant blast of frigid air, their bodies were sheened with sweat, and the sheets felt like they'd been left out overnight in a tent during a rainstorm. With each day, the humidity was creeping up, and by May, the monsoon rains would start to fall, making life almost unbearable.

But she wouldn't think about that now. The album playing on her reel-to-reel, Led Zeppelin II, ended and the next one began to play—Bert Sommer's *Road to Travel*. Cindy listened to his achingly sweet tenor, remembering his performance at Woodstock. What had Quin been doing back then? What road had he traveled to get here to her? She would ask him someday. Right now, she just wanted to listen to Bert singing about sailing into the sun with his girl, hearts and souls as one. Maybe it was a cliché but that's exactly how she felt about Quin. *This should be our song.*

When the song ended, and "Jennifer" began to play, she kissed the bottom of Quin's chin, her hand stroking the prickly reddish-blond stubble on his jaw. "Why is your hair brown, but your beard is red?" she murmured.

Quin chuckled, his lips brushing her forehead. "You should've seen me when I was two. My hair was so red, Dad's nickname for me was Flame." He kissed her nose. "It comes from my mother's side. She's a fiery redhead." His lips brushed against her ear. "But as I grew older, my hair darkened. Now you can only see the red in the sunlight." His hand traveled down her back, creating a shiver of pleasure along its trail. His mouth nibbled at one ear. "You know where I want to take you after we get home?" he murmured. "Hawaii. I *know*!" He lifted his head and grinned at her. "I just had the greatest idea. We'll get married here by a chaplain, but once we're home, we'll go to Hawaii and renew our vows. I know the perfect place."

Cindy stared at him. "In Hawaii? What do *you* know about Hawaii?"

He chuckled and brushed his lips against her eyelids, one after the other. "Ah, so little you know about me. I spent four years there as a teenager. My dad was a naval rear admiral at Pearl Harbor. One day, while exploring the island, I found a place called the Valley of the Temples on the windward side." His eyes took on a faraway look as he played with her hair. "It's a cemetery...no, don't freak out...it's a cool place. There's a place called Byodo-In Temple, a Buddhist sanctuary...it's probably the most peaceful place I've ever seen in my life. There're waterfalls, ponds filled with Japanese koi, rabbits and peacocks running wild...and the most haunting sound of a gong when visitors ring it for good fortune." His eyes warmed. "That's where I want to say my vows to you...in a place of peace."

"Then why not just wait and get married there? Once we both get back home."

His face grew solemn. "Do you *want* to wait?"

Cindy traced a finger over his arching eyebrow, her heartbeat accelerating. "Of course not. Besides..."

His mouth fused with hers, taking her breath away. He lifted his head and grinned down at her. "You'll love this place, Cindy. I promise. It'll be our real wedding—we'll just make it official with the chaplain...just in case something happens—"

Cindy covered his mouth with her fingers. "Don't say it. Don't even *think* it. Yes, that's what we'll do...renew our vows at this...what did you call it?"

"Byodo-In Temple."

"It sounds beautiful." Cindy traced his lips with a finger. "But we're not Buddhists. You think they'll still let us do it?"

He laughed. "Honey, if you've got the green

to offer, you can talk anyone into almost anything."

Grinning, she cupped his face in her hands. "And speaking of green…where did you get those gorgeous green eyes? Those from your mother, too?"

He shook his head. "Nope. Dad." He kissed her nose. "And where did *you* get those adorable freckles, Cinnamon? They remind me of brown sugar melting in a bowl of oatmeal," he said, exaggerating his down-home Texas accent.

Cindy laughed. "You sweet-talking devil. What're you trying to do? Get me into bed?"

He gave her a lazy smile, his eyes smoldering. "'Pears it's a little too late to be worried about that, little lady." His mouth settled onto hers with sure confidence.

Cindy arched into his kiss, feeling his arousal. Twice tonight, and he was ready for a third round? She definitely was. All he had to do was look at her with that sexy twinkle in his eyes.

He broke the kiss and nuzzled her neck. "What time is it?" he whispered.

Cindy glanced at the illuminated hands of the clock on her bedside table. "Almost 0300."

"Good." His lips lowered for another kiss. "We have an hour before I have to go."

Cindy stiffened and pulled away from him. "Wait! Why do you have to leave in an hour? You're supposed to go into Saigon with me tomorrow. Remember, we're shopping for your sister's birthday present?"

Quin rolled away from her and sat up, running his fingers through his tousled curls. "Damn, Cinnamon. I forgot about that. But it'll have to wait. I'm on first-up duty tomorrow. Well…today. I have to report at 0500."

Cindy's stomach plunged. Silly, she knew. This was his job; it was what he was here for, flying dust offs to pick up the wounded. But usually, they weren't together when he was on "first up" duty. Only once—that time in the hotel in Saigon had he ever been summoned to duty while with her. Most of the time, she didn't actually know he was gone on a mission. Well, she knew he was, but it was easy to put it in the back of her mind as long as she didn't know for sure. Now, hearing that he had a scheduled early morning mission, made her fear more visceral.

On the stereo, Bert Sommer's "Tonight Together" ended and "The Road to Travel" began to play. Cindy sat up and pulled the clammy sheet up to cover her nudity. He'd explored every inch of her body, yet, she still felt shy with him. "Do you know where you're going?"

He nodded, glancing up at the neon poster of Jim Morrison as if it were the most interesting thing he'd ever seen. I really should take that down, she thought. *He's going to think I'm stuck in my adolescent past.*

"You're familiar with Nixon's policy of

'Vietnamization, right?"

Cindy nodded. On the stereo, Bert Sommer sang about things goin' his way. "I think so. He wants to get the South Vietnamese to gradually take over combat operations, so we can get out of this mess, right?"

"Yeah, that's the idea." Quin reached for a pack of cigarettes on the bedside table. He flicked one out and offered it to her. She took it. "Well, don't know how much you've heard about this, but last month, ARVN troops, backed by air and tactical support launched an incursion into Laos." He lit their cigarettes and took a long drag. "It worked at first, but the NVA launched a counteroffensive and took back all the ground the ARVN gained. Things are desperate there for the ARVN troops, and we've been ordered to go in and get them out. Word has it there are lots of wounded, so that's where I come in."

Cindy's heart began to pound. "It sounds dangerous." She regretted the words the minute they left her mouth. *Imbecile! Of course it's dangerous. It's war.*

Quin shrugged, then apparently seeing the concern on her face, gave her a confident smile. "Piece of cake, Cinnamon. It's nothing I haven't done a hundred times before. Drop in, pick up the wounded, and get them out." He gave her a wink, and then drawled in a bad imitation of John Wayne. "Don't you worry about a thing, little lady." He took the cigarette from her fingers, ground it out in the ashtray on the bedside table, and did the same with his own. Then, with a growl, he was upon her, wrestling her down on the bed. He tugged the sheet away from her body. "You're too beautiful to cover up, Cinnamon. Don't you know that?" He kissed her neck, her face, her breasts and finally, her mouth.

As they made slow, sweet love to the sound of Bert Sommer's soaring voice, Cindy forgot to worry.

CHAPTER TWENTY-ONE

Jenny saw the choppers first. The rhythmic thrum of the UH-1 Huey in which they'd hitched a ride had put Cindy into a light doze. The lack of sleep from the night before with Quin, and an all-day shopping trip with Jenny in Saigon's popular marketplace had finally caught up with her, and as soon as they'd lifted off from Headquarters, her head had started to bob. Her last thought before she'd drifted off had been how thankful she was that she didn't have to go on duty until 0700 tomorrow.

Jenny's nudge jolted her awake. As the helicopter descended toward Bien Hoa Air Field, Jenny pointed off in the direction of Long Binh, and through the smudgy, heat-simmering skies, Cindy could just make them out— five…no…seven dust offs churning toward the red cross landing strip next to the hospital. Her first thought was one of elation.

Quin's back!

But immediately following was a second, more sobering thought. Seven choppers–each had the capacity to hold eight casualties plus four crew members, but that was a rule of thumb which was often bent. Sometimes, in extreme circumstances, they packed in another eight casualties. And God only knew how many had landed already—or how many more might be on the way.

Cindy and Jenny exchanged a look of alarm. Mass-cal. A big one. In all the mass-cals each of them had worked, there had never been more than five dust offs coming in at the same time. Just thinking about what lay ahead for the next hours brought moisture to Cindy's palms and queasiness to her stomach. Looking at Jenny's pale face, Cindy could tell she felt the same.

"Guess we'd better haul ass and get back to the 24th," Jenny said. "You think we'll be able to find a ride?"

Cindy glanced out the window as the helicopter lost altitude. "Eventually. Trouble is, we need to get there *now*."

It was standard practice for nurses to hitch rides to Saigon from Bien Hoa—so much faster and less dangerous than catching a ride on a transport truck or Jeep. Sometimes, if they were lucky, they could get a hop on a chopper from Long Binh. Getting back, though, was a different story. Most of the hops they caught at

Headquarters in Saigon went directly to Bien Hoa. Under ordinary circumstances, it wouldn't take long to find someone heading from the air field to Long Binh, but if the ER was being bombarded with casualties, they would need every available nurse *stat*.

Cindy looked up front to the chopper pilot and made her decision. She stumbled forward, trying to keep her balance so she wouldn't fall out the open door and die a horrible death in the jungle below. "Hey!" she yelled over the chopping blades and thrum of the engine. Startled, the pilot turned to look at her. "We need to get to the 24th Evac Hospital ASAP. You saw the incoming dust offs. We're nurses. Can you just take us over there?"

"It's against regulations," he yelled back. Cindy's heart dropped. Then he grinned and gave her a wink. "Good thing I don't give a shit about regulations."

The chopper banked to the southeast, and moments later, descended into the chaos.

Ω

They kept coming, and coming—and coming. Cindy worked triage with David Ansgar, assessing the wounded and directing where they'd go— directly to surgery, to pre-op to await surgery—or to the yellow curtain. Her civilian clothes—a sleeveless top and a long paisley-print cotton skirt and sandals—were saturated with blood. She hadn't had time to go to her dorm to get into her uniform. The present she'd bought for Quin's sister, a turquoise silk Vietnamese robe, had ended up tossed on a desk in the ER, possibly never to be seen again. Dr. Stalik, somehow noticing her attire in the pandemonium, had screamed at her to get into uniform. But just at that moment, a G.I. coded on the gurney in front of her, and she grabbed the crash cart to try to save him. It was no use. He was gone.

When the whopping drum of incoming dust offs signaled more wounded, Dr. Charley Moss sent Cindy and David out to take over triage duties from other nurses and corpsmen who'd been at it for five hours nonstop. The appalling stench of white phosphorous burns permeated the ER, forcing Cindy to choke back the bile that threatened to erupt from her esophagus. The last time she'd glanced at a clock, it had been after 2200 hours. Eyes burning with fatigue, she moved from one patient to another, working essentially on auto-pilot, encouraging the conscious G.I.s, no matter how damaged they were, and efficiently examining the unconscious with clinical detachment before sending them off to their destinations.

Sometimes, a fleeting thought drifted through her mind. *Who am I to determine who lives or who dies? How can a 21-year-old girl have such a responsibility? What if I send someone to the yellow curtain who _can_ be saved?* But she knew she had no choice but to shut down these thoughts. She just had to do her job.

In the distance, she heard the ominous chop-chop of a helicopter, and her heart fell. It had finally started to slow down, but just like always, it seemed, just when you thought things were under control, and soon, you'd be able to go get some sleep, it all began again.

David looked up from his patient, and his eyes met hers. She could see the fatigue dwelling in their depths, and wondered how long he'd been on duty. Probably long before she'd left for Saigon this morning. She released a frustrated sigh. "God, I hate the sound of those chopper blades!"

Sometimes, she dreamed she heard them, and she'd awake in a panic only to find blessed silence—nothing but the roar of the air conditioner in her room. Would it always be like this? Once back in The World, would she hear a helicopter fly over, and be overcome with nausea?

David tagged his patient and directed a corpsman to take him to pre-op. "I do, too," he said. "But you know what I remind myself? That the sound of those chopper blades are a Godsend to the troops lying wounded out in the field."

His matter-of-fact statement sent a wave of shame through Cindy. She knew he hadn't meant it like that; he was much too kind to reprimand her in any way, but that was exactly how she took it. Because that was exactly what she needed—a reprimand. Here she was, feeling sorry for herself because she hadn't slept in over 24 hours, and she was exhausted and bloody and pissed off at the world and the war—and she just wanted to fall into bed and sleep and sleep and sleep. Blot out this horror of maimed and dying boys, many even younger than her. But that blessed drug of sleep wasn't going to happen any time soon. For these guys—these poor, mangled young men, lack of sleep and bone-weary fatigue were the least of their problems. Some of them would be going home in body bags. Others, if they were lucky—or unlucky, depending on how you looked at it--would be going home with missing limbs, shot-off faces and brains that no longer worked.

Grow up, bitch, and just do your job.

The dust off landed on the giant red cross 30 yards from the triage area. The doors opened and the wounded were off-loaded. Cindy examined the first one—GSW, right shoulder—and sent him to pre-op. Lucky guy—the bullet appeared to have missed any vital organs. The second one was DOA. The third writhed in pain, his face blackened with grime and blood. Another GSW, this one to the left thigh, nicking the femoral artery. A corpsman in the field had applied a tourniquet, saving him from bleeding to death. Cindy tagged him for immediate surgery, hoping they'd be able to save the leg. Just as she started to send him off to the OR, the G.I. reached out and grabbed her wrist.

"Cindy Sweet, it's you, right?" he gasped, eyes wide with panic. "Cinnamon?"

Cindy's heart plunged to her toes. For a hideous moment, she thought the blood-splattered G.I. was Quin. That she hadn't recognized him because of the blood and jungle grime. But then sanity returned when she saw his sweat-dampened white-blond hair and brown eyes. Not the ocean-green eyes she'd gazed into last night when they'd made love.

Oh, thank God, thank God, thank God!

She searched for his name on his fatigue shirt, and finally made it out through the dirt and blood. *Clancy.* Her heart skipped a beat. Quin's dust off corpsman—the one who'd driven them to Bien Hoa the time Quin took her up in the chopper.

She bent over him, trying desperately to quell her panic. "Quin! Is he okay? What happened? Where is he?"

Sgt. Clancy closed his eyes, wincing from pain. "He's…oh, Jesus…"

Cindy clutched his hand, squeezing it. Her blood turned to ice when she saw a tear trickling down his muddy face. "Sgt. Clancy, please tell me what's going on!"

He shook his head, writhing on the stretcher. "I'm sorry…so sorry, Cindy. They got him. Quin is dead."

Two corpsman appeared and swept Sgt. Clancy into pre-op as Cindy stood motionless, staring after him. She felt weightless, almost as if she were in a dream, a place where gravity didn't exist. Around her, people seemed to move in slow-motion. Behind her, a voice floated to her, "L.T.! Need some help over here!"

David.

The world righted itself, and again, she was weighted to the earth; around her, action had resumed its normal speed. Slowly, she turned and made her way over to David where he was working on a convulsing boy with extensive injuries.

Do your job, do your job, do your job.
And that's what she did.

CHAPTER TWENTY-TWO

Sergeant Clancy gazed up at Cindy from his hospital bed, his brown eyes welling with tears. He'd come through surgery with his leg intact, and would be shipping back to the World, barring any complications, within the week. Cindy was happy for him, but she couldn't help thinking about how Quin would be going home once they found his body. He was officially listed as Missing in Action, but according to Sgt. Clancy, there was no hope he was still alive.

"Tell me how it happened," Cindy said, her nails digging into her palms.

She didn't know if she was ready to listen; maybe she'd never be. But Sgt. Clancy would be gone soon, and then she'd never know. For 24 hours, Cindy had see-sawed between total despair and wild hope that the corpsman was wrong. They hadn't found Quin's body, so couldn't he be alive? Couldn't the VC have captured him, and though it tore her apart to think of him in a POW camp, tortured and confined to a cramped bamboo cage in a rice paddy somewhere, at least he'd be alive. At least he could come back to her someday. But now, looking at Sgt. Clancy's mournful face, she knew she was fooling herself.

He nodded, his eyes haunted. "It should've been me, too. If I hadn't jumped out…"

"Start at the beginning, Todd. You'd landed to pick up the injured…"

"Yeah, it was a hot LZ. The VC were crawling all over the place, like cockroaches, damn them to hell!" With a trembling hand, he reached for his water bottle. Cindy took it from him and poured him a glass of water, then lifted it to his lips. He took a sip then fell back onto his pillow. "Quin knew it could be a suicide mission, but he went in anyway. There were scores of wounded on the ground, under heavy fire from the VC. We almost made it, too. We *would* have if not for me. It's my fault!" A strangled sob issued from his throat.

Cindy squeezed his hand, trying to quell a sudden nausea. Her heart felt like a snowball lodged in her ribcage. She couldn't really feel anything—hadn't been able to feel anything since she'd first gotten the news. She knew this wasn't right—that sooner or later, grief would cut through her numbness like an ice pick, stabbing away at the snowball that encased her heart, and then she'd surely die from the pain. It would be Gary all over again, only this time...*this* time...

She shook her head to banish the thought, and then gave Todd Clancy's hand another reassuring squeeze. "You've got to stop blaming yourself, Todd. Go on...tell me the rest."

He took a deep, shuddering breath and nodded. "Just as Quin was lifting off with the wounded, another guy stumbled out of the jungle, screaming for help. His arm had been severed just above the elbow, and he was jetting arterial blood. I didn't think, I just acted. I yelled for Quin to hold on, and then jumped out to get him. I grabbed the guy; he practically collapsed in my arms, and we were stumbling back to the chopper. And that's when it happened. An RPG hit the chopper. It blew up right in front of me. Twelve men killed because I had to save one." He gave a choked laugh, his eyes glinting with anguish. "A moment later, he died in my arms. And that's when I got hit by gunfire. A real fucking success, that mission."

Motionless, Cindy digested his words. Even when he began to sob, she couldn't move a muscle to comfort him. The horrifying image of Quin's dust off exploding flared in her mind's eye, and she felt a sickening shift inside her, and knew it for what it was. The snowball was starting to melt.

Ω

"Cindy, are you okay?"

Cindy stood at the supply cabinet, mechanically sorting and organizing the contents. *Running low on syringes. Need to order more.*

"Cindy!"

The voice seemed far away. But when she turned in its direction, she was startled to see Cap Bren just a few inches away. Her sapphire eyes revealed her concern. "I said, are you okay?"

Cindy stared at her. Was she *serious*? And just like that, a hot-white rage gripped her. "Fuck, *no*! I'm not okay!" Even as she spat out the words, she couldn't believe she was doing it. "My fiancé is *dead*! But then, I'm not *you*, Major. I'll bet when *your* fiancé bought the farm, you handled it just fine and dandy with that stiff, upper lip you Scandinavians are so famous for. I'll bet you just waved the grand old flag, and sang "The Army Goes Rolling Along," didn't you?" Cindy's mouth snapped closed as the blood drained from Cap Bren's face. She knew she'd gone too far and now she'd pay for it.

But incredibly, Cap Bren's eyes softened. "I know what you're going through," she said quietly. "I remember it like it was yesterday."

Cindy felt the snowball shift again. But she wasn't ready. She couldn't...*wouldn't* break down in front of the Major. Turning back to the supply cabinet, she said, "I'm sorry, Major. That was a horrible thing to say. I'll understand if you want to write me up."

Cap Bren touched her shoulder. "Cindy, look at me."

Reluctantly, Cindy turned to meet her gaze. The look of sympathy and understanding on the older woman's face almost undid her. Cindy stiffened against it.

"You're due for an R&R," the head nurse said. "I want you to take it. I want you out of here as soon as you can get a flight."

Cindy shook her head. "Quin and I were going to Bangkok at the end of the month. I can't go there without him."

"Not Bangkok," Cap Bren said. "Hawaii. I have a friend who owns an estate near Diamond Head. It's right on the ocean with a swimming pool...and it's unoccupied. One phone call, and I'll arrange for you stay there for R&R. You can hole up there all week, and never have to see a soul except for his staff. It will help, Cindy. I promise."

Cindy stared blankly. "I don't know...I just can't...I can't think..."

"You don't have to. Just leave everything to me. Pack your bag and get ready to go." She turned to walk away, and then turned back. "Oh! I almost forgot. Someone in the ER said this belonged to you." She held out a rice paper bag.

Cindy felt another twinge in her chest as she recognized it as the bag containing Quin's sister's silk robe. She took it with hands that felt curiously detached from her body. Cap Bren stared at her a moment longer, then said, "I'm sorry, Cindy. For saying what I did that day you showed off your engagement ring. I know it didn't cause Quin to die, but I feel guilty all the same." She didn't wait for Cindy to respond, but went on, "We're slow here. Take off the rest of the day, and pack for your R&R." When Cindy opened her mouth to protest, one eyebrow rose imperiously, and the old Cap Bren was back. "That's an order, Lieutenant."

Ω

Cindy left the hospital with the rice paper bag, but instead of heading to the nurse's quarters, she went in the other direction toward the swimming pool. The hour was just after high noon, and the sauna-like temperatures were keeping anyone with a choice inside. Within seconds, sweat pooled from Cindy's underarms, saturating her olive-grey T-shirt. Her panties, inside her fatigue pants, felt as if she'd wet them. She was conscious of these things, but strangely detached. Clutching the rice paper bag, she strode with purpose, not thinking, not feeling, yet, driven by an internal compulsion.

The pool glimmered, dazzling blue, in the sunlight. Yet, Cindy knew the cool comfort it promised was a facade. In the heat of day here in the tropics, it would feel like tepid bathwater.

The pungent smell of chlorine hung heavily in the humid air.

At the pool's edge, she opened the bag and took out the silk robe. It slid through her fingers like a caress. She studied the bright turquoise color, the pink and peach Bird of Paradise design. She closed her eyes and imagined Quin's grin as he proclaimed how delighted his sister would be with the gift. *He never even got to see it.* She buried her face in the silk fabric. Why, she didn't know. No scent of Quin here. Nothing of Quin here.

With a soft cry, she let it drop from her fingers. It slithered to the asphalt and lay there in graceful neglect. Cindy sat down on the hot cement and took off her combat boots and socks. Then, standing, she unzipped her fatigue pants and stepped out of them, leaving them lying next to the robe. In her T-shirt and panties, she dove into the pool.

The water was way too hot, yet, it offered oblivion. It closed over her head, encasing her in its warm, comforting grasp. She swam from one end to the other, counting each time she touched the tiles…twelve…twenty…twenty-five.

Exhaustion began to slow her. At thirty-one, she knew she'd reached her limit. Panting, she held onto the side of the pool, waiting for her heart to resume its normal pace. She lifted a hand to smooth back her hair, and then stiffened, sensing someone watching her.

She turned to the other end of the pool and

saw David Ansgar, still in uniform, sitting on the pool's edge, his feet dangling in the water. His combat boots rested behind him. When he saw she was aware of him, he pulled his feet from the water and stood. Cindy hauled herself out of the pool and walked around to him, uncaring that she was practically nude, that he could probably see everything through her wet T-shirt and skimpy panties.

He watched her approach, and that's when she realized what he was holding in his hands—the silk robe. Neither of them spoke as she reached him. He held out the robe, helping her as she slid her arms into it. The silk against her wet skin felt like a soothing balm. Methodically, she tied it around her waist then turned to David.

"What? Were you waiting to save me from a suicide attempt?"

He didn't answer, just looked at her with blue eyes awash with tenderness and sympathy. And that's when it happened. The snowball inside her ribcage exploded into fragments of ice.

She began to sob–harsh, ragged, ugly explosions that burst from her throat with savage fury and heartrending pain. David still didn't say a word. He took her into his arms and held her while she cried.

TWENTY-THREE

On the flight to Honolulu, Cindy ate half of a ham sandwich and just made it to the bathroom before throwing it up. By the time she landed at the airport and found a driver and limousine waiting to take her to the home of Cap Bren's rich and powerful "friend," she knew she could no longer deny what she'd been suspecting since the trip to China Beach.

She was pregnant.

Following the driver into the ocean-front Spanish-California-style house with beautiful archways and a brick-red stucco roof, Cindy gazed around in amazement. She'd never seen such a gorgeous place. The sofa, chairs and loveseat in the family room were off-white silk, accented by dark koa nut wood end tables holding pale blue porcelain lamps, a matching bookshelf and an entertainment center with a huge TV and a state-of-the art stereo system. An oval mirror framed with silver-carved wood leaves hung over a massive gas fireplace, which, Cindy suspected, was rarely, if ever, used. Opposite the entrance to the room, floor-to-ceiling windows looked out onto a marble-floored lanai and a huge, oval swimming pool, shimmering turquoise in the sun. Beyond that, the ocean in its blue-green magnificence, framed by a cluster of graceful coconut palms with fronds swaying in the trade winds, provided the perfect backdrop, like a location scene out of a Hollywood movie.

The driver, a friendly local, judging by his swarthy skin and pidgin language, touched a switch on the wall, and with a soft whir, the central windows facing the lanai opened, and a plumeria-scented sea breeze drifted into the room, sending the sheer white curtains billowing. Loki, as he'd introduced himself, grinned, revealing a gold-tipped front tooth. "Nice, fresh air, huh? Put some color in dose white cheeks of yours, yeah?"

A wave of exhaustion swept over Cindy, and she dropped to the sofa, knowing if she stood a moment longer, she'd surely pass out. *I must look as bad as I feel.* Sensing her fatigue, she guessed, Loki showed her a print-out from the owner, explaining everything in detail—how things worked, where everything was, and important phone numbers such as the nearest hospital and fire department. He'd also left a map of Honolulu and—incredibly—the keys to a red Mustang convertible, accompanied by a note and several tourist brochures: *Thank you, Cindy, for your service to our country. I'm so sorry for your loss. Brenda told me all about it. Please use this week to feed your soul and see the island on me. Ted.*

Cindy stared at the note in amazement. Who *was* this Ted, and what was his relationship to Brenda? *He must be one hell of a good friend.* Without warning, tears filmed her eyes as gratitude consumed her for Cap Bren's kindness—and Ted's. To lend out his beautiful home to her like this.

Feed your soul.

She wondered how that was possible. Her soul felt dead. Losing Quin had killed it as surely as that inferno had killed him.

Loki gave a soft cough. "I go, now, miss? You be okay, yeah?"

Cindy looked up at the Hawaiian and summoned a smile. "Yes. Thank you, Loki. I'll be fine." She shakily got to her feet. "I just need a long nap, and something to eat."

He grinned, his brown eyes kind. "Das why Mr. Ted stocked fridge and pantry, yeah? You eat, you rest. You call Loki if you need anyting, yeah? My numba on dat sheet. I take you anywhere, yeah?" His grin widened. "If you crazy 'nuth not to wanta drive that mean Mustang."

"Thank you."

She started to walk him to the door, but he waved her back. "You rest. Mebbe go for swim, yeah?" He gave her a wink. "De ocean nice and warm, yeah?"

The front door closed behind him, and all was silent. Not a sound in the house except for the soft tinkling of wind chimes on the lanai. Cindy dropped onto the sofa and looked around. The ceiling soared high overhead to the second floor where an etched-glass oval balcony held court. Behind the sofa, two levels of carpeted stairs led to the second floor and the bedrooms, she presumed. To her right, sprawled a large kitchen with the same koa nut cabinets and granite counters—a dream kitchen for someone who loved to cook. The built-in oven and even the refrigerator were finished in koa nut wood. A wallpaper border of palm trees lined the top of the walls; the slate floor was finished in varied shades of beige and brown. *Oh, how Mom would love this kitchen.*

Cindy took a deep breath and prepared to get up, fighting the dizziness which immediately assaulted her. It passed after a moment, and she began to move. Several needs had to be addressed, and the first one was a bathroom. She found it past the kitchen, and it was breathtaking. A large bay window looked out onto the ocean, and below it, a huge soaking tub graced the sanctuary. Oh, yes, Cindy thought. A bath. How long had it been since she'd had a bath?

Not since before she'd arrived in 'Nam, that was for sure.

Later, she decided. After some food, a swim and a nap. After using the bathroom…no, still no period…she stepped into the kitchen and opened the refrigerator. Her gaze lit on a bottle of Pinot Grigio. *Now, that's the ticket.* Despite her grumbling stomach—she hadn't been able to eat a bite on the flight from Tokyo—she pulled out the bottle of wine and began searching for a corkscrew. It was in the first drawer she pulled open.

A moment later, she stepped out onto the lanai with a crystal goblet of wine in her hand and settled onto a chaise lounge. She took a sip of the crisp Italian wine and gazed around at the beauty of Hawaii—the swaying coconut trees, the pearly yellowish-white blossoms of plumeria growing on the tree beyond the pool, Diamond Head soaring to her left—and the opalescent blue-green ocean–the exact color of Quin's eyes– straight ahead. Her heart panged as the thought whispered through her mind, but she took another sip of wine to push it away.

Oh, Hawaii, you are beautiful. The blossom-scented air smelled so sweet—a marked contrast to the fetid air she'd been breathing in 'Nam for the past six months. A pinkish-gray gecko skittered over the lanai, and Cindy watched it with interest. There had been a time when she would've jumped up screaming at the sight. But not anymore. She'd lost her innocence, had realized there were much more terrifying sights than a bug or a lizard. A little bird fluttered past, landing in the branches of a hibiscus bush. The bird was black, white and gray with a little red beak. *Looks like he's wearing a tuxedo*. It took a moment before she realized she was smiling.

Perhaps she *would* be able to heal here in this place known as Paradise. If not here, then *where?*

But what to do about the baby?

It had to have happened that very first time at the hotel in Saigon. That had been the only time they hadn't used protection. After that, Quin had always made sure he had condoms. But apparently, that had been too late. Cindy had missed three periods, but she'd just chalked that up to the emotional upheaval of being a combat nurse. It had happened once before, shortly after her arrival at Long Binh. She'd missed her period in October, but then it had come like clockwork...up until January, a month after she and Quin had started sleeping together. And then, earlier this month, she'd started getting other symptoms—tender nipples, morning sickness, dizziness.

She'd intended to tell Quin that last night before he'd left for Laos. But when she'd heard how dangerous the mission might be, she'd decided against it. She hadn't wanted to burden him with another worry when he already had enough to deal with. Besides, she'd wanted to have the test first, and hadn't figured out how to do it. She couldn't go to the lab at the 24th. If word got out about her condition, they'd ship her home, and no way had she wanted to leave Quin behind. Better to be in 'Nam with him than home without him.

Now, that didn't matter anymore, did it?

She finished her wine and swung her legs off the chaise lounge. *Better to get it over with right now.* Fighting dizziness—from the wine or the pregnancy, she didn't know—she stood and went inside. In the kitchen, she found a phone and dialed information. When the operator answered, she spoke crisply into the receiver. "I'd like the number for Tripler Army Medical Center, please. OB/GYN."

Ω

The plumeria-scented wind tousled Cindy's hair as she sped down the coastal highway in the red Mustang convertible. On her right, Hanauma Bay came into startling view—a gorgeous expanse of turquoise green cradled in an ancient volcanic basin populated with tropical fish and sea turtles. An oasis for snorkelers, Cindy had read in a brochure. She hoped to get there before she left Hawaii, but today, she was driving the coastal road around the island. She didn't expect to complete the circuit, but wanted to at least reach the North Shore to see the big waves rolling in at

Waimea Bay. Of course, it was the wrong time of year for the really big waves, but no matter.

For the first time since she'd heard the news about Quin, she felt a semblance of peace entering her soul. Maybe it was something to do with the wind in her face, the power of the Mustang as it hugged the curves of the cliff highway, the beauty of the ocean—the beauty that still existed in a world of ugliness. She had the car radio turned up full-blast, the only way she could hear it with the top down and the engine humming. She even found herself singing along with Neil Diamond's "Sweet Caroline." It had been a long time since she'd sang anything.

But just as the song faded away, another song began to play, and Cindy felt as if a dark cloud had suddenly obliterated the sun.

Good sense, innocence, crippling' and kind...

Her hands clenched on the steering wheel; her eyes filled with tears. Years ago, this had been the song that reminded her of Gary—the innocence of first love and first loss. Now, though, it embodied Quin. She remembered nights in her room, lying entwined, sharing a joint, and singing along with the song when it played on her reel-to-reel. He'd always said it was his favorite hippie song because of his love for peppermints—and pot.

Incense and peppermints, the color of time...

By the second verse, tears were streaming down her face, and she knew she had to pull off.

She saw an overlook ahead and put on her signal. The Mustang rolled to a stop. She put the gearshift in Park, folded her arms on the steering wheel, dropped her head and began to sob.

The song finally ended, and Elton John's "Your Song" came on. *It's a little bit funny…*

Cindy sobbed harder. She cried so hard she thought her tears were somehow soaking her arms and hair. But when she raised her head, she saw it was raining. Just a moment ago, the sun had been shining in all its glory. Tilting her face toward the sky, she felt the soft, gentle rains of Hawaii bathe her like a kiss from heaven.

The rain stopped as quickly as it had arrived, and once again the sun smiled. Cindy ran her fingers through her damp hair, started the car and pulled out onto the highway, heading toward the North Shore.

Ω

Cindy stared down at the USS Arizona resting in the shallow depths of Pearl Harbor, and thought of all the men still entombed in the wreckage. The morning sunlight pierced down from a cloudless sky, turning the water an impossible shade of sea green. A sheen of iridescent oil moved on the surface, still leaking from the sunken battleship, even after thirty years, according to the brochure she'd picked up in the visitor center. Nearby, several leis floated, tossed by tourists paying homage to the memorial. Curiously, many of those tourists were Japanese.

How did they feel, Cindy wondered. Saddened by so many lost lives, and the horrors of war, or secretly gloating at their country's victory behind those somber faces? She imagined how she'd feel if she went to Nagasaki or Hiroshima—and realized it would be the same as she felt here. So many lost lives in so many wars. In her head, she heard Edwin Starr's hit record, "War." If ever a song was appropriate for the Vietnam War, it was this one.

War…what is it good for?

"Excuse me, miss. Can you take our picture?" A big man wearing a cheap nylon Aloha shirt with a surfboard and palm tree print held out a Polaroid camera to her. He looked painfully sunburned, and so did his companion, an overweight woman in a *muu muu* matching his shirt. "This is our first trip to Hawaii, and we need to take home a lot of pictures," he said in a thick Midwestern twang.

Cindy nodded and took the camera. As she snapped off a shot and waited for the camera to issue the photo, he said, "So, where y'all from, little lady?"

"Indiana," Cindy said, resisting the urge to look around to see who else he might be talking to besides her. She really didn't feel like chatting, and she especially wasn't about to reveal any information as to why she was here alone.

A look of delight flashed across his lobster-colored face. "Why, we're from Illinois, just a hop, skip and a jump from y'all. This is my wife, Agnes, and we're here celebrating our 35th anniversary."

"That's wonderful." Cindy held out his camera along with the photo which hadn't fully developed.

He took it but before she could get away, he went on, "Seeing the Arizona was number one on my list. I served in the Navy in WWII, but I was stationed in Norfolk when those bastards attacked us. We lost a lot of good men on that day."

Cindy nodded, feeling a twinge in her abdomen. *Oh, please...I don't want to talk about the war.* "Well, I..." What excuse could she come up with to escape this guy and his wife? She glanced out at the anchored launch which had ferried them out to the memorial. "Well, enjoy your vacation," she said weakly.

"Yeah, a lot of fine men died...just like what's happening over at 'Nam right now," he went on, oblivious to her attempt to end the conversation. His wife stood at his side, a blank look on her pudgy face. Cindy wondered if she was mute, deaf or just bored.

"Yes, well..." Cindy backed away.

"But that's what sacrifice is all about. And at least we're kicking some ass over there.

Yesiree. Kicking some ass. The body count for those yellow monkeys just keep going up. We watch it on the news every night."

Bile rose in her throat, and clamping her hand over her mouth, she whirled around and stumbled away. *Oh, God, I can't throw up here. Not here.* No restrooms on the memorial. She had no choice but to fight back the nausea. She crossed the gangway to the boat and boarded, praying they'd soon get everyone onboard so they could get back to the visitor center.

Once seated, her stomach settled down, but she still felt some discomfort, an occasional cramping sensation. *Stupid man…believing everything he saw on the nightly news.* Didn't he realize the body count for the VC was inflated by the American government, hoping to keep some kind of support for the war? Was all of America so deluded?

She glanced at her wristwatch. Almost eleven. Her appointment at Tripler was at three. Still plenty of time to get back to the Mustang and drive over to the other side of the island. She'd been saving the trip to the Byodo-In Temple for the end of the week. Truth be told, she just wasn't sure she could handle it. How could she go to this place that Quin had loved so much? The place he'd intended to exchange vows with her. It would tear her heart out to see it without him.

But then she'd remembered the look in his

eyes when he'd described the peace of the place. Maybe this was exactly what she needed. Maybe there, at this tranquil Buddhist sanctuary, she'd feel his spirit, and somehow, allow the peace to soak into her soul. Maybe then she could go on.

She dug into her black military handbag and drew out the brochure of the Byodo-In Temple she'd found at the house among many others and gazed down at the color images of red pagoda meditation temples surrounded by reflecting pools and waterfalls. It looked exactly as Quin had described, even the gigantic *bon-sho*—sacred bell—as the brochure called it. She could almost hear its gentle, sonorous peal.

Yes, that's what she'd do. As soon as the boat docked at the visitor center, she'd make her way out of Pearl City and head for the Pali Highway that snaked through the Nu'uanu Valley to the windward side of the island. She hoped she wasn't being too ambitious to try to fit this in before her appointment at Tripler, but tomorrow was her last day in Hawaii, and the weather forecast was calling for intermittent rain.

The motor from the launch rumbled beneath the bench she sat on, and she looked up, startled to see the boat full of quiet tourists. The sight of the oil-leaking Arizona beneath the aquamarine waters of the harbor had apparently left them somber and reflective. Cindy wondered if someday there would be a memorial to all the men dying right now in Vietnam. To Quin.

No! Don't think about that. The launch moved away from the Arizona Memorial and began to head back across the harbor toward the visitor center. Cindy gazed up at the hillside rising behind Pearl City with its sprinkling of homes among the verdant green landscape. The morning sun baked upon her back and shoulders, exposed by the green and white polka-dot halter top she'd bought at the International Marketplace on her first day of exploring.

Just as the launch neared the dock at the visitor center, another cramp ricocheted through Cindy's stomach. She grimaced. Maybe breakfast at that greasy diner in Waikiki this morning hadn't been the smartest idea. It had sure tasted good, though.

"Thank you for joining us for the tour of the Arizona Memorial," the guide said through the loudspeaker. "Please watch your step disembarking."

Tourists stood and began to file toward the gangplank. Cindy got to her feet, and fought off a sudden dizziness as the blood rushed to her head. *Just the heat.* She'd grab an ice-cold soda to take on the drive.

Across from the aisle, a little girl, about six, holding the hand of her mother, looked at Cindy and her big brown eyes widened. "Mommy!" she said, her voice sounding unnaturally loud over the tourists silently edging their way to the exit. "That girl is *hurt.*"

The little girl's disquieted gaze was fixed upon Cindy's pelvic area. At that moment, Cindy felt the warmth between her thighs, and with a curious detachment, she looked down to see bright red blood saturating her white shorts. Like a kaleidoscope, the edges of her vision closed to a small circle, and then went black.

Ω

As the Pan Am airliner climbed into the sky above Hawaii, a weakened and frail Cindy watched the misty green Ko'olau mountain range grow smaller with each passing second. Down there somewhere among the green lushness was Quin's Byodo-In Temple.

A tear trickled down her cheek, and she forced herself to look away from the peace and beauty of the Hawaiian Islands as the airliner took her back to the war.

April 1971

March 30, 1971

Dear Cindy,

Well, I suppose I should congratulate you on your engagement. But honey, I just hope you know what you're doing. If you ask me, you're rushing into this way too fast. This Quin-guy could be perfectly nice for all I know, but you haven't known him all that long. And what are you thinking??? Getting married over there! Can't you at least wait until you both get back home? Even Terri thinks you should wait. She made some cockamamie remark about the two of you getting married in a double wedding in December. I had to bite my tongue to hold back some choice words. Like you'd want to share your wedding with a woman nearly twice your age. But the point is, she thinks you're making a mistake getting married over there. Not that she'll speak out and actually agree with me! You know Terri…she wants you to think she's so groovy or hip…or whatever the word is these days. But I know she's against it as much as I am. Still, I know I'm wasting my breath. You've always been so headstrong, and you're going to do exactly what you want to do. I just hope you don't regret it. Look what happened to me and your father. All those years I worked my fingers to the bone, trying to please him, and he up and leaves me for some young blonde the first chance he gets.

Okay, I'll shut up. (I can read your mind from 3,000 miles away…or however far it is.) So, what do you think about Lt. Calley getting the guilty verdict? He's supposed to be sentenced tomorrow, and the newspaper says he'll most likely get life in prison. I think it's a crying shame. Poor guy. He was just doing his duty, following orders— and they're going to put him away for it. It just makes me sick! What's wrong with our country? I have half a mind to go out and buy "Free Calley" T-shirts for everyone I know. Except I can't. This move into the new apartment has practically bankrupted me. I swear, I've barely got enough in this week's paycheck to buy groceries. Do you know how much a dozen eggs sell for right now? $1.18. Can you believe it? And milk is $1.32 a gallon. It's a good thing I have my employee discount at Kroger, I'll tell you that. Anyway, Joanie loves having more room, and I guess I do, too. At least I don't have to watch that sleazy "Laugh-In" anymore. Terri just loves Goldie Hawn, and I think she's the most scatterbrained blonde I've ever seen. Can't stand her! Maybe because she reminds me so much of Lesley. Your father always did like the little blondes. God knows why he ever married me!

Anyway, don't you worry about me and Joanie. We're doing fine. And I hope you are, too. You take care of yourself, Cindy, and please…just think about what I said. Bring your Quin home and marry him here. I'm your mother, and I want to help you pick out your wedding gown and do all the stuff mothers are supposed to do. God knows I can't afford to pay for a wedding for you, but maybe your father will put some money toward it. You *know he has it...after all, they live in that big mansion down there while me and Joanie have to settle for this little apartment. Doesn't seem fair, does it? Oh, well...nobody said life <u>was</u> fair.*

Love you, Cindy. Keep safe. (And write me, for God's sake. I hardly ever hear from you!)

Mom

CHAPTER TWENTY-FOUR

Cindy stood at attention in Colonel Kairos' office as the grim-faced chief nurse pinned the double silver bars on her dress uniform. "Congratulations, Captain Sweet," she said, stepping back, her eyes as dark and cold as a mausoleum.

Cindy gave her a smart salute, wondering what the woman would look like if she'd remove the bamboo stick from up her bony ass. Colonel Kairos returned her salute with one of her own that somehow suggested contempt.

"Dismissed, Captain." The chief nurse turned and moved to her desk. Waves of Chanel trailed her movement.

If she were a cartoon, the waves would be visible, Cindy thought. *And I'd have a clothespin on my nose.*

Relieved, she headed for the door. It was 1600

hours, and she'd just got off a twelve-hour shift at 1500. Friends and colleagues—the ones who weren't on-duty—would be waiting at the O Club, along with a cold Pabst Blue Ribbon with her name on it. Time to celebrate her promotion.

Yee haw! I'm a captain now. And that meant exactly jack-shit to her. Oh, it was a little more money, and that was good. She could send more home to help Mom and Joanie out. And the rest, she'd put into beer, wine and weed.

"Captain!" Colonel Kairos barked just as she reached the door.

Cindy stiffened and turned. "Yes, Ma'am?" Was it her imagination or did she actually see the colonel's lips quirk in what might pass for a smile...on a different planet far, far away.

"Stay out of trouble!"

Cindy nodded. "Yes, Ma'am."

Colonel Kairos dropped into the chair at her desk. "Go on! Get the hell out of here."

Cindy left her office, marveling over the woman's gall. She touted herself as such a pious officer, patrolling the nurse's quarters with her big, black, man-hating dog, always waiting to pounce on a nurse if she so much as smiled at a member of the opposite sex, or heaven-forbid, utter the mildest of curse words—and yet, she could turn the air blue with crude words if she was angry enough. Such a hypocrite. This war was full of hypocrites. And the war itself was the worst of the hypocrisy.

As she headed back to her quarters to change into civvies, she thought about Mom's letter, unanswered since she'd received it almost a week ago. Her reference to William Calley had boiled her blood. Talk about hypocrisy! *Is that why we came here? To kill innocent women and children in cold blood? No excuse, no fucking excuse for that!* But even as she thought that, she saw the young Vietnamese girl who'd died in the ER after killing several marines, and the sniper who'd killed the nurse—and Mai, her hairdresser who'd intended to blow up three soldiers after seducing them. Yes, they weren't all innocents. But no one could tell her that those two and three-year-old babies Calley and his men had mowed down had been VC.

Of course, they might've grown up to be VC.

She hated herself for that thought…yet, those kind of thoughts kept on coming. Quin's death and her miscarriage had changed her…irrevocably, she was afraid. Everything just seemed so…pointless. Like these stupid silver bars pinned upon her lapel.

In her quarters, she changed into jeans and a Led Zeppelin T-shirt. The jeans were too loose; since the miscarriage and the subsequent D&C they'd done at Tripler, she'd lost several pounds. Mainly because she had no appetite. The unexpected two nights in the hospital hadn't extended her stay in Hawaii as she'd feared, and weakened and pale, she'd made it to the airport for her flight to Tokyo on Saturday as scheduled. Arriving at Bien Hoa on Sunday morning to the familiar stomach-turning stench of Vietnam, hearing the ominous rumble of artillery in the not-distant-enough distance, Cindy felt an overwhelming urge to run, screaming, into the plane's lavatory and cower there in hysteria until the men in white coats came to cart her away. But instead, she straightened her shoulders, put on her big-girl, appropriately stoic military face and stepped off the plane.

Leaving her quarters, Cindy walked the couple of yards to the O Club and Jenny met her at the door with a welcoming smile. "Oh, I was just coming to check on you. So, did all go as planned? Or did old Ramrod Butt change her mind about promoting you?"

Cindy gave her a sardonic smile. "You're looking at Captain Sweet, Lieutenant Yu. I'll out-rank you for what? A week?"

"Four days." Jenny grinned. "I got my notification this morning. So, we'll get to celebrate all over again on Saturday." Her gaze swept Cindy's face, and her voice lowered, "You feeling okay?"

Cindy nodded. "As good as new." Her words rang with irony.

Jenny's almond-shaped brown eyes glimmered with sympathy. "It'll get better," she said softly.

Jenny had been the only one Cindy had shared her secret with. On her first night back, she'd wept in her friend's arms, the first time since the pool incident with David that she'd really cried. She'd cried for the loss of Quin, the loss of their baby…the loss of any innocence she'd possessed before coming to Vietnam. And then her grief had turned to rage—at God, at Vietnam, at war in general—even at Quin for leaving her, for letting himself get killed. Jenny had been there through it all, holding her, wiping away her tears, listening to her vent. Not judging, not attempting to give answers or reassurance, and most importantly, not delivering that old platitude—*you have to pick up the pieces and move on.*

But wasn't that exactly what she was doing?

"You ready?" Jenny said. "Everyone's waiting."

They stepped into the O Club, and a cheer went up. Cindy looked around at all the smiling familiar faces—Charley Moss, Shyanne Rooney, even Cap Bren. *Damn it.* She couldn't think of the woman by any other name. Even the Ward 2 corpsmen were here—including David and Jenny's boyfriend, Simon. Cindy had made sure they would be allowed into the O Club— threatening not to show up if they weren't. New faces, too—Lt. Ariane Mitchell, the pretty brunette from South Dakota that had taken Rosalie's slot, and the FNG who'd just arrived a mere two weeks ago, Lt. Sharon Falley, a naïve strawberry blonde from Fort Wayne, Indiana. With Cindy's state of mind, she'd barely had a chance to talk to the girl, much less bond over being from the same state. But Sharon was here, shell-shocked from her first full week on duty, but smiling, and seemingly ready to party.

And so was Cindy. Once the cheers and congratulations died down, Cindy raised her glass of Pabst, already beaded with sweat from the heat that even the club's air conditioning barely affected, and yelled, "Here's to getting *wasted*!"

Ω

Steppenwolf's "Born to be Wild" blared out in the smoky club. During the chorus, everyone who wasn't too drunk or off in a dark corner making out, sang along. Sloshing the beer out of its glass—she'd lost count how many beers she'd had—Cindy danced and sang at the top of her lungs. *"Booorrrnnn to be wiiillddd."* And when the guitars and drums set in with the next verse, she bopped her head with the beat, spilling more beer. Didn't matter. There was more where that came from. And it was dirt-cheap.

When the song ended, replaced by George Harrison's "My Sweet Lord," she headed to the bar for a refill. "Another Pabst, Jake." She leaned on the bar, her head spinning. No more head-bopping, she told herself.

"You okay, L.T.?"

Cindy turned to see David Ansgar sitting three barstools down, nursing a beer. A light overhead shone down on his blond hair, freshly washed and gleaming. Cindy smiled at him. Man, what a looker. Those blue eyes. That little bit of blond stubble on his jaw.

She paid for her beer and moved down the bar to join him. "I'm great, David. Don't I look okay?" She settled on the stool next to him.

"You always look great," he said, and then blushed. He took a quick slurp of his beer. "I mean…you look a little wobbly."

Cindy threw back her head and laughed. "Yeah, I probably am. I lost count of how many beers I've had. But what the hell? It's not every day you become a *captain*."

David's face grew even redder. "And I just called you L.T. Sorry, Captain."

Poor guy. He looked so bashful, Cindy wanted to kiss him. *Really* give him something to be embarrassed about. Instead, she reached out and gave his blond head a ruffle. "Silly boy! Like I care about stuff like that!" Relief crossed his face, and she laughed again. Her gaze traveled to his full, firm lips and lingered.

She really *did* want to kiss him.

But that was the alcohol talking. She straightened up and ran her fingers through her short bob. "Man, can it *be* any hotter in here? Look at this!" She tugged at her T-shirt, damp with perspiration. "Hey! I have an idea. Let's go for a swim."

David's expression told her he clearly thought she'd lost her mind. "The pool is off-limits at night."

"Who gives a fuck?" She gave a harsh laugh. "What are they going to do if they catch me? Send me to Vietnam?" She jumped up from the bar stool and shouted over George Harrison. *"Who's up for some skinny-dipping?"*

A cheer went up from the people close enough to hear her, most of which were males. Cindy grinned and started toward the door. A hand grabbed her arm and she whirled to meet David's concerned gaze. "You don't want to do this, L.T…I mean, Captain."

"The hell I don't!" She tried to wrench her arm away, but his grasp tightened.

"Cindy, you've had too much to drink. Maybe you should just go back to your quarters and sleep it off."

Her jaw tightened. "Let go of me, Sergeant Ansgar. You're not my father, and you're damn well not the boss of me. Now, *let go!*" She glared at him until she saw his resignation. He released her arm. Guilt swept through her, and she almost changed her mind. But then she remembered—this was *her* night. And she was hot and wanted to swim.

"Come on, everybody," she yelled, heading for the door. "Last one in the pool has to buy a round of drinks!"

She stepped out into the sauna-like night. A waxing moon glowed with an eerie greenish cast through a cluster of clouds. The ever present artillery boomed in the distance. In the northwest, intermittent flares lit up the skies. Heading toward the pool, Cindy began to strip off her clothes, first her T-shirt, then her jeans, leaving them on the ground behind her. She heard drunken voices and laughter, and knew that most of the club's occupants had got the word, and wanted to see the show.

Then she'd damn well give them a show!

By the time she reached the pool's edge, she wore only her panties. Wolf whistles pierced the night interspersed with salacious comments from masculine voices.

"Hey, baby! Wait up! I want to check out those tits."

"Got your bra here, sweetheart. What are these? C-cups?"

"Wait for me, honey. Got something here for you to float on!"

Standing at the deep end of the pool, a memory flashed through her mind—of Quin sitting right here with her, munching on peppermints. It seemed so very long ago.

She slipped her panties down her legs and stepped out of them, almost losing her balance. She giggled, her head spinning. *Guess maybe I have had too much to drink.*

Male figures burst out of the darkness, cat-calling and whistling. Cindy dived into the pool, and its delicious, tepid water closed around her naked body. She surfaced to a cauldron of activity as male officers—at least a dozen of them--jumped in around her.

She shook her head and rubbed the sting of chlorine out of her eyes, treading water. The men surrounded her, naked—at least naked above the waist; she couldn't tell. But they each wore an identical hungry look in their eyes as they taunted her.

"Hey, Captain Sweet…why don't you show us just how sweet you can be."

"Yeah, honey, why don't you show us those sweet tits of yours. Can't see 'em under all that water."

Reality set in, and Cindy felt the first ripple of fear. She searched the pool's edge for help, but saw only more men, laughing, ogling, hungry-eyed. Like sharks surrounding a wounded porpoise. But no, there was Jenny and Shyanne, horrified expressions on their faces. *Oh, my God. What am I doing?*

Suddenly, strong male hands gripped her around the waist, and pulled her up against a hot, muscular body. She cried out in protest as she felt his erection against her buttocks. His hands slid up to cup her breasts.

She shrieked and pushed away from him. *"No! Leave me alone!"*

Another man grabbed her and then another; they pushed her from one man to another, each taking a turn to touch her in intimate places. Cindy sobbed, pushing them away and twisting to get out of their grasps.

"Hey, Sweet." One officer held her tight around the waist, his lips brushing against her ear. "Isn't this what you wanted?" His fingers slipped between her thighs. "Don't advertise what you don't want to sell." Roughly, he grabbed her chin and brought his mouth down on hers.

Cindy thrashed and pushed at him, her fingernails clawing. She wanted to kill him. She *would* kill him if she had a gun.

As if echoing this thought, a gunshot pierced the night. All activity stopped in the pool, and Cindy felt herself floating free. The moon broke through the clouds for a moment, playing hide-and-seek on the animal-like faces of the men in the pool. Sobbing, Cindy looked toward the end of the pool and saw two military policemen standing there with David Ansgar.

He was the most beautiful sight she'd ever seen.

CHAPTER TWENTY-FIVE

"**H**ere, drink this." David shoved a cup of steaming black coffee at her; it was the color of mud, even after milk had been added to it.

Cindy forced herself to take a sip. In this tropical heat, hot coffee was the last thing she wanted, but seeing as how David had saved her from being gang-raped—of that, she was sure—she wasn't going to argue. It tasted awful. One of the corpsmen whose ancestors came from Bolivian coffee farmers, had told her of a coffee bean made from some kind of bird dung, so rare and sought after that it was the most expensive coffee ever produced. She figured he'd been pulling her leg, but if it *was* true, she wondered if it could possibly taste any worse than this crap? She took another tentative sip and tried not to grimace.

"Where did you get this?" she asked. "It tastes like you scraped it off Highway 1."

David shrugged. "Where do you think? The ward. Guess who's on duty tonight?"

Cindy sighed. "Appleby. That guy couldn't make a decent cup of coffee if his life depended on it. But thank you, David." She took another tentative sip then placed the cup down on the step next to her. No, not even for David could she finish it.

They were sitting on the steps of her barracks, and except for going to hunt down some coffee, he hadn't left her side since he'd walked her back from the pool. The night was still ridiculously hot, and even that nightmare swim hadn't cooled her down. Oh, she'd been shivering when he'd helped her out of the pool, but not because she was cold. David had stripped off his T-shirt and helped her into it to cover her nudity before walking her back to her quarters.

She reached down and grabbed his T-shirt, still damp from her wet body. While he was getting the coffee, she'd gone inside to change into shorts and a tank top.

"Here, don't forget this." She tossed him the T-shirt.

He caught it and dropped it to the step, then took another drag of his cigarette, his face pensive. Cindy wanted to thank him and apologize at the same time, but was afraid her words would sound inane.

The two military policemen had dispersed the crowd, and she'd watched, feeling sick, as the guys in the pool—the bastards who'd man-handled her—climbed out, all of them naked. One of them had been that red-haired lieutenant who'd beat her at ping pong the night she'd met Quin.

One MP asked if she wanted to press charges, but she'd adamantly refused. She just wanted to forget the whole thing. It was too…despicable. And it had been her fault. She'd practically offered herself on a silver platter. Lucky that David…

She looked at him. He sat two steps below her, a cigarette dangling from his lips, his tawny chest sweat-dampened in the muted light off the corner of the barracks roof. Nice muscles, she thought. He obviously worked out during his time off.

"How did you do it?" she finally said. "How did you get the SPs there so quickly?"

He glanced back at her. "As soon as you left the O Club, I called my buddy, Smitty. After I told him what was up, I booked it to the pool, and saw what was happening." He ground out his cigarette then began to tear at the paper to discard the leftover tobacco. "I knew I couldn't take them on. Not all of them. And they were officers…I couldn't order them to leave you alone." He shook his head, unwrapping a breath mint and popping it into his mouth, then offered her one. She took it, hoping to rid her mouth of the rank taste of the coffee. "If Smitty and his friend hadn't shown up, I don't know what I would've done." He turned to look at her, his blue eyes stormy. "I don't know if I could've stopped them, Cindy."

She took a deep, staggering breath. "You would've, David. You wouldn't have let them hurt me."

He stared at her for a long moment, and Cindy felt her heartbeat pick up. Something had changed between them. But whatever it was—this electricity–and face it, it had been there from the beginning, even before Quin–she didn't want it! It hadn't even been a month since Quin had died. She felt disloyal to him, just glancing at David's toned, muscular arms.

In the distance, towards the northwest, artillery fire sent flashes of light across the dark sky. Flares floated to earth—a sight that never failed to give Cindy goose bumps. What was going on out there in the jungle? How many able-bodied men were alive and well right now, but would soon be on a dust off heading for the 24th?

She shook the thought away and glanced back at David. "Anyway, let's just put it behind us, okay? I did something really stupid, and you were there to save the day." She gave a mirthless laugh. "Just like Superman…or is it Mighty Mouse?"

David's solemn expression didn't change. He

grabbed his T-shirt and stood. "Take care, L.T.—I mean, Captain." He strode off into the darkness.

Cindy got to her feet, staring after him. "Oh, for God's sake, David! You've seen me *naked*! Can't you just call me *Cindy*?" Something about that sounded so ludicrous she started to laugh. She knew her laughter was tinged with hysteria, but it felt good anyway. Through the gloom, she saw David stop and turn.

"I think that qualifies us to be on a first-name basis, don't you think?" she said, between giggles.

He reappeared into the light from the barracks roof, his face solemn, eyes guarded and sad. "Cindy?" he said quietly. "Are you okay?"

The tenderness in his voice broke her. Her giggle turned to a sob. A visceral pain gripped her midsection and she clutched herself, knees buckling. David sprang forward and caught her. She dissolved into his arms, weeping against his damp, bare chest. "I lost his baby, David. In Hawaii. I...barely had time to think about it...to decide what to do..." She pressed her face against his shoulder, sobbing.

He didn't speak, just held her, stroking her tangled, wet hair.

She realized how ridiculous it was—an officer bawling her eyes out in the arms of a corpsman. If anyone saw them, what would they think? And God *knew* what kind of rules they were breaking.

But his warmth felt so good, so comforting. She could feel his heart thudding against her hand. He smelled of beer, tobacco and raw masculinity. Or maybe that was the jungle scent of 'Nam she inhaled every single day. Whatever, she found it incredibly, unmistakably erotic.

She felt it in every nerve of her body—that stirring, pooling sensation in her womb…something she hadn't felt since…

No. She wouldn't think of him now. Her tears spent, she drew away from David and met his gaze. She caught her breath at the heat in his blue eyes. She'd never noticed before their unusual shape—slightly tilted down, etched with laugh Lines. But he wasn't laughing now. In fact, as his gaze moved over her face, Lingering on her lips, he looked sad…almost resigned.

She moved instinctively, her fingers threading through his dark blond hair. He stiffened, but didn't pull away. She searched his face, waiting…not sure for what. He bit his bottom lip. "Captain, we…" And then he started to pull away.

"No." She cupped his face in her hands and kissed him.

He stood like a statue, unresponsive. But Cindy felt his heart thudding against hers, and knew he wanted her. He'd always wanted her; she knew that. She explored his lips leisurely. They tasted like wintergreen, the breath mint he'd slipped into his mouth after smoking. She deepened the kiss, sliding her tongue between his lips, and finally, his mouth surged against hers. And she knew she'd won.

They kissed for an exquisite eternity on the steps of the barracks. When he finally tore his mouth away, and Cindy came up for air, she realized her body was molded to his and her hands were clutching the belt loops of his fatigue pants. She felt his erection against her groin. *Almost the same height.* A perfect match.

He gazed at her, eyes stormy. "Cindy, we can't."

She traced his bottom lip with her index finger, and felt a heady sense of power when his eyes darkened with lust. "Why the hell not?" she asked.

She kissed him again, and he responded immediately, sending her blood sky-rocketing. After a long moment, she drew away from him and took a ragged breath. She waited for him to protest again, but he didn't say anything, just gazed at her with those melting blue eyes.

She took his hands in hers. Holding her breath, still expecting him to come to his senses and bolt, she turned and led him into the barracks and down the hall to her room.

Ω

She lay in the darkness, curled up in the fetal position. David slept next to her, the damp heat from his naked body, a comfort. She could hear him breathing–slow, even, rhythmical breaths, and that, too, was a comfort. He was alive, and she was alive—and her body felt as if it had awakened from a coma. The sex had been good. More than good; it had been mind-blowing. And she almost felt guilty about that. As if she were betraying Quin because she'd enjoyed it. Wouldn't it have been better if it had been awkward or boring or even just mediocre? Would she still feel like she was betraying Quin if she'd hated it?

Nonetheless, it probably had been a mistake. Now that she could think, she realized that. How weird would it be to work with David on the ward now that they knew each other's bodies so intimately? How could she ask him to empty a bedpan after he'd brought her to climax more times than she could remember? How could she look at him in his scrubs and not remember the bold heft of his penis in her hand?

That's why you don't mix sex and work.

It couldn't happen again. Tonight had been an anomaly. She'd been distraught after the incident at the pool. She'd been lonely and vulnerable— and God, she missed Quin so much, it felt like she'd lost a limb. David had been there, a warm, masculine body…tender and so very sweet. And yes, she knew he had a crush on her. She'd known that for a long time. So, she'd used him. Flat-out used him. And it was wrong—she knew that, too. But she wasn't sorry. Her body wasn't sorry; it felt fluid and alive and...nurtured.

But they couldn't do it again.

He stirred next to her, and she felt the warmth of his breath on her neck. He nestled up against her, spooning her into his flat, toned belly. She thought about drawing away, putting a stop to things right now. But she just couldn't do it.

Just this one night. Tomorrow we'll talk.

His lips nibbled at her neck, and she started. She'd been so sure he was asleep. His penis hardened against her buttocks. *Oh, God.* Yes, she wanted him again. How many times tonight already? Three? Four?

One more time.

She turned in his arms and pressed her body against his. But instead of kissing her, he took her face in his hands, and gazed into her eyes. Through the approaching light of dawn through the window, she could just make out their glimmering blue.

"I love you, Cindy," he whispered. "I tried to deny it, but when I saw your engagement ring that day you came back from China Beach...I knew. And it was too late." He kissed her lips tenderly, then drew back to gaze at her. "And now, you're here. A miracle. Do you know how long it's been since I stopped believing in miracles?"

Cindy felt as if her heart had frozen solid in her chest. Love? He was talking *love*? The look in his eyes was so sincere, so…authentic. She knew he believed it. That he loved her.

But couldn't he see how ridiculous that was? Not because he was a corpsman and she was an officer. No…*fuck* that. If she loved him, that wouldn't matter in the slightest. Couldn't he see…didn't he understand that she *couldn't* love? Not anymore. The two men she'd loved had both died. And she liked David too much to put that curse on him.

But she couldn't tell him that—not now. Not with that earnest "I'm-the-luckiest-man-in-the-world" look on his face. There was only one thing to do.

She drew his head down and kissed him. And the talking stopped.

CHAPTER TWENTY-SIX

She saw the note on the floor the next morning. He must've written it while she slept.

Last night
I put my hands on your skin
And my heart in your hands
I know you will keep it safe
My soul, my secrets
yours for the asking
I am ready to trust
In whatever comes next
As long as you are by my side
I am not afraid of loving you
But I am afraid of losing you

Tears streaked down her cheeks as she read it. *Oh, David, no. Don't love me. Not because you'll lose me. You can't lose something you don't have.*

You can't have my heart.

Because you're not Quin.

Ω

A quiet night shift for once. All of the patients were asleep, except for one whose morphine hadn't kicked in yet. He thrashed and moaned periodically, and although his cries tore at Cindy's heart, she could do nothing more except pray that the medication would start working soon.

It was just four of them on the shift tonight—another nurse, the FNG from Fort Wayne, Indiana, and two corpsmen, Appleby…and David. It had been the first time Cindy had seen him since he'd left her room that morning. He'd been as earnest as a puppy, and more light-hearted than she'd ever seen him as he kissed her goodbye, telling her again how much the night had meant to him. Cindy had smiled and kissed him back, knowing they needed to have "the talk," but unable to make herself do it. So she'd swallowed her guilt and sent him on his way.

Sitting at the nurse's station, she glanced up at the clock on the stark military grey wall. 0238. In the ward, monitors bleeped and respirators hissed. She listened. The moaning had stopped. Better go check on him.

She stood and glanced over at Appleby. He had his curly red head buried in an anatomy

277

textbook. A 20-year-old from Seattle, he had dreams of becoming a doctor once he got out of the military, and planned to use the GI bill to finance his schooling. Meanwhile, he read medical books and journals copiously. Lt. Sharon Falley sat at the other end of the nurse's station, jotting down notes in patients' charts. David had taken a cigarette break.

"I'll be right back," Cindy said. Sharon nodded and returned to her chart.

Try not to knock yourself out being friendly, you butter bar bitch. It was the weirdest thing. The nurse from Indiana had a big chip on her shoulder or something. No matter how many attempts Cindy had made to find common ground with the girl, she'd been rebuffed. Cindy supposed it was what had happened last night. Sharon had been among the crowd at the pool and had apparently witnessed the whole thing. Probably thought Cindy was some kind of slut or something. *Well, screw you, Indiana girl. Talk to me after you've been here a few months, and we'll see if you're still so judgmental.*

Cindy went over to check on the patient who'd fallen silent. PFC Kenneth Walker had been hit in the chest by an armor-piercing shell just a week before he was due to ship home. It had been a miracle he'd made it through surgery, and it was still touch-and-go, but so far, he was hanging on. Tubes snaked from his body, and he had a trach that needed suctioning every hour or so. He appeared to be sleeping. The morphine had finally done its job.

Cindy checked the tube from the trach leading to the ventilator where water built up. It had to be emptied periodically so it wouldn't back up and drown the patient. She saw a little bit of pink-tinted water. Not a big concern. It was just blood leaking a bit from the trach. She made a mental note to mention it to Appleby and David to keep an eye on it.

On the way back to the nurse's station, she decided to stop in the supply room and see what needed to be ordered. The last time she'd worked, she'd noticed they were getting low on syringes. Might as well use this rare quiet time to see what needed re-stocking.

Standing with clipboard in hand, she sensed him before she heard him. It was almost as if the temperature in the tiny supply closet rose a degree or two. Catching her breath, she turned, and there he stood in the threshold. David. Her heart contracted at the soft look in his eyes. With his blond hair rumpled from the breeze, and his face golden from the sun, he looked like a California surfer boy. He smiled, and a dimple she'd never noticed before appeared near his mouth.

"Hi," he whispered.

She cleared her throat. "Hi."

For a long moment, they gazed at each other. Cindy realized her heart was pounding. Why? Because she knew she had to break it off? Or because–the real truth—she hadn't been able to get him out of her mind? That, face it, she wanted him again.

He glanced back toward the ward then looked at her. "Cindy, when can I see you again? Last night was so amazing."

She shook her head, chewing on her bottom lip. "I don't know...I..." Her words fell silent. She swallowed. "I don't have a night off again until Saturday. What about you?"

"I start days on Saturday. I'll meet you outside your barracks."

Just as Cindy nodded, they both heard a footfall. David turned, and past his shoulder, Cindy saw Sharon Falley. The strawberry-blonde stared at them, and something in her expression made Cindy wonder if she'd overheard their conversation. *Shit.* That would be just her luck. It would be all over the hospital before noon tomorrow.

"Yes, Lieutenant?" Cindy said crisply. *If all else fails, pull rank.*

Sharon drew herself up to her full 5-foot, four-inches. "Oh, just wondering where you'd got off to, Captain. I thought maybe there was a problem."

"No problem, Lieutenant." Inwardly, Cindy grimaced. *Don't over-do it, idiot, or she'll know you've got something to hide.* She summoned a smile. "Just thought I'd take this opportunity to order supplies. While it's quiet." She turned to David.

"Sgt. Ansgar, keep an eye on Private Walker's trach tube. It was looking a little pink last time I checked."

Sharon's gaze shot from Cindy to David, and Cindy realized she'd made another tactical mistake. No one called the corpsmen by their ranks and last names. It was always a first-name basis, except for rare cases like Appleby who went by no other name.

"Yes, Captain," David said. He left the supply closet and brushed past Sharon to head for Walker's bed.

Even after Cindy turned back to her clipboard, she could still feel Sharon Falley's speculative gaze on her back.

Ω

"Captain, you need to come take at look at this."

Cindy looked up and saw the urgency on David's face. Her heart skipped a beat. She followed him over to Private Walker's bed. He showed her the tube leading from the patient's trach to the ventilator. The water that had been pink just a few moments ago had turned to a brackish rust color.

"Damn! We need to suction him out."

When she pulled the plug from the GI's trach, foam and blood bubbled up from the hole. With David assisting, she suctioned him out, but it just kept coming, no matter how much she sucked out. "*Shit!* What's going on?" she muttered. "David, what's his urine output?"

He checked. "Not good. Hardly anything in the last hour."

Clearly, the patient was crashing.

"I think he's got a pulmonary edema. Help me get him upright."

It was an unsophisticated treatment, but sometimes it helped in getting the fluid down to the legs. The two of them managed to get Walker upright, then they put rotating tourniquets on his arms and legs to keep extra blood from returning to his heart, giving it more time to clear out the fluid from his lungs.

But it didn't seem to be helping.

"Go wake up Stalik," Cindy ordered. "Tell him we have a patient that's *fucked up.*" Code for on his way out. What rotten luck that Stalik was the doctor on call. She hadn't been able to stomach the man since he'd refused to intubate the expectant back in November, but had been lucky not to have any more run-ins with him since. Well, it was only a matter of time.

David raced out of the ward. Minutes ticked by, and still, the fluid bubbled up from the patient's trach, and Cindy continued to fruitlessly suction. *Where the fuck is Stalik?*

Footsteps pounded outside, and David rushed into the ward, out of breath.

"He's on his way. I had to hunt him down.

Found him playing poker with some other docs. But Cindy…?"

"What?" Cindy searched David's face, and saw his eyes were bright with anger. "What is it, David?"

He glanced over his shoulder just as the ward doors banged open again. "I think he's been drinking," he said quickly, then straightened as Stalik entered.

"What's going on, Captain?" Stalik barked, casting her a dark glance. He hadn't forgotten the time she'd confronted him. Not only did he hate her for that, he probably also held her responsible for his break-up with Cap Bren.

Cindy's gaze swept over him. His eyes were blood-shot and his mouth slack. Not necessarily signs of drinking, but it didn't bode well. If David thought he had been, then he probably was right.

"Pulmonary edema, I think, sir," she said. "No matter how much I suction, fluid just keeps bubbling   up."

"You *think*?" he said, sarcasm heavy in his tone. He brushed past her to examine the patient.

Cindy tried to remain professional even though she wanted to reach out and brain him with the patient's chart. "No urine output and low blood pressure. What do *you* think?"

He gave her a dark scowl, and her stomach sank. No *way* that didn't sound insubordinate. Oh, hell…who gave a fuck?

"Hang some Ringers." Stalik straightened and turned to leave.

Cindy looked at David. His face wore the concern she felt. Ringers? What the *fuck*? Lactated Ringers was a saline-based solution used during surgery to hydrate patients. It was the last thing Walker needed; it would be like drowning him.

"Doctor," Cindy protested as Stalik headed for the doors. "I don't think that's the answer. Could I give him a diuretic to relieve the fluid in his lungs?"

Stalik whirled around, his face like a gathering storm. "You're questioning *me*? I've had just about enough of your insolence, Captain Sweet. Listen, you smart-ass little twat, I didn't go through twelve years of medical school, graduating magna cum laude from Brown University, to be interrogated by an upstart little nurse who probably got her degree from a Cracker Jack box. Now, *hang the fucking Ringers and open it wide*! That's a *goddamn* order!" He turned and stalked off.

White-hot fury shot through Cindy. Teeth bared, she lunged after him, but strong hands caught her from behind.

"*Don't.*" David's urgent whisper drilled into her ear.

She watched Stalik go. Sharon Falley looked up from her desk and gave him a worshiping smile which was immediately followed by a blush.

The bastard had winked at her, Cindy guessed. She wanted to *kill* him. Wanted to scratch out his beady little blood-shot eyes with her fingernails. The ward doors slammed behind him.

"You can let me go now," Cindy muttered through clenched teeth. David released her then headed for the supply room. "Where are you going?"

He didn't look back. "To get the Ringers."

"David, we can't do that!" She followed after him. "It will kill him."

He kept going. "Doesn't matter, Cindy." Then he stopped, and turned around, resignation written on his face. "He's dead anyway."

Twenty minutes later, PFC Kenneth Walker flat-lined. Without orders, Cindy injected a shot of intercardiac epinephrine into his heart to try to revive him, knowing it wouldn't work, but unable to just stand by and do nothing.

She covered him with the sheet, then looked up at the bottle of Ringers on the IV stand, valve still open wide, dripping the useless—and probably fatal--solution into the soldier's vein.

Her gaze moved to a somber David, standing on the other side of the bed. "I don't care what happens to me, but I'm going to report his ass."

CHAPTER TWENTY-SEVEN

"Explain yourself, Captain Sweet. What's the meaning of all this nonsense?"

Cindy stood at attention in front of Colonel Kairos, wondering why the witch was still here. Wasn't it about time for her to ship back to some unfortunate hospital in the States to terrorize young nurses and orderlies? As always, the woman's flowery perfume in the tight quarters of the small office made it difficult to breathe. What did she do? *Bathe in it?* The colonel's dark eyes flashed indignance as she waited for Cindy's response.

Cindy lifted her jaw in resolve, acutely aware of David's presence next to her. He'd insisted on going with her to report Stalik, and she'd agreed, realizing she needed back-up when accusing a doctor of drunken incompetence. "I said he appeared to be drunk, ma'am. My corpsman was the one who first noticed it, and when I saw him, I agreed."

Colonel Kairos skewered David with her piercing gaze. "How do you know he was drunk, Sergeant?"

David stood stiffly, staring beyond the colonel's left shoulder. "He was playing poker and drinking when I found him, ma'am. He smelled of whiskey. His eyes were blood-shot, and...well, it was just obvious."

"Was he stumbling? Was he slurring his words?" Colonel Kairos shot back, her words like bullets. "What makes you an expert, Sgt. Ansgar? Experience?"

Cindy couldn't look at David, but guessed his face had reddened with anger. She could feel hot spots on her own cheeks. "Colonel Kairos," she cut in, amazed at her nerve. But then, she was a totally different girl than the one who'd stood cowering in front of the woman back in September. "Everyone knows Major Stalik drinks. He drinks a lot. That's no secret. But last night he made a horrible mistake that resulted in the death of a patient."

Silence. At the look on Colonel Kairos' face, Cindy felt like the temperature in the air conditioned office had dropped another degree. Her heart pounded. Maybe this hadn't been a good idea.

"Well? Don't stop now, girl. Spit it out. What did he do?"

287

Cindy took a deep breath. "He ordered us to hang Ringers for a patient with pulmonary edema."

Something flickered in the lieutenant colonel's eyes, and Cindy knew she understood what that meant. Hope rose inside her. Maybe, after all, she'd made the right decision in reporting the bastard. Maybe something would finally be done, and they'd kick his ass out of here.

"And you followed orders, Captain?"

When Cindy hesitated, David cut in, "Permission to speak, ma'am." At her brusque nod, he went on, "The captain protested, Colonel, and he reamed her out for it. When he left, I hung the Ringers. Even knowing it would probably kill the patient."

Kairos stared at him, and then nodded. "You did the right thing, Ansgar." Her gaze shot to Cindy. "And *you* are lucky I'm not going to write you up for insubordination, Captain. What you need to understand…and what you obviously *don't*…is that Major Stalik outranks you. And when he gives you an order, it's your duty to carry it out."

Every muscle in Cindy's body quivered in outrage. And she could no more stop herself from speaking than she could decide not to draw in another breath. "Even when the officer giving you an order is an *incompetent jackass*?"

Colonel Kairos' jaw tightened, sending her corkscrew curls trembling. "You're lucky I don't write you up for that remark, Captain. There is such a thing as military protocol, but you obviously don't give a flying fig for that."

Realizing it was too late to go backwards, Cindy decided she might as well plow ahead. "You do what you have to do, Colonel Kairos." She allowed a sardonic smile to come to her lips. "What are they going to do? Send me to Vietnam?"

"*Silence, Captain Sweet!*" Her eyes blazed. "I will *not* stand for this insubordination in my own office!" She took a deep breath and released it. When she spoke again, her voice was calmer but lined with steel. "As for Major Stalik, I'll decide who is incompetent and who isn't, Captain Sweet. Now, is there anything else you want to add?"

"No, ma'am," Cindy barked, the anger and contempt in her voice obvious to anyone with half a brain.

As Colonel Kairos had a fully-functional one, she picked up on it, and her eyes glittered. "You have an attitude problem, Captain Sweet. If I were you, I'd adjust it." A grim smile flickered on her full Greek lips. "An ugly rumor reached my ears yesterday about an incident involving you at one of the base pools on Monday night."

Cindy's stomach sunk to her toes. She tried desperately to keep her expression neutral.

"The details were vague," the lieutenant colonel went on, "but my sources will keep digging until they get at the truth. You'd just better hope I don't find out something that will bring you here in front of me again, Captain. You understand what I'm saying?"

"Yes, ma'am." Her response still sounded bitter to her own ears, but maybe that was her imagination.

Colonel Kairos' cold gaze moved from Cindy to David. "Dis-*missed*! Get the hell out of my office."

Ω

Through the grapevine, Cindy learned that the hospital commander brought Stalik into his office. Twenty minutes later, Stalik was back on duty at the hospital. Simon Forester, Jenny's boyfriend, had an admin friend in the commander's office, and agreed to try to find out what happened. That's how Cindy discovered that the commander had ordered Stalik to lay off the booze or his ass would be shipped back to The World on a platter. He'd been allowed to go back to work because he was due to transfer out in June anyway, and after all, there was a shortage of doctors.

Apparently, it was better to have an incompetent, alcoholic doctor than no doctor at all.

Ω

Just as Cindy was about to get off the night shift on Saturday morning, Cap Bren called to her from her desk. "Hey, Sweet. Need to talk to you a minute."

Oh, shit. What now? Had that butter bar Sharon Falley said something to her about the pool incident? That's all Cindy needed after her run-in with Kairos. Cap Bren had been pretty easy to get along with since Cindy had returned from Hawaii, but she never felt fully comfortable in her presence. You never knew when the arctic ice queen would make an appearance.

Cap Bren scribbled something in a chart, and then looked up at Cindy. Her sapphire eyes lacked their usual frostiness, and in fact—dare she believe it—held something that might be considered warmth. "You know I'm leaving in June, right?"

"Yes." Of course, she'd known it. It was all the younger nurses had been talking about— when they were getting rid of Cap Bren. They'd been planning the party for months. Not the going-away party—the "she's gone" party. There had been a time when Cindy would've felt the same way, but after Brenda's generosity in getting her friend to let Cindy stay in the house in Hawaii Kai, she'd realized how much she was going to miss the taciturn nurse.

Cap Bren closed the chart with a snap, and in an off-hand manner, said, "The Prince has asked me to marry him, and I've accepted his proposal.

I'll be flying directly to Honolulu for the wedding."

The Prince? Dumbfounded, Cindy stared at her.

Cap Bren responded with a cool smile. "No need for congratulations. It's strictly a business arrangement—I give him sex and he gives me mansions, cars and designer clothing. He's been pestering me about marriage for years, and I've finally decided to take him up on it. But that's not what I wanted to talk to you about. Sit down."

Cindy took a seat next to her desk, her nerves on red alert. *What on earth does she want?*

"As you know...or maybe you don't...Charley got me involved in his med caps shortly after he arrived. He could use another volunteer to replace me after I leave, and I thought of you. He goes out every couple of weeks, and he likes you. I think you'd be a real asset to him."

Although Cindy had never been on a med cap, she knew about them. The acronym stood for Medical Civil Action Projects, or, in other words—medical outreach. Army doctors went into Vietnamese villes to give rudimentary medical care, and sometimes, emergency care to civilians. Charlie Moss was one of the few doctors who not only enjoyed med caps, but who relished in them. He did at least one every week.

Cindy nodded. "It sounds interesting. What about my schedule?"

"Don't worry. We'll work it out. As a matter

of fact, we're going to an orphanage outside of Saigon this afternoon. It's run by Vietnamese nuns in an old French monastery. The kids speak fluent French as well as Vietnamese. Did you take French in school?"

"Two years in high school. I can manage the basics."

"Then you'll do fine. I know you just got off duty, but go get a few hours sleep and be ready to leave with Charlie and me at 1430." Cap Bren turned back to her charts.

"Yes, Major." Cindy stood, trying not to show her frustration. What time would they get back? She'd agreed to meet David at 2000. And damn it, she was looking forward to spending another night with him—right or wrong. As long as she was upfront with him about…well, whatever was going on. They were just having fun. Finding comfort in each other to get through this hell. No one would get hurt. Not if she told him it could never be anything more than…what it was.

But now, she had to deal with this scheme of Cap Bren's. Her "suggestion" may have been delivered in a conversational "hey, why don't you check this out" kind of way, but Cindy knew it for what it was—an order.

Outside in the courtyard, she sighed and trudged toward the nurse's hooches. Might as well get some sleep. Who knew what this afternoon would bring?

Ω

Cindy gasped at the beauty of the white stone French monastery set amidst lush palm trees down a dirt road just south of Saigon. With its bell tower topped by a massive stone cross and its arched doorways, it looked graceful and imposing from the Jeep. But when she followed Charlie Moss and Cap Bren inside, she saw by the crumbling tile and the encroachment of the jungle where the walls had fallen away that the beauty was just a façade. Clearly, at one time, it had been a place of tranquility, but now, it was anything but.

Charlie had filled her in on the drive to the orphanage. Up to 40 children, ranging from infants to ten-year-olds, filled the three-story former monastery, looked after by a dozen Vietnamese nuns, overworked and understaffed in primitive conditions—no electricity, no running water, no medical facilities except for what Charlie delivered during his med caps. A well provided the only water. The children read by candlelight or lanterns. The older children were the luckier ones—the nuns taught classes each day so they received some semblance of normality in their lives since their parents had died or disappeared. It was the younger children, especially the babies, who were neglected and starved of love, not because the nuns were unkind, but simply because there were too many of them—and two few nuns.

When they arrived, children appeared from everywhere, gathering around Cap Bren, faces wreathed in smiles, all chattering in French or Vietnamese. Charlie, too, drew his fair share of attention. Clearly, they adored their *Bac Si.* But it was Cap Bren who was the real star in their eyes. Cindy watched in amazement as they hugged her and vied for her attention. She knelt on the damaged tile floor, allowing them to stroke her honey blonde hair, her blue eyes shining in a way Cindy had never seen before. As little fingers plucked at her locks, she pulled the pins out of her sleek French roll and allowed her hair to fall to her shoulders. The children squealed with delight as if she'd just presented them with a basket of spun gold.

Feeling Cindy's gaze, Cap Bren looked up and smiled. "They don't see blonde hair often."

It was then that a little boy of about three years old turned away from Cap Bren, his almond-shaped eyes the color of dark cognac alighting upon Cindy. He gave her a smile of such pure sweetness that Cindy felt her heart spasm. As he approached her, she saw that not only his eyes were an unusual color for a Vietnamese, his skin was paler, and his hair lighter. A Eurasian, she guessed. No doubt fathered by an American G.I. What had happened to his mother?

"Den xem xe cu'u ho'a cu'a toi," he said in

Vietnamese, taking her hand and leading her into the next room where rows of pallets had been laid out on the floor.

He knelt near one of them and reached his small hand beneath it, pulling out a Matchbox fire truck. His smile broadened as he handed it to her.

"See? Fire truck," he said in perfect English.

Cindy looked from the Matchbox toy in her palm to the little boy's earnest cognac-brown eyes—and for the third time in her life, she fell passionately, irrevocably in love.

May 1971

May 10, 1971

Dear Cindy:

First, a big happy birthday to you! Yeah, I know it's not for four more days, and I also know you probably won't even get this by your birthday, but I hope you like the card anyway. Pretty funny, huh? I know it's been a really sad time for you, so I hope this card makes you laugh.

So, Mom let me stay up last night to watch the Emmy Awards. Can you believe it? I don't know what's going on with her, but she's a lot more chill since she started dating the produce manager at Kroger. (Oh, did she tell you about that?) Anyway, it really ticked me off! Not Mom dating this Ted-guy, but the Emmy's. Can you believe that Peggy Lipton got <u>robbed</u>? She's the coolest actress on TV, and she got beat out by that old lady on **All in the Family**. *I mean, can you <u>believe</u> that? I just love* **The Mod Squad***, especially Michael Cole. He's <u>so</u> hunky! But I want to <u>be</u> Peggy Lipton. What I wouldn't give to have her long, straight blonde hair. (I'm going to try Summer Blonde hair color if Mom will let* *me.) You know my friend, Sherry? She comes over to watch **The Mod Squad** with me because…get this…her dad won't let her watch it because of the Negro on it. (Of course, he doesn't say "Negro.") He's so prejudiced. A real life Archie Bunker. But you'd never know it if you just met him. Seems like a real nice guy, but watch out if he sees a Negro on TV. People are so weird!*

Just three more weeks of school! YAY!!! I just love summer—drive-in movies, fish fries on Friday nights, trips to Dairy Queen in the evenings, swimming at Westlake. And in July, my 15th birthday! Wahoo!!! Wouldn't it be great if I were turning 16, though? I'd get my driver's license and I could go to all these places by myself. But that's a whole nother year away. Geez! How can I stand the wait? I want to be grown up like you and do what I want without someone always bossing me around.

Mom just yelled that dinner is almost ready, so I've got to go. (See what I mean? I have to eat when she says it time to eat.) Hey, Cindy, I'm really sorry about Quin. I know I didn't know him, but he must've been a special guy if you fell in love with him. It's not fair what happened. I cry about it every night…not just because he…you know…didn't make it, but because I miss you. When you come home, I'm going to be the best little sister ever, I promise! I love you SO much. XOXOXO.

Joanie

CHAPTER TWENTY-EIGHT

Cindy:

Lying beside you as the morning rain drums against the corrugated tin

Your tousled hair and the curve of your shoulder make me smile

You sleep

And the rhythm of your breathing calms me after last night's tempest.

Never has my heart felt so full.

Where does this path lead?

I hope it's long and full of wonder

with a hint of danger to stir our spirits

and the thrill of fire to melt our souls together

Finding my shoes, I slip away, leaving behind a piece of myself.

--David

The monsoon rains of May began in earnest the week of Cindy's 22nd birthday. Within hours, the post turned into a quagmire of stinking, oozing, greenish-gray mud, and no matter how sturdy the buildings--and none were all that sturdy--they leaked from every crevice. Including the hospital. But oddly enough, the casualty load had lightened. Whether or not it had anything to do with the deluge, Cindy didn't know. She was just glad she didn't have to pull any double shifts.

The music of raindrops plunking into buckets placed strategically around her room competed with the din on the roof, intensifying as the rain fell harder. Naked and sitting Indian-fashion on her cot, Cindy reached out to turn the reel-to-reel stereo louder when Neil Young's "Down by the River" came on.

David took a drag from the joint of Mantagnard Gold Cindy had passed him, and gazed at her through heavy-lidded eyes. She smiled. He was even cuter than usual when he was stoned.

His lips twisted in a grin. "I broke up with Ingrid yesterday," he said, his voice mellow. "In a letter. Mailed it this morning."

Cindy took the joint from him and brought it to her lips. She took a drag and released a trail of blue smoke into the air, watching it curl and disappear into the wan light. "Who's Ingrid?" She peered at him. His blond head wavered and pulsed.

"My girlfriend. Since Junior year. I told her I was in love with someone else."

That struck Cindy as funny. Even though she knew, somewhere in the back of her stoned mind, that it was anything *but*. It wasn't a laughing matter at all, but a tragedy. Like everything else. A fucking tragedy.

But she laughed anyway. "And who are you in love with?"

He handed the joint back after taking another hit. "Some nurse at the hospital," he said, his glazed eyes dancing. "But she doesn't know I'm alive."

"Oh, really?" Cindy smirked. "If you're talking about who I *think* you're talking about, Ansgar, she knew you were alive a few minutes ago. Very *much* alive, I might add."

"I *am* in love with you," David said, his smile fading. "That's why I broke up with Ingrid."

She took a last hit of the joint, and passed it back to him. "Well, that probably wasn't the best idea you ever had," she said. "What's going to happen when you go back to Minnesota and the love of your life has married some big Norwegian farmer?"

He ground out the last bit of the joint in the ashtray, then lay back on the bed, folding his hands behind his blond head. "She's not the love of my life. I know that now."

"If you say so."

Led Zeppelin's "Whole Lotta Love" blared

out. Eyes closed, David grinned, his head moving to the music. "This song makes me want to…you know…"

Cindy laughed, her gaze flicking down to his hardening penis. "You can't even say the word, can you, David? Fuck me again?"

He blushed. Stoned or not, David couldn't shed his upper Midwest Lutheran upbringing. Instead of blushing, Quin would've laughed—and then fucked her again.

No. You will __not__ think of him now.

She lay down next to him, her hand moving over his muscled chest. "But I get it. Led Zeppelin always makes me horny, too. Must be that long, curly blond hair of Robert Plant." Her hand traveled down to his erection. "I'd love to see you with your hair grown out. Bet it's gorgeous."

He kissed her, his mouth urgent. "I'll show you someday," he said in a ragged whisper after breaking the kiss. "After we're back in the World."

Cindy held back a sigh. Why did he keep referring to the future? Like they *had* one together. *This situation is a mistake.* The thought went through her mind for the millionth time. But no matter how many times it did, she couldn't seem to end it. Still…did it really matter? It was all temporary, anyway. David had less than two months left; he'd ship home the end of July. So, why not take advantage of the comfort of his body until then? Making love to him was the only way to drive away the loss, even if only for a few minutes. She just wished he'd quit talking about love. His poetry was beautiful, but he didn't really love her! He was just a romantic boy who *thought* he was in love. Didn't he know the difference between sex and love?

Oh, what the hell? She allowed the marijuana buzz to take her away. Nothing mattered except *now*.

She crawled on top of him, easing down on him. He gasped, and then cupped her face between his hands, and motionless, gazed at her, his blue eyes hazy from the pot. For a breathless moment, Cindy gazed back. She felt some kind of shift, an almost audible click as something homed into place, as if it had always been there, had been lost but was back where it belonged.

I could love him.

It was as if he could read her mind. "You may not know it yet," he whispered. "But you love me. Even if you won't admit it." He didn't give her a chance to respond. His mouth covered hers and he began to arch into her.

Cindy was close to climaxing when the music changed from Led Zeppelin to Bert Sommer's "Road to Travel." Her hands slackened on David's shoulders as all desire dissipated like cotton candy on a tongue.

She was back in this same room, but with Quin, not David. She could almost feel his presence, smell his Pub aftershave. *Our last night together. How come I didn't know it was our last night?* Her eyes misted with tears.

David reached his climax, his eyes closed, hands tightening on her buttocks. He has no idea, Cindy thought. *That I'm not here…not with him.* Finally still, he opened his eyes and gazed at her; the tenderness on his face sent a shaft of guilt through her. His fingers brushed at the tears on her cheeks, and he gave a tremulous smile. "You *do* love me…I know it."

Cindy couldn't respond. She just eased off him, then turned on her side and curled into the fetal position. With David's body cupped around her, she stared into the darkness, listening to the rain on the roof, the droplets of water plunking into buckets—and the sound of Bert Sommer's voice, taking her back to Quin.

Ω

The rain was still falling in horizontal sheets the next morning when Cindy met Charley Moss in front of the hospital. An Army green van with a red cross on its side waited outside the entrance with two naval advisors and two Vietnamese officers wearing rain ponchos and armed with M16s. It would be Cindy's third med-cap with Charley, her first one without Cap Bren. Today's trip would be to a ville north of Saigon on Highway One—an area ripe with Vietcong activity.

Charley grinned as she approached. "Flying solo today, huh? You sure you're ready for this?"

Cindy shrugged. "We'll see. But I think I've got the idea."

He put a friendly arm around her and gave her a hug. "Not exactly what you wanted to do on your birthday, huh?"

Surprised, she smiled. "Who *told* you?"

He laughed. "I'm not giving any secrets away. But a little bird told me about a celebration at the O Club tonight."

Cindy shrugged, climbing into the second row bench seat of the van, running her fingers through her wet mop of hair. "Any excuse to party."

Charley gave her a wink as he settled onto the seat next to her. "Hey, a birthday is always an excuse to party."

The Vietnamese officers and one of the naval advisors climbed into the back row of the van. The driver, a three-striper, and the other naval advisor settled into the front. A moment later, they were rumbling down the muddy road in the driving rain. Potholes and tire grooves made for a jostling ride. Cindy gripped the back of the seat in front of her, but that didn't stop her from bumping against Charley's rock-hard bicep. He laughed, his dark brown eyes sparkling. He loved going on med-caps. Would do it every day if he could, Cindy suspected. But she knew the gleam in his eyes these days was because of one thing—

he was short–going home the end of the month to his wife, his twin little girls and his baby boy that he'd never seen. She was happy for him, but sad for herself—and for the boys he'd never treat. He was, by far, the best doctor at the 24th.

"So, I hear you have a new love in your life," he said with a knowing grin.

Her heart plunged. How did he know about David? They'd tried hard to keep things discreet.

"Hey, don't pass out on me," Charley said. "It's no crime to fall for one of the kids at the orphanage. Just don't get too attached. It'll break your heart when you have to leave."

Relief rushed through her. The van hit a pothole as big as a child's swimming pool, and it felt like the bottom was going to cave under her feet. The clack of the windshield wipers kept rhythm with the driving rain.

"Oh, An Li," Cindy said. "Yeah, I guess you could say I've fallen in love with him. He's a sweetheart."

"And Brenda tells me he's quite taken with you."

"Yeah, it's weird. We had this…connection…from the beginning. And Cap Bren tells me he's never responded to any other nurse like he has with me. I don't get it but…" She shrugged. "He's been the light of my life since…" Her voice faltered, and she closed her eyes.

Charley gave her hand a squeeze. "I'm glad."

An Li <u>and</u> David. If it hadn't been for them, she didn't think she would've made it through these past months.

Trying to drive the thoughts of Quin away, she filled the silence. "The nuns told me An Li's father was American. His mother was a 15-year-old prostitute. Abandoned him right after she gave birth. Guess she was anxious to get back to work." Her voice betrayed her disgust.

Charley remained silent for a moment, and then said, "Well, don't be too harsh on her. You don't know what may have driven her to prostitution." He glanced out the window even though there was nothing to see but the driving rain. "Look at what we've done here. Years of occupation…destroyed villages, land ravaged by Agent Orange…with their ancestral lands gone, the people had no choice but to go to refugee camps. Family structure and values collapsed. Young girls turned to prostitution to feed their families." He shook his head, a grim look on his face. "After we leave…*whe*n we leave, there will be a proliferation of Eurasian kids growing up without fathers, and like in An Li's case, without mothers. *'Bui doi*,'" the Vietnamese call them. 'The dust of life.' Unwanted…drifting about like dust."

Cindy bit her bottom lip. She thought of An Li's sweet, heart-shaped face, his beautiful cognac-brown eyes. How could anyone think of him as "dust?" But besides the indignation, she felt shame at her own callous thinking, assuming that An Li's mother was just a selfish whore who'd abandoned her baby so she could get back to her job of pleasuring American soldiers.

"You're right," Cindy murmured. "I'm a bitch."

"No, you're not." He squeezed her hand, giving her a wink. "You're just an emotional young lady who sometimes doesn't think things through before sharing the way you feel. But Cindy…?" His eyes grew serious. "Be careful about An Li. Not just for your sake, but for his. If you get too close, when you leave, it'll be devastating for him. It's not fair to make him love you only to go away."

Her heart panged at the thought. In the back of her mind, she'd always known they'd have to say goodbye, but now, for the first time, she actually imagined what it would be like.

"What should I do?" she asked quietly. "Should I stop going to the orphanage? That seems cruel in itself. You should see his face light up when he sees me." And she suspected her own looked as bright.

Charley shook his dark head. "No, keep going to the orphanage. Brenda says he's learning English at an astonishing pace with you. So, just prepare him. Let him know you'll be leaving in…what's your DEROS?"

"September."

"So, you have plenty of time. Start talking

about going home. He's four, right?"

Cindy nodded. "That's what the nuns think. Three going on four, maybe. But he's so smart! He speaks perfect French—full sentences. And Cap Bren is right. He's learning English so fast it would make your head spin."

They hit another pot-hole, jostling Cindy against Charley.

He grinned, steadying her with a hand on her knee. "You sound like a proud mama." He paused, and then went on, "I think he'll be fine as long as you don't spring it on him. You, I'm not so sure about. It's going to hurt like hell when you have to leave him. Believe me, I know. When Janet and the girls saw me off at the airport, it just about killed me to look into Kirby and Kaitlen's big brown eyes, thinking about how much they'd grow before I saw them again. But at least I knew I'd see them again, God willing. With you, when you say goodbye to An Li, it'll be for good."

The van stopped to allow a water buffalo to amble across the muddy road. Cindy watched an old Vietnamese farmer nudge the animal with a long stick, and the thought blossomed in her mind like a spring flower. "Why can't I adopt him?"

Charley looked at her in astonishment. "You can't be serious."

Her heart began to drum. "Why not? It makes sense, doesn't it? He's an orphan; he loves me. I love him."

It's crazy, though. You're single. Once you get out of the Army, you won't have a job. Not to mention, you're probably screwed up in the head—or will be—after spending a year in this godforsaken country.

Charley shook his head. "Well, if you can pull it off, I think it would be a wonderful thing to do for the kid. But I don't have any idea how you'd go about it. If it's even possible."

The water buffalo and his farmer finally out of the way, the van started up again, throwing Cindy against Charley as it hit another pothole.

"One thing's for sure," Charley said. "If you have any hope of making this work, you're going to have to find someone high up to help you." He looked at her. "You know anybody like that?"

Ω

"Look at this place," Charley said, climbing out of the van. "A pig-sty."

He wasn't kidding. The place looked like a dump. The stench of garbage and raw sewage competed with the almost as rotten smell of *nuoc ma*, the decayed fish delicacy so popular with the Vietnamese. Grass-thatched hoochesrested parallel to a small brown river, its current swift with the monsoon rains. As Cindy glanced around, she saw a villager moving along a walkway built out onto the river. He reached the end, dropped his loose pants and squatted.

"Oh, my God," Cindy whispered.

Charley followed her gaze and nodded. "And *that's* one reason we see so much diarrhea and skin abscesses. Look!"

He pointed to a woman doing her laundry downstream of the defecating man. Near her, several children played in the shallows.

Aghast, Cindy turned to Charley. "Can't we do anything about that? Teach them about hygiene?"

He shrugged. "We try. But it's almost impossible to get through. They've been living like this for centuries."

"*Bac Si, Bac Si!*"

A crowd of villagers had gathered around them, all eager for medical attention. Cindy wasn't surprised he was as popular here as he was at the 24th. Everyone loved *Bac Si* Charley. Cindy and Charley grabbed their medical bags. He flashed the villagers a grin and strode through the rain toward a small open-sided hut where he'd receive his patients.

"You know the drill," he said to the villagers. "Form one line and Nurse Cindy and I will see you one at a time." The Vietnamese advisor translated his words, and the group turned obediently to follow Charley. "You'd think they'd find a place for us to work that isn't exposed to the elements, huh?" Charley said, throwing Cindy a disgruntled glance.

But there wasn't any other choice. The ville didn't have electricity, and it would be too dark in an enclosed hooch to examine, let alone treat, a patient. They just had to make do.

In the first hour, they saw several patients with a variety of problems--diarrhea, skin infections, an abscess from a cut. With relief, Cindy saw the line growing shorter. Miserable from the pellets of rain hitting her face and dripping beneath her poncho down her back, she looked forward to getting back to the post. Maybe get a nice hot shower before meeting David at the NCO Club for a drink before her birthday party. Have a private celebration with him. Nurses in the NCO Club didn't raise any eyebrows, but David couldn't step foot into the O Club. Heaven forbid an enlisted man should sully the hallowed atmosphere of officer territory.

As she injected a dose of penicillin into the arm of a young woman with a probable urinary tract infection, she felt a wave of guilt wash over her at the memory of the soft look in David's eyes last night as he'd murmured he loved her. She wished she *could* love him, but even if she did—and maybe she did—could it ever compare with the way she'd felt about Quin? And was it fair to David to give him hope when she might not ever love him the way she'd loved Quin?

"*Bac sĩ! Danh từ!*"

The urgency of the young girl's voice needed

no translation. A lovely teenage girl ran up to Charley as he bandaged a cut on a boy's foot, her dark eyes wide with panic. She shouted out a stream of Vietnamese, beckoning the doctor to follow her.

"She says her mother is in labor," the translator explained. "Something is wrong. The baby is stuck."

"Come on, Cindy," Charley said. "Let's see what we've got."

When it was clear that the teenage girl was leading them to a hooch near the river, Charley called out to the van's driver to pull up as close to the structure as possible and turn his headlights on bright.

Even before they entered the hooch, they could hear the woman screaming. Charley followed the teenage girl inside with Cindy on his heels. Headlights flashed over her shoulder as the driver pulled the van up behind her. Still, it was so dim inside, she couldn't see anything in the first seconds. But she heard a shrill stream of Vietnamese, and it didn't sound welcoming at all.

As the van drew closer, she saw a teenage boy, the girl's brother, she guessed, gesturing at Charley, his eyes enraged as he spewed out venomous words. Cindy didn't have to know Vietnamese to understand he was demanding that they leave. The teenage girl tugged on her brother's arm, shouting back at him, tears running down her face. And all the time, a woman…their mother?…writhed on the dirt floor, screaming non-stop.

Ignoring the boy, Charley dropped onto his knees at the woman's side. Cindy crouched nearby with her medical bag, ready to help however she could. But when Charley peered between the woman's legs and began to examine her, the teenage boy's voice rose in fury. He flung himself on Charley, trying to pull him away from the laboring woman. The girl screamed and grabbed at her brother. Charley pushed him away, cursing. The scrawny Vietnamese boy was no match for a six-foot-three American, and he went flying backward, hitting his head on an iron wok, and lay there, dazed.

"I hope to God I didn't kill him," Charley muttered, turning his attention back to the woman. Her screams had grown more intense.

Cindy looked toward the boy. "Shall I…?"

"No, I need you here," Charley said grimly. "The cord is wrapped around the baby's neck. We need to deliver her *now*." He positioned himself between her legs. "Give me the forceps."

Cindy reached for them and handed them over, then she cuffed the woman and took her blood pressure. "180/110."

"Eclampsia," Charley muttered. "Try to get her to push."

She scrambled up to the woman's head. "Do you know the word? I don't know it." Even in the dim light, Cindy could see the Vietnamese woman's face was red with exertion. Or was it agony? Tears leaked out of her half-closed eyes, trickling down her weathered face. She looked too old to be having a baby. At least fifty. But then, Vietnamese women aged prematurely. Thirty looked like fifty here.

"Where the fuck is the translator?" Charley snarled, carefully easing the forceps into the woman's vagina.

"Here." One of the Vietnamese officers stepped into the hooch.

Charley glared at him. "Tell her how to say 'push,' and then get that kid out of here. When he comes to, explain to him that the baby is in distress, and I have to deliver it or it's going to die. And keep him *the fuck* out of here! Take the girl out, too. Then get back in here *pronto*!"

The translator nodded and barked to the woman, "*Giúp sức!*"

Of course. It couldn't be _easy_ to say. But Cindy tried her best to repeat it the way he said it. The woman screamed louder, grimaced and strained. Charley squatted on his heels and with the forceps, eased the baby out of the birth canal. "You've got the suction bulb ready? This baby is going to be blue."

"Yes, doctor."

"Take her blood pressure again. It goes much higher, we're going to lose her."

"190/120."

"Shit. We should be doing a C-section.

Almost there. Come on…one more push should do it."

"*Giúp súc,*" Cindy said to the gasping woman. "*Giúp súc!*"

The woman's scream sounded like an air siren as she strained to relieve her womb of its occupant.

"That's it! It's out," Charley growled. "Tell her it's a boy. Let's just hope we can get him breathing."

Cindy looked over at the translator who'd come back in after getting rid of the teenagers.

"*Cậu bé,*" he said.

She looked down at the mother. Her dark eyes stared up at her, still apprehensive, but at least she'd stopped screaming. "*Cậu bé,*" Cindy said. "You have a little boy."

Suddenly the woman began to thrash. "*She's seizing, doctor!*" Cindy reached for a tongue depressor to prevent the woman's brown-mottled teeth from gnashing at her mouth, but before she could get it in, the woman stiffened and became still. Cindy stared into her fixed and dilated pupils.

"Charley, I think she stroked out," she whispered. When he didn't respond, she looked up at him.

He held the lifeless blue baby in his hands, his gaze locked on the woman's vaginal area. Even in the dim light, she could tell his face was ashen. "It's no use," he said quietly. "She's bleeding out.

Placental abruption. There's nothing we can do. Not here."

Cindy stared at him, her heart thudding. "The baby?"

He shook his head. "My guess is he's been dead for hours. There's nothing we could've done."

They stepped out of the hooch into the pelting rain. Cindy saw the boy and his sister standing with the Vietnamese officers and the naval advisors. Rain pelted down out of a slate sky. The boy stared balefully at Charley, hatred etched on his rain-streaked face. *Oh, God...this is not going to go well.* The girl chewed on a fingernail, her oval face pale, her eyes alight with hope. She spoke a stream of Vietnamese, and without waiting for the translation, Cindy knew she was asking about her mother and the baby. The boy continued to glower at them.

Charley turned to the translator. "Explain to them that we did everything we could, but his mother died giving birth. And the baby didn't make it either. Tell him I'm very sorry. We tried to save them both, but..." His gaze went to the boy and his sister. "I'm very sorry for your loss."

"I'm sorry," Cindy echoed, her voice sounding hollow even to herself.

The translator began to speak, but before he said a few words, the girl screamed and fell to the ground, sobbing. The blood drained from the boy's face and with an anguished cry, he ran into the hooch.

Charley's sober gaze met Cindy's. "Sometimes I hate being a doctor," he said. "Come on, let's go see the rest of the patients and get the hell out of here."

They headed back to the medical hooch, sloshing through puddles of ankle-deep water and blinking rain out of their eyes. Charley gave her a sidelong glance. "Usually, I love these med-caps. They make me feel like I'm giving back in some little way to these people after we've fucked them over. But times like today, it just feels so futile. You know?"

Cindy nodded. "Believe me, I often feel like that."

"Well, thank God, the line is short. We should get out of here---"

Cindy saw the puff of red mist explode from his chest before she heard the gunshot. She screamed, hurling herself toward Charley as he toppled to the ground in slow motion. Another burst of gunfire, and she flinched, not knowing if the shots were aimed at them, but not caring. She just knew she had to help Charley. He lay prone, the bullet hole on the right side of his upper back darkening his poncho with blood. She turned him over, panic lodged in her throat. His hands clawed at his chest, his eyes panicked. A horrible wheezing sound came from his lips.

"Captain Sweet, are you okay?"

Cindy couldn't spare a glance at the naval officer hovering over her. "I am, but Charley's been hit!" She ripped open the doctor's fatique shirt and stared at the fist-sized exit wound on the right side of his chest. The bullet had punctured the lung—a sucking chest wound. She went into action, her mind a curious void. First, and most important, the wound had to be sealed to keep the lung from collapsing. She grabbed the rain-soaked plastic fabric of his poncho, and pressed the inside of it against the gaping hole, holding it securely with the flat of her palm. Still she felt his hot, slick blood seeping out. He stared up at her, eyes wide with shock. "Stay with me, Charley!" she pleaded, holding his gaze. "You hear me?"

He gasped and tried to talk. Blood streamed out of his mouth.

She looked up at the naval advisor, still hovering, his face a mask of horror. "What's your name, Gunny?"

"Anthony Peroni, ma'am."

"Anthony, we need to get him back to base. It's the only chance he has. But I have to keep the pressure on the wound while we move him, so we're going to need everybody to help!"

Anthony scrambled to his feet. "Right away, ma'am."

For the first time, Cindy became aware of the screaming behind them. She glanced back and saw the teenage girl on her knees next to her brother. Even from the distance of several yards, Cindy could see his blood-splattered clothing.

She tried to feel some empathy for the girl and her dead brother, but couldn't. Not after what he'd done to Charley. *All he ever wanted to do was help these people.* Why hadn't they realized what the kid was going to do when he ran back into his dead mother's hooch? What good was it to have armed escorts if they weren't able to stop…

She choked back a sob.

"Cin…dy," Charley gasped, an odd whistle escaping through his lips.

The plastic of the poncho wasn't working. His lung was collapsing. She pressed harder on the wound, wanting to brush back his dark, wet curls from his grey face, but needing both hands to try to save him. "Shhhh…don't talk, Charley. Save your strength."

"No…" He shook his head, and a fresh flow of blood seeped from his mouth. "Do…it…Cin…dy."

She shook her head, tears blurring her eyes. A lump grew in her throat, threatening to choke her. "Do *what?*" she finally managed to say.

Incredibly, he grinned. It was a grin ravaged by pain, but definitely a grin. "A…adopt An…Li. Kids are…" He struggled to speak and more blood bubbled from his mouth. "…are what it's…all about." His eyes fluttered closed.

Tears spilled down Cindy's cheeks, mixed with the relentless rain. She pressed harder on his chest. "Dammit, don't you die on me, Charley

Moss! Your family needs you!"

His eyes opened, and the clarity in them gave her hope. His grip tightened on her wrist. "Tell...Janet..." he whispered. His hand fell from her wrist, his eyes glazing over.

"*No!*" Cindy screamed, taking her hands off his wound and shaking him violently. "No, Charley! You *will not die on me!*"

The two naval advisors and the driver had to pry her off him so they could transport his body back to the post.

CHAPTER TWENTY-NINE

The rain pelted down out of a grim, gray sky. As a gurney rolled Charley's body toward the morgue, David held Cindy in his arms, apparently uncaring that practically everyone in the hospital had gathered outside, most of them crying, the rest stunned and shaken. Cindy clung to him, dry-eyed, but trembling. The reality of Charley's murder had started to sink in. They'd left together from this very spot just a few hours ago. He'd been grinning and teasing her about her birthday. And now...

She gasped as a visceral pain stabbed through her. "He died on my birthday," she whispered into David's shoulder.

His palms pressed into her back, his lips brushing her wet forehead. She pulled away to look at him. "I tried to save him, David. I tried everything…"

"I know." Tears glistened in his blue eyes.

"He…the bullet…it went right through his chest." She shook her head. "His lung collapsed…I tried…I used his poncho, but…Jesus, David, what else could I have *done*?"

His hands tightened on her shoulders. "You did everything you could."

She shook her head. "I should've known…that kid was furious. You should've seen the hatred in his eyes when he yelled at Charley. When he went back into that hooch, I should've realized---"

"*Look at me!*" His fingers dug into her. When she finally met his solemn gaze, he said, "You know as well as I do that even if it had happened here, we might not have been able to save him. Out there…" He shook his head. "As for knowing what that kid was going to do…well, you're not psychic, are you?"

Tears blurred her eyes. "Charley was just trying to help them. And he gets killed for it. *Why are we here, David? What good are we doing?*"

He didn't answer, but held her closer.

"I keep thinking about Janet…and those little kids," Cindy murmured. "The last thing he said was her name."

"*Captain Sweet!*"

Cindy jerked away from David. Lieutenant Colonel Kairos strode up to them, her black eyes flashing fire. Even in the rain-drenched air,

Cindy could smell her obnoxious fragrance. "I'm sure you have something more important to do than stand around here canoodling with…" Her gaze flicked over David as if he were some kind of reptile that had just crawled out of the sewage Line. "…an *enlisted man*! *Get back to work, Sergeant!*"

To David's credit, he kept his dignity, but it took every bit of Cindy's self-control not to reach out and slap the bitch. David released her with a look that clearly told her to hang in there, and headed toward the hospital doors.

"I don't know what you think you're doing, missy," Kairos went on in a caustic tone. "But I won't have you putting on a spectacle in front of these new young nurses, corrupting them and their morals. I've heard rumors about you and that corpsman, Sweet, and I'm not going to put up with your flagrant fraternization! So help me, God---"

"You are a callous *witch*!" Without really knowing how it had happened, Cindy found herself nose-to-nose with Kairos. The blood had drained from the colonel's face, but before she could speak, Cindy went on, "We just lost the best doctor I've ever worked with, *ma'am*, and instead of showing a little compassion, all you're concerned with is who I'm sleeping with! Well, it's *none of your goddamn business!*" Cindy started to brush past her, but then paused, thinking *what the fuck do I have to lose now?* "Maybe if *you* got laid, you wouldn't be so concerned with everyone else's love life."

As she headed toward the hospital doors, she came face-to-face with Cap Bren, and it was clear she'd overheard the entire exchange. Wearing her usual expression of ice-queen stoicism, she gestured toward the doors, and then headed for Colonel Kairos.

Cindy went inside the doors then leaned against the wall, her heart pounding.

I don't care. I just don't care anymore. They can all go straight to hell.

Ω

The order came down the next morning. Nurses were not to converse with enlisted men outside of the line of duty. If they were caught doing so, the enlisted men would be punished, not the nurses. The perfect reprisal—because the nurses who were friendly with corpsmen genuinely liked them, if not loved them. Cindy knew three or four other nurses dating corpsmen, and now, they wouldn't even be allowed to speak to them. All because of her.

Yet, when she thought back to that moment when she'd stared that Greek bully in the eyes and essentially told her to go fuck herself—because she doubted that anyone would do it *for* her—it felt damn good. The price, though, for that satisfaction would be her affair with David. And the thought that she'd no longer have those sanity-saving moments in his arms filled her with despair. But she couldn't—*wouldn't*—have him punished just to fulfill her needs. She loved—no...too strong a word...*cared* for him—too much for that.

So for the next few days, she avoided him. Until on the night shift, he cornered her in the supply room. When she turned and saw him standing in the doorway, his face solemn, eyes wounded, her heart began to race.

"I know you think you're protecting me by avoiding me," he said quietly. "But not being with you is killing me."

She looked past him into the dim light of the ward. "David, you shouldn't be following me in here," she stage-whispered. "Falley is Kairos' spy. I'm sure of it, and you can believe she saw you and is ready to report you."

He took a step toward her, anger flashing across his face. "I don't give a damn what they do to me, Cindy. I'll wash floors, I'll clean blood off the walls, I'll do latrine duty every damn day until they send me home. Anything they throw at me, I'll do." By this time, he'd reached her, standing just inches away. "But I won't give you up, Cindy Sweet. I *can't*. I need you too much." His hands fastened around her head, and his lips claimed hers.

Cindy kissed him back for what seemed like a long moment, her head spinning. *I can't give this up either. I just can't!* Finally, she forced herself to break the kiss. "David! We can't *do* this," she said breathlessly. "Didn't you hear what I said? Sharon Falley is—"

He covered her lips with his fingers. "Sharon Falley is taking a cigarette break. I checked first before I followed you. Listen, babe, you're the only thing that's keeping me sane here…and I think it's the same for you. I'm not going to give you up. Not for anything." With another hard kiss, he released her, turned and strode out of the supply room.

Cindy watched him go, her mouth tender from his bruising kiss. I *could* love him, she thought.

A few moments later, when she'd got her breathing under control, she left the supply room. A moment later, Lt. Sharon Falley strode into the ward. She glanced from Cindy to David, attending to a patient a few feet away. Then she looked back at Cindy, her gaze speculative.

Cindy gave her a bright smile. "You'll be happy to know that David and I have broken up. You can report *that* to Colonel Kairos, you sneaky little bitch."

June 1971

May 29, 1971

Dear Freckleface:

Joanie told me what happened to your boyfriend, and damn, honey, I'm just so sorry. Did you get the sympathy card Lesley sent? I know I should've written before now, but you know I'm no good at this stuff. It's hard to find the right words to say. You're way too young to be going through this. (But as a father, I have to say I think you're way too young to be falling so hard for a guy you've only known a few months. And Joanie says you were planning to marry him. When were you going to tell <u>me?</u>)

Anyway, no lectures! It's beside the point now, isn't it? What you have to do, Cindy, is buck up, be a strong girl and do your job—and come back home safe and sound. You know, I've been thinking...you should come on down here to Myrtle Beach. There's a nice new hospital being built in Conway, and with your experience, I'll bet you can get a good job there. Think about it, okay? Lesley and I would love to have you living close. (You aren't planning on re-upping in the Army, are you? I can't tell you what to do, but hon, you've done your duty by giving them two years out of your life. That's enough.) But I said no lectures, didn't I? You probably get enough of those from your mom.

The kids are growing like weeds. You should see them. (I've enclosed some pictures.) Scotty will be starting first grade in the fall, and Nancy rules the roost around here. She wears her princess dress every day and screams bloody murder when Lesley takes it away to be washed.

I'm still flying the Charleston/Atlanta/New York route. Boring as hell, but what can you do? It's a job— and it keeps Lesley in the fancy duds she wears to all her Junior League meetings. Oh! Hey, guess what I got her for her birthday last month? A brand new bright blue 1971 Thunderbird—four on the floor and black leather seats. What a ride! Got it for a great deal before the 72's come out. Lesley loves it. Maybe she'll let you drive it when you come down. Hey, the Indianapolis 500 is about to start on TV. Wonder if your Aunt Terri is there? I know she was always crazy about that race, and so was your mom. She always used to say she'd take me someday, but we never got around to it. Maybe you and I should go next year when you're back. Just the two of us—a daughter/dad thing. Take care of yourself, Freckleface. And remember…your old dad loves you.

Daddy

CHAPTER THIRTY

A skinny corporal behind the desk looked up as Cindy walked into General Hopper's office at Headquarters in Saigon. "Yes, ma'am? How can I help you?"

She swallowed hard, trying to calm the butterflies in her stomach. "I have an appointment with General Hopper," she said in a calm, hopefully confident voice. *I can't believe I'm doing this*! She prepared herself to have to explain further, but the corporal glanced down at a notebook on the desk.

"Are you Captain Sweet?"

She nodded. "Yes, sir...I mean, yes, I am." Her cheeks grew warm.

I must be nuts. This is crazy! In about two minutes, the general himself would be telling her so. *What are you talking about, girl? Adopt a Vietnamese national? Impossible!*

But she remembered Charley's last words to her. *Adopt An Li…kids are what it's all about.* Okay, so, what did she have to lose? Her dignity? *Yeah, when the general has you escorted out of his office by security police and shipped back to the World in a strait jacket.*

But he'd agreed to see her. That was a good sign, wasn't it?

The corporal—Decker, his nametag read—looked up from his notebook and picked up the phone. "I'll let him know you're here. Please have a seat."

But before she could do so, Sgt. Decker called out to her. "Captain, the general will see you now." He jumped up from his desk and ushered her toward a door with a brass nameplate: General Joseph K. Hopper.

Cindy's heart thudded like the blades of an incoming chopper. *You idiot. You must be out of your mind. What are you doing here? Just because you saved his life…*

But he <u>said</u> anything I need…

Well, she'd soon find out if he meant it or not. *<u>Idiot</u>. Of <u>course</u> he didn't mean it; he was just being nice.* Suddenly panic gripped her by the throat and she almost turned right around to make a beeline for the closest one-holer so she could upchuck her breakfast. But it was too late. The corporal tapped on the general's door then opened it. "Captain Sweet to see you, sir."

General Hopper looked up, and the twinkle in

his blue eyes immediately squelched her panic. She came to attention and gave him a smart salute.

He smiled. "At ease, Captain." His gaze slid to the corporal. "Thank you, Decker. Bring us a couple of coffees, will you? And make it fresh, huh? Don't want any of that sludge at the bottom of the pot." He gave Cindy a wink. "And I'm betting this young lady here knows what a good cup of coffee tastes like, am I right, dear?"

"Yes, sir." Cindy had relaxed into the "at ease" position, hands clasped behind her back, feet shoulder-width apart. Funny, how infrequently she had to follow military protocol working in the hospital. While she was stationed at Walter Reed in 1970, she and a couple other nurses had gone down to Dupont Circle to watch a movie called "MASH" with Donald Sutherland and Elliott Gould, about a mobile field hospital in Korea. She'd enjoyed the film, but found the lack of military protocol among the medical unit to be largely a figment of Hollywood's imagination. After serving nine months at the 24th, she'd realized it hadn't been that much of a fantasy, after all.

The door closed behind the corporal, leaving Cindy alone with the general. A quick glance around the spacious office assured her that the foul-tempered attaché, Colonel Simpson, was nowhere in sight, and she relaxed a bit more. But then she remembered why she was here, and tensed again. Affable, the general might be, but when he heard what she wanted, she could very well find herself kicked out on her butt in two minutes flat.

General Hopper gestured to a chair in front of his desk. "Well, sit yourself down, young lady. Cindy, right? Mind if I call you Cindy?" He smoothed one of his gigantic hands over his bristle of white hair and grinned.

"Of course I don't mind," she said, moving to the chair. She sat on the edge of it, her two-inch heels flat on the floor. She'd worn her light green summer cords for this meeting, eschewing the ridiculously hot dress "blues," which were actually dark green; not even for the General could she suffer such discomfort. Besides, she looked better in the cords. "Thank you for seeing me, sir."

"Not at all! Been wondering why you haven't stopped in before." He opened his desk drawer and pulled out a bottle of Jameson Irish whiskey. His smile deepened the crinkly lines around his sparkling blue eyes. "How about a little pick-me-up while we wait for our coffee?" He poured a couple of fingers of whiskey into two etched crystal tumblers and slid one over to her.

Cindy wasn't a whiskey drinker, but she couldn't very well refuse it. "Thank you." She took the tumbler, toasted to his "down the hatch" and tossed back the liquor. It burned down her

throat and exploded in her stomach like a small
bomb. Somehow, she managed not to cough, but
her eyes blurred with tears that he surely couldn't
miss. To his credit, he didn't laugh, but his smile
widened.

"That'll clean out your sinuses, yeah?" He
placed his tumbler on the desk, folded his arms
and leaned toward her. "So, Miss Cindy, how's
that young man of yours? Quinlan, isn't that his
name?"

And just like that, the tears in her eyes had
nothing to do with the whiskey. She blinked,
fighting the thickening lump in her throat that
threatened to cut off her air supply. Hearing
Quin's name—especially from General Hopper—
had been totally unexpected. As was the pain
that enveloped her at the sound of it. And she'd
started to believe she was making progress.

Somehow, she found her voice. It came out
raspy. "He...didn't make it, sir." She fixed her
gaze on a photograph on his desk—the General
with an elegant blond woman and a teenage
daughter who could pass for a **Seventeen
Magazine** model.

General Hopper's smile disappeared. "Aw,
Jesus Christ! I'm damn sorry to hear that, Cindy.
How did it happen?"

Oh, please. No. Don't make me go through this.

But he was waiting for an answer, his face
solemn, eyes sympathetic.

"The incursion into Laos," she said softly.

"His chopper was hit by a RPG."

"Aw, *shit*. Excuse my language, Miss Cindy." He ran both hands through his bristle and stood. "I'm just so damn sorry. He was a fine young man. We're losing too many fine young men in this war." He strode over to a window overlooking the parade field. "Too many fine young men."

Silence. Cindy couldn't speak. Her throat had closed like a vault. *Great. All this is for nothing. I can't speak, so how can I ask him to help me adopt An Li?*

General Hopper turned and met her gaze. "God rest his soul. He was a brave man, an American hero." He shook his head then ambled back to his chair. "So, tell me, Miss Cindy, what brings you hear today? What is it I can do for you?"

Cindy took a deep breath, gave a quick, silent prayer, looked him in the eyes and said, "I've fallen in love, General. With a little Eurasian boy named An Li. And I need your help to take him back to the U.S. with me."

CHAPTER THIRTY-ONE

No matter how bad a mood Cindy was in, no matter how exhausting and horrendous her shift on Ward 2 had been, no matter what a crap day she'd had, the sight of Cahoney's neon sign between the base and Bien Hoa always made her smile. The bar was owned by an aging hippie expat from Haight-Ashbury, a taciturn, bearded man called Snag who looked like he'd rather kill you than serve you a beer. No one knew much about him, but rumors ran rampant—he'd served with one of the first units in 'Nam and had been dishonorably discharged after putting his commanding officer in the hospital because of a difference of opinion. He lived with a Vietnamese woman and had fathered four or five kids with her. He was a junkie, an alcoholic, a card shark, a black market dealer and ran a cathouse in Saigon.

Cindy didn't know if all—or any—of these

things were true. But one thing was for sure. Snag had cajones. And the beer was cold, the French fries crisp and golden—and unlike at the O Club, officers and enlisted could mingle without fear of being dressed down. Because of course, the only officers who had the guts to go to a dive like Cahoney's weren't the "Frank Burns" dressing-down types. Hawkeye and Trapper John would've fit right in.

On Saturday night, the place was jumping. Over the blare of Mick Jagger belting out "Brown Sugar," military personnel stood shoulder to shoulder at the greasy bar and filled the tables tucked into dark corners around an oval-shaped dance floor–drinking, laughing, toasting, arguing and singing along with the music. Every half-hour or so, a fight would break out, and Snag, with the help of his bulldog-faced bartender, affectionately known as Baby, would kick them out on their butts, then complacently go back to work. As always, men outnumbered women, (mostly nurses) 10-1, and GIs were dancing together on the dance floor, with only the lucky ones finding female partners.

Cahoney's was the only place where Cindy and David could hang out socially since Colonel Kairos had issued the ridiculous rule prohibiting nurses from *conversing* with enlisted men outside the line of duty. That hadn't stopped them from sleeping together, of course, but it had curtailed any social activity, so Cahoney's had been the answer.

Across the sticky table from Cindy and David, Simon Forester, Jenny's boyfriend, raised his can of Pabst Blue Ribbon, an ear-to-ear grin on his smooth chocolate face. "Cheers to Cindy and her success with the general!"

Beside him, Jenny beamed and lifted her beer. David did the same. Cindy was a few seconds slower. Smiling, she clinked her can against the others. "Nothing is definite. He said he'd look into it. So, I guess what we're really toasting is that he didn't say a flat-out *no*."

Simon swallowed his beer, and then chuckled. "Hey, if a four-star general wants something, chances are he'll make it happen. I wouldn't worry if I were you."

David gave her shoulder a squeeze, smiling. "Simon's right. Sounds like General H will move hell and high water for you, Cindy. And why not? You saved his life. He owes you."

Cindy shook her head, her index finger tracing a wet circle of condensation on the table from her cold beer. "Well, I'm trying not to get my hopes up. Even for a general, the red tape just might be too much."

Jenny, already a little drunk, laughed. "The boys are right. Bet we'll be calling you 'Mom' before too long." Her brown, almond-shaped eyes danced as she glanced over at David. "And will we be calling *you* 'Dad?'"

Cindy shot her a glare. *You did not just say that!*

A slow flush creeping over his face, David reached for his beer and took a gulp. Simon laughed. "Jumping the gun, a bit, aren't you, babe?"

"What?" Jenny's grin widened. "Hey, it's clear they're crazy about each other! What's wrong with putting the idea in his head?"

Poor David looked like he wanted to crawl under the table and hide. The first notes of The Association's "Cherish" began, and Simon looked expectantly at Jenny. "Dance?"

She smiled, took his hand and got to her feet. A bit wobbly, she followed him to the dance floor. Cindy watched as the tall, lanky black officer took the petite Asian girl into his arms, and they began to move to the music.

Thank God it's not "Never My Love." Cindy had heard "their song" only twice since Quin's death, and it had undone her both times.

Next to her, David fidgeted, still embarrassed by Jenny's flippant remark, Cindy guessed. She was about to ask him if he wanted to dance when he stood, mumbling something about getting another round of beers, then headed for the bar. Cindy watched him, her cheeks warm. She hoped she wasn't as red as he was. Crazy about each other? Well…she knew he was crazy about *her*; he'd made that clear. Made it clear every time he touched her. But how did *she* feel?

She stared at the back of his blond head as he waited for Baby to notice him. She loved the way he looked in his jeans and olive green Army T-shirt…his broad back and trim waist. Nice, firm, *pinchable* behind. He might only be her height, even shorter when she wore her pumps, but every inch of him was muscular and male. And oh, my, he was attentive between the sheets. Quiet and gentlemanly in the hospital, the boy was a tiger in bed. Her cheeks grew hotter, just thinking about what they'd done last night, and would do again tonight.

But good sex didn't mean they were crazy about each other, did it? Crazy about *it*, but not necessarily about each other. She watched him lean toward Baby who'd finally noticed him, and saw the dimple flicker in his right cheek as he smiled. Cindy's stomach took a little dip. When he glanced back, caught her gaze and gave her a wink, she felt as if she were on a roller coaster starting down a gigantic hill. She looked away in sudden confusion.

David arrived back at the table with a tray of beers as "Cherish" was fading out. "Here you go." He placed a beer in front of her.

Cheeks still warm, and feeling the effects of a wild roller coaster ride she hadn't known she'd bought tickets for, Cindy felt shyness creep over her. She stared at the cold can of Pabst in front of her, unable to look at David, but feeling his gaze upon her. The tantalizing aroma of grilling burgers drifted her way, and she opened her mouth to suggest ordering a couple.

But then it happened. The opening drums and guitar chords of Neil Young's "Cinnamon Girl" began to play, and the roller coaster slammed to earth. Cindy felt the impact through every tissue, through bone and muscle and artery and vein. She went ice-cold. How could that be possible? It had to be 90 degrees in here with only that overhead rattan fan spinning half-heartedly, moving the saturated tropical air from one spot to another. But Cindy felt paralyzed by the cold moving inexorably through her body.

"Want to dance, Cindy?" David asked.

She tried to answer him but couldn't. Her voice had frozen with the rest of her being.

Jenny, walking off the dance floor, hand in hand with Simon, looked at her and her smile faltered. She disengaged herself from Simon and rushed over to the table. "Jesus, Cindy! What's wrong? You look like you've seen a…" Her voice drained away as comprehension came to her face. "Oh." She placed a hand on Cindy's shoulder. "Come on, honey. Let's go to the little girl's room."

Cindy found herself getting to her feet and moving with Jenny through the crowd of GIs, ignoring their cat-calls and invitations to dance. They'd learned a long time ago it was best to ignore their entreaties because an engagement of any kind only encouraged them. But when a drunk lieutenant reached out and blatantly placed a hand on Jenny's breast, she shoved him with every bit of her 5'1" strength, and since he was a skinny Beetle Bailey type, and drunk out of his mind, he toppled backwards into a beefy Green Beret who hauled off and gave him an upper cut to the chin. And the fight was on.

Amid crashing glass, tables toppling, blows exchanging, and Neil Young singing a song that would forever break Cindy's heart, Jenny led her to the ladies' restroom, a filthy hole in the floor—Vietnamese style—that stank of old urine and fresh feces surrounded by crumbling tile. Cindy had never used the facilities—even after a long night of drinking and didn't intend to unless she was so drunk she didn't care. Luckily, she apparently had the bladder of a camel and had always been able to wait until they were back at post.

Nasty as it was, the stench and filth had the effect of a smelling salt. The cold inside her was already starting to thaw, and she was beginning to feel again. Over the enraged shouting and noise of the fight in the bar, she could still hear "Cinnamon Girl." She hoped David and Simon had had the good sense to get the hell out of the bar, but knowing them, they wouldn't go anywhere without them. At the thought, panic rushed through Cindy.

"We've got to get back to the guys!" she shouted over the noise. "They're probably looking for us!"

"They're okay," Jenny yelled back. "Question

is…are you?"

"I'll live. I just wasn't prepared when…that song came on. It…brings Quin back so vividly."

Jenny nodded, her oval face sympathetic. "I know."

"Jen, will it…" Cindy swallowed hard, and then found her voice again. "Do you think it will…always hurt this bad?"

Jenny reached out and squeezed her hand. "I think it will always hurt, but it won't always be this bad. And you know something else? I didn't know Quin all that well, but I do know this just from the few times I hung out with him…he'd want you to be happy."

Cindy stared into Jenny's soft brown eyes for a long moment. "I know he would. But…"

"But what?"

Cindy looked away from her, feeling her cheeks growing hot. "Would he want me to be happy…this soon?"

Jenny squeezed her hand tighter. "He loved you. I think that's *exactly* what he'd want." She released Cindy's hand. "Come on. Simon told me if we ever got separated by a fight to get out and meet him outside behind the bar. I'll bet they're waiting for us."

They were. When David caught his first glimpse of Cindy, his tense face relaxed and he gave her a smile that sent her pulse racing. "Thank God!" In three strides, he reached her and took her into his arms. She could feel his heart pounding beneath her palm.

"I told you they'd be okay, my man," Simon growled in the darkness. "My girl knows how to take care of herself. You did good, sweetheart...just like I taught you."

Still harbored in David's arms, Cindy heard Jenny giggle. "What you *don't* know, honeycakes, is I was probably the one who started the fight."

Probably? Cindy had to stifle a laugh. No doubt that was something they should probably keep between the two of them. She drew away from David to gaze at him. No cuts and bruises, thank God.

"I was worried about you," she said, stroking his jaw where tiny blond whiskers were starting to sprout.

He smiled and his dimple flickered. "And I was worried about *you*." He planted a kiss on the tip of her nose, then placed an arm around her. "Come on, let's head back to the post. Maybe have a...nightcap...or something."

Cindy grinned and slipped her arm about his waist. She was pretty sure it would be the *something*. The four of them headed toward the gate a click down the road. They walked silently for a few moments, occasionally glancing up at a hazy full moon. Cindy wondered if her folks back home were staring at this same moon. Somehow, the thought was comforting.

They would love David. Mom, Aunt Terri, Joanie. Even Dad. How could they not?

Her hand tightened on his waist. "David? I have to ask you something."

He looked down at her, and the love on his face outshined the moon. "Anything, babe."

She had to look away from his radiance. "You're off until 1900 tomorrow, right? Would you…uh…like to come with me to the orphanage to meet An Li?"

CHAPTER THIRTY-TWO

An Li grinned up at David from his sleeping mat, and spoke in a mixture of English and French. "*Monsieur* Daveed, can you tell me story about little boy lost in cold white sand? *S'il vous plaît?*"

"You mean lost in the snow, right?" David glanced over at Cindy, smiling at the running joke between him and the four-year-old.

An Li giggled and kicked his skinny legs against his coarse blanket. "*No!* Cold white *sand!*"

On their last visit, David had brought photos from Minnesota of ten-foot snowdrifts and snowmen, sleighs gliding through tall pines and firs, their boughs laden with snow—sights that a three-year-old orphan from a tropical climate could barely comprehend. Since then, the boy had been fixated on the white stuff he insisted on calling "sand." On this visit—the third one since Cindy had first brought David to the orphanage,

David had told An Li the "lost boy in the snowstorm story" twice, with only minor alterations, and always a happy ending.

"Okay," David said now, brushing back An Li's coal black hair from his forehead. "One more time. But then you have to go to sleep. *Mademoiselle* Cindy and I have to get back to the post."

An Li nodded, his eyelids already heavy. Bet he wouldn't make it through the story, Cindy thought. And no wonder! She and David had worn him and the other children out with games of Tag and Kick the Can. If Cindy had had any doubts about David's ability to connect with children—and An Li in particular–they had disappeared within moments of his first visit. The children adored him. David had immediately fell into play with them, unconcerned if he looked silly or awkward, giving them piggyback rides and making them laugh with his comical antics. In fact, on his first visit, An Li had been so fascinated with David that Cindy felt practically invisible. But a goodbye kiss and cuddle had reassured her that she was still Mademoiselle Number One with him. It was clear, though, that David was Number Two.

An Li's eyes closed before the fictional little boy had been rescued from the snowstorm. David looked over at Cindy and smiled. "Out like a light."

Cindy couldn't resist stroking the little boy's

silky hair, her heart tight with love. His outrageously long, black eyelashes fluttered with every measured breath. His pursed lips reminded her of a perfect rosebud. She looked up and met David's gaze. The tender expression on his face made her catch her breath.

After a long moment, she looked away, uncomfortable and confused. *He's leaving next month! That is...if nothing happens to him before he gets on that Freedom Bird.*

At the thought of what her life was going to be like without David, Cindy felt almost nauseous. And then angry. *Damn it!* She wasn't supposed to do this. Fall in love again. That wasn't part of the plan. It made her feel disloyal to Quin. To Quin's memory, she amended. What kind of girl could be so head over heels in love with someone, get engaged to him, get impregnated by him, and then fancy herself in love with someone else three months later—just because the first guy died? Didn't that make her a slut? Or at the very least, a frivolous, boy-crazy chick that had to fancy herself in love in order to justify her existence?

Jenny and Shyanne both thought she was nuts when she talked like this—which had been often lately. Jenny had been the first one to bring up the "L" word. Love, not lust—although lust was clearly part of the package. But when Jenny had suggested she'd fallen in love with David, Cindy had hotly denied it. "You are nuttier than those gorks you work on," she'd snapped, feeling ashamed of herself even as the words left her mouth.

But Jenny had just shrugged. "Must be my imagination then…the way your face lights up whenever he's near you. Maybe those gorks *are* rubbing off on me."

"I'm sorry," Cindy murmured, chastened.

Jenny ignored her apology. "Hey, you can deny it all you want if it makes you feel better, but one thing you can't deny—David Ansgar is crazy in love with you. He's one of the sweetest guys I've ever met. I just hope you're not going to break his heart."

"You ready?" David asked now as An Li turned onto his side and curled into the fetal position, inserting a thumb into his mouth.

David got up from the floor and reached down to help Cindy to her feet. "We'd better get back. Don't want to be caught on Highway One after dark."

Cindy nodded and took his hand. Since their visits to the orphanage weren't official, they didn't travel with armed escorts. David had worked out a deal with one of his friends in the motor pool to sign out a Jeep, and then he and Cindy had pooled their money to hire an off-duty GI to ride with them, armed with an M-16. So far, they hadn't run into any trouble, but they'd always got back to the post well before sunset.

Walking hand in hand to the Jeep, David

asked, "Heard anything more from the general?"

Cindy shook her head. "Not since what I told you on Monday. It's making its way through the channels, and is looking good. I'm trying not to get my hopes up, though."

"But it *sounds* good," David said. "We've got to stay positive."

Cindy didn't miss the "we." She bit her lip. She knew what was happening. David was gearing himself up to ask "the question." And Cindy didn't know how she was going to respond. It might not even be *the* question, she told herself. Maybe he would just ask if he could come to Indiana to see her when she got home. At the most, maybe he'd suggest moving in together. Everybody was doing it these days, after all. Trying it out, seeing if it worked.

But no, she couldn't see David suggesting that. They might be going at it like bunny rabbits here in 'Nam, but from what she'd learned about David's small town Minnesota life and his staid Midwestern upbringing, there would be no "living in sin" for the two of them.

David was going to propose marriage, and he was going to do it before he got on that Freedom Bird home. And Cindy had no idea how she was going to answer him.

Ω

Cindy had just gone on duty when an

explosion in the distance shook the foundation of the hospital and sirens began going off. Red alert! Immediately everyone went into action, pulling on flak jackets and helmets, then began covering the patients with mattresses. Cursing like a sailor, Cap Bren started at one end of the ward, and Cindy at the other, with three corpsmen and Shyanne Rooney hitting the middle. Cindy knew exactly why Cap Bren was so mad. It was her last shift before she caught her Freedom Bird tomorrow. Nothing Cap Bren had ever said had given Cindy cause to think she was superstitious in any way, but she *had* to be worried. Many a soldier had died on his last mission, his last patrol or his last trip into Saigon for drunken revelries to celebrate his last night in Hell. So it was definitely possible that a nurse could die on her last day of duty.

At first, Cindy thought they were under mortar attack. Heart pounding and gut churning, she dragged extra mattresses out of the supply cabinet but suddenly realized there had been no more explosions, just sporadic gunfire. Maybe whatever was happening wasn't all that serious.

The doors to the ward burst open and David rushed in, followed by more off duty medical personnel. Standard red alert procedure called for all personnel to report to their duty stations until the all clear. As Cindy covered a delirious, protesting GI with a mattress, she glanced up to try to catch David's eye. *Thank God he's okay.* Just having him in the same room calmed her. He hadn't seen her yet. He scanned the room, his eyes worried; his sober expression changed to relief when he found her. Giving her a brief smile, he jumped in to help the nurses and other corpsmen cover the patients.

The siren continued to blare, and gunfire punctuated the night. The doors burst open again, and two gigantic MPs armed with M16s strode in, stationing themselves one on each side of the double doors. Cap Bren glanced over at them, and her face grew even grimmer than it had been before. Her lips tight, she looked away, her gaze stopping on Cindy. Something flickered in her eyes…sadness…regret? But before Cindy could identify the emotion, she got back to work, settling a mattress over an unconscious GI.

When all the patients were protected and nothing more could be done, Cindy watched Cap Bren make her way over to the MPs.

"Do you know what's happening out there?" she asked, her voice carrying.

The MPs exchanged a grim look, and then one of them said, "A sapper blew up the guard shack. Killed two grunts. In the chaos, about a dozen VC stormed the gate. We've killed most of them but some are still at large."

"Oh, good Lord!" Shyanne's big green eyes widened. "That's *terrifying*! Thank the Lord they sent y'all here to protect us." She stood next to the larger MP, looking like a pretty GI JoAnn doll in her Army fatigues, flak jacket and much too large helmet.

He looked down at her and a slow, red tide crept up his neck and over his face.

"Lieutenant Rooney!" Cap Bren snapped. "You think you can find something worthwhile to do other than stand here and flirt with MPs?"

It was Shyanne's turn to blush. Cindy knew her well enough to know that flirting wasn't anything Shyanne did intentionally; it was just part of her personality, and she could no more turn it off than she could stop the sun from shining. Cindy also knew that Shyanne would never in a million years try to defend herself to the major. She, alone, was the only nurse on Ward 2 that gave Cap Bren the differential treatment that her rank demanded. She scurried away, her helmet slipping on her head like an unruly wig.

The siren stopped suddenly, and the silence in its place seemed almost menacing. The two MPs stared at each other, and then the smaller one said, "I'll check it out." Cindy and the rest of the team continued to do the tasks that had to be done—checking vitals, IVs, drainage tubes. The MP wasn't gone long. When he reappeared, he gave a nod and barked, "All clear."

The large MP tipped a finger to his helmet and said, "Looks like everything is back to normal, ladies and gentlemen. Thanks for your cooperation." And with that, the two MPs strode out of the hospital.

"Okay, people! Let's get these mattresses off the troops," Cap Bren said, taking off her helmet and tossing it into a supply closet. The flak jacket followed.

David had sidled his way over to Cindy. "You okay?" he asked under his breath, keeping a watchful eye on Cap Bren.

"Yeah, you?" She took off her helmet, running a hand through her sweaty bob.

With another glance at the charge nurse, he reached down and squeezed her hand, releasing it immediately. "See you when you get off in the morning?"

Cindy grinned, shrugging out of her flak jacket. "I'll be exhausted, but what the hell? I'm sure you'll think of something to energize me."

He blushed, and Cindy was glad Cap Bren was busy on the other side of the ward. It would be clear to anyone with anything resembling a brain that there was more going on between them than a patient consultation.

David gave her a smile that made her heart feel like ice cream on a hot summer day. "See you at seven...or shortly thereafter." Shedding his flak jacket and helmet, he dropped them in the supply cabinet and began to help take the mattresses off the patients.

As Cindy worked her way toward Cap Bren's side of the ward, she heard Shyanne chatting with one of the corpsmen. "Well, I just think it was the sweetest thing to send those MPs over to guard us during the red alert. It sure made me feel a lot safer. I'll tell you that!"

A harsh laugh erupted from Cap Bren, a few feet away. "Rooney, you've got to be the most naïve young woman I've ever met! Are all the girls in Kentucky as innocent as you are?"

Shocked and a little irritated at Cap Bren's cruelty, Cindy started to protest, but before she could, Cap Bren went on, "You don't really think the MPs were here to protect *us*, do you, Lieutenant?" She laughed again, her eyes hard, and somehow, bleak. "Not even close, honey. You know what would've happened if the VC had broken in? The MPs would've shot us before they'd let them take us hostage. Orders from the top. And you know something else, if that had happened, we'd be better off dead."

July 1971

June 27, 1971

Dear Cindy,

I got into a fight with this freaky hippie girl at camp yesterday. We all were talking about the war, and she called our soldiers a bunch of baby-killing drug addicts, and said she hopes they all die over there. I couldn't keep my mouth shut, Cindy. This is what I said... yelled, actually, "You'd better shut your ignorant, fat mouth, you stupid-ass communist! My sister is a nurse over there, serving her country for morons like you!" And you know what that bitch said? "She should be ashamed of herself, fixing up those druggies so they can go out and kill more innocent babies!" Well, that did it. I punched her. Of course, I ended up in trouble. The camp counselor called Mom, but it was worth it. Now I'm grounded when I get home. But I don't care; I'd do it again. Nobody gets away with saying things like that about my sister. Gotta go. Love you, Cindy.

Joanie

July 5, 1971

Dear Cindy,

Well, we really missed you at the 4th of July celebration

yesterday. We all went to the Lebanon park, and spent most of the afternoon in the pool. It's hotter than blazes here. What did you do to celebrate the fourth?

Guess you heard about Joanie getting into that fight at camp. Sounds like she was justified in hitting that girl, but I can't condone it. I grounded her for two weeks. I didn't even let her bring a friend to the park with us yesterday; she was lucky I let her go at all. This darn war is really riling everybody up…people feel strongly on both sides. But it seems to me that we all should just be patriotic and trust our government. I know Nixon is doing everything he can to bring this war to an end. In fact, I read in the newspaper the other day that the peace talks are going well. Apparently, the Viet Cong have proposed an agreement that they'll release all the POWs in North and South Vietnam by the end of this year as long as we withdraw all our troops. That won't affect you, of course, because you'll already be home, thank God. Still, it sounds like a step in the right direction. I just wish these darn war protestors would quit marching on Washington. Did you read about the Vietnam veterans who camped on the mall down from the Capitol? Yeah, protesting against the war. They threw medals they'd won and ribbons at the foot of the statue of Chief Justice John Marshall. Doesn't that just beat all? You'd think if you served over there, it would make you more patriotic.

Well, the mailman will be here soon, so I'll close for now. Keep safe, Cindy.
I love you. Mom

357

CHAPTER THIRTY-THREE

Cindy folded her mother's letter and slipped it back into the envelope. She shook her head, her lips twisting in an ironic grin. *What was I doing on the 4th of July? Well, Mom, I was working a 16-hour push...cutting the uniform off the body of a boy who looked about sixteen, trying to find out where all the blood was coming from...turns out it was coming from pretty much everywhere. He was just one of the many who didn't make it. And after it was finally over, I got to tag bodies and place them in plastic bags. So, that's how I spent the 4th of July. Glad to hear you enjoyed the fireworks. We see and hear them every night from mortar rounds. Lucky us!*

She felt guilty as these thoughts traveled through her mind. Poor Mom just had no idea what it was like here. How could she? No one back home understood. Probably didn't *want* to know what it was really like.

Reaching down for her half-smoked

Virginia Slim on the bench next to her, she lifted it to her lips and took a long drag. Her break was almost over. Amazing, actually, that she was even able to take one. It had been so crazy on the ward since the push on the 4th. When she'd finally got off duty at 0400 on the 5th, she'd gone back to her hooch and slept for a straight ten hours. Now she was back on the day shift after one night off. David was working the 1900/0700 shift, and not because Cap Bren had wanted to separate them. No, this had all been Cindy's doing; she'd drawn up the schedule this week.

After Cap Bren caught her freedom bird home on July 1st, Cindy had taken over head nurse duties on Ward 2. True to her aloof personality to the very end, Cap Bren had wasted no time in sentimental goodbyes and "look me up when you get back to the World" trivialities. She'd made sure everyone knew she didn't want any going away parties planned for her. Everyone took her at her word; when she'd said goodbye to her colleagues, it had been like she was leaving after her shift.

On the afternoon of her last day, Cindy had been doing inventory in the supply closet when she heard a footfall behind her, followed by Cap Bren's no-nonsense voice. "Hey, Sweet, I hear you're adopting one of those little brats from the orphanage."

Cindy turned from her list, anger flaring, but just as she opened her mouth to defend An Li, she realized that Cap Bren's blue eyes were twinkling. She hadn't known they were *capable* of twinkling. She smiled. "That's right. You've met him. Little An Li...and he's not a brat," she couldn't help adding.

Cap Bren returned her smile. It wasn't *much* of a smile, more like an uncomfortable twisting of the lips, but Cindy recognized it for what it was. "Yeah, I know him. He's a cute little brat, but a brat all the same. They *all* are, aren't they? Little rugrats. Why anyone would *choose* to have them...or *adopt* them...is beyond me."

It wasn't Cindy's imagination; the twinkle was still there. The woman was *teasing* her. And Cindy couldn't help accepting the challenge. "Well, you're getting married to your Hawaiian prince. Before you know it, you might have a couple of rug-rats of your own running around that mansion of his."

Cap Bren shook her blonde head. "God forbid. I'm not exactly the motherly type."

Cindy's lips twitched. "Really? I hadn't noticed."

Cap Bren's not-quite-a-smile became a real one—and it made her an exceptionally beautiful woman. Too bad she didn't smile more often. "Sweet, you are the worst liar I've ever met. Anyway, I think it's great you're adopting An Li. You'll be a wonderful mother. It's just too bad all those children..." Her voice trailed away.

Cindy nodded. "Yeah...I wish that, too. But

thanks. It's not a done deal yet. Still waiting for final word from General Hopper."

Cap Bren turned to go. "It'll happen. If the general is behind it, he'll *make* it happen. Keep your head down, Sweet, and come back home in one piece." Her gaze fastened on Cindy, then swerved away. "You're a good nurse. It was an honor serving with you."

Cindy's throat tightened. Cap Bren turned and strode toward the door. Cindy found her voice before she disappeared. "Cap Bren! Brenda."

She paused and turned back. "What is it, Sweet?"

Cindy cleared her throat. "It was my honor to work with *you*. You taught me so much. Thank you."

Cap Bren's eyes, usually so hard and arctic, softened. For the briefest of moments, a semblance of emotion crossed her perfect features, and then it was gone. She gave a stiff nod. "You'd better get back to your inventory. We're running low on Foleys." She turned and headed out the door, but just as she reached the threshold, she paused and looked back. "Oh, I know all about that affair you've been carrying on with Ansgar. You two weren't fooling anybody."

Cindy opened her mouth to say…*what* she didn't know. Before she could speak, Cap Bren went on, "He's a good guy, Sweet, and he's crazy about you. Don't break his heart or I'll track you down in Indiana or Idaho…or *wherever* the hell you're from, and kick your ass. You got that?"

And she was gone.

Ω

Twenty days until David's DEROS. He would leave on the last day of July. Cindy tried to put it out of her mind. Tried not to think about what it would be like working on a ward without David. With sleeping in a bed without David. With living in Vietnam without David. Yes, it would only be for another month, but without him, that month would feel like a year. And who knew if, when she returned to the World, she'd ever see him again? He would be going back to Minnesota, and she'd be in Indiana. Anyway, even if that weren't true...even if they lived in the same state, nothing would be the same. Once back in his old life, he'd want to put Vietnam behind him...and everything that had to do with Vietnam. That meant *her*.

She wasn't so young and naïve to believe that what they felt for each other was true love, and *not* powered by the intensity of their situation here, the knowledge of the fragility of life, the raw emotion brought out by dealing with death every day, and the danger they were in from sapper attacks and incoming shells. Love affairs in the midst of danger couldn't help but be more intense; but what happened to that passion once the danger was gone?

When these thoughts weighed upon her, she had to find a way to turn them off. Her choices were slim: she could: A) immerse herself in work on the ward or B) make love to David, and give herself up to the warmth and sensation of his body against hers. C) A&B. She chose C.

But it was those times when he was working and she was off that played havoc with her mind. Then it wasn't so easy to turn off those thoughts. So, since she was now the head nurse, and answered to no one except Cruella, she'd taken to going back to the ward to unofficially help out while David was on duty. So much for her first week's schedule where she'd felt it wouldn't be fair—or subtle—if she'd had them working together on the same shift. But she'd quickly realized she just couldn't handle it. Instead of changing the schedule, though, she'd simply returned to the ward after a few hours of sleep. No one seemed to care, and for that, Cindy was grateful.

On the second week's schedule, she'd given up all pretense, and scheduled their shifts and time off together. No one said a word. When Cindy realized she was starting to count down the days, it had hit her like a sledgehammer. Their time was running out. And suddenly, every moment with David became precious; every sunrise meant one day less. Every sunset broke her heart.

On the 14th—17 days left—they made love with an intensity that verged upon desperation to the music of Joni Mitchell's "Blue" album. Afterwards, still inside her, he dropped his head to her neck, clutching her like he'd latched onto driftwood after a shipwreck, his body trembling. But when Cindy felt the wetness on her neck, she knew his convulsions had nothing to do with passion.

"David! Honey…" She tried to lift his face from her neck, but he clung to her. "Babe, what's wrong? You're scaring me!"

"I'm sorry," he murmured. His hands relaxed, and slowly, he lifted his head.

Cindy caught her breath at the sight of the tears tracking down his face. "Oh, sweetheart," she said softly. "What is it?"

He shook his head. "I just…have this feeling I can't shake…that after I get back home…I'm never going to see you again."

Cindy stared at him, biting her bottom lip. It would be so easy to say the right words—the ones he wanted to hear. *Don't be silly! Of course we'll see each other again. All we have to do is make it happen.* But she just couldn't do it. The one thing she'd learned in this year in Vietnam was to never make plans. She'd done that with Quin, and look what had happened.

She wasn't going to jinx things with David.

Gazing into his eyes, she drew his head down and kissed his lips softly. "We can't know what's going to happen in the future," she said. "Let's just enjoy what we have this very moment."

He stared at her, and after a long moment, nodded. He withdrew from her, and turning onto his side, he pulled her into his arms. She anchored her chin into the crook of his neck, her hand stroking the light carpet of hair on his muscular chest. Beneath her palm, she felt the strong, even beating of his heart. On the reel-to-reel stereo, Gordon Lightfoot began to sing "If You Could Read my Mind."

Long after David's grip on her eased, and his easy, rhythmical breathing told her he'd fallen asleep, Cindy lay awake, staring into the darkness. On her bedside table, the illuminated clock's hands moved past midnight.

Sixteen days.

CHAPTER THIRTY-FOUR

Nine days left. David had reached the status of a single-digit midget. Cindy didn't have much time to think about it that morning. She'd been on duty for only a few moments when the incoming call came. After the dust off settled onto the landing pad near the ER doors, rumors began to circulate about the wounded. They weren't Americans but captured VC who'd been rooted out of one of their infamous tunnels and shot up by American forces as they tried to make a run for it. Only four had survived, and two of them were hanging onto life by a gossamer thread.

When an OR tech rolled in the gurney with the first survivor who'd had a bullet removed from his chest, he shrugged when Cindy asked how many other patients they could expect. "One fucker died on the table; they put the other behind the yellow curtain. Hope he's dying *painfully*. The other one's still in surgery. He's more serious than this bastard. We'll probably have him to you in an hour."

David helped Cindy situate the VC prisoner toward the emptier part of the ward. He was still unconscious, but when he did come to, Cindy didn't want him upsetting the other patients. She checked his vitals, his chest tube and drainage tube. All looked good. An MP had been sent in to keep and eye on him, but since the patient was clearly unconscious, and would be for some time, he drew up a chair near the bed, propped his M16 against the wall and began to read a paperback novel, Louis L'Amour's *Galloway*. For a moment, Cindy considered saying something. *Hey, you're supposed to be guarding him, not lost in the wild, wild west.* But another glance at the torpid VC made her realize the absurdity of dressing down the MP. Let him have his escape from 'Nam. *God knows we can all use one.*

She went on to the next patient, making her rounds with the brain-numbing routine of checking vitals, hanging IVs, suctioning traches, changing dressings, and in some cases, exchanging banter with soldiers who were recovering from their injuries and soon to be sent on to other wards. Most of them would return to the field; some, the luckier ones would be going home.

Across the length of the ward, Cindy watched David making his rounds, doing the exact same patient care duties as she. It seemed unfair; he had so much knowledge and skill, yet, he was making a fraction of what she did. He stood at the bed of Pfc. Ortello M. Mitchell, a nineteen-year-old black boy from Mississippi who'd lost half his upper face in a mortar attack. Amazingly, the teenager's spirits were high, and had been since he'd come to after surgery. When he'd first learned about his disfigurement, his remaining brown eye had dimmed only a moment, and then his smile returned as he proclaimed in a melting Mississippi drawl, "Glory be to God that's *all* I lost. I reckon I can still be of service to the Lord with what I've got left."

Cindy had smiled and nodded, but inside, she was thinking *Uh huh. You just wait until the shock wears off, hon. In a day or two, you'll be singing a different song.* But she'd been wrong. Private Mitchell never wavered in his positive attitude. Every time she went to check on him, he greeted her with a toothy smile and a "How's my favorite nurse today?"

When she'd commented to David about his almost too good to be true attitude, even suggesting they should get someone from Psych down to talk to him, he'd looked at her like *she* was crazy. "Ortello doesn't need a psych evaluation," he said calmly. "He's the most together guy I've ever met. His father and grandfather are ministers. And that's what he's planning to be, too."

Cindy didn't get the connection. "Yeah, so? You think ministers don't go off their rockers?"

David gave her an odd look, and then said, "He doesn't need psych, Cindy. Ortello has faith in God's plan for him."

Feeling an uncustomary irritation at David's brush-off of her suggestion, she snapped, "Well, Dr. Ansgar, if that's your *professional* opinion…"

The blush that spread over David's face immediately made her regret her flippant remark. She touched his shoulder. "I'm sorry, David. I didn't mean that."

He moved away from her but not before she saw the hurt in his blue eyes.

Damn it…why am I such a bitch?

That night she tried to make it up to him, apologizing again and again before and after lovemaking, but she was still haunted by the memory of the hurt on his face. He'd accepted her first apology, being the consummate gentleman that he was, but later, just before they fell asleep, he said quietly, "Do you believe in God, Cindy?"

Taken aback, it took her a moment to find a response. "Well…yeah, I guess. I mean…I *used* to. I guess I'm not so sure anymore." When he didn't reply, she went on, "It's hard, you know.

When you see some of the things we have to deal with…I have to admit, my faith isn't as strong as it used to be." Still no response. If his arms hadn't tightened around her, she would've thought he'd fallen asleep. "It's not like my parents were big church goers, anyway. When Joanie and I were little, Mom used to drop us off at the local Baptist church for Bible school. But when my parents got divorced and we moved to Indiana, Mom didn't go to church, and didn't make us go. What about you, David? Do *you* believe in God?"

"I do," he said quietly. "And this year in Vietnam has made my faith stronger."

He went on to tell her that his father was a Lutheran minister, and so was his older brother, Finn. His mother was the church pianist and head of the women's fellowship group. His younger sister, Ingrid, ran a youth ministry at Finn's church in the next town.

"My plan was to follow in Pop's and Finn's footsteps when I come home. Become a minister like them…find my own little parish somewhere in Minnesota, hopefully, not too far from Bethel…"

Cindy's heart sank. *Great. Another whopping difference between us. He wants to be a preacher, and I'm practically an atheist. And just when I was starting to think there might be a future for us.*

"But you remember what you told me after we saved that boy with the RPG in his abdomen? You said I should use the GI bill to go to medical school." He paused, and then said, "You still think I should do that, Cindy?"

Cindy turned in his arms and took his face in her hands. In the dim light of dawn, she gazed into his eyes. "I think you'd be a wonderful doctor. But...I think you'd be a wonderful minister, too. David, whatever you decide to do, you're going to be fantastic at it."

And that, she was sure of. She watched him now as he laughed down at Ortello Mitchell. He was just one of the many patients who loved and respected David. Not to mention the nurses and doctors. Every last one of them would choose to have David at their side during a dicey situation. And it hadn't escaped Cindy's notice that all the FNG nurses who rotated in always immediately developed huge crushes on him. Not that he'd noticed. Cindy knew she was the only nurse who existed for him beyond a professional level.

The double doors leading to surgery burst open and the same lanky corpsman Cindy had spoken to earlier pushed in a patient on a gurney. The other surviving VC, she assumed. David and one of the newer nurses, Kay, were closer to the doors, so they went to accept him. Seeing that they had everything under control, Cindy decided to check on the first VC patient. It had been about a half-hour since he'd been brought in. He'd probably be coming to soon.

At his bedside, she glanced down at the prisoner. His eyes were closed, his face bloodless, but his respirations were even. She checked his pulse and blood pressure. Pulse was thready and B/P a bit on the low side, but that wasn't unusual for a GSW recovering from surgery. Still, it was odd he showed no signs of awakening yet. Cindy examined the tube inserted into the wall of his chest and saw it needed milking to make sure it was stripped of blood clots. She bent over to get started.

It happened quickly and without warning. She felt a movement and heard a guttural growl. Gut instinct propelled her backwards, but too late, she saw the VC lunging at her with a pair of sharp scissors, his black eyes murderous. Cindy shrieked and again, instinct set in. She yanked at his chest tube with every ounce of her strength. The scissors clattered to the floor as the VC screamed and fell back onto his bed, fresh blood oozing from the incision where the chest tube had been inserted. Cindy stared at him in shock, her heart pounding. She heard shouts behind her and footsteps scrambling toward her. The MP appeared, leveling his M16 at the prisoner. He looked as shaken as Cindy felt. Reaction had set in and she'd begun to shake.

"*What happened? You okay?*" David grabbed her by the shoulders, his eyes frantic. On the bed, the VC writhed, screaming out in Vietnamese. The other nurses and corpsmen gathered around. Cindy stared at David, nausea churning in her stomach.

"He tried to kill me!" Her gaze focused on the scissors on the floor. "With my own scissors!"

The nurses all carried scissors in their front left pockets. When had he grabbed them? And how had he done it without her knowing? David stared at her, and slowly, his expression changed from concern to pure rage. He released her and bent down to pick up the scissors. Before anyone could stop him, he had the VC by his thatch of black hair, the tip of the scissors at his pulsating throat. "You *fucking bastard*! I'm going to *kill* you!"

"David, *no*!" Cindy screamed.

The scissors pierced into the prisoner's skin, and a trickle of blood appeared on the man's throat. David's hand shook as he glared into the VC's panicked eyes.

"*Release him, Corpsman*!" the MP ordered, but in a voice so ineffective that David probably didn't even hear him.

"You don't want to do this, Dave," one of the corpsman said behind her.

"Jackson is right, David," Cindy said softly. She was afraid to touch him, afraid any movement would make him thrust the scissors into the man's throat. She didn't know why she cared. The creep had tried to kill her. But she just knew David wouldn't be able to live with himself if he took a life.

His hand trembled on the scissors. Cindy felt the tension in his body. "David," she urged, keeping her voice low. "You're not a killer. Please give me the scissors."

She felt the change come over him. Slowly, he withdrew the scissors from the man's neck, and with a disdainful jerk, released the man's hair. He backed away from the bed and turned to Cindy. The rage had disappeared from his face, and now he just looked shell-shocked. Cindy held out her hand for the scissors. Meeting her gaze, he gave them to her, and then he turned and strode to the nurse's station.

Cindy placed the scissors back into the slit in her front pocket, and then turned to Corpsman Jackson, a lanky red-haired boy from Illinois. "Jackson, get some restraints on the prisoner. *Both* prisoners." She fastened a cold gaze on the MP. "And you. Do your job."

His face reddened. "Yes, Ma'am. I'm sorry, Ma'am, I---"

Cindy turned and walked away, leaving him still stuttering out excuses. She had to know if David was okay. She found him sitting at the desk in the nurse's station, his head cradled in his hands. She touched his shoulder. "You okay?"

He looked up at her, his eyes wounded. "If he had killed you, I would've torn him apart with my bare hands. The only thing that saved him was that I knew you were okay. I never knew I could feel rage like that."

Cindy reached out and touched his lean, stubbled jaw, uncaring if anyone was watching them. "You're only human, David."

He gazed up at her. "I'm just glad…" He swallowed hard, and Cindy knew he was holding back tears. "…you're alright."

"Uh…Captain? I'm sorry…" The voice came from behind her.

She turned and saw the MP, a look of abject misery and embarrassment on his face. Before she could speak, he went on, "I know you told me to watch the gook, but…well, Ma'am…I just need to…well, relieve myself."

Cindy held back a sigh. The guy looked so mortified that she couldn't help but feel sorry for him. "*Go,* for God's sake!"

She'd barely got the words out before all hell broke loose on the ward. Screams and shouting, one of them a female. One of the nurses! *Oh, Jesus Christ! What now?* The MP whipped around and ran toward the sounds. Cindy and David were right behind him.

The screams were coming from the area of the VC's bed. The first thing Cindy saw was the new nurse, Kay, her brown eyes wide with horror, sobbing in near hysterics. Jackson held her, cradling her brown head to his chest. Next to the bed stood Pfc. Ortello M. Mitchell, grinning, looking like he'd just been awarded a gold medal in the Olympics. He held a Bowie knife in one hand, still dripping blood. When he saw Cindy, his grin widened.

"The Lord told me to do it," he said. "Glory hallelujah!"

Beside her, she felt David stiffen. She looked from Private Mitchell to the VC on the bed. The sheets were stained red from the gaping wound that went from ear to ear across his throat.

Next to her, the hapless MP drew in a deep breath and muttered, "Oh, shit."

CHAPTER THIRTY-FIVE

Two days left.

And this one was almost over, so really, she should be thinking *one day left*. She and David had got off-duty this morning at 0700, but instead of going back to their quarters to sleep, they'd headed over to the motor pool and found an off-duty sergeant willing to serve as an armed escort to the orphanage—for a price, of course. It would be David's last visit with An Li. Cindy had known saying goodbye to the little boy was going to be tough for him. They'd established a real bond in the last few months. As for An Li, she wasn't sure if the youngster really understood that he might never see David again.

They'd told the boy nothing about the possibility of adoption. Word still hadn't come down from the General, and with each day that passed without news, Cindy's hope grew a little dimmer. So, it really might be—probably *would* be—the last time David ever saw An Li.

The day had flown by. David had stopped by the PX before he'd gone on duty the night before and bought the boy a soccer ball. All morning he and Cindy had kicked the ball around with An Li and the other children. An Li had shown an exceptional talent, despite his young age. Maybe his father had played soccer, Cindy thought, watching him maneuver the ball better than the seven and eight-year-olds.

1500 hours arrived all too soon—nap-time for the orphans, and time for David to say goodbye. He hugged An Li, tears glimmering in his eyes. Cindy took in the sight of David's flaxen head nestling against An Li's black one, and her eyes burned. She couldn't imagine being in his shoes—or combat boots–saying goodbye to the little boy they'd come to love. Yet, in another month, she could well *be* in his combat boots. It didn't bear thinking about. She *wouldn't* think about it. Just like she wouldn't think about the fast-approaching moment on the flight line when she'd have to say goodbye to David.

"*Oww!* You squeezing me too hard, Daveed!" An Li struggled to get out of David's grip. In the months since Cindy had started visiting him, the child had grown fluent in English. It boggled her mind—how smart he was.

David reluctantly let go. "I'm sorry, bud. It's your fault, though. You're just so darn squeezable." He gave An Li's belly a tickle.

The little boy giggled. "Tickle *more!*"

David drew away from him, a sad smile on his face. "No, bud. It's time for your nap. I've got to…say goodbye now." His voice cracked a little on the goodbye.

An Li rolled onto his sleeping mat, clutching his soccer ball to his skinny chest. He rubbed his eyes, a clear sign he was ready for his nap. "You come tomorrow, Daveed?"

Cindy's heart panged. Poor kid still didn't get it. They'd been preparing him for this for a couple of weeks, and today had mentioned several times that David was going home to America.

David swallowed hard, his solemn gaze connecting with Cindy's. She ran a hand through An Li's silky black hair. "Sweetie, David has all kinds of things he has to do on the post tomorrow. You know… before he gets on the big airplane to fly home to America. That's why he came to say goodbye to you today."

An Li blinked sleepily, a soft smile creeping over his lips. "You take freedom bird?" he murmured.

"That's right," David said, covering Cindy's hand on the boy's head. "My freedom bird home." A tear crept down his stubbled cheek, and he made no attempt to wipe it away.

The lump in Cindy's throat grew. *Oh, God! How am I ever going to say goodbye to this man?*

An Li yawned and rolled over onto his side, curling up in the fetal position. His petal-like lips parted in a soft sigh as he closed his eyes. David leaned over and kissed his tawny cheek. As he drew away, the little boy spoke again, his eyes still closed. "I want to go on freedom bird with Daveed."

Tears tracked down Cindy's face as she leaned down to kiss An Li. David was already on his feet. She got up and he took her hand. They silently made their way out of the old French orphanage. In the courtyard, the sergeant sat in the Jeep parked under a banana tree, reading a paperback. Instead of heading toward him, David took Cindy's elbow and guided her to an old stone fountain that probably hadn't seen a drop of water in ten years—except for what fell out of the sky during this time of year--monsoon season. Today had been unusual because it had rained only early this morning. Which meant they were due for a downpour—and it would probably happen as they drove in the open Jeep back to the post.

But David, apparently, wasn't ready to go yet. When they reached the fountain, he circled around it, leading her to where they were hidden from the sergeant. Grasping her shoulders, he turned her to face him, gazing at her through moist eyes. Something in his expression made Cindy's heart beat faster.

"You've never told me you loved me," he said

quietly.

Cindy opened her mouth to respond, but he pressed his fingers to her lips, giving his head a slight shake. "No. Let me finish. I don't want you to say it until you're ready. I love *you*, Cindy, and I think…I'm pretty sure…you love me, too. And I love that little boy in there. I know we don't know if the adoption will go through or not. I hope to hell it does. Because that little guy needs a family. Not just a mother, Cindy. A *family*. A mom and a dad…and maybe someday, a brother and sister." His hands tightened on her shoulders; his blue eyes blazed into hers. "I want to be that man. I want to ask you to marry me, Cindy. But I'm not going to do it now. You know why? Because I know what's going on in that beautiful brain of yours. You're afraid if you admit you love me, the plane is going to get shot down before we leave Vietnam airspace. I don't know if you think God is out to get you or if you're some kind of bad luck charm." He shook his head, his jaw tightening. "I'm going to prove to you that's not true. I'm not Gary, and I'm definitely not Quin. I'm the man who is going to love you for the rest of your life. I'm the man who wants to grow old with you."

Cindy blinked back tears. "David, I---"

"No, I'm not finished. I know what else you're thinking. Even if I make it back home in one piece, you're going to start doubting what we have. You'll be thinking…*how can he know he's in love with me? He's in love with the idea of love. It's the extraordinary circumstances we're under here...the living on the edge...the romance, the danger.* But I'm telling you now, Cindy Sweet, it's not that for me. I love *you.* I've loved you from the first moment you walked onto the ward, looking shell-shocked from your first encounter with Cruella." A sheepish smile crossed his face. "Okay, so maybe that's an exaggeration; maybe I was just attracted to you. But that attraction turned to love that night when you broke into tears, telling me how that soldier died on your watch." He finally ran out of breath and paused.

"Can I speak now?" Cindy asked.

"No, you cannot. Still not finished." He smiled, took a deep breath and went on. "So, that's why I'm not going to ask you to marry me now. But this is what I'm going to do. When you step off your freedom bird at Travis Air Force Base on September 5th, I'm going to be there to meet you, and *that's* where I'm going to ask you to marry me, Cynthia Marie Sweet. So, just prepare yourself for that."

Without giving her a chance to respond, he took her head in his hands and planted a deep, passionate kiss on her. As if on cue, the skies opened up, and the monsoon rains pelted down.

A few minutes later, soaked to the skin, they walked to the Jeep, arms entwined. The sergeant glared at them, probably wondering what had taken them so long. They climbed in the Jeep, and David started the engine. Before he shifted into gear, he glanced at her and smiled. Cindy felt like an invisible hand had reached into her chest and given her heart a squeeze. He looked so adorable with his hair all wet and eyelashes spiked with rain droplets.

And she realized something. If he *had* asked her to marry him, she might well have said yes.

CHAPTER THIRTY-SIX

Wet and bedraggled, Cindy walked down the corridor of the nurse's quarters, still thinking about David's "almost" proposal. She smiled. For the first time, it seemed like a future with him could be a real possibility. But he was smart—delaying the proposal until she was back in the World. That way, if he changed his mind, he simply wouldn't be at Travis when she arrived. And she would graciously let him off the hook, knowing she'd been right all along—that what they had was fueled by the extreme circumstances here.

She'd understand—but face it, her heart would be broken. Something had happened in these past weeks. And the turning point had been that night at Cahoney's—the night the fight had broken out.

She still remembered the exact moment she'd fallen in love with David—he'd been leaning against the bar, waiting for his drinks; he'd turned and smiled at her. And she'd fallen. It wasn't the kind of wild, head-spinning love she'd felt for Quin. That had been like a hurricane, sweeping her off her feet and taking her for a tumultuous, exhilarating ride. Nor was it the kind of wide-eyed, innocent, though heartfelt, love she'd felt for Gary. The love she felt for David was calm and encompassing, like the eye of the storm. A safe harbor.

Oh, dear God. How will I get through this last month without him?

A door opened down the corridor, and Creedence Clearwater Revival blared from the room, singing "Susie-Q." A glance at her watch revealed it was almost 1630 hours. David had headed back to his hooch to shower. They were meeting Jenny, Simon and some of the other nurses and corpsmen at Cahoneys for his going away party. Cindy felt almost resentful that she had to share David with others even if it were only for a couple of hours. But that was a couple of hours she'd never get back. Her heart panged. This time tomorrow, he'd probably be landing in the Philippines for refueling.

A woman in a bathrobe stepped out into the hall—Sarah, a nurse from Ward 5. She saw Cindy and smiled. "Hey, I put a message on your door a few minutes ago. It's from General Hopper's office."

Cindy's heart dropped to her toes. "Oh, thanks, Sarah." She was amazed at how calm her voice sounded.

"Hope it's good news," Sarah said, passing her to head for the showers. "See you at Cahoney's."

Clearly, everyone in the hospital knew about An Li and her request to adopt him. Sometimes, living on the post felt like Mayberry. Heart pounding, Cindy stared at the pink message note taped to her door. **Call Gen. Hopper. 76303.**

She walked to the phone at the end of the hall. *Please, please, please, please.* She visualized An Li's sweet little face, his endearing smile, his almond-shaped, gamin eyes twinkling with mischief only a four-year-old could get away with. *Please God, I love him so much.*

She dialed with trembling fingers.

"General Hopper's office."

"This is Captain Sweet, returning the general's call." Again, she found herself amazed at how calm she sounded.

As if this were just an ordinary phone call, and not one that could change the course of her life.

Ω

When Cindy saw David waiting for her outside the nurse's quarters, she burst into tears. His expression changed from a welcoming smile to concern. She ran into his arms and nestled against him, breathing in the scent of Palmolive soap and Old Spice aftershave.

"Oh, babe, what is it?" He kissed her forehead, then drew back to meet her gaze.

She smiled at him, her eyes still blurred with tears. "He's ou…mine, David. I got the call from General Hopper. The adoption has gone through." She'd almost said, "he's ours." That's how she thought of An Li. As *theirs*. But it was presumptuous to say that. Anything could happen between now and the time she stepped off that plane at Travis.

David's face sagged in relief. "Oh, sweetheart!" He grabbed her in a bear hug. "Didn't I tell you? I *knew* it would happen. I prayed for it. God is good!" He cupped her face in his hands and gave her a soft, urgent kiss. Then he drew away, and the love in his eyes warmed her from head to toe. "Now, we'll be a real family. You, me, An Li…and all the other babies we'll have." He grinned. "Come on. Tonight we really have something to celebrate."

Ω

Three hours.

Cindy had been calm since awakening at 0600. Even ushering David out of her room, knowing the next time she saw him would be as he said his goodbyes at the hospital before leaving for Bien Hoa hadn't broken her. Sometime in the night, lying sheltered in his arms after the storm of goodbye lovemaking, she'd realized she had to be strong for him. He was catching his Freedom Bird home today! He'd probably been counting down the days since he'd first stepped foot on Vietnam soil, just as she had. How could she let him see her heartbreak? Her fear that she'd never see him again? It wouldn't be fair to ruin this for him.

And she wouldn't. She'd be a big girl and put on a happy face for him. After all, she was a mother now. Well, *almost* a mother. It helped to know that when she caught her own Freedom Bird home, she'd have An Li with her. Even if David realized that their romance had been simply that—a romance that had flared under the extraordinary conditions of war, only to burn out once he'd returned to normal life, at least she'd still have An Li.

All she had to do was get through the next hours. And then the next days...thirty-five of them, to be exact, until September 5th, her own DEROS. It would be a long month and four days, but the welcome news she'd received from General Hopper yesterday had given her strength. She *would* get through it.

And then as she was tying the laces of her combat boots, a song came on the AFN-- American Forces Network—that froze her fingers and immediately blurred her eyes with tears. Not one of the myriad of songs she associated with Quin—*Cinnamon Girl… Incense & Peppermints…Never my Love…*Bert Sommer's *Road to Travel.* This one, she'd heard a million times and had never thought much about it, but now, on this morning, she knew it would forever make her think of David. Peter, Paul and Mary's "Leaving on a Jet Plane."

She cried until it was over, then wiped her tears, ran a brush through her tousled bob, then left her room to meet David at the hospital.

Ω

Five minutes.

"It's time, babe," David said, his hand tightening on hers.

Cindy swallowed hard to try to dislodge the thickening lump in her throat. *I'm not going to cry…I'm not going to cry.* She'd managed to stay composed since she'd met him at the hospital where he'd said his final goodbyes to the staff. She'd remained calm through the short drive to Bien Hoa. She'd been stoic as they stood silently in the terminal while soldiers milled around them, waiting for the final call to board the 727 that had arrived earlier, vomiting out green troops wearing various expressions of resignation, bravado, anxiety and outright terror. A few of them were women, new nurses. Cindy recognized their fear, remembered the moment she'd first step foot in this place. A life-time ago. She didn't even know that naïve young girl anymore.

The call came again over the intercom for the outgoing troops to Line up for boarding. Cindy's heart plunged. It was really happening. *He was leaving.*

David turned to her, clasping her hands. She drew in a sharp breath at the sight of his blue eyes shimmering with tears. *Oh, crap. Not fair! If you cry, how will I ever hold it together?* She felt the lump in her throat grow thicker, threatening to cut off her air supply.

He squeezed her hands. "Thirty-five days," he said, his voice husky. "And I'll be waiting for you in another airport. You take care of yourself, Cindy. Promise me you won't do any med-caps, that you'll stay on post, don't take any unnecessary risks. I don't know what I'd do if..." His voice broke.

Somehow, Cindy managed to speak through her choking throat. "Don't worry about me, David. I'll be fine." She didn't mention the obvious reason why she couldn't possibly do what he asked of her. An Li. She *had* to leave post to see him. He was her child now, and she wouldn't neglect him.

As if reading her mind, David gave a slight smile, smoothing her hair away from her face. "I know you'll go to the orphanage, but promise me you won't go alone. Get Larry from the motor pool to protect you. Just don't go off to

Saigon…and *definitely* don't go to Cahoney's." His smile widened, incongruous with the tears in his eyes. "I don't want you anywhere near some of those crazy GIs who hang out there."

"Come on, Ansgar, time to go!" shouted a sergeant, ushering out the last of the troops. "That bird ain't gonna wait forever!"

Cindy's heart skipped a beat. *This was it.* "David, I…" Her voice drained away as her nerve faltered. She bit her bottom lip, and then went on, "Be careful, David. And write me…if you can."

He cupped her face in his hands and kissed her, a surging kiss that left her head reeling. She clung to him, drinking in his essence. Impossible that within moments, he'd be gone. He drew away, his gaze sweeping her face, as if he were trying to memorize every freckle. "And remember this, Cindy Sweet…I love you."

He released her and turned to go. Cindy watched him stride away, lean and handsome in his jeans and light blue oxford shirt. With all the animosity for troops at the airports these days, wearing uniforms home was strongly discouraged. Ironic—the difference between the reception of the boys from WWII and the troops from Vietnam. *No ticker tape parades for any of us.*

Her heart began to pound as David moved toward the airliner. *No! Too fast!* She'd thought she had more time. That's why she hadn't told him…but no, she hadn't *intended* to tell him. Why put that pressure on him? If he changed his mind after he returned to the pastoral green pastures of Minnesota…if he decided to return to Ingrid, his high school sweetheart–whom she imagined to be a buxom Norwegian blonde, ready to crank out babies and simultaneously serve pot-luck dinners at Wednesday night church suppers–Cindy didn't want to make it difficult for him. And if he *were* to show up at Travis, she wanted it to be because he really loved her and saw a future for them— not because of three little words she'd muttered as he walked away.

She watched him step out the door. Her heart sank. She closed her eyes. *Too late…too late…too late.*

But it wasn't. Not yet.

Her combat boots grew wings. She raced after him, her heart thundering, and burst through the door. The morning sunlight pierced her eyes. A cacophony of noise assaulted her—choppers whopping, jets shrilling, people shouting, sergeants yelling orders—and in the distance, the inevitable artillery fire.

When her eyes finally adjusted to the brightness, she saw David. He was halfway across the tarmac, heading for the gigantic Pan Am jetliner on the flight line. A stream of troops were inching their way up the rolling staircase and disappearing inside.

"*David!*" Cindy screamed as loud as she could,

knowing he'd never hear her in all this tumult. Suddenly, it was imperative she get to him before he boarded that plane. She knew she'd never forgive herself if she let him go like this. She ran, again depending on the imaginary wings attached to her combat boots. "*David!*"

His step faltered, and she knew that somehow, he'd heard. Maybe his God really *was* listening. She called out to him again, wanting to make sure it wasn't a pebble in his boot or a muscle cramp that had made him hesitate.

But no, he stopped and looked over his shoulder. The GI behind him almost body-slammed him. Even from a distance, Cindy saw the smile cross David's face. He dropped his duffle bag, side-stepped around the GI and broke into a run. Her heart thudded. The look of love on his handsome face was more than she could bear, and she burst into tears. And she didn't care.

He reached her and gathered her into his arms, burrowing his fingers into her hair.

"I love you," she gasped, her tears wetting his shirt. "I love you, I love you, David. I do. I'm sorry I couldn't tell you." She drew away to look into his moist blue eyes. "But I really *do* love you."

He smiled. "I know. I never doubted it for a moment." He gave her a hard, urgent kiss then released her. "I'll see *you* at Travis on September 5th."

He turned and strode off toward the plane, a bounce in his step that hadn't been there before. Trembling, she watched as he climbed the steps, reached the door, and then turned to look back at her. Even from that distance, she could almost feel his gaze burning into her soul. He lifted a hand, gave her a wave, then turned and disappeared into the jetliner.

CHAPTER THIRTY-SEVEN

February 2011
Memphis, Tennessee

Someone is playing a cruel joke on me.

Cindy sat at her computer, her eyes blurry with fatigue. She couldn't draw her gaze away from his name. *Ryan Paul Quinlan.* Who could possibly hate her that much? Not anyone she'd known in 'Nam—that was for sure. Well, except for Cruella—Colonel Kairos. But she'd died some seventeen years ago.

Ignore it. Why dredge up the past? But something—some small shred of hope—made her click on the message.

Cinnamon, I'm sorry I let you think I was dead. At the time, I thought it was for the best...

Cindy lurched up from her chair, bile rising in her throat. It felt like an icy hand had reached into her mid-section and taken a death grip on her stomach. *Quin is alive! He's <u>alive</u>! But how can that <u>be</u>?*

Struggling to catch her breath, she stumbled to the window that looked out on the front street of their cul de sac. The sleet had turned to snow—unusual for Memphis. In some part of her brain, she felt concern for David, hoping he'd made it to the hospital safely. He was working his last day shift before they left for the cruise. This time next week, they'd be soaking up the sun in St. Maarten.

But…oh, God. Quin!

Trembling, she turned back to the computer. No way on earth could she ignore the message now. *Cinnamon.* He'd been the only one who ever called her Cinnamon. She sank into her chair, and scrolled down to read on.

I'll try to explain without writing **War and Peace, Volume 2**.

Cindy couldn't help but smile through the tears that misted her eyes. That line was *so* Quin. She began to believe…

When the chopper went down, I was thrown clear, but that's when my luck ran out. A piece of burning wreckage hit me, taking half my face off. Before the good guys could airlift me out, Charlie got me. They put me in one of their shithole hospitals…guess I should be thankful for that, though. Otherwise, I would've died in one of their POW camps. Needless to say, the medical care was a step above Civil War standards, and when I finally healed, my face…well, don't want to gross you out, Cinnamon, but my face would've made Frankenstein look like Brad Pitt…well, half of it, anyway. So when the war ended in 1973, and they exchanged me for a NVA prisoner, I went back to Texas.

I wanted like hell to contact you, Cinnamon. But I just couldn't do that to you. It wasn't just my face, you know. I was a different man. Not the guy you fell in love with. Being in a NVA POW camp does that to you. I'm not going to go into detail, but it takes the humanity out of you. I just knew you'd be better off thinking I was dead. But I never forgot you, Cinnamon. I even called your family home once…guess it was in 1974. Your mom answered…I guess it was your mom. I got so far as to ask for you…told her I was an old friend from 'Nam. She said you were living in Minnesota…got married to a guy from there. She volunteered to give me your number, but I hung up without giving her my name.

So…why am I contacting you now after all these years? Did you see that movie "The Bucket List?" Came out a few years ago. Well, Cinnamon, you're on my bucket list. Seeing you again. Listen, I don't want a pity party or anything. But last month I was diagnosed with Non-Hodgkin's lymphoma. The doc says I can expect to live maybe three to five years if I do the chemo. Not sure I want to go that route. The wife and kids want me to, but…oh, hell…I'm not going to get into this.

I just want to see you. I know you're married…yeah, I read all about you on Facebook. You know, you really should make your page private; there's a lot of crazies out there. I liked David. He was a good guy. Told you he was in love with you, didn't I? It's a curse…being right all the time.

Anyway, Lynn and I…that's my wife, Lynn…we're going to DC in April to visit the Vietnam Memorial. Another thing on my bucket list. And I was wondering if you've ever been there? I've heard it's healing—and God knows we can all use some healing, right?

So…give it some thought, Cinnamon. I'd love to see you—and David, of course. But if you can't do it…I'll understand. Maybe we can just be friends on Facebook.

Take care,

Quin

Cindy didn't know how long she sat there at the computer. Or how long the tears streamed down her face. But finally, she reached for a tissue and dried her eyes. She picked up her Iphone and touched David's name in her contacts file.

He answered immediately. "Hey, babe, what's up?"

At the sound of his familiar, loving voice, Cindy smiled through fresh tears. "What do you think about taking a few days off and going to Washington in April?"

CHAPTER THIRTY-EIGHT

April 2011

Cindy inhaled the sweet fragrance of cherry blossoms, pausing for a moment before entering the final area of the Vietnam Memorial—the one she'd saved for last. It had been emotional walking down the endless column of black granite engraved with the names of men she'd known and loved, nursed and consoled. Gary…Charley…and so many other names unknown to her, but belonging to boys with whom she'd spent their final moments. Just walking along that wall brought it all back.

She and David had stood, hand-in-hand, gazing at Charley's name etched into the granite. *Charles E. Moss.* Closing her eyes, she could see his friendly, smiling face and gentle brown eyes. She wondered if his wife had remarried. His children probably had kids of their own by now. Sometime later, she found Gary's name. *Gary R. McCartney.* And in her mind's eye, she was back on the dock of a small lake in Plainfield, Indiana, falling in love with the blond, blue-eyed soldier who'd entered her life on a hot night in August of 1965.

Birdsong surrounded her now as she stood at the entrance to the enclosure surrounded by beech and maple trees. She stared at the bronze statue sculpted by Glenna Goodacre. The Vietnam Women's Memorial.

Her heart pounded and perspiration dampened her neck under the collar of her short-sleeved cotton blouse. It was unseasonably warm in Washington DC this spring, more like May than April. But it wasn't the temperature making her feel light-headed and heart-fluttery, nor was it the thyroid medication or even the hot flashes she still sometimes suffered. It was this trip down Memory Lane.

That's why she'd put it off for so long. She just wasn't sure she wanted to go there...to go *back.* But when the Facebook "friend request" from Quin came out of the blue in February, she knew she could no longer postpone the inevitable. And her family had been in full support. David had arranged the trip for the upcoming Cherry Blossom Festival. But if it hadn't been for Quin, Cindy would've waited until fall when the nation's capitol was cooler and less crowded. Her heart panged at the thought that he might not make it until fall if he didn't choose to have chemo. *The stubborn idiot!*

For years, she'd wanted to go to the memorial, but had never really pursued it. After all, why dredge up the past? It had taken her decades to put it all behind her. For the first few years after her return to "the World," she'd bolted for cover every time she heard a car backfire. The sound of an approaching helicopter had turned her insides to jelly. The stench of Napalm would sometimes come out of the blue—all in her head, of course, but stinging her nostrils all the same, and she'd have to fight back nausea. But finally, through the years, those memories of 'Nam—good and bad—receded, became like an old movie seen on cable late at night. Belonging to a different life, a different person.

Yet, here she stood, and the first sight of the statue—the three nurses surrounded by sandbags, one of them cradling a wounded soldier—brought tears to her eyes. She stepped onto the red granite terrace and moved slowly toward the memorial. Slowly, not because she was 62–elderly, she supposed, by society's standards, but thankfully, still healthy and in good shape, thanks to yoga classes and work-outs at the local gym—but because she was almost afraid to go closer, afraid she couldn't contain the emotion welling inside her. Others strolled around—people who'd surely think that the tall, silver-haired lady was going to have a nervous breakdown and have to be carted away by the men in white.

She stopped in front of the nurse cradling the wounded soldier, and gazed at the woman's anguished face. She recognized that expression, had seen it on the faces of Rosalie, on Jenny, on Shyanne…even on Cap Bren when the hardened nurse hadn't known anyone was watching. And she knew she'd worn that very expression herself. Amazing that a woman who hadn't been there had captured it so perfectly.

Cindy had researched Glenna Goodacre and the memorial on the internet, and she knew that the sculptor's intent for this wounded soldier had been that he was a survivor. His name wouldn't have ended up on that black wall; this monument was for the living. She studied his bandaged face, and the memories of those who'd survived their wounds and gone home drifted through her mind.

She remembered faces, not names—the blond, blue-eyed boy from Massachusetts, a double amputee who always wore a smile and loved to tell knock-knock jokes. The boy from Tennessee, left a quadriplegic from a bullet wound in the spine. And the one she remembered most—Patrick Cummings from Stowe, Vermont, who'd lost half his face, an arm and a leg. He'd survived—a miracle, really—but how had he fared when he returned home? She'd always worried about how he'd adapted to life back in Vermont. He'd been terrified his girlfriend wouldn't be able to handle his deformity. So many stories with no endings.

Tears welled again, and this time, she didn't bother to try to hold them back. They tracked down her face as she moved around the statue. Now she stood in front of the nurse looking up to the heavens. What was she looking for? An incoming dust off? Or perhaps for God or a guardian angel to take her away from the horror of war?

Wiping a tear away, she walked on. Stopped at the kneeling nurse who stared forlornly at the helmet in her hand. No confusion here. This was the nurse who mourned the dead. All the ones they'd tried to save, but couldn't. Oh, those faces were vivid in Cindy's memory. The boy from Conway, South Carolina—her very first expectant, the one she'd left to die alone while she ran his blood to the lab. The one whose last request had been for a Coke—forbidden by policy, but nonetheless, delivered to him in an act of defiance. The boy Stalik had condemned to death by ordering the bottle of Ringers. Of course, he would've died anyway, but she'd never been able to shake the feeling of being an accessory to murder.

Those eternally young boys. Not silver-haired and brittle-boned like she was. No worrying about high cholesterol and Type II diabetes for them. No looking back at children and grandchildren and retirement from jobs they'd hated—or loved. No worrying about deteriorating funds in 401K plans or thinking forward to burial plots and funeral insurance to take the burden off their children. No experiencing the joy of graduations, and weddings and the births of grandchildren. No growing old with the one they loved. No wondering how they'd possibly live on if their mate died first.

What was it all for?

The sound of laughter drifted toward her, and like a swirl of autumn leaves, a group of school children stepped into the enclosure, gathering around the statue. A young, harried-looking teacher tried to quiet them, but the kids were too excited, happy to be on a field trip on this beautiful spring day filled with the perfume of cherry blossoms. From the looks of them, they were eight and nine-year olds, and Cindy knew from her work at St. Jude's Children's Hospital that this was not an age easy to quiet. Even an eight-year-old sick child could be boisterous. Another teacher, older by the looks of her, arrived, and clapped her hands sharply. The group immediately grew silent.

"This is a place that demands respect," she said with the no-nonsense tone of a seasoned teacher. "No less respect than the wall we just left, ladies and gentlemen. This is a memorial to the women who served in Vietnam. They were every bit as important—and courageous—as the men who fought and died there. When you look at this statue, I want you to remember one thing. Without the service of these women—the nurses—that black wall over there…would be much longer." As she finished, her brown eyes connected with Cindy's.

Cindy smiled, her eyes awash with fresh tears. *She knew.* Somehow, she knew. But the teacher wasn't going to put her on the spot and proclaim to the kids that here was one of those nurses. And for that, Cindy was grateful.

She looked down at her wrist, and turned her gold bangle bracelet so she could see the word spelled out in crystal. HOPE. It had been a birthday present from the grandchildren last year, and it had never seemed more appropriate than at this very moment.

"*Grandma!*"

She turned and saw Luke, her three-year-old grandson, running toward her, a joyous grin on his face. Behind him, her son-in-law, Zac, kept a close eye on him.

"Want to ride the merry-go-round, Grandma?" Luke called out, his elfin eyes sparkling. "Daddy says we can!"

Cindy knelt and held out her arms. He ran into them and snuggled against her. She buried her nose in his silky dark brown hair. Oh, how she loved this boy. Loved all five of her grandchildren.

Zac gave her an apologetic grin. "Sorry,

Cindy. I tried to tell him you needed some time alone, but you know how he is."

Cindy chuckled. "I do, indeed. Strong-willed. He gets it from his mother."

"Who gets it from you," Zac said with a grin.

Cindy straightened and took Luke by the hand. "Okay, young man. We'll go on the merry-go-round soon. I promise." She glanced at her wristwatch. 2:10.

Quin was ten minutes late. Maybe he'd changed his mind and wasn't coming. Disappointment warred with relief. Maybe it was all for the best. Better to remember him the way he'd been than to see how much the war—and age—had changed him. Her hand tightened on Luke's and they headed out of the memorial and down the sidewalk toward the Washington Monument. Up ahead, gathered around a park bench, stood a group of people.

The people she loved.

Her gaze moved over each endearing face as she approached them. Dear, sweet An Li, who was born in a war-torn country but whose name meant "peace," had grown from a sweet-natured orphan into a sweet-natured, beautiful man. Like his adoptive father, he worked as an oncologist at St. Jude's. There, he'd met and married Kim-ly, a tiny Vietnamese nurse, giving Cindy her first granddaughters—11-year-old Lien, and nine-year-old Lucy.

She smiled when she saw her first-born

son, Stephen, a happy-go-lucky bachelor. He looked almost exactly like his father had at the age of 34. Tall, blond, blue-eyed. Incredibly handsome. He'd graduated from the Air Force Academy and flew fighter jets out of Andrews Air Force Base.

The next face—her daughter's. Leah, a fashion designer in New York, had married a really good man, even if he *was* a lawyer, and a Republican, to boot. And they'd given Cindy her two grandsons—Luke, and Zealand, a 15-month sweetheart with red-gold hair and blue eyes.

She was a lucky woman to have such a wonderful family.

Her gaze rested on the final face—the most beloved of all. David. He sat on the park bench, watching her approach. His hair was silver-blond now, but his glittering blue eyes were the same as they'd been all those years ago in Vietnam, filled with warmth, humor, and love.

In December, God willing, they'd celebrate their 40th wedding anniversary. It hadn't been a perfect marriage, but it had been a good one. There had been occasional arguments—one in particular, a peanut butter sandwich throwing incident in the car during a road trip—but they'd never gone to bed angry in all these years.

He smiled at her now, and her heart skipped a beat. His smile still had that power. He got to his feet, and held out a freckled hand to her. "He didn't show?"

Cindy shook her head and started to speak. But then her phone beeped, alerting her to a text message. "Wait," she said. She drew her cell phone out of her purse.

On my way. Got hung up at the wall.

Her heart lurched, reminding her of the old days when just the thought of Quin had given her palpitations.

"He's on his way," Cindy said. "Guess I'll head back to the memorial."

David nodded. "We'll wait for you here."

She turned to go, and then hesitated before turning back to her husband. "David...I'm scared. I don't know if I can do this."

His eyes softened as he took her hands. "You can, Cindy. I think you need to see him...and I think he needs it, too."

She looked down toward the black wall and saw a man and woman slowly approaching. Something about his gait, though much slower than she remembered, reminded her of Quin. Her heart began to pound. But it couldn't be. He'd said nothing about bringing his wife to their meeting. But then again, she'd said nothing about bringing her entire family.

David leaned toward her and gave her a gentle kiss. "Go, babe. We'll be right here."

Cindy nodded, and biting her bottom lip, turned and headed back the way she'd come. She reached the entrance to the Vietnam Women's Memorial and waited, her heart racing.

As the couple grew closer, she began to make out the man's features—gray hair, tall and still lean, a crooked smile on the right side of his face. The other side of his face was scarred, but not hideously so. His green eyes—so familiar—held the twinkle she remembered--*so* Quin. But it wasn't until he was almost upon her that she saw the glass eyeball that had replaced his left eye. The woman with him, gray-haired and beautiful, clutched his hand, a look of curiosity mixed with something else—hope?—on her carefully made-up face.

"Hey, Cinnamon," Quin said, his grin widening. "You look beautiful."

"Hello, Quin." Her voice came out in a raspy whisper. She cleared her throat, clenching her moist hands. Her heart still pounded. She felt light-headed. Was she having a heart attack?

Quin glanced from Cindy to his companion. "This is my wife, Lynn. Lynn, this is Cindy Sweet...I mean, Cindy Ansgar. Sorry, Cinnamon."

Lynn Quinlan's brown eyes met hers. "It's good to finally meet you, Cindy. Ryan told me all about you."

Ryan? It took Cindy a moment to remember that was Quin's real name. "Happy to meet you," she murmured, shaking the woman's hand. *What the hell am I doing here? This is nuts. I should never have agreed to this.*

Lynn turned from Cindy to her husband.

"I'm going to take a walk. Be back in fifteen minutes?"

He nodded. "Thanks, hon."

She turned and strode back toward the black wall. Suddenly she stopped and whirled back to Cindy, her eyes blazing with what looked like a mixture of anger and despair. "Do me a favor, Cindy. Talk some sense into this stubborn ass of a man, and get him to take the chemo. God knows I can't do it! Maybe *you* can." She strode away, her sturdy low heels tapping angrily on the asphalt.

Cindy's gaze connected with Quin's. Incredibly, he still had that twinkle in his eye. And just like that, her anxiety drained away. "So," she said, "you're a stubborn ass of man, huh?" She smiled. "Some things never change, do they?"

He shrugged. "Some things do, and some things don't."

Her smile faltered. She stared at him a long moment, then shook her head. "I should hate you, you know."

He nodded, a sober look on his face. Then he grinned. "But you don't."

Cindy laughed. And the years melted away; she felt as if it had been just yesterday that she'd last seen him instead of over forty years ago. But one thing was missing—that heady, over-the-top, roller coaster love that had encompassed every moment she'd spent in his presence. She still felt love for him, a love she knew would always be with her, but not the deep, eternal love that had grown between her and David.

She looked toward a bench on the perimeter of the statue. "Want to sit for awhile?"

He nodded, and together, they moved to the bench.

When he settled down beside her, she reached over, took his hands in hers and gazed into his green eyes. "Okay, Quinlan, what do I have to do to convince you to have the chemo and live a few more years?"

He stared at her, his face solemn, and in the depths of his good eye, she could see the love he still felt for her. Her heart panged...because all she wanted to do was get back to David.

Suddenly, Quin's grin returned, as did the twinkle in his eye. "All you had to do was ask, Cinnamon. I'd do anything for you."

A breeze tousled his hair, and for just the tiniest moment, Cindy thought she detected the scent of incense. But it was just the perfume of cherry blossoms.

The End

About INCENSE & PEPPERMINTS

A note from Carole Bellacera

Dear Readers:

*I don't think I've ever been so terrified and intimidated in my life as I was while I was researching this book. For two years, I read every book I could find about women in Vietnam—and about the Vietnam War itself (**The Vietnam War for Dummies** was one of my favorites.) I watched a documentary about the combat nurses who served so bravely there—**Vietnam Nurses with Dana Delany**, and I watched every movie I could find about the Vietnam War, including the entire series of **Tour of Duty**. The more I read and watched, the more terrified and inadequate I felt. How could I...a former medical technician in the Air Force, who served during the Vietnam War...but who didn't know the slightest thing about serving during combat...how could I write this book? What gave me the right to write this book? Could I do justice to it, and be able to honor all the women who served there?*

I just knew I had to try. I felt directed to write this novel...God, the Universal Spirit, Mother Goddess...whatever, I knew I had to do it.

The inspiration first came from a photograph—the one of the marine on the lower left corner of the cover. This boy had been my pen-pal in high school. I came across this torn photo of him one day while I was reorganizing my photo albums. Honestly, I didn't remember much about him. I knew his name was Danny and he was from Indiana. My best friend, Susie, had given me his address and told me he was going to Vietnam and would I write him? (I seem to recall he was a cousin or related to her family somehow.) I was a flighty sixteen-year-old, and madly in love with a senior named Gary Baldauf. And perhaps the only reason I even agreed to write Danny was because he bore a remarkable resemblance to Gary. Of course, I knew there was a war going on somewhere in southeast Asia. (I'm not even sure, though, I knew Vietnam was in southeast Asia.) But the war hadn't affected me. Oh, in the back of my mind, I guess I worried that Gary might be drafted and get sent there, but the chance was small. After all, he was heading off to college at Purdue.

So that's how I began writing chatty, scatter-brained letters to this "older man" who looked like my high school crush. I'm sure my letters were filled with all kinds of gems like how much I loved Mark Lindsay of Paul Revere and the Raiders, and how cute my new white go-go boots were, and how groovy I looked after drawing Twiggy eyelashes around my eyes and dotting freckles on my cheeks with eyeliner—following the how-to instructions in **Teen Magazine***.*

Danny replied to my letters, and even sent me the photo of himself taken in Vietnam, but I can't tell you what he said. I have absolutely no memory of anything he wrote. When I think back on it, I believe I received only one or two letters. When they stopped coming, I didn't think about it; I doubt if I even noticed or wondered. After all, I was 16…going to basketball games, and dances, and pep rallies. It didn't even occur to me to worry about Danny and what may have happened to him. It was only after I found his photo a few years ago that it hit me. What <u>had</u> happened to him? And how could I find out? I didn't even remember his last name.

I turned the photo over and saw that half of it had been torn away. I knew he'd sent it to me like that because there hadn't been another person in the picture. Only half of the inscription on the back was visible.

ny Bruce
Nam '69

Danny Bruce. That had to be his name. So I got online and did a web search. When a page popped up on my screen, my stomach dipped, and I could feel the blood draining from my face. It was a website about the Vietnam Memorial Wall, and his name was on it.

http://www.vvmf.org/Wall-of-Faces/6358/DANIEL-D-BRUCE

Even as I write this, I have tears in my eyes, and I can't bring myself to put down in words what happened to him. But here's a clip from Wikipedia.

While participating in combat at Fire Support Base Tomahawk, Quang Nam Province, on March 1, 1969, he was killed in action — for his gallantry on this occasion, which saved the lives of three fellow Marines, he was awarded the Medal of Honor. He was on night watch when an enemy explosive was thrown at his position. He caught the charge, held it to his body, and ran from his position — away from fellow Marines who would have been killed by the explosion. Seconds later, the charge exploded and the full force of the blast was absorbed by Bruce.

He had been in Vietnam for a little over a month before he was killed. And me? I was busy partying, having sleepovers, eating burgers at the **Dog 'N Suds,** *and just going about my happy teenage life. I know…I was just doing what any teenager would be doing. But Danny had been a teenager, too. He was 18 when he died.*

This is why I was driven to write this book—to honor Danny, and the courageous nurses who saved thousands of

"Dannys." I hope I've done them the honor they so deserve.

Out-Takes from INCENSE & PEPPERMINT

The original version of **INCENSE & PEPPERMINTS** *began at an earlier point than the revised version. I was still obsessed with Danny Bruce and what I'd learned about him. Later, I realized that this was all back-story, and the novel really begins when Cindy is arriving in Vietnam. However, I still loved the first original chapters, so I'm sharing them with you here.*

Plainfield, Indiana

August 18, 1965

Dear Diary:

It happened today! I fell in love. His name is Gary, and he's 18. He's so sweet—and unbelievably cute! Tall, blond, gorgeous blue eyes. He came into my life at 4:00 this afternoon. I know. It sounds crazy. How can I be in love? I've only known him for five hours and forty-seven minutes.

Okay, it happened like this. I was just finishing up my shift at The Lovin' Spoonful…filling the salt shakers *when Susie told me I had a customer at table seven. I looked over—and almost died. He was SO cute, even if his hair was short—not like most of the guys around here. But he looked so sad...like his dog had died or something. I hurried over and took his order—pecan pie and coffee. Well, it <u>was</u> only four—way too early for supper.*

He gave me the sweetest smile, but still, there was such sadness in his eyes—and something else. He looked scared! Anyway, when I brought him his order, he asked me to sit with him awhile. And that's when he told me. He was leaving for an army camp in California on the 9:00 bus. It gets worse. After that, he was going to Vietnam!

By the time he was done with his pie and coffee, my shift was over, so instead of going home, I went with him to the park. No point in going home. Mom's working the evening shift, and I'll bet Aunt Terri has a date with that weirdo Tommy-guy. And as usual, Twerpface would be spending the night with that snotty little Sherry friend of hers. Nobody is going to miss me. Gary and I just talked and talked for hours. Gary. G-A-R-Y. I just love writing his name. Gary & Cindy. Mrs. Gary McCartney. Yes, that's his last name, and no, he's not related to Paul. I asked him. Anyway, he got dumped by his girlfriend just like Donny dumped me after we moved to Indiana. She left him for some college guy at Purdue. Talk about dumb! What college guy could compare to Gary? Her loss, my gain! Can you believe it? My height didn't even bother him. He said he liked tall girls. But here's the cool thing—he's an inch taller than me. He played varsity basketball at PHS. Before I got here, of course. He graduated this spring.

Anyway, we ate burgers at Dairy Queen, and ended up back on that park bench, watching the sun set. It was so romantic! A crescent moon rose over the pond, and he held my hand. I love his hands—they're big and callused—a farmer's hands. That's where he's been all my life—on a farm just outside of town. (Who knew farmers could be so sexy???) Oh, why couldn't I have met him sooner? It's not fair! Before we knew it, it was time to walk over to the bus station. And wouldn't you know it? The bus was early. By about three minutes. Just before he got on it, he kissed me. A soft, sweet kiss—the best kiss ever! Much better than those slimy ones of Donny's. God, I can't believe I ever thought he was a good kisser. It was like he was digging for gold or something! Gross-out!!!! Gary's kiss, though, was...mmmm...just perfect! He kisses better, I bet, than even Paul McCartney does. His lips tasted like the peppermint Lifesaver we'd had earlier. We exchanged addresses and promised to write each other— and I'm going to do that right now. He said he probably wouldn't be getting much mail from home because his mom died years ago, and his brothers and father are really busy on the farm. So I'm going to make sure he gets a ton of mail. I'm going to write him every day!

God, I miss him so bad. Isn't that weird? How can you miss someone you didn't even know existed when you woke up this morning?

October 24, 1965

Dear Diary:

Oh, my God!!! There was a letter from Gary waiting for me when I got home from school today! I grabbed it and raced to the bedroom, locking the door against Joanie and her prying eyes. Of course, she went screaming to Mom about being locked out of our room. I turned up the stereo really loud—Herman's Hermits "Can't You Hear my Heartbeat"—and opened his letter. Before I could even start reading it, Mom was banging at my door, yelling at me to let Joanie in. God!!! I can't have any privacy here in this horrible place.

I still don't get why Mom had to leave Daddy and move up here into Aunt Terri's house. Yeah, he was no saint. I know that. He drank too much and, well, I don't know if he was messing around with Lesley like Mom said he was. Still, all she was thinking about was herself—not me and Joanie. It wasn't fair—yanking us out of school and moving us up here to this deadbeat town, and I lost all my friends—and Donny. Not that I care now, but still...it's just so annoying living on top of each other in this little house. We had such a nice big house in Myrtle Beach.

Oh, well...back to Gary's letter. I tucked it under the pillow and opened the door so Mom could come in. I thought Joanie was with her, but she wasn't. Probably cramming her face with peanut butter in the kitchen. I couldn't believe it when Mom made herself comfortable on my bed like she was going to stay for hours, and then she started in about the homecoming dance and why I wasn't going with Ricky Bullock who asked me a few weeks ago, even though he and everyone else at school knows I'm madly in love with Gary. So, I'm sitting there, trying to drown out Mom's lecture about how I can't stop living my life because of a boy in Vietnam. She just doesn't get it. I love him. I'm going to marry him when he comes home. He's already sort of asked me. It's clear he's as crazy about me as I am about him. Look at that bottle of "Emeralde" he sent me from the PX in California. "To match those gorgeous green eyes of yours," he wrote. (My eyes aren't really green, but hazel, but that's okay.)

Anyway, Mom was going on and on about how I'm too young to be in love with some boy I barely know, and finally, I just exploded. Said some really mean things about how she drove Daddy away, and if he had been cheating with Lesley, then maybe it was because she'd driven him to it. I think she wanted to slap me. But then her face changed from anger to hurt, and it made me feel bad for what I'd said, but I couldn't apologize. I should've but I didn't. She finally left the room, and thank God, Joanie must've went over to Sherry's because she was nowhere around, so I finally got to read Gary's letter.

It made me cry. He's so sweet. Look what he wrote:

When I get home, I'm going to show you how much you mean to me—and that's a promise. Well, I'd better get this in the mail. Just so you know…I might not be able to write for a while. New orders have come in, and we're heading out tomorrow. Don't know where. But I promise I'll be in touch as soon as I can. You keep yourself safe for me, Cindy. I've got someone to come home to now, and that's what keeps me going. I love you, Cindy Sweet. Don't you forget that.

Yours Forever,
Gary

Oh, God. I love him…love him. LOVE HIM!!!!!

***

November 1965

The glaring lights on the football field washed over Cindy as she marched down the 40-yard-line, playing "Zorba the Greek" on her clarinet with the Plainfield Marching Band. It was half-time at the Friday night game between Plainfield and Brownsburg with the home team ahead 14-6.

Not that she cared about the stupid football game. She didn't understand it, and didn't want to. As far she could tell, it was just a bunch of over-grown boys piling up on the ground and fighting over a stupid ball. If it weren't for the marching band, she wouldn't even be here.

The half-time show ended, and with the band, Cindy marched off the field. She could hardly wait to get out to the parking lot. Mom had let her borrow the car for the night—a shiny big white Buick that she'd won in the divorce settlement—as long as Cindy promised she'd come straight home after the game. No problem. She wasn't even going to stay until the end. What was the point? She didn't care if Plainfield won or lost...and besides, she'd rather be in her room, writing a heartfelt letter to Gary.

Just as the marching band broke formation, the loudspeaker crackled and Principal Wolfe's booming voice reverberated over the field, "Ladies and Gentlemen, before the third quarter begins, we'd like to take a moment of silence to honor the latest list of Indiana boys who've bravely given their lives in service to our country over in Vietnam."

Cindy's step faltered. *No!* She didn't want to hear this! It was just too scary! But still, her pace slowed. *Don't worry. It'll be fine. Gary is okay. You just got that letter from him yesterday. He's fine! But you owe it to him and his buddies to give respect to the ones who...won't be coming back.*

She stopped in her tracks and turned to face the field with several other members of the marching band. The principal's voice rang out through the sudden stillness in the stadium.

"Eric Arnold Baker…"

Cindy's heart lodged in her throat as the names lingered on the brisk autumn night. She reached into the pocket of her band uniform and withdrew Gary's latest letter. He'd finally enclosed a picture—after she'd bugged him to death for one in her last few letters. In the small photo, he leaned against a green jeep, wearing a green and brown-splotched uniform and combat boots. Hands clasped, he stared into the camera with a hardened expression that seemed impossible to reconcile with the scared boy he'd been in the bus station on that summer night three months ago. But it *was* him; that was for sure. There was no mistaking those soulful blue eyes and his golden blond hair. But he looked older.

"Bruce David Freeman…"

"Aaron Daniel Matthews…"

She traced a finger over the photograph, lingering on Gary's sharp cheekbones, trying to imagine he was really here…that she was really touching him. Had he lost weight? Yes, he definitely looked skinnier than she remembered. Probably the food wasn't that great over there. In one of his letters, he'd mentioned something called C-Rations—kits of canned food left over from World War II, he swore. Sounded disgusting! There was no way in the world she'd survive if she had to eat stuff like--

"Gary Ronald McCartney…"

Cindy's head shot up, her stomach plunging. *Oh, God!* Had she *really* heard his name? Or was she so consumed with thoughts of him that she'd imagined it? *Oh, please, God, let that be the case!*

"James Albert O'Connell…"

"Christopher Leon Petty…"

Fear lodged in her throat; her palms grew clammy. She tried to swallow, but her suddenly dry mouth made it impossible. She'd heard his name. She knew in her heart she had! But maybe it was a mistake! Maybe it was *another* Gary McCartney from Indiana. Yes, that was it! She didn't know Gary's middle name, but she was *sure* it wasn't Ronald. Fighting the panic bubbling up inside her, she brought out the envelope she'd thrust back into her pocket and stared down at the return address. Her stomach turned to ice. *PFC Gary R. McCartney.* Her cold, trembling fingers tightened on the letter. She closed her eyes and tried to draw in a calming breath. *Don't jump to conclusions. So his middle name starts with an "R," but that doesn't mean it's him. Maybe his middle name isn't Ronald. Maybe it's Randy or Roger or Roy or…*

Heart racing, knees weak, she turned to the oboe player standing a few feet away. "Did you hear that name? Did they say Gary McCartney?"

The oboe player, Tom Childs, she thought his name was, gave her a blank look. Frustrated, she grabbed his sleeve and shook it. "Did you *hear* the name the principal just called out?"

He rolled his eyes. "Uh...the dude called out a *lot* of names."

Cindy had already pivoted away from him.

Clutching her clarinet as if it were a lifeline, Cindy ran toward the building perched above the stands where Principal Wolfe's funereal voice continued to intone the names of Indiana's Vietnam dead.

"Daniel Evan Warner..."

"James Bruce Waters..."

Meet Carole Bellacera

Carole Bellacera wrote her first novel, "The Vaughn's Daughters," in a loose-leaf notebook, drawing her own illustrations for it at the age of 12. Summers were really boring in a rural area of Indiana in the days before driver's licenses. With both parents working, Carole and her younger sisters, Kathy, and Sharon, had to drum up their own entertainment to while away the hours of the long, hot summers. Kathy and Sharon liked the outdoors, but Carole preferred making up stories in her cozy little bedroom. One summer she wrote a play, and forced her sisters and several neighborhood kids to perform it. (Some probably would remember her as a "control freak.")

In her teens, Carole continued writing novels in notebooks, and some were passed around her high school. Even then, she was eager to read the "reviews" on the blank pages left for that purpose—and luckily, most of them, if not all, were glowing. One of her favorite teachers, Mrs. Regina Scott, wrote a review that encouraged Carole to pursue writing as a career—something she wouldn't do for another couple of decades.

At 16, Carole wrote her best work yet—THE SWEDE, a romance inspired by growing up near the famous Indianapolis 500 race track. (At the time, she was madly in love with race car driver, Peter Revson.) Confident that it would be the next big best-seller, she packed it up and sent it off to **Doubleday.** It was promptly rejected with a form letter–and Carole officially became a professional writer—although she didn't know it yet. At the time, she was too naïve to realize that being rejected was a necessary, though unpleasant, aspect of a writer's life; she just assumed that New York knew what they were talking about, and apparently, she had no writing talent at all, so she gave up her dream. (And discovered boys, and ultimately, a husband.)

Fast-forward to the 1980's. Several momentous things happened that reminded Carole that she *did* have a talent for writing. She went back to college and did well in a creative writing course. This inspired her to start writing a romance novel about a race car driver (of course) and a news reporter. It never got published, but writing it did the job of getting her creative juices flowing again. And then…*drum roll*…something *really* exciting happened. Carole met Princess Di at Andrews Air Force Base. She hadn't wanted to get up early that morning to go to the flight line to see the royal couple arrive, but her friend,

Diana, talked her into it. Who knew that meeting would be the start of a real writing career? Carole wrote about the encounter, and months later, the article appeared in the military magazine, **Family**, earning her $100. (And no, she didn't frame it; she spent it.)

Thus, ambition was born. Carole began to get published on a fairly regular basis—and began collecting *a lot* of rejections along the way. This time, though, she didn't let them deter her. Although she was doing well in publishing short fiction and articles, earning credits in magazines such as **Woman's World**, **Endless Vacation** and **The Washington Post**—(even publishing a story about how she met her husband in **Chicken Soup for the Couples' Soul)**, her dream to publish a novel remained elusive for 13 long years.

But finally, in February, 1998, she got the call she'd been fantasizing about from her agent, and a year later, her first novel, BORDER CROSSINGS, hit the shelves, earning glowing reviews and awards such as a 2000 RITA Award nominee for Best Romantic Suspense and Best First Book and a nominee for the 2000 Virginia Literary Award in Fiction. Seven more novels followed, including the one you just read— INCENSE & PEPPERMINTS.

Carole is presently at work on an 8th novel, HOWLING AT THE MOON, the story of four new-rich women trying to fit into the old-rich society of Charleston.

She lives in Myrtle Beach with the most wonderful man in the world, Frank, her husband of 39 years, and is blessed to be the mom of a talented daughter, Leah, also a writer, (www.mommiesneedsleeptoo.com) and a fantastic son, Stephen, and Grandma to the two most beautiful boys in the world, Luke, 5, and Zealand, 4.

Questions for Reading Group Discussion

❖ What would you say was the incident that made Cindy begin to change from a wide-eyed innocent young woman into the hardened, cynical nurse she'd become by the end of her year in Vietnam?

❖ How did Cap Bren play a part in Cindy's transformation?

❖ How did you feel about Cap Bren's character?

❖ Who was your favorite secondary character? Dr. Moss? Cap Bren? Colonel Kairos? Lindy? The General? Rosalie? David? Quin?

❖ This novel had lots of brutal, heartbreaking scenes. Which one made you reach for a box of Kleenex©?

❖ When Cindy went to Hawaii and met the Midwestern couple on the Arizona Memorial, discuss why she felt such disgust for them and their flag-waving.

❖ At the beginning of each new month Cindy spent in Vietnam, she reads a letter from home. What was the author's purpose in including these letters? Did you think this was a good decision? If so, why?

❖ How did you feel about Quin and what happened to him?

❖ How did you feel about David?

❖ Did the inclusion of the original first chapter make you understand Cindy's motives better in her decision to join the military?

❖ Which beginning did you like better? The published version or the original "diary entry" version?

❖ In the last chapter, how did you feel about Cindy's realization that life had worked out exactly like it was supposed to?

❖ How did you feel about Quin's decision to let Cindy think he was dead? Did it make you angry?

❖ How do you think nurses who served in Vietnam will feel about this novel? Will

Cindy's cynicism and later anti-war
sentiments be controversial?

Acknowledgements

I couldn't have written this novel without the help and encouragement of many different people. First, I'd like to thank real life combat nurse, Barbara Pendleton, who served at Long Binh from January 1968-February 1969. Barb was so forthright in telling me stories of her year in Vietnam. She was also helpful with the medical details, and in describing what the nurse's quarters looked like. Also, remember the colonel's big black dog who hated men? That was a true story from Barb's experience there. Thank you, Barb. I honor and respect you for serving our country.

Other combat nurses, Susan O'Neill, who served from May of '69-June '70, and Jill Mishkel who served from July '70-July '71, were also helpful with details and the endless questions I asked.

Thank you to Robert Robeson, a dust-off pilot with the 236th Medical Detachment, who served from July 1969-July 1970 out of Da Nang. Without your help, I wouldn't have been able to write about Quin as vividly as I did.

Thanks to Debi O'Neille who critiqued the book. She was good at finding some of the little mistakes. Also, big thanks to the Bull Run Writers Group that listened to a chapter every two weeks. Their feedback was priceless. Miss you guys!!!

And finally, thank you to Leigh Giza for writing the poem, "Last Night" for the book. And another big thank to Robert Bensen who wrote the poem, "Beside You." Both poems brought to life the love David felt for Cindy, and I very much appreciate the gifts you shared for my books.

As always, thanks to my husband, Frank, for listening to every chapter and giving me feedback. And for doing a wonderful job with the cover. I love you, honey. You are my Quin and my David, all wrapped into one.

An excerpt from Carole's next novel,
HOWLING AT THE MOON.

The doorbell rang just as Ashleigh opened the box labeled "kitchen items." Doug had already left for his office in Charleston, leaving her to unpack the boxes and get their new lives at Hawk Moon Estates off to a smooth start.

Typical Doug. He hadn't taken a day off from his legal firm since they'd first put the down payment on the five-bedroom custom-built McMansion in the new sub-division on the previously uninhabited barrier island, Salamander Cay, just northwest of Isle of Palms. Despite lawsuits that had delayed ground-breaking for two years, Doug and his development company had finally won the battle—as he always did— and at last, they were moving into their new home. Ironic that other families on the cul de sac had beaten them to it by eleven months. Also typical Doug, the perfectionist, had caused delay after delay during the building process because, for example, one nail was a centimeter off from where he thought it should be. It was exhausting. But finally, here they were—first morning in their new home.

Navigating the moving boxes in the hallway, Ashleigh reached the etched-glass front door, and opened it to see an overweight woman with silky long brown hair and an oval, freckled face smiling at her. A beautiful freckled face, Ashleigh realized. If she'd take off about thirty pounds, she'd be a stunner.

"Hi," the woman said, beaming a generous smile. "Welcome to the neighborhood. I'm Michaela, but everyone calls me Micki." She stuck out a pudgy hand.

"Hello," Ashleigh said, smiling back, and extending her hand. "I'm Ashleigh."

Micki's smile widened. "Ah! You're a southerner! Everyone else in the cul de sac is from the north. I'm from Rehoboth, Delaware. Cathy is from Minnesota…God knows why *anyone* would live in a place that cold. And Sam hails from Virginia, but you can't call her a southerner. Manassas, Virginia, close to DC. Are you a local?"

"I was born in Charleston," Ashleigh said, feeling the usual butterflies in her stomach when people probed about her past. She looked at the aluminum foil-covered tray in the woman's hands. "What you got there?"

"Oh!" Micki thrust it at her. "Homemade chocolate chip cookies. I love to bake!"

Well, that's obvious, Ashleigh thought, and immediately felt ashamed of herself. After all, she wasn't the poster child of good health.

Super-model thin she might be, but that came with a price—bulimia. Oh, not anymore. With a year of therapy, she'd overcome that particular problem. But sometimes, deep inside, she still felt like that insecure bulimic teen.

"Thank you." She took the cookies. Maybe she'd freeze them and serve them for guests.

Micki beamed. "That's not the only reason I came by. I'm having a little get-together this evening with Cathy and Sam—Samantha. She's a woman, obviously, not a guy. We call it our monthly 'howl party.' Been doing it ever since we moved in. Jeez, I didn't think you guys were *ever* going to move in. The house looks perfect from outside." Her eager brown eyes glanced around at what she could see from the front porch.

Ashleigh realized how rude she'd been in not immediately inviting her in. She stood back from the door. "Please come in. It's chilly out this morning."

Micki didn't hesitate. Grinning, she stepped into the foyer. "Wow! This is gorgeous! And I thought our houses were stunning!"

"That's why it took so long," Ashleigh said dryly. "Perfectionist husband wanting only the best. For example, these tiles here in the foyer and kitchen came from a quarry in Pompeii at $5,000 per square foot."

Immediately, Ashleigh realized how that

sounded. Bragging. Why did she always do this? What was *wrong* with her?

But amazingly, Micki's smile brightened. "Too cool! Anyway, I'd love to have you join us tonight."

Ashleigh led Micki into the enormous kitchen with its Italian granite counters, stainless steel appliances and the before-mentioned "Tuscan sand" Pompeian tiled floor and double-sink island. "Want some coffee?" she asked, gesturing toward the mahogany bar stools.

Micki clumsily slid into one. "Awesome!"

"So, what is this 'howl party?" Ashleigh asked, punching "brew" on the Keurig.

Micki's brown eyes danced, and a dimple flickered in her right cheek. "Well, it's kind of hard to describe. Let's just say it's a way we let off steam. De-stress."

Ashleigh stared at her, waiting for her to go on. The coffee maker sputtered and fragrant dark coffee streamed into a Polish Cermika Boleslawiec mug.

"Oh, you just have to see for yourself," Micki said as Ashleigh brought the coffee to her. "Cream and sugar…if you have it." Her humorous gaze flicked down Ashleigh's trim body. "You don't look like you eat much sugar."

Ashleigh's lips quirked. She liked this down-to-earth woman. "Not anymore," she said dryly. She took a china creamer from the cabinet and poured in some Half & Half from the refrigerator, then got out its matching sugar bowl filled with raw sugar. "Hope this is okay." She slid the creamer and sugar bowl in front of Micki along with a heavy silver teaspoon.

"Cathy and Sam can't wait to meet you," Micki said, adding several teaspoons of sugar to her coffee. "So, will you come? Appetizers and wine at seven."

Well, why not? Ashleigh smiled. "Thank you. I'd love to come."

Micki beamed. "Great! I'm right next door on the left. I mean, *your* left. Cathy is on the right. *Your* right. Oh, hell! I'm right there!" She pointed out the window over the sink. "I'm so excited you're coming!" She glanced pointedly at the foiled-covered plate Ashleigh had put on the counter. "How about if we break into those chocolate chip cookies?"

∞

Ashleigh wasn't sure how to dress for this get-together. She'd forgotten to ask. Well, it was a pretty highfalutin' neighborhood. Her lips quirked. *Highfalutin.* Her North Carolina country roots were showing with her thoughts. She'd have to make sure things like that didn't come out in her conversation with these obviously rich women.

But Micki had seemed down-to-earth and friendly, she reminded herself. Not at all what she'd expected. She wondered what the other two women on the cul de sac would be like.

She decided to choose something elegant yet casual for the "howl party"—sleek black jersey slacks with a flowing silk top in sea green and teal, and her four-inch Jimmy Choo strappy sandals. Thank God she'd had time to run to Mount Pleasant for a pedicure this afternoon.

Ashleigh climbed the stone steps to Micki's front door, her heartbeat quickening. Meeting new people always filled her with trepidation. All the lies she'd built since Doug had rescued her from that sleazy topless club in Myrtle Beach made her uneasy. What if she slipped and betrayed who...*what*...she really was. Doug would never forgive her.

She rang the doorbell and a voice called out from inside. "It's open!"

Ashleigh stepped into the foyer and saw that the lay-out was similar to her own—a dining room to the left, a formal living room to the right, and a grand staircase beyond leading up to the second floor. But there, the similarity ended. No extravagant Italian tiled floors, no frescoed walls, no opulent lighting. Still, Micki's home was warm and inviting—and fragrant with something cinnamon-scented. More to Ashleigh's taste, really, than her own home of which Doug had chosen everything down to the last detail.

"We're in the kitchen, Ashleigh" the same voice called out. "Straight ahead and to the left."

A different lay-out, after all. Ashleigh followed her instructions, stepping into a huge great room with its enormous floor-to-ceiling stone two-sided fireplace that separated it from the kitchen on the left.

Three women stood around the granite island, two of them sipping wine. Immediately, Ashleigh realized she was over dressed. The others wore jeans with white T-shirts depicting a grey wolf and a full moon. "Howling at the Moon" the T-shirts read.

What the hell?

Micki's warm smile lit up her face. "Ashleigh! Welcome! Don't worry. We'll order you a T-shirt."

The other two women, a blonde and a brunette, turned to her, smiling. The brunette seemed a bit older than the rest of them, and the other looked vaguely familiar.

"This is Cathy," Micki said, indicating the more mature-looking woman. "And this…" She looked at the younger one. "…is Sam. If you haven't already seen her on Channel 8 News, you will. She's Samantha Peroni, the entertainment anchor on the morning show."

"Yeah." Sam grinned. "In other words, I get all the fluff jobs."

So, *that* was why she looked so familiar. Ashleigh watched Channel 8 News, and now remembered how she'd thought Samantha was the typical blonde local reporter that every mini-market had. Long on looks and short on brains. *Man, it sucks to be so judgmental.* She needed to work on that; apparently Doug was wearing off on her after seven years of marriage.

"Ladies, this is our new neighbor, Ashleigh. Would you like some wine, Ashleigh?"

"White," Ashleigh said, smiling. "It's sure nice to meet y'all."

Sam smiled. "Ah, a real Southern belle. I just love that Charleston accent. Micki tells us you're a hometown girl."

Ashleigh's stomach tightened as she took the glass of chardonnay Micki had poured for her. She forced a smile. "Born and raised. And Micki tells me you're all northern transplants." She took a sip of wine and tried not to grimace. She preferred sweet wines like a Riesling or Moscato but she knew if she'd asked for a sweet wine these women would see through to her pedestrian roots. She probably should've asked for red instead of white, but she had to draw the line at room temperature wine. Doug, a real wine connoisseur, had tried to develop her palate to an acceptable taste level, but hadn't been too successful, much to his chagrin.

She noticed though, that Sam didn't appear to be drinking wine like the others. Instead, she held a glass that looked like it held iced tea. Probably because she had to get up early to go to the studio. She was on live every morning when Ashleigh turned on her TV.

Micki brought out appetizers—spinach dip with bagel chips, cream cheese cylinders wrapped in pastrami, tiny crab cakes with dill sauce and an assortment of sweets—chocolate chip cookies (one of which Ashleigh had forced herself to eat this morning, and was, admittedly, delicious, oozing with milk chocolate still warm from the oven.) In addition to the cookies, a dense carrot cake slathered in rich cream cheese frosting held court on a stoneware pedestal and fudgy dark chocolate brownies towered on a crystal plate.

Ashleigh eyed the array of food and wondered how many other people had been invited to the party. Surely Micki didn't expect the four of them to eat all this.

But apparently so.

The four women sat at the dining room table, sipping wine and nibbling on the appetizers and desserts, and Ashleigh began learning about her neighbors. She realized she was enjoying herself, despite growing more and more perplexed. What was this "howl party?" And what was the significance of the "howling at the moon" T-shirts?

As the wine flowed, so did the conversation, getting increasingly less inhibited. As far as Ashleigh could tell, this "howl party" was nothing more than women getting together and venting about what was going on in their lives. Sam, the only single woman, was bitching about her love-life…or…on the other hand bragging about the great sex she'd had with her off-and-on Brazilian guitarist lover. Cathy talked about the problems of raising twin teen boys, and how she felt like a single mother because her husband, a top executive at Boeing, was always working. Micki lamented about her weight gain, and how no matter how good she tried to be, she always broke down and ate something laden with calories.

A bitch session—that's what these "howl parties" were all about, Ashleigh surmised. And why not? Maybe once she got to know these women better, she'd be comfortable enough to vent. God knows she had enough to vent about. Of course, she'd have to be careful. She could never entirely open up to anyone.

The evening sped by and Ashleigh was shocked when the clock struck midnight. Dear God, Doug would be wondering where the hell she was…despite the fact she'd left a note for him about her plans.

As the grandfather clock pealed, Micki stood, a grin spreading across her face. "Okay, ladies. You ready?"

Mystified, Ashleigh watched as the others got up and stretched, then one by one, they headed out to the deck overlooking the Atlantic Ocean where a full moon bathed them in white-washed light.

And as Ashleigh watched in astonishment, the other three women turned their faces toward the luminous moon and began to howl.

Made in the USA
Columbia, SC
23 June 2019